THE WIGWAM AND THE CABIN

WILLIAM GILMORE SIMMS

THE WIGWAM AND THE CABIN

(LIFE IN AMERICA)

BY THE AUTHOR OF

" THE YEMASSEE," " GUY RIVERS," &c.

William Gilmore Simms

———

" The ancient tales
Which first I learn'd,
Will I relate."
EDDA OF SAEMUND.

———

THE GREGG PRESS / RIDGEWOOD, N. J.

First published in 1845 by George Clark & Son
Republished in 1968 by
The Gregg Press Incorporated
171 East Ridgewood Avenue
Ridgewood, New Jersey U.S.A.

Copyright© 1968 by
The Gregg Press, Inc.

Printed in United States of America

AMERICANS IN FICTION

In the domain of literature the play may once have been the chief abstract and chronicle of the times, but during the nineteenth and twentieth centuries the novel has usurped the chief place in holding the mirror up to the homely face of society. On this account, if for no other, the Gregg Press series of reprints of American fiction merits the attention of all students of Americana and of librarians interested in building up adequate collections dealing with the social and literary history of the United States. Most of the three score and ten novels or volumes of short stories included in the series enjoyed considerable fame in their day but have been so long out of print as to be virtually unobtainable in the original editions.

Included in the list are works by writers not presently fashionable in critical circles—but nevertheless well known to literary historians—among them Joel Chandler Harris, Harriet Beecher Stowe, Thomas Bailey Aldrich, and William Gilmore Simms. A substantial element in the list consists of authors who are known especially for their graphic portrayal of a particular American setting, such as Gertrude Atherton (California), Arlo Bates (Boston), Alice Brown (New England), Edward Eggleston (Indiana), Mary Wilkins Freeman (New England), Henry B. Fuller (Chicago), Richard M. Johnston (Georgia), James Lane Allen (Kentucky), Mary N. Murfree (Tennessee), and Thomas Nelson Page (Virginia). There is even a novel by Frederic Remington, one of the most popular painters of the Western cowboy and Indian—and another, and impressive minor classic on the early mining region of Colorado, from the pen of Mary Hallock Foote. The professional student of American literature will rejoice in the opportunity afforded by the collection to extend his reading of fiction belonging to what is called the "local-color movement"—a major current in the development of the national belles-lettres.

Among the titles in the series are also a number of famous historical novels. Silas Weir Mitchell's *Hugh Wynne* is one of the very best fictional treatments of the American Revolution. John Esten Cooke is the foremost Southern writer of his day who dealt with the Civil War. The two books by Thomas Dixon are among the most famous novels on the Reconstruction Era, with sensational disclosures of the original Ku Klux Klan in action. They supplied the grist for the first great movie "spectacular"—*The Birth of a Nation* (1915).

Paul Leicester Ford's *The Honorable Peter Stirling* is justly ranked among the top American novels which portray American politics in action—a subject illuminated by other novelists in the Gregg list—A. H. Lewis, Frances H. Burnett, and Alice Brown, for example. Economic problems are forcefully put before the reader in works by Aldrich, Mrs. Freeman, and John Hay, whose novels illustrate the ominous concern over the early battles between labor and capital. From the sweatshops of Eastern cities in which newly arrived immigrants toiled for pittances, to the Western mining camps where the laborers packed revolvers, the working class of the times enters into various other stories in the Gregg list. The capitalist class, also, comes in for attention, with an account of a struggle for the ownership of a railroad in Samuel Merwin's *The Short-Line War* and with the devastating documentation of the foibles of the newly rich and their wives in the narratives of David Graham Phillips. It was Phillips whose annoying talent for the exposure of abuses led Theodore Roosevelt to put the term "muck-raker" into currency.

While it is apparent that local-color stories, the historical novel, and the economic novel have all been borne in mind in choosing the titles for this important series of reprints, it is evident that careful consideration has also been given to treatments of various minority elements in the American population. The Negro, especially, but also the Indian, the half-breed, Creoles, Cajuns—and even the West Coast Japanese—appear as characters in various of these novels or volumes of short stories and sketches. Joel Chandler Harris's *Free Joe* will open the eyes of readers who know that author solely as the creator of humorous old Uncle Remus. And there is a revelatory volume of dialect tales, written by a Negro author, *The Conjure Woman* by Charles W. Chesnutt.

In literary conventions and the dominating attitudes toward life, the works in the Gregg series range from the adventurous romance illustrated so well by Mayne Reid or the polite urbanity of Owen Wister to the mordant irony of Kate Chopin and the grimmer realism of Joseph Kirkland's own experiences on bloody Civil War battlefields or the depressing display of New York farm life by Harold Frederic. In short, the series admirably illustrates the general qualities of the fiction produced in the United States during the era covered, just as it generously mirrors the geographical regions, the people, and the problems of the times.

PROFESSOR CLARENCE GOHDES
Duke University
Durham, North Carolina

December, 1967

WILLIAM GILMORE SIMMS

William Gilmore Simms was born in Charleston, South Carolina in 1806. He received very little education, and was apprenticed to a druggist. Simms' mother died while he was a child. His father was an Irishman; a soldier of fortune who left his son with a grandmother while he wandered in Alabama, Tennessee, Florida, and Mississippi. For a short while, the boy lived with his vagrant father, and received impressions of frontier and Indian life which he used as raw material for his stories and poems. He read law, but never practiced at the bar, and turned to journalism, becoming part owner and editor of the *City Gazette* in Charleston, while continuing to write verse sporadically. For a while he lived in New York and New Haven, but in 1835 he returned to the South, which he had never ceased to love, and married Chevillette Roach, the daughter of a wealthy, aristocratic planter. He lived happily with her in her ancestral home, the "Woodlands," where he wrote *The Scout,* as well as other novels, non-fiction, and verse. In the North, he was praised as "the Southern Cooper, the American Scott," in the South, he was completely neglected. From 1844 to 1846 he served in the state legislature, and was an outspoken Secessionist. The Civil War ruined him. His wife died, stragglers from Sherman's army burned the "Woodlands," and Simms was forced to do hack writing for magazines to support his six remaining children. He died of overwork in 1870.

Simms once said of his native city: "Charleston, sir, was the finest city in the world; not a large city, but the finest. South Carolina, sir, was the flower of modern civilization. Our people the most hospitable, the most accomplished, having the highest degree of culture and the highest sense of honor of any people, I will not say of America, sir, but of any country on the globe. And they are so still, even in their temporary desolation." Simms was elected to the St. Cecilia Society of Charleston, one of the highest social honors which that city bestows upon its citizens, but this did not solve his financial problems.

Like Thomas Nelson Page, Simms believed in the God-given right of "superior" races to enslave their "inferiors," as long as the masters assumed the responsibility of clothing and feeding their charges. To question this prerogative would be absurd, for Simms found in the universe a "great chain of being," a graduated scale of hierarchy or degree, in which everything had its assigned place. In human society there was an aristocracy, a middle class, and slaves. Whatever one's opinion of Simms' world-view, it would be as wrong to criticize his art, which is frequently excellent, because of his social philosophy, as it would be to condemn the Elizabethan writers who believed in Divine Right of Kings.

The Wigwam and the Cabin is a collection of nine short stories set in the Carolina swamps just after the Revolutionary War, when this area was still inhabited by "the planter, the squatter, the Indian, and the negro — the bold and hardy pioneer, and the vigorous yeoman." In spite of the misleadingly prosaic subtitle "Life in America," these tales have a strong flavor of the macabre, the uncanny, and the exotic. Simms has created a remarkable imaginative world, where characters whose lives are harsh, drab, and devoid of cultural richness move across a background of sinister glamour and romantic, Gothic decadence. Much attention is given to Nature, but Simms' woodlands, rivers, and lakes are the antithesis of the New England of Thoreau and Emerson, and consist of dismal, feverish swamps, forests which swallow up the traveller, ramshackle cabins in lonely clearings, and forgotten graveyards. The Indian, defeated and rotten with disease and alcohol, treads his wretched way through these stories, almost unrecognizable as the brother of the warlike and proud Sioux of Frederic Remington's *John Ermine*. With these ingredients, and the ability to tell a good ghost story such as "Grayling; or Murder Will Out," it is no wonder that Poe lauded Simms as the writer who had "more vigor, more imagination, more movement and more general capacity than all our novelists (save Cooper) combined."

F. C. S.

CONTENTS

LIFE IN AMERICA.

GRAYLING; OR, "MURDER WILL OUT."

CHAPTER I.

THE world has become monstrous matter-of-fact in latter days. We can no longer get a ghost story, either for love or money. The materialists have it all their own way; and even the little urchin, eight years old, instead of deferring with decent reverence to the opinions of his grandmamma, now stands up stoutly for his own. He believes in every "ology" but pneumatology. "Faust" and the "Old Woman of Berkeley" move his derision only, and he would laugh incredulously, if he dared, at the Witch of Endor. The whole armoury of modern reasoning is on his side; and, however he may admit at seasons that belief can scarcely be counted a matter of will, he yet puts his veto on all sorts of credulity. That cold-blooded demon called Science has taken the place of all the other demons. He has certainly cast out innumerable devils, however he may still spare the principal. Whether we are the better for his intervention is another question. There is reason to apprehend that in disturbing our human faith in shadows, we have lost some of those wholesome moral restraints which might have kept many of us virtuous, where the laws could not.

The effect, however, is much the more seriously evil in all that concerns the romantic. Our story-tellers are so resolute to deal in the real, the actual only, that they venture on no subjects the details of which are not equally vulgar and susceptible of proof. With this end in view, indeed, they too commonly choose their subjects among convicted felons, in order that they may avail themselves of the evidence which led to their conviction; and, to prove more conclusively their devoted adherence to nature and the truth, they depict the former not only in her condition of nakedness, but long before she has found out the springs of running water. It is to be feared that some of the coarseness of modern taste arises from the too great lack of that veneration which belonged to, and elevated to dignity, even the errors of preceding ages. A love of the marvellous belongs, it appears to me, to all those who love and cultivate either of the fine arts. I very much doubt whether the poet, the painter, the sculptor, or the romancer, ever yet lived, who had not some strong bias—a leaning, at least,—to a belief in the wonders of the invisible world. Certainly, the higher orders of poets and painters, those who create and invent, must have a strong taint of the superstitious in their composition. But this is digressive, and leads us from our purpose.

It is so long since we have been suffered to see or hear of a ghost, that a visitation at this time may have the effect of novelty, and I propose to narrate a story which I heard more than once in my boyhood, from the lips of an aged relative, who succeeded, at the time, in making me believe every word of it; perhaps, for the simple reason that she convinced me she believed every word of it herself. My grandmother was an old lady who had been a resident of the seat of most frequent war in Carolina during the Revolution. She had fortunately survived the numberless atrocities which she was yet compelled to witness; and, a keen observer, with a strong memory, she had in store a thousand legends of that stirring period, which served to beguile me from sleep many and many a long winter night. The story which I propose to tell was one of these; and when I say that she not only devoutly believed it herself, but that it was believed by sundry of her contemporaries, who were themselves privy to such of the circumstances as could be known to third parties, the gravity with which I repeat the legend will not be considered very astonishing.

The revolutionary war had but a little while been concluded. The British had left the country; but peace did not imply repose. The community was still in that state of ferment which was natural enough to passions, not yet at rest, which had been brought into exercise and action during the protracted seven years' struggle through which the nation had just passed. The state was overrun by idlers, adventurers, profligates, and criminals. Disbanded soldiers, half-starved and reckless, occupied the highways,—outlaws, emerging from their hiding-places, skulked about the settlements with an equal sentiment of hate and fear in their hearts;—patriots were clamouring for justice upon the tories, and sometimes anticipating its course by judgments of their own; while the tories, those against whom the proofs were too strong for denial or evasion, buckled on their armour for a renewal of the struggle. Such being the condition of the country, it may easily be supposed that life and property lacked many of their necessary securities. Men generally travelled with weapons which were displayed on the smallest provocation; and few who could provide themselves with an escort ventured to travel any distance without one.

There was, about this time, said my grandmother, and while such was the condition of the country, a family of the name of Grayling, that lived somewhere upon the skirts of "Ninety-six" district, Old Grayling, the head of the family, was dead. He was killed in Buford's massacre. His wife was a fine woman, not so very old, who had an only son named James, and a little girl, only five years of age, named

A 5

Lucy. James was but fourteen when his father was killed, and that event made a man of him. He went out with his rifle in company with Joel Sparkman, who was his mother's brother, and joined himself to Pickens's Brigade. Here he made as good a soldier as the best. He had no sort of fear. He was always the first to go forward; and his rifle was always good for his enemy's button at a long hundred yards. He was in several fights both with the British and tories; and just before the war was ended he had a famous brush with the Cherokees, when Pickens took their country from them. But though he had no fear, and never knew when to stop killing while the fight was going on, he was the most bashful of boys that I ever knew; and so kind-hearted that it was almost impossible to believe all we heard of his fierce doings when he was in battle. But they were nevertheless quite true for all his bashfulness.

Well, when the war was over, Joel Sparkman, who lived with his sister Grayling, persuaded her that it would be better to move down into the low country. I don't know what reason he had for it, or what they proposed to do there. They had very little property, but Sparkman was a knowing man, who could turn his hand to a hundred things; and as he was a bachelor, and loved his sister and her children just as if they had been his own, it was natural that she should go with him wherever he wished. James, too, who was restless by nature —and the taste he had enjoyed of the wars had made him more so—he was full of it; and so, one sunny morning in April, their waggon started for the city. The waggon was only a small one, with two horses, scarcely larger than those that are employed to carry chickens and fruit to the market from the Wassamaws and thereabouts. It was driven by a negro fellow named Clytus, and carried Mrs. Grayling and Lucy. James and his uncle loved the saddle too well to shut themselves up in such a vehicle; and both of them were mounted on fine horses which they had won from the enemy. The saddle that James rode on—and he was very proud of it—was one that he had taken at the battle of Cowpens from one of Tarleton's own dragoons, after he had tumbled the owner. The roads at that season were excessively bad, for the rains of March had been frequent and heavy, the track was very much cut up, and the red clay gullies of the hills of "Ninety-six" were so washed that it required all shoulders, twenty times a day, to get the waggon wheels out of the bog. This made them travel very slowly—perhaps not more than fifteen miles a day. Another cause for slow travelling was, the necessity of great caution, and a constant look-out for enemies both up and down the road. James and his uncle took it by turns to ride a-head, precisely as they did when scouting in war, but one of them always kept along with the waggon. They had gone on this way for two days, and saw nothing to trouble and alarm them. There were few persons on the high road, and these seemed to the full as shy of them as they probably were of strangers. But just as they were about to camp, the evening of the second day, while they were splitting light-wood, and getting out the kettles and the frying-pan, a person rode up and joined them without much ceremony. He was a short thick-set man, somewhere between forty and fifty: had on very coarse and common garments, though he rode a fine black horse of remarkable strength and vigour. He was very civil of speech, though he had but little to say, and that little showed him to be a person without much education and with no refinement. He begged permission to make one of the encampment, and his manner was very respectful and even humble; but there was something dark and sullen in his face—his eyes, which were of a light grey colour, were very restless, and his nose turned up sharply, and was very red. His forehead was excessively broad, and his eyebrows thick and shaggy—white hairs being freely mingled with the dark, both in them and upon his head. Mrs. Grayling did not like the man's looks, and whispered her dis-

extra show of confidence and courage. He did not relish the
stranger from the first, any more than his sister; and having
subjected him to a searching examination, such as was considered, in those days of peril and suspicion, by no means in-
consistent with becoming courtesy, he came rapidly to the
conclusion that he was no better than he should be.

"You are a Scotchman, stranger," said Joel, suddenly
drawing up his feet, and bending forward to the other with
an eye like that of a hawk stooping over a covey of partridges.
It was a wonder that he had not made the discovery before.
The broad dialect of the stranger was not to be subdued; but
Joel made slow stages and short progress in his mental jour-
neyings. The answer was given with evident hesitation, but
it was affirmative.

"Well, now, it's mighty strange that you should ha' fou't
with us and not agin us," responded Joel Sparkman. "There
was a precious few of the Scotch, and none that I knows on,
saving yourself, perhaps,—that didn't go dead agin us, and
for the tories, through thick and thin. That 'Cross Creek
settlement' was a mighty ugly thorn in the sides of us whigs.
It turned out a raal bad stock of varmints. I hope—I reckon,
stranger—you aint from that part."

"No," said the other; "oh, no! I'm from over the other
quarter. I'm from the Duncan setttlement above."

"I've hearn tell of that other settlement, but I never know'd
as any of the men fou't with us. What giniral did you fight
under? What Carolina gineral?"

"I was at Gum Swamp when General Gates was defeated;"
was still the hesitating reply of the other.

"Well, I thank God, I warn't there, though I reckon things
wouldn't ha' turned out quite so bad, if there had been a leetle
sprinkling of Sumter's, or Pickens's, or Marion's men, among
them two-legged critters that run that day. They did tell
that some of the regiments went off without ever once

emptying their rifles. Now, stranger, I hope you warn't among them fellows."

" I was not," said the other, with something more of promptness."

" I don't blame a chap for dodging a bullet if he can, or being too quick for a bagnet, because, I'm thinking, a live man is always a better man than a dead one, or he can become so ; but to run without taking a single crack at the inimy, is downright cowardice. There's no two ways about it, stranger."

This opinion, delivered with considerable emphasis, met with the ready assent of the Scotchman, but Joel Sparkman was not to be diverted, even by his own eloquence, from the object of his inquiry.

" But you ain't said," he continued, "' who was your Carolina gineral. Gates was from Virginny, and he stayed a mighty short time when he come. You didn't run far at Camden, I reckon, and you joined the army ag'in, and come in with Greene ? Was that the how ?

To this the stranger assented, though with evident disinclination.

" Then, mou't be, we sometimes went into the same scratch together ? I was at Cowpens and Ninety-Six, and seen sarvice at other odds and eends, where there was more fighting than fun. I reckon you must have been at ' Ninety-Six,'— perhaps at Cowpens too, if you went with Morgan ?"

The unwillingness of the stranger to respond to these questions appeared to increase. He admitted, however, that he had been at " Ninety-Six," though, as Sparkman afterwards remembered, in this case, as in that of the defeat of Gates, at Gum Swamp, he had not said on which side he had fought.— Joel, as he discovered the reluctance of his guest to answer his questions, and perceived his growing doggedness, forbore to annoy him, but mentally resolved to keep a sharper lookout than **ever** upon his motions. His examination concluded

with an inquiry, which, in the plain-dealing regions of the
south and south-west, is not unfrequently put first.

" And what mout be your name, stranger ?"

" Macnab," was the ready response, " Sandy Macnab."

" Well, Mr. Macnab, I see that my sister's got supper ready
for us ; so we mou't as well fall to upon the hoecake and
bacon."

Sparkman rose while speaking, and led the way to the spot,
near the waggon, where Mrs. Grayling had spread the feast.—
" We're pretty nigh on the main road here, but I reckon there's
no great danger now. Besides, Jim Grayling keeps watch for
us, and he's got two as good eyes in his head as any scout in
the country, and a rifle that, after you once know how it
shoots, 'twould do your heart good to hear its crack, if so be
that twa'n't your heart that he drawed sight on. He's a per-
digious fine shot, and as ready to shoot and fight as if he had
a nateral calling that way."

" Shall we wait for him before we eat ?" demanded Macnab, anxiously.

" By no sort o' reason, stranger," answered Sparkman.—
He'll watch for us while we're eating, and after that I'll
change shoes with him. So fall to, and don't mind what's a
coming."

Sparkman had just broken the hoecake, when a distant
whistle was heard.

" Ha! that's the lad now !" he exclaimed, rising to his feet
" He's on trail. He's got sight of an inimy's fire, I reckon.—
'Twon't be onreasonable, friend Macnab, to get our we'pons
in readiness ;" and, so speaking, Sparkman bid his sister get
into the waggon, where the little Lucy had already placed
herself, while he threw open the pan of his rifle, and turned
the priming over with his finger. Macnab, meanwhile, had
taken from his holsters, which he had before been sitting
upon, a pair of horseman's pistols, richly mounted with figures
in silver. These were large and long, and had evidently seen

service. Unlike his companion, his proceedings occasioned no comment. What he did seemed a matter of habit, of which he was himself scarcely conscious. Having looked at his priming, he laid the instruments beside him without a word, and resumed the bit of hoecake which he had just before received from Sparkman. Meanwhile, the signal whistle, supposed to come from James Grayling, was repeated. Silence then ensued for a brief space, which Sparkman employed in perambulating the grounds immediately contiguous. At length, just as he had returned to the fire, the sound of a horse's feet was heard, and a sharp, quick hallo from Grayling informed his uncle that all was right. The youth made his appearance a moment after, accompanied by a stranger on horseback, a tall, fine-looking young man, with a keen, flashing eye, and a voice whose lively, clear tones, as he was heard approaching, sounded cheerily like those of a trumpet after victory. James Grayling kept along on foot beside the newcomer; and his hearty laugh, and free, glib, garrulous tones, betrayed to his uncle, long ere he drew nigh enough to declare the fact, that he had met unexpectedly with a friend, or, at least, an old acquaintance.

"Why, who have you got there, James?" was the demand of Sparkman, as he dropped the butt of his rifle upon the ground.

"Why, who do you think, uncle? Who but Major Spencer —our own major?"

"You don't say so!—what!—well! Li'nel Spencer, for sartin! Lord bless, you, major, who'd ha' thought to see you in these parts; and jest mounted too, for all natur, as if the war was to be fou't over ag'in. Well, I'm raal glad to see you.— I am, that's sartin!"

"And I'm very glad to see you, Sparkman," said the other, as he alighted from his steed, and yielded his hand to the cordial grasp of the other.

"Well, I knows that, major, without you saying it. But

you've jest come in the right time. The bacon's frying, and here's the bread;—let's down upon our haunches, in right good airnest, camp fashion, and make the most of what God gives us in the way of blessings. I reckon you don't mean to ride any further to-night, major?"

"No," said the person addressed, "not if you'll let me lay my heels at your fire. But who's in your waggon? My old friend, Mrs. Grayling, I suppose?"

"That's a true word, major," said the lady herself, making her way out of the vehicle with good-humoured agility, and coming forward with extended hand.

"Really, Mrs. Graylin, I'm glad to see you." And the stranger, with the blandness of a gentleman and the hearty warmth of an old neighbour, expressed his satisfaction at once more finding himself in the company of an old acquaintance. Their greetings once over, Major Spencer readily joined the group about the fire, while James Grayling—though with some reluctance—disappeared to resume his toils of the scout while the supper proceeded.

"And who have you here?" demanded Spencer, as his eye rested on the dark, hard features of the Scotchman. Spark-man told him all that he himself had learned of the name and character of the stranger, in a brief whisper, and in a moment after formally introduced the parties in this fashion—

"Mr. Macnab, Major Spencer. Mr. Macnab says he's true blue, major, and fou't at Camden, when General Gates run so hard to 'bring the d—d militia back.' He also fou't at Ninety-Six, and Cowpen—so I reckon we had as good as count him one of us."

Major Spencer scrutinized the Scotchman keenly—a scrutiny which the latter seemed very ill to relish. He put a few questions to him on the subject of the war, and some of the actions in which he allowed himself to have been concerned; but his evident reluctance to unfold himself—a reluctance so unatural to the brave soldier who has gone through his toils honourably

—had the natural effect of discouraging the young officer, whose sense of delicacy had not been materially impaired amid the the rude jostlings of a military life. But, though he forebore to propose any other question to Macnab, his eyes continued to survey the features of his sullen countenance with curiosity and a strangely increasing interest. This he subsequently explained to Sparkman, when, at the close of supper, Janes Grayling came in, and the former assumed the duties of the scout.

"I have seen that Scotchman's face somewhere, Sparkman, and I'm convinced at some interesting moment: but where, when, or how, I cannot call to mind. The sight of it is even associated in my mind with something painful and unpleasant; where could I have seen him?"

"I don't somehow like his look myself," said Sprakman, "and I mislists he's been rether more of a tory than a whig; but that's nothing to the purpose now; and he's at our fire and we've broken hoecake together; so we cannot rake up the old ashes to make a dust with."

"No, surely not," was the reply of Spencer. "Even though we know him to be a tory, the cause of former quarrel should occasion none now. But it should produce watchfulness and caution. I'm glad to see that you have not forgot your old business of scouting in the swamp."

"Kin I forget it, major?" demanded Sparkman, in tones which, though whispered, were full of emphasis, as he laid ear to the earth to listen.

"James has finished supper, major—that's his whistle to tell me so; and I'll jest step back to make it cl'ar to him how we're to keep up the watch to-night."

"Count me in your arrangements, Sparkman, as I am one of you for the night," said the major.

"By what sort of means," was the reply. "The night must be shared between James and myself. If so you wants to keep company with one or t'other of ns, why that's another thing, and, of course, you can do as you please."

"We'll have no quarrel on the subject, Joel," said the officer, good-naturedly, as they returned to the camp together.

CHAPTER II.

THE arrangements of the party were soon made. Spencer renewed his offer at the fire to take his part in the watch ; and the Scotchman, Macnab, volunteered his services also ; but the offer of the latter was another reason why that of the former should be declined. Sparkman was resolute to have everything his own way ; and while James Grayling went out upon his lonely rounds, he busied himself in cutting bushes and making a sort of tent for the use of his late commander. Mrs. Grayling and Lucy slept in the waggon. The Scotchman stretched himself with little effort before the fire ; while Joel Sparkman, wrapping himself up in the cloak, crouched under the waggon body, with his back resting partly against one of the wheels. From time to time he rose and thrust additional brands into the fire, looked up at the night, and round upon the encampment, then sunk back into his perch and stole a few moments, at intervals, of uneasy sleep. The first two hours of the watch were over, and James Grayling was reliev- ed. The youth, however, felt in no mood for sleep, and taking his seat be the fire, he drew from his pocket a little volume of Easy Reading Lessons, and by the fitful flame of the resinous light-wood, he prepared, in this rude manner, to make up for the precious time which his youth had lost of its legitimate employments, in the stirring events of the preceding seven years consumed in war. He was surprised at this employment by his late commander, who, himself sleepless, now emerged from the bushes and joined Grayling at the fire. The youth had been rather a favourite with Spencer. They had both been reared in the same neighbourhood, and the first military achievments of James had taken place under the eye, and had met the approbation of his officer. The difference of their ages was just such as to permit of the warm attachment of the lad without diminishing any of the reverence which should be felt by the inferior. Grayling was not more than seventeen, and Spencer was perhaps thirty-four — the very prime of manhood. They sat by the fire and talked of olden times and told old stories with the hearty glee and good nature of the young. Their mutual inquiries led to the revelation of their several objects in pursing the present journey. Those of James Grayling were scarcely, indeed, to be considered his own. They were plans and purposes of his uncle, and it does not concern this narrative that we should know more of their nature than has already been revealed. But whatever they were, they were as freely unfolded to his hearer as if the parties had been brothers, and Spencer was quite as frank in his revelations as his companion. He, too, was on his way to Charleston, from whence he was to take passage for England.

"I am rather in a hurry to reach town," he said, "as I learn that the Falmouth packet is preparing to sail for England in a few days, and I must go in her."

"For England, major!" exclaimed the youth with unaffected astonishment.

"Yes, James, for England. But why—what astonishes you?"

"Why, lord!" exclaimed the simple youth, "if they only knew there, as I do, what a cutting and slashing you did use to make among their red coats, I reckon they'd hang you to the first hickory."

"Oh, no! scarcely," said the other, with a smile.

"But I reckon you'll change your name, major?" continued the youth.

"No," responded Spencer, "if I did that, I should lose the

object of my voyage. You must know, James, that an old
relative has left me a good deal of money in England, and I
can only get it by proving that I am Lionel Spencer; so you
see I must carry my own name, whatever may be the risk."

"Well, major, you know best; but I do think if they could
only have a guess of what you did among their sodgers at
Hobkirk's and Cowpens, and Eutaw, and a dozen other
places, they'd find some means of hanging you up, peace or
no peace. But I don't see what occasion you have to be
going cl'ar away to England for money, when you've got a
sight of your own already."

"Not so much as you think for," replied the major, giving
an involuntary and uneasy glance at the Scotchman, who was
seemingly sound asleep on the opposite side of the fire.
"There is, you know, but little money in the country at any
time, and I must get what I want for my expenses when I
reach Charleston. I have just enough to carry me there."

"Well, now, major, that's mighty strange. I always
thought that you was about the best off of any man in our
parts; but if you're strained so close, I'm thinking, major,—
if so be you wouldn't think me too presumptuous,—you'd
better let me lend you a guinea or so that I've got to spare
and you can pay me back when you get the English money."

And the youth fumbled in his bosom for a little cotton wal-
let, which, with its limited contents, was displayed in another instant to the eyes of the officer.

"No, no, James," said the other, putting back the generous
tribute; I have quite enough to carry me to Charleston, and
when there I can easily get a supply from the merchants.
But I thank you, my good fellow, for your offer. You *are* a
good fellow, James, and I will remember you."

It is needless to pursue the conversation farther. The
night passed away without any alarms, and at dawn of the
next day the whole party was engaged in making preparation for a start. Mrs. Grayling was soon busy in getting

breakfast in readiness. Major Spencer consented to remain
with them until it was over; but the Scotchman, after returning thanks very civilly for his accommodation of the
night, at once resumed his journey. His course seemed, like
their own, to lie below; but he neither declared his route
nor betrayed the least desire to know that of Spencer. The
latter had no disposition to renew those inquiries from which
the stranger seemed to shrink the night before, and he accordingly suffered him to depart with a quiet farewell, and
the utterance of a good-natured wish, in which all the parties
joined, that he might have a pleasant journey. When he was
fairly out of sight, Spencer said to Sparkman,

"Had I liked that fellow's looks, nay, had I not positively
disliked them, I should have gone with him. As it is, I will
remain and share your breakfast."

The repast being over, all parties set forward; but Spencer,
after keeping along with them for a mile, took his leave also.
The slow waggon-pace at which the family travelled, did not
suit the high-spirited cavalier; and it was necessary, as he
assured them, that he should reach the city in two nights
more. They parted with many regrets, as truly felt as they
were warmly expressed; and James Grayling never felt the
tedium of waggon travelling to be so severe as throughout the
whole of that day when he separated from his favourite captain. But he was too stout-hearted a lad to make any complaint; and his dissatisfaction only showed itself in his unwonted silence, and an over-anxiety, which his steed seemed
to feel in common with himself, to go rapidly ahead. Thus
the day passed, and the wayfarers at its close had made a progress of some twenty miles from sun to sun. The same precautions marked their encampment this night as the last, and
they rose in better spirits with the next morning, the dawn of
which was very bright and pleasant, and encouraging. A
similar journey of twenty miles brought them to a place of
bivouac as the sun went down; and they prepared as usual

for their securities and supper. They found themselves on the
edge of a very dense forest of pines and scrubby oaks, a portion
of which was swallowed up in a deep bay—so called in the
dialect of the country—a swamp-bottom, the growth of which
consisted of mingled cypresses and bay-trees, with tupola,
gum, and dense thickets of low stunted shrubbery, cane grass,
and dwarf willows, which filled up every interval between
the trees, and to the eye most effectually barred out every human intruder. This bay was chosen as the background for
the camping party. Their waggon was wheeled into an area
on a gently rising ground in front, under a pleasant shade of
oaks and hickories, with a lonely pine rising loftily in occa-
sional spots among them. Here the horses were taken out,
and James Grayling prepared to kindle up a fire; but, looking
for his axe, it was unaccountably missing, and after a fruitless
search of half an hour, the party came to the conclusion that
it had been left on the spot where they had slept last night.
This was a disaster, and, while they meditated in what manner to repair it, a negro boy appeared in sight, passing along
the road at their feet, and driving before him a small herd of
cattle. From him they learned that they were only a mile or
two from a farmstead where an axe might be borrowed; and
James, leaping on his horse, rode forward in the hope to obtain
one. He found no difficulty in his quest; and, having obtained
it from the farmer, who was also a tavern-keeper, he casually
asked if Major Spencer had not stayed with him the night before. He was somewhat surprised when told that he had not.

"There was one man stayed with me last night," said the
farmer, "but he didn't call himself a major, and didn't much
look like one."

"He rode a fine sorrel horse,—tall, bright colour, with white
fore foot, didn't he?" asked James.

"No, that he didn't! He rode a powerful black, coal black,
and not a bit of white about him."

"That was the Scotchman! But I wonder the major didn't

stop with you. He must have rode on. Isn't there another
house near you, below!"

"Not one. There's ne'er a house either above or below for
a matter of fifteen miles. I'm the only man in all that distance
that's living on this road ; and I don't think your friend could
have gone below, as I should have seen him pass. I've been
all day out there in that field before your eyes, clearing up the
brush."

CHAPTER III.

SOMEWHAT wondering that the major should have turned aside
from the track, though without attaching to it any importance
at that particular moment, James Grayling took up the borrowed axe and hurried back to the encampment, where the toil
of cutting an extra supply of light-wood to meet the exigen-
cies of the ensuing night, sufficiently exercised his mind as well
as his body, to prevent him from meditating upon the seeming
strangeness of the circumstance. But when he sat down to
his supper over the fire that he had kindled, his fancies crowded
thickly upon him, and he felt a confused doubt and suspicion
that something was to happen, he knew not what. His con-
jectures and apprehensions were without form, though not altogether void ; and he felt a strange sickness and a sinking at
the heart which was very unusual with him. He had, in short,
that lowness of spirits, that cloudy apprehensiveness of soul
which takes the form of presentiment, and makes us look out
for danger even when the skies are without a cloud, and the
breeze is laden, equally and only, with balm and music. His
moodiness found no sympathy among his companions. Joel
Sparkman was in the best of humours, and his mother was so
cheery and happy, that when the thoughtful boy went off into
the woods to watch, he could hear her at every moment breaking out into little catches of a country ditty, which the gloomy

events of the late war had not yet obliterated from her memory.

"It's very strange!" soliloquized the youth, 'as he wandered along the edges of the dense bay or swamp-bottom, which we have passingly referred to,—"it's very strange what troubles me so! I feel almost frightened, and yet I know I'm not to be frightened easily, and I don't see anything in the woods to frighten me. It's strange the major didn't come along this road! Maybe he took another higher up that leads by a different settlement. I wish I had asked the man at the house if there's such another road. I reckon there must be, however, for where could the major have gone?"

The unphilosophical mind of James Grayling did not, in his farther meditations, carry him much beyond this starting point; and with its continual recurrence in soliloquy, he proceeded to traverse the margin of the bay, until he came to its junction with, and termination at, the high road. The youth turned into this, and, involuntarily departing from it a moment after, soon found himself on the opposite side of the bay thicket. He wandered on and on, as he himself described it, without any power to restrain himself. He knew not how far he went; but, instead of maintaining his watch for two hours only, he was gone more than four; and, at length, a sense of weariness which overpowered him all of a sudden, caused him to seat himself at the foot of a tree, and snatch a few moments of rest. He denied that he slept in this time. He insisted to the last moment of his life that sleep never visited his eyelids that night,—that he was conscious of fatigue and exhaustion, but not drowsiness,—and that this fatigue was so numbing as to be painful, and effectually kept him from any sleep. While he sat thus beneath the tree, with a body weak and nerveless, but a mind excited, he knew not how or why, to the most acute degree of expectation and attention, he heard his name called by the well-known voice of his friend, Major Spencer. The voice called

B

him three times,—" James Grayling!—James!—James Grayling!" before he could muster strength enough to answer. It
was not courage he wanted,—of that he was positive, for he
felt sure, as he said, that something had gone wrong, and he
was never more ready to fight in his life than at that moment,
could he have commanded the physical capacity; but his
throat seemed dry to suffocation,—his lips effectually sealed
up as if with wax, and when he did answer, the sounds
seemed as fine and soft as the whisper of some child just born.

" Oh! major, is it you?"

Such, he thinks, were the very words he made use of in reply; and the answer that he received was instantaneous,
though the voice came from some little distance in the bay,
and his own voice he did not hear. He only knows what he
meant to say. The answer was to this effect.

" It is, James!—It is your own friend, Lionel Spencer, that
speaks to you; do not be alarmed when you see me! I have
been shockingly murdered!"

James asserts that he tried to tell him that he would not be
frightened, but his own voice was still a whisper, which he
himself could scarcely hear. A moment after he had spoken,
he heard something like a sudden breeze that rustled through
the bay bushes at his feet, and his eyes were closed without
his effort, and indeed in spite of himself. When he opened
them, he saw Major Spencer standing at the edge of the bay,
about twenty steps from him. Though he stood in the shade
of a thicket, and there was no light in the heavens save that
of the stars, he was yet enabled to distinguish perfectly, and
with great ease, every lineament of his friend's face.

He looked very pale, and his garments were covered with
blood; and James said that he strove very much to rise from
the place where he sat and approach him;—"for in truth,"
said the lad, " so far from feeling any fear, I felt nothing but
fury in my heart; but I could not move a limb. My feet were
fastened to the ground; my hands to my sides; and I could

only bend forward and gasp. I felt as if I should have died with vexation that I could not rise; but a power which I could not resist, made me motionless, and almost speechless. I could only say, ' Murdered !'—and that one word I believe I must have repeated a dozen times.

" ' Yes, murdered !—murdered by the Scotchman who slept with us at the fire the night before last. James, I look to you to have the murderer brought to justice ! James!—do you hear me, James ?' "

" These," said James, " I think were the very words, or near about the very words, that I heard; and I tried to ask the major to tell me how it was, and how I could do what he required; but I didn't hear myself speak, though it would appear that he did, for almost immediately after I had tried to speak what I wished to say, he answered me just as if I had said it. He told me that the Scotchman had waylaid, killed, and hidden him in that very bay; that his murderer had gone to Charleston; and that if I made haste to town, I would find him in the Falmouth packet, which was then lying in the harbour and ready to sail for England. He farther said that everything depended on my making haste,—that I must reach town by to-morrow night if I wanted to be in season, and go right on board the vessel and charge the criminal with the deed. ' Do not be afraid,' said he, when he had finished ; ' be afraid of nothing, James, for God will help and strengthen you to the end.' When I heard all I burst into a flood of tears, and then I felt strong. I felt I could talk, or fight, or do almost anything; and I jumped up to my feet, and was just about to run down to where the major stood, but, with the first step which I made forward, he was gone. I stopped and looked all around me, but I could see nothing ; and the bay was just as black as midnight. But I went down to it, and tried to press in where I thought the major had been standing; but I couldn't get far, the brush and bay leaves were so close and thick. I was now bold and strong enough, and I called out, loud enough to be heard half a mile. I didn't exactly know what I called for, or what I wanted to learn, or I have forgotten. But I heard nothing more. Then I remembered the camp, and began to fear that something might have happened to mother and uncle, for I now felt, what I had not thought of before, that I had gone too far round the bay to be of much assistance, or indeed, to be in time for any, had they been suddenly attacked. Besides, I could not think how long I had been gone; but it now seemed very late. The stars were shining their brightest, and the thin white clouds of morning were beginning to rise and run towards the west. Well, I bethought me of my course,—for I was a little bewildered and doubtful where I was; but, after a little thinking, I took the back track, and soon got a glimpse of a camp-fire, which was nearly burnt down ; and by this I reckoned I was gone considerably longer than my two hours. When I got back into the camp, I looked under the waggon, and found uncle in a sweet sleep, and though my heart was full almost to bursting with what I had heard, and the cruel sight I had seen, yet I wouldn't waken him; and I beat about and mended the fire, and watched, and waited, until near daylight, when mother called to me out of the waggon. and asked who it was. This wakened my uncle, and then I up and told all that had happened, for if it had been to save my life, I couldn't have kept it in much longer. But though mother said it was very strange, Uncle Sparkman considered that I had been only dreaming; but he couldn't persuade me of it; and when I told him I intended to be off at daylight, just as the major had told me to do, and ride my best all the way to Charleston, he laughed, and said I was a fool. But I felt that I was no fool, and I was solemn certain that I hadn't been dreaming ; and though both mother and he tried their hardest to make me put off going, yet I made up my mind to it, and they had to give up. For, wouldn't I have been a pretty sort of a friend to the major, if, after what he had told me, I could have stayed behind, and gone on only at a waggon-pace to look after the murderer! I don't think if I had done so that I should ever have been able to look a white man in the face again. Soon as the peep of day, I was on horseback. Mother was mighty sad, and begged me not to go, but Uncle Sparkman was mighty sulky, and kept calling me fool upon fool, until I was almost angry enough to forget that we were of blood kin. But all his talking did not stop me, and I reckon I was five miles on my way before he had his team in traces for a start. I rode as briskly as I could get on without hurting my nag. I had a smart ride of more than forty miles before me, and the road was very heavy. But it was a good two hours from sunset when I got into town, and the first question I asked of the people I met was, to show me where the ships were kept. When I got to the wharf they showed me the Falmouth packet, where she lay in the stream, ready to sail as soon as the wind should fa-vour."

CHAPTER IV.

JAMES GRAYLING, with the same eager impatience which he has been suffered to describe in his own language, had already hired a boat to go on board the British packet, when he remembered that he had neglected all those means, legal and otherwise, by which alone his purpose might be properly effected. He did not know much about legal process, but he had common sense enough, the moment that he began to reflect on the subject, to know that some such process was necessary. This conviction produced another difficulty; he knew not in which quarter to turn for counsel and assistance; but here the boatman who saw his bewilderment, and knew by his dialect and dress that he was a back-countryman, came to his relief, and from him he got directions where to find the merchants with whom his uncle, Sparkman, had done business in former years. To them he went, and without circumlocution, told the whole story of his ghostly visitation. Even as a dream, which these gentlemen at once conjectured it to be, the story of James Grayling was equally clear and curious; and his intense warmth and the entire absorption, which the subject had effected, of his mind and soul, was such that they judged it not improper, at least to carry out the search of the vessel which he contemplated. It would certainly, they thought, be a coincidence—believing James to be a veracious youth—if the Scotchman should be found on board. But another test of his narrative was proposed by one of the firm. It so happened that the business agents of Major Spencer, who was well known in Charleston, kept their office but a few rods distant from their own; and to them all parties at once proceeded. But here the story of James was encountered by a circumstance that made somewhat against it. These gentlemen produced a letter from Major Spencer, intimating the utter impossibility of his coming to town for the space of a month, and expressing his regret that he should be unable to avail himself of the opportunity of the foreign vessel, of whose arrival in Charleston, and proposed time of departure, they had themselves advised him. They read the letter aloud to James and their brother merchants, and with difficulty suppressed their smiles at the gravity with which the former related and insisted upon the particulars of his vision.

"He has changed his mind," returned the impetuous youth; "he was on his way down, I tell you,—a hundred miles on his way,—when he camped with us. I know him well, I tell you, and talked with him myself half the night."

"At least," remarked the gentlemen who had gone with James, "it can do no harm to look into the business. We can procure a warrant for searching the vessel after this man,

Macnab; and should he be found on board the packet, it will
be a sufficient circumstance to justify the magistrates in de-
taining him, until we can ascertain where Major Spencer
really is."

The measure was accordingly adopted, and it was nearly
sun-set before the warrant was procured, and the proper officer in readiness. The impatience of a spirit so eager and so
devoted as James Grayling, under these delays, may be imagined; and when in the boat, and on his way to the packet
where the criminal was to be sought, his blood became so excited that it was with much ado he could be kept in his seat.
His quick, eager action continually disturbed the trim of the
boat, and one of his mercantile friends, who had accompanied
him, with that interest in the affair which curiosity alone inspired, was under constant apprehension lest he would plunge
overboard in his impatient desire to shorten the space which
lay between. The same impatience enabled the youth, though
never on shipboard before, to grasp the rope which had been
flung at their approach, and to mount her sides with catlike
agility. Without waiting to declare himself or his purpose,
he ran from one side of the deck to the other, greedily staring,
to the surprise of officers, passengers, and seamen, in the faces
of all of them, and surveying them with an almost offensive
scrutiny. He turned away from the search with disappointment. There was no face like that of the suspected man
among them. By this time, his friend, the merchant, with
the sheriff's officer, had entered the vessel, and were in conference with the captain. Grayling drew nigh in time to hear
the latter affirm that there was no man of the name of Macnab, as stated in the warrant, among his passengers or crew.

"He is—he must be!" exclaimed the impetuous youth.
"The major never lied in his life, and couldn't lie after he was
dead. Macnab is here—he is a Scotchman—"

The captain interrupted him—

"We have, young gentleman, several Scotchmen on board, and one of them is named Macleod—"

"Let me see him—which is he?" demanded the youth.

By this time, the passengers and a goodly portion of the crew were collected about the little party. The captain turned his eyes upon the group, and asked,

"Where is Mr. Macleod?"

"He is gone below—he's sick!" replied one of the passengers.

"That's he! That must be the man!" exclaimed the youth. "I'll lay my life that's no other than Macnab. He's only taken a false name."

It was now remembered by one of the passengers, and remarked, that Macleod had expressed himself as unwell, but a few moments before, and had gone below even while the boat was rapidly approaching the vessel. At this statement, the captain led the way into the cabin, closely followed by James Grayling and the rest.

"Mr. Macleod," he said with a voice somewhat elevated, as he approached the berth of that person, "you are wanted on deck for a few moments."

"I am really too unwell, captain," replied a feeble voice from behind the curtain of the berth.

"It will be necessary," was the reply of the captain. "There is a warrant from the authorities of the town, to look after a fugitive from justice."

Macleod had already begun a second speech declaring his feebleness, when the fearless youth, Grayling, bounded before thr captain and tore away, with a single grasp of his hand, the curtain which concealed the suspected man from their sight.

"It is he!" was the instant exclamation of the youth, as he beheld him. "It is he—Macnab, the Scotchman—the man that murdered Major Spencer!"

Macnab,—for it was he,—was deadly pale. He trembled like an aspen. His eyes were dilated with more than mortal apprehension, and his lips were perfectly livid. Still, he found strength to speak, and to deny the accusation. He knew nothing of the youth before him—nothing of Major Spencer—his name was Macleod, and he had never called himself by any other. He denied, but with great incoherence, everything which was urged against him.

" You must get up, Mr. Macleod," said the captain; " the circumstances are very much against you. You must go with the officer !"

" Will you give me up to my enemies ?" demanded the culprit. " You are a countryman—a Briton. I have fought for the king, our master, against these rebels, and for this they seek my life. Do not deliver me into their bloody hands !"

" Liar !" exclaimed James Grayling—" Didn't you tell us at our own camp-fire that you were with us ? that you were at Gates's defeat, and Ninety-Six ?"

" But I didn't tell you," said the Scotchman, with a grin, " which side I was on !"

" Ha ! remember that !" said the sheriff's officer. " He denied, just a moment ago, that he knew this young man at all ; now, he confesses that he did see and camp with him."

The Scotchman was aghast at the strong point which, in his inadvertence, he had made against himself ; and his efforts to excuse himself, stammering and contradictory, served only to involve him more deeply in the meshes of his difficulty. Still he continued his urgent appeals to the captain of the vessel, and his fellow-passengers, as citizens of the same country, subjects to the same monarch, to protect him from those who equally hated and would destroy them all. In order to move their national prejudices in his behalf, he boasted of the immense injury which he had done, as a tory, to the rebel cause ; and still insisted that the murder was only a pretext of the

B 5

youth before him, by which to gain possession of his person,
and wreak upon him the revenge which his own fierce performances during the war had naturally enough provoked.
One or two of the passengers, indeed, joined with him in en-
treating the captain to set the accusers adrift and make sail at
once; but the stout Englishman, who was in command, rejected instantly the unworthy counsel. Besides, he was better
aware of the dangers which would follow any such rash proceeding. Fort Moultrie, on Sullivan's Island, had been already
refitted and prepared for an enemy ; and he was lying, at that
moment, under the formidable range of grinning teeth, which
would have opened upon him, at the first movement, from the
jaws of Castle Pinckney.

" No, gentlemen," said he, " you mistake your man. God
forbid that I should give shelter to a murderer, though he were
from my own parish."

" But I am no murderer," said the Scotchman.

" You look cursedly like one, however," was the reply of
the captain. " Sheriff, take your prisoner."

The base creature threw himself at the feet of the Englishman, and clung, with piteous entreaties, to his knees. The
latter shook him off, and turned away in disgust.

" Steward," he cried, " bring up this man's luggage."

He was obeyed. The luggage was brought up from the
cabin and delivered to the sheriff's officer, by whom it was
examined in the presence of all, and an inventory made of its
contents. It consisted of a small new trunk, which, it afterwards appeared, he had bought in Charleston, soon after his
arrival. This contained a few changes of raiment, twenty-six
guineas in money, a gold watch, not in repair, and the two
pistols which he had shown while at Joel Sparkman's camp
fire ; but, with this difference, that the stock of one was broken
off short just above the grasp, and the butt was entirely gone.
It was not found among his chattels. A careful examination
of the articles in his trunk did not result in anything calcu-

lated to strengthen the charge of his criminality; but there was not a single person present who did not feel as morally certain of his guilt as if the jury had already declared the fact. That night he slept—if he slept at all—in the common jail of the city.

———

CHAPTER V.

His accuser, the warm-hearted and resolute James Grayling, did not sleep. The excitement, arising from mingling and contradictory emotions,—sorrow for his brave young commander's fate, and the natural exultation of a generous spirit at the consciousness of having performed, with signal success, an ardous and painful task combined to drive all pleasant slumbers from his eyes; and with the dawn he was again up and stirring, with his mind still full of the awful business in which he had been engaged. We do not care to pursue his course in the ordinary walks of the city, nor account for his employments during the few days which ensued, until, in consequence of a legal examination into the circumstances which anticipated the regular work of the sessions, the extreme excitement of the young accuser had been renewed. Macnab or Macleod,—and it is possible that both names were fictitious, —as soon as he recovered from his first terrors, sought the aid of an attorney—one of those acute, small, chopping lawyers, to be found in almost every community, who are willing to serve with equal zeal the sinner and the saint, provided that they can pay with equal liberality. The prisoner was brought before the court under *habeas corpus*, and several grounds submitted by his counsel with the view to obtaining his discharge, It became necessary to ascertain, among the first duties of the state, whether Major Spencer, the alleged victim, was really dead. Until it could be established that a man should be imprisoned, tried, and punished for a crime, it was first necessary to show that a crime had been committed, and the attorney made himself exceedingly merry with the ghost story of young Grayling. In those days, however, the ancient Superstition was not so feeble as she has subsequently become. The venerable judge was one of those good men who had a decent respect for the faith and opinions of his ancestors; and though he certainly would not have consented to the hanging of Macleod under the sort of testimony which had been adduced, he yet saw enough, in all the circumstances, to justify his present detention. In the meantime, efforts were to be made, to ascertain the whereabouts of Major Spencer; though, were he even missing,—so the counsel for Macleod contended, —his death could be by no means assumed in consequence. To this the judge shook his head doubtfully. " 'Fore God !" said he, " I would not have you to be too sure of that." He was an Irishman, and proceeded after the fashion of his country. The reader will therefore *bear* with his *bull.* " A man may properly be hung for murdering another, though the murdered man be not dead ; ay, before God, even though he be actually unhurt and uninjured, while the murderer is swinging by the neck for the bloody deed !"

The judge,—who it must be understood was a real existence, and who had no small reputation in his day in the south,— proceeded to establish the correctness of his opinions by authorities and argument, with all of which, doubtlessly, the bar were exceedingly delighted ; but, to provide them in this place would only be to interfere with our own progress. James Grayling, however, was not satisfied to wait the slow processes which were suggested for coming at the truth. Even the wisdom of the judge was lost upon him, possibly, for the simple reason that he did not comprehend it. But the ridicule of the culprit's lawyer stung him to the quick, and he muttered to himself, more than once, a determination " to lick the life out of that impudent chap's leather." But this was not his only resolve. There was one which he proceeded to put into instant execution, and that was to seek the body of his murdered friend in the spot when he fancied it might be found—namely, the dark and dismal bay where the spectre had made its appearance to his eyes.

The suggestion was approved—though he did not need this to prompt his resolution—by his mother and uncle, Sparkman. The latter determined to be his companion, and he was farther accompanied by the sheriff's officer who had arrested the suspected felon. Before daylight, on the morning after the examination before the judge had taken place, and when Macleod had been remanded to prison, James Grayling started on his journey. His fiery zeal received additional force at every added moment of delay, and his eager spurring brought him at an early hour after noon, to the neighbourhood of the spot through which his search was to be made. When his companions and himself drew nigh, they were all at a loss in which direction first to proceed. The bay was one of those massed forests, whose wall of thorns, vines, and close tenacious shrubs, seemed to defy invasion. To the eye of the townsman it was so forbidding that he pronounced it absolutely impenetrable. But James was not to be baffled. He led them round it, taking the very course which he had pursued the night when the revelation was made him; he showed them the very tree at whose foot he had sunk when the supernatural torpor—as he himself esteemed it—began to fall upon him; he then pointed out the spot, some twenty steps distant, at which the spectre made his appearance. To this spot they then proceeded in a body, and essayed an entrance, but were so discouraged by the difficulties at the outset that all, James not excepted, concluded that neither the murderer nor his victim could possibly have found entrance there.

But, lo! a marvel! Such it seemed, at the first blush, to all the party. While they stood confounded and indecisive, undetermined in which way to move, a sudden flight of wings was heard, even from the centre of the bay, at a little distance above the spot where they had striven for entrance. They looked up, and beheld about fifty buzzards—those notorious domestic vultures of the south—ascending from the interior of the bay, and perching along upon the branches of the loftier trees by which it was overhung. Even were the character of these birds less known, the particular business in which they had just then been engaged, was betrayed by huge gobbets of flesh which some of them had borne aloft in their flight, and still continued to rend with beak and bill, as they tottered upon the branches where they stood. A piercing scream issued from the lips of James Grayling as he beheld this sight, and strove to scare the offensive birds from their repast.

" The poor major! the poor major!" was the involuntary and agonized exclamation of the youth. " Did I ever think he would come to this!"

The search, thus guided and encouraged, was pressed with renewed diligence and spirit; and, at length, an opening was found through which it was evident that a body of considerable size had but recently gone. The branch were broken from the small shrub trees, and the undergrowth trodden into the earth. They followed this path, and, as is the case commonly with waste tracts of this description, the density of the growth diminished sensibly at every step they took, till they reached a little pond, which, though circumscribed in area, and full of cypresses, yet proved to be singularly deep. Indeed, it was an alligator-hole, where, in all probability, a numerous tribe of these reptiles had their dwelling. Here, on the edge of the pond, they discovered the object which had drawn the keen-sighted vultures to their feast, in the body of a horse, which James Grayling at once identified as that of Major Spencer The carcass of the animal was already very much torn and lacerated. The eyes were plucked out, and the animal completely disembowelled. Yet, on examination, it was not difficult to discover the manner of his death. This had been effected by fire-arms. Two bullets had passed through his skull, just above the eyes, either of which must have been fatal. The murderer had led the horse to the spot, and committed the cruel deed where his body was found. The search was now continued for that of the owner, but for some time it proved ineffectual. At length, the keen eyes of James Grayling detected, amidst a heap of moss and green sedge that rested beside an overthrown tree, whose branches jutted into the pond, a whitish, but discoloured object, that did not seem native to the place. Bestriding the fallen tree, he was enabled to reach this object, which, with a burst of grief, he announced to the distant party was the hand and arm of his unfortunate friend, the wristband of the shirt being the conspicuous object which had first caught his eye. Grasping this, he drew the corse, which had been thrust beneath the branches of the tree, to the surface ; and, with the assistance of his uncle, it was finally brought to the dry land. Here it underwent a careful examination. The head was very much disfigured ; the skull was fractured in several places by repeated blows of some hard instrument, inflicted chiefly from behind. A closer inspection revealed a bullet-hole in the abdomen, the first wound, in all probability, which the unfortunate gentleman received, and by which he was, perhaps, tumbled from his horse. The blows on the head would seem to have been unnecessary, unless the murderer—whose proceedings appeared to have been singularly deliberate,—was resolved upon making " assurance doubly sure." But, as if the watchful Providence had meant that nothing should be left doubtful which might tend to the complete conviction of the criminal, the constable stumbled upon the butt of the broken pistol which had been found in Macleod's trunk. This he picked up on the edge of the pond in which the corse had been discovered, and while James Grayling and his uncle, Sparkman, were engaged in drawing it from the water. The place where the fragment was discovered at once denoted the pistol as the instrument by which

parated. The dull travelling waggon-gait at which he himself
was compelled to go, was a source of annoyance to him; and
he became sullen, all the day, after the departure of his friend.
When, on the evening of the next day, he came to the house
where it was natural to expect that Major Spencer would
have slept the night before, and he learned the fact that no
one stopped there, but the Scotchman, Macnab, we see that he
was struck with the circumstance. He mutters it over to
himself, "Strange, where the Major could have gone!" His
mind then naturally reverts to the character of the Scotchman;
to the opinions and suspicions which had been already expressed of him by his uncle, and felt by himself. They had
all, previously, come to the full conviction that Macnab was,
and had always been, a tory, in spite of his protestations.
His mind next, and very naturally, reverted to the insecurity
of the highways: the general dangers of travelling at that period; the frequency of crime, and the number of desperate
men who were everywhere to be met with. The very employment in which he was then engaged, in scouting the
woods for the protection of the camp, was calculated to bring
such reflections to his mind. If these precautions were considered necessary for the safety of persons so poor, so wanting
in those possessions which might prompt cupidity to crime,
how much more necessary were precautions in the case of a
wealthy gentleman like Major Spencer! He then remembered
the conversation with the major at the camp fire, when they
fancied that the Scotchman was sleeping. How natural to
think then, that he was all the while awake; and, if awake,
he must have heard him speak of the wealth of his companion.
True, the major, with more prudence than himself, denied that
he had any money about him, more than would bear his expenses to the city; but such an assurance was natural
enough to the lips of a traveller who knew the dangers of the
country. That the man, Macnab, was not a person to be
trusted, was the equal impression of Joel Sparkman and his

nephew from the first. The probabilities were strong that he would rob and perhaps murder, if he might hope to do so with impunity; and as the youth made the circuit of the bay in the darkness and solemn stillness of the night, its gloomy depths and mournful shadows, naturally gave rise to such reflections as would be equally active in the mind of a youth, and of one somewhat familiar with the arts and usages of strife. He would see that the spot was just the one in which a practised partizan would delight to set an ambush for an unwary foe. There ran the public road, with a little sweep, around two-thirds of the extent of its dense and impenetrable thickets. The ambush could lie concealed, and at ten steps command the bosom of its victim. Here, then, you perceive that the mind of James Grayling, stimulated by an active and sagacious judgment, had by gradual and reasonable stages come to these conclusions: that Major Spencer was an object to tempt a robber; that the country was full of robbers; that Macnab was one of them; that this was the very spot in which a deed of blood could be most easily committed, and most easily concealed; and, one important fact, that gave strength and coherence to the whole, that Major Spencer had not reached a well-known point of destination, while Macnab had.

" With these thoughts, thus closely linked together, the youth forgets the limits of his watch and his circuit. This fact, alone, proves how active his imagination had become. It leads him forward, brooding more and more upon the subject, until, in the very exhaustion of his body, he sinks down beneath a tree. He sinks down and falls asleep; and in his sleep, what before was plausible conjecture, becomes fact, and the creative properties of his imagination give form and vitality to all his fancies. These forms are bold, broad, and deeply coloured, in due proportion with the degree of force which they receive from probability. Here, he sees the image of his friend; but, you will remark—and this should almost

conclusively satisfy any mind that all that he sees is the work
of his imagination,—that, though Spencer tells him that he is
murdered, and by Macnab, he does not tell him how, in what
manner, or with what weapons. Though he sees him pale and
ghostlike, he does not see, nor can he say, where his wounds
are! He sees his pale features distinctly, and his garments
are bloody. Now, had he seen the spectre in the true appearances of death, as he was subsequently found, he would not
have been able to discern his features, which were battered,
according to his own account, almost out of all shape of humanity, and covered with mud; while his clothes would have
streamed with mud and water, rather than with blood."

" Ah!" exclaimed the old lady, my grandmother, " it's hard
to make you believe any thing that you don't see; you are
like St. Thomas in the Scriptures; but how do you propose to
account for his knowing that the Scotchman was on board the
Falmouth packet? Answer to that!"

" That is not a more difficult matter than any of the rest.—
You forget that in the dialogue which took place between
James and Major Spencer at the camp, the latter told him that
he was about to take passage for Europe in the Falmouth
packet, which then lay in Charleston harbour, and was about
to sail. Macnab heard all that."

" True enough, and likely enough," returned the old lady ;
" but, though you show that it was Major Spencer's intention
to go to Europe in the Falmouth packet, that will not show
that it was also the intention of the murderer."

" Yet, what more probable, and how natural for James
Grayling to imagine such a thing! In the first place, he knew
that Macnab was a Briton; he felt convinced that he was a
tory ; and the inference was immediate, that such a person
would scarcely have remained long in a country where such
characters laboured under so much odium, disfranchisement,
and constant danger from popular tumults. The fact that
Macnab was compelled to disguise his true sentiments, and

affect those of the people against whom he fought so vindic-
tively, shows what was his sense of the danger which he in-
curred. Now, it is not unlikely that Macnab was quite as
well aware that the Falmouth packet was in Charleston, and
about to sail, as Major Spencer. No doubt he was pursuing
the same journey, with the same object, and had he not murdered Spencer, they would, very likely, have been fellow-passengers together to Europe. But, whether he knew the fact
before or not, he probably heard it stated by Spencer, while he
seemed to be sleeping; and, even supposing that he did not
then know, it was enough that he found this to be the fact on
reaching the city. It was an after-thought to fly to Europe
with his ill-gotten spoils; and whatever may have appeared a
politic course to the criminal, would be a probable conjecture
in the mind of him by whom he was suspected. The whole
story is one of strong probabilities, which happened to be veri-
fied; and if proving any thing, proves only that which we
know, that James Grayling was a man of remarkably sagacious judgment, and quick, daring imagination. This quality
of imagination, by the way, when possessed very strongly in
connection with shrewd common sense, and well-balanced general faculties, makes that particular kind of intellect which,
because of its promptness and powers of creation and combi-
nation, we call genius. It is genius only which can make ghosts,
and James Grayling was a genius. He never, my son, saw
any other ghosts than those of his own making !"

I heard my father with great patience to the end, though he
seemed very tedious. He had taken a great deal of pains to
destroy one of my greatest sources of pleasure. I need not
add that I continued to believe in the ghost, and, with my
grandmother, to reject the philosophy. It was more easy to
believe the one than to comprehend the other.

THE TWO CAMPS.

A LEGEND OF THE OLD NORTH STATE.

" These, the forest born
And forest nurtured—a bold, hardy race,
Fearless and frank,u nfettered, with big souls
In hour of danger."

CHAPTER I.

IT is frequently the case, in the experience of the professional novelist or tale-writer, that his neighbour comes in to his assistance when he least seeks, and, perhaps, least desires any succour. The worthy person, man or woman, however,—probably some excellent octogenarian whose claims to be heard are based chiefly upon the fact that he himself no longer possesses the faculty of hearing,—has some famous incident, some wonderful fact, of which he has been the eye-witness, or of which he has heard from his great-grandmother, which he fancies is the very thing to be woven into song or story.. Such is the strong possession which the matter takes of his brain, that if the novelist whom he seeks to benefit does not live within trumpet-distance, he gives him the narrative by means of post, some three sheets of stiff foolscap, for which the hapless tale-writer, whose works are selling in cheap editions at twelve or twenty cents, pays a sum of one dollar sixty-two cents postage. Now, it so happens, to increase the evil, that, in ninety-nine cases in the hundred, the fact thus laboriously stated is not worth a straw—consisting of some simple deed of violence, some mere murder, a downright blow with gun-butt or cudgel over the skull, or a hidden thrust, three inches deep, with dirk or bowie knife, into the abdomen, or at random among the lower ribs. The man dies and the murderer gets off to Texas, or is prematurely caught and stops by the way—and still stops by the way! The thing is fact, no doubt. The narrator saw it himself, or his brother saw it himself, or his brother saw it, or—more solemn, if not more certain testimony still—his grand-mother saw it, long before he had eyes to see at all. The circumstance is attested by a cloud of witnesses—a truth solemnly sworn to—and yet, for the purposes of the tale-writer, of no manner of value. This assertion may somewhat conflict with the received opinions of many, who, accustomed to find deeds of violence recorded in almost every work of fiction, from the time of Homer to the present day, have rushed to the conclusion that this is all, and overlook that labour of the artist, by which an ordinary event is made to assume the character of novelty; in other words, to become an extraordinary event. The least diffi-cult thing in the world, on the part of the writer of fiction, is to find the assassin and the bludgeon ; the art is to make them appear in the right place, strike at the right time, and so adapt one fact to another, as to create mystery, awaken curiosity, inspire doubt as to the result, and bring about the catastrophe, by processes which shall be equally natural and unexpected. All that class of sagacious persons, therefore, who fancy they have found a mare's nest, when they are only gazing at a goose's, are respectfully counselled that no fact—no tradition —is of any importance to the artist, unless it embodies certain peculiar characteristics of its own, or unless it illus-trates some history about which curiosity has already been awakened. A mere brutality, in which John beats and bruises Ben, and Ben in turn shoots John, putting eleven slugs, or thereabouts, between his collar-bone and vertebræ— or, may be, stabs him under his left pap, or any where you please, is just as easily conceived by the novelist, without the help of history. Nay, for that matter, he would perhaps rather not have any precise facts in his way, in such cases, as then he will be able to regard the picturesque in the choice of his weapon, and to put the wounds in such part of the body as will better bear the examination of all persons. I deem it right to throw out this hint, just at this moment, as well for the benefit of my order as for my own protection. The times are hard, and the post-office requires all its dues in hard money. Literary men are not proverbially prepared at all seasons for any unnecessary outlay—and to be required to make advances for commodities of which they have on hand, at all times, the greatest abundance, is an injustice which, it is to be hoped, this little intimation will somewhat lessen. We take for granted, therefore, that our professional brethren will concur with us in saying to the public, that we are all provided with " disastrous chances" for some time to come—that our " moving accidents by flood and field" are particularly numerous, and of " hair-breadth 'scapes" we have enough to last the century. Murders, and such matters, as they are among the most ordinary events of the day, are decidedly vulgar; and, for mere cudgelling and bruises, the taste of the belles-lettres reader, rendered delicate by the monthly magazines, has voted them to be equally gross and unnatural.

But, if the character of the materials usually tendered to the novelist by the incident-mongers, is thus ordinarily worthless as we describe it, we sometimes are fortunate in finding an individual, here and there, in the deep forests,—a sort of recluse, hale and lusty, but white-headed,—who unfolds from his own budget of experience a rare chronicle, on which we delight to linger. Such a one breathes life into his deeds. We see them as we listen to his words. In lieu of the dead body of the fact, we have its living spirit—subtle, active, breathing and burning, and fresh in all the provocations and associations of life. Of this sort was the admirable characteristic narrative of Horse-Shoe Robinson, which we owe to Kennedy, and for which he was indebted to the venerable

the country, and struck down some of its game,—tasted of its
bear-meat and buffalo, its deer and turkey,—all, at that time,
in the greatest abundance,—they returned for the one thing most
needful to a brave forester in a new country, a good brisk, fearless wife, who, like the damsel in Scripture, would go whitherso-
ever went the husband to whom her affections were surrendered.
They had no fear, these bold young hunters, to make a home and
rear an infant family in regions so remote from the secure walks
of civilization. They had met and made an acquaintance and a
sort of friendship with the Indians, and, in the superior vigour of
their own frames, their greater courage, and better weapons,
they perhaps had come to form a too contemptuous estimate of
the savage. But they were not beguiled by him into too
much confidence. Their log houses were so constructed as to
be fortresses upon occasion, and they lived not so far removed from one another, but that the leaguer of one would be
sure, in twenty-four hours, to bring the others to his assistance. Besides, with a stock of bear-meat and venison always
on hand, sufficient for a winter, either of these fortresses
might, upon common calculations, be maintained for several
weeks against any single band of the Indians, in the small
numbers in which they were wont to range together in those
neighbourhoods. In this way these bold pioneers took possession of the soil, and paved the way for still mightier gene-
rations. Though wandering, and somewhat averse to the
tedious labours of the farm, they were still not unmindful of
its duties; and their open lands grew larger every season, and
increasing comforts annually spoke for the increasing civilization of the settlers. Corn was in plenty in proportion to the
bear-meat, and the squatters almost grew indifferent to those
first apprehensions, which had made them watch the ap-
proaches of the most friendly Indian as if he had been an
enemy. At the end of five years, in which they had suffered
no hurt and but little annoyance of any sort from their wild

neighbours, it would seem as if this confidence in the security of their situation was not without sufficient justification.

But, just then, circumstances seemed to threaten an interruption of this goodly state of things. The Indians were becoming discontented. Other tribes, more frequently in contact with the larger settlements of the whites,—wronged by them in trade, or demoralized by drink,—complained of their sufferings and injuries, or, as is more probable, were greedy to obtain their treasures, in bulk, which they were permitted to see, but denied to enjoy, but only in limited quantity. Their appetites and complaints were transmitted, by inevitable sympathies, to their brethren of the interior, and our worthy settlers upon the Haw, were rendered anxious at signs which warned them of a change in the peaceful relations which had hitherto existed in all the intercourse between the differing races. We need not dwell upon or describe these signs, with which, from frequent narratives of like character, our people are already sufficiently familiar. They were easily understood by our little colony, and by none more quickly than Daniel Nelson. They rendered him anxious, it is true, but not apprehensive; and, like a good husband, while he strove not to frighten his wife by what he said, he deemed it necessary to prepare her mind for the worst that might occur. This task over, he felt somewhat relieved, though, when he took his little girl, now five years old, upon his knee that evening, and looked upon his infant boy in the lap of his mother, he felt his anxieties very much increase; and that very night he resumed a practice which he had latterly abandoned, but which had been adopted as a measure of strict precaution, from the very first establishment of their little settlement. As soon as supper was over, he resumed his rifle, thrust his *couteau de chasse* into his belt, and, taking his horn about his neck, and calling up his trusty dog Clinch, he proceeded to scour the woods immediately around his habitation. This task, performed with the stealthy caution of the hunter, occupied some time, and, as the night was clear, a bright starlight, the weather moderate, and his own mood restless, he determined to strike through the forest to the settlement of Jacob Ransom, about four miles off, in order to prompt him, and, through him, others of the neighbourhood, to the continued exercise of a caution which he now thought necessary. The rest of this night's adventure we propose to let him tell in his own words, as he has been heard to relate it a thousand times in his old age, at a period of life when, with one foot in his grave, to suppose him guilty of falsehood, or of telling that which he did not himself fervently believe, would be, among all those who knew him, to suppose the most impossible and extravagant thing in the world.

CHAPTER III.

" WELL, my friends," said the veteran, then seventy, drawing his figure up to its fullest height, and extending his right arm, while his left still grasped the muzzle of his ancient rifle, which he swayed from side to side, the butt resting on the floor—" Well, my friends, seeing that the night was cl'ar, and there was no wind, and feeling as how I didn't want for sleep, I called to Clinch, and took the path for Jake Ransom's. I knew that Jake was a sleepy sort of chap, and if the redskins caught any body napping, he'd most likely be the man. But I confess, 'twarn't so much for his sake, as for the sake of all—of my own as well as the rest;—for, when I thought how soon, if we warn't all together in the business, I might see, without being able to put in, the long yellow air of Betsy and the babies twirling on the thumbs of some painted devil of the tribe—I can't tell you how I felt, but it warn't like a human, though I shivered mightily like one—'twas wolfish, as if the the hair was turned in and rubbing agin the very heart within me. I said my prayers where I stood, looking up at the stars, and thinking that, after all, all was in the hands and the marcy of God. This sort o' thinking quieted me, and I went ahead pretty free, for I knew the track jest as well by night as by day, though I didn't go so quick, for I was all the time on the look-out for the enemy. Now, after we reached a place in the woods where there was a gully and a mighty bad crossing, there were two roads to get to Jake's—one by the hollows, and one jest across the hills. I don't know why, but I didn't give myself time to think, and struck across the hill, though that was rather the longest way.

" Howsomedever, on I went, and Clinch pretty close behind me. The dog was a good dog, with a mighty keen nose to hunt, but jest then he didn't seem to have the notion for it. The hill was a sizeable one, a good stretch to foot, and I began to remember, after awhile, that I had been in the woods from the blessed dawn; and that made me see how it was with poor Clinch, and why he didn't go for'ad; but I was more than half way, and wasn't guine to turn back till I had said my say to Jake. Well, when I got to the top of the hill, I stopped, and rubbed my eyes. I had cause to rub 'em, for what should I see at a distance but a great fire. At first I was afeard lest it was Jake's house, but I considered, the next moment, that he lived to the left, and this fire was cl'ar to the right, and it did seem to me as if 'twas more near to my own. Here was something to scare a body. But I couldn't stay there looking, and it warn't now a time to go to Jake's; so I turned off, and, though Clinch was mighty onwilling, I bolted on the road to the fire. I say road, but there was no road; but the trees warn't over-thick, and the land was too poor for undergrowth; so we got on pretty well, considering. But, what with the tire I had had, and the scare I felt, it seemed as if I didn't get for'ad a bit. There was the fire still burning as bright and almost as far off as ever. When I saw this I stopt and looked at Clinch, and he stopt and

looked at me, but neither of us had any thing to say. Well,
after a moment's thinking, it seemed as if I shouldn't be
much of a man to give in when I had got so far, so I pushed
on. We crossed more than one little hill, then down and
through the hollow, and then up the hill again. At last we
got upon a small mountain the Indians called Nolleehatchie,
and then it seemed as if the fire had come to a stop, for it was
now burning bright, on a little hill below me, and not two
hundred yards in front. It was a regular camp fire, pretty
big, and there was more than a dozen Indians sitting round it.
'Well,' says I to myself, 'it's come upon us mighty sudden,
and what's to be done? Not a soul in the settlement knows
it but myself, and nobody's on the watch. They'll be sculped,
every human of them, in their very beds, or, moutbe, waken up
in the blaze, to be shot with arrows as they run.' I was in
a cold sweat to think of it. I didn't know what to think and
what to do. I looked round to Clinch, and the strangest
thing of all was to see him sitting quiet on his haunches,
looking at me, and at the stars, and not at the fire jest before
him. Now, Clinch was a famous fine hunting dog, and jest
as good on an Indian trail as any other. He know'd my
ways, and what I wanted, and would give tongue, or keep it
still, jest as I axed him. It was sensible enough, jest then,
that he shouldn't bark, but, dang it!—he didn't even seem to
see. Now, there warn't a dog in all the settlement so quick
and keen to show sense as Clinch, even when he didn't say a
word;—and to see him looking as if he didn't know and
didn't care what was a-going on, with his eyes sot in his
head and glazed over with sleep, was, as I may say, very on-
natural, jest at that time, in a dog of any onderstanding. So
I looked at him, half angry, and when he saw me looking at
him, he jest stretched himself off, put his nose on his legs, and
went to sleep in 'arnest. I had half a mind to lay my knife-
handle over his head, but I considered better of it, and though
it did seem the strangest thing in the world that he shouldn't

the core ; for, in the midst of the redskins, I could see a white
one, and that white one a woman. There was no mistake.
There were the Indians, some with their backs, and some
with their faces to me ; and there, a little a one side, but still
among them, was a woman. When the smoke blowed off, I
could see her white face, bright like any star shining out of the
clouds, and looking so pale and ghastly, that my blood cruddled in my veins to think lest she might be dead from fright.
But it couldn't be so, for she was sitting up and looking about
her. But the Indians were motionless. They jest sat or lay
as when I first saw them—doing nothing—saying nothing, but
jest as motionless as the stone under my elbow. I couldn't
stand looking where I was, so I began creeping again, getting
nigher and nigher, until it seemed to me as if I ought to be
able to read every face. But what with the paint and smoke,
I couldn't make out a single Indian. Their figures seemed
plain enough in their buffalo-skins and blankets, but their faces
seemed always in the dark. But it wasn't so with the
woman. I could make her out clearly. She was very young;
I reckon not more than fifteen, and it seemed to me as if I
knew her looks very well. She was very handsome, and her
hair was loosed upon her back. My heart felt strange to see
her. I was weak as any child. It seemed as if I could die
for the gal, and yet I hadn't strength enough to raise my rifle
to my shoulder. The weakness kept on me the more I
looked ; for every moment seemed to make the poor child
more and more dear to me. But the strangest thing of all
was to see how motionless was every Indian in the camp. Not
a word was spoken—not a limb or finger stirred. There they
sat, or lay, round about the fire, like so many effigies, looking
at the gal, and she looking at them. I never was in such a
fix of fear and weakness in my life. What was I to do? I
had got so nigh that I could have stuck my knife, with a jerk,
into the heart of any one of the party, yet I hadn't the soul to
lift it; and before I knew where I was, I cried like a child.

only a sort of quickening, I knew there was nothing to fear. In a moment he started off, and went boldly ahead. I followed him, but hadn't gone twenty steps down the hill and into the hollow, when I heard something like a groan. This quickened me, and keeping up with the dog, he led me to the foot of the hollow, where was a sort of pond. Clinch ran right for it, and another groan set me in the same direction. When I got up to the dog, he was on the butt-end of an old tree that had fallen, I reckon, before my time, and was half buried in the water. I jumped on it, and walked a few steps for'ad, when, what should I see but a human, half across the log, with his legs hanging in the water, and his head down. I called Clinch back out of my way, and went to the spot. The groans were pretty constant. I stooped down and laid my hands upon the person, and, as I felt the hair, I knew it was an Indian. The head was clammy with blood, so that my fingers stuck, and when I attempted to turn it, to look at the face, the groan was deeper than ever; 'twarn't a time to suck one's fingers. I took him up, clapped my shoulders to it, and, fixing my feet firmly on the old tree, which was rather slippery, I brought the poor fellow out without much trouble. Though tall, he was not heavy, and was only a boy of fourteen or fifteen. The wonder was how a lad like that should get into such a fix. Well, I brought him out and laid him on the dry leaves. His groans stopped, and I thought he was dead, but I felt his heart, and it was still warm, and I thought, though I couldn't be sure, there was a beat under my fingers. What to do was the next question. It was now pretty late in the night. I had been all day a-foot, and, though still willing to go, yet the thought of such a weight on my shoulders made me stagger. But 'twouldn't do to leave him where he was to perish. I thought, if so be I had a son in such a fix, what would I think of the stranger who should go home and wait till daylight to give him help! No, darn my splinters, said I,—though I had just done my prayers,—if I leave the lad—and, tightening my girth, I give my whole soul to it, and hoisted him on my shoulders. My cabin, I reckoned, was good three miles off. You can guess what trouble I had, and what a tire under my load, before I got home and laid the poor fellow down by the fire. I then called up Betsy, and we both set to work to see if we could stir up the life that was in him. She cut away his hair, and I washed the blood from his head, which was chopped to the bone, either with a knife or hatchet. It was a God's blessing it hadn't gone into his brain, for it was fairly enough aimed for it, jest above the ear. When we come to open his clothes, we found another wound in his side. This was done with a knife, and, I suppose, was pretty deep. He had lost blood enough, for all his clothes were stiff with it. We knew nothing much of doctoring, but we had some rum in the cabin, and after washing his wounds clean with it, and pouring some down his throat, he began to groan more freely, and by that we knew he was coming to a nateral feeling. We rubbed his body down with warm cloths, and after a little while, seeing that he made some signs, I give him water as much as he could drink. This seemed to do him good, and having done every thing that we thought could help him, we wrapped him up warmly before the fire, and I stretched myself off beside him. 'Twould be a long story to tell, step by step, how he got on. It's enough to say that he didn't die that bout. We got him on his legs in a short time, doing little or nothing for him more than we did at first. The lad was a good lad, though, at first, when he first came to his senses, he was mighty shy, wouldn't look steadily in our faces, and, I do believe, if he could have got out of the cabin, would have done so as soon as he could stagger. But he was too weak to try that, and, meanwhile, when he saw our kindness, he was soft-ened. By little and little, he got to play with my little Lucy, who was not quite six years old; and, after a while, he seemed to be never better pleased than when they played together. The child, too, after her first fright, leaned to the lad, and was jest as willing to play with him as if he had been a cl'ar white like herself. He could say a few words of English from the beginning, and learnt quickly; but, though he talked tolerable free for an Indian, yet I could never get him to tell me how he was wounded, or by whom. His brow blackened when I spoke of it, and his lips would be shut together, as if he was ready to fight sooner than to speak. Well, I didn't push him to know, for I was pretty sure the head of the truth will be sure to come some time or other, if you once have it by the tail, provided you don't jerk it off by straining too hard upon it.

CHAPTER V.

" I suppose the lad had been with us a matter of six weeks, getting better every day, but so slowly that he had not, at the end of that time, been able to leave the picket. Meanwhile, our troubles with the Indians were increasing. As yet, there had been no bloodshed in our quarter, but we heard of murders and scalpings on every side, and we took for granted that we must have our turn. We made our preparations, repaired the pickets, laid in ammunition, and took our turns for scouting nightly. At length, the signs of Indians got to be thick in our parts, though we could see none. Jake Ransom had come upon one of their camps after they had left it; and we had reason to apprehend every thing, inasmuch as the outlyers didn't show themselves, as they used to do, but prowled about the cabins, and went from place to place, only by night, or close skulking in the thickets. One evening after this, I went out as usual to go the rounds, taking Clinch with me, but I hadn't got far from the gate, when the dog stopped and gave a low bark;—then I knew there was mischief, so I turned round quietly, without making any show of scare, and got back safely, though not a minute too soon. They trailed me to the gate the moment after it had got fastened, and were pretty mad, I reckon, when I found their plan had failed for surprising me. But for the keen nose of poor Clinch, with all our skill in scouting,—and it was not small, even in that early day,—they'd 'a had me, and all that was mine, before the sun could open his eyes to see what they were after. Finding they had failed in their ambush, they made the woods ring with the war-whoop, which was a sign that they were guine to give us a regular siege. At the sound of the whoop, we could see the eyes of the Indian boy brighten, and his ears prick up, jest like a hound's when he first gets scent of the deer, and hears the horn of the hunter. I looked closely at the lad, and was dub'ous what to do. He mout be only an enemy in the camp, and while I was fighting in front, he might be cutting the throats of my wife and children within. I did not tell you that I had picked up his bow and arrows near the little lake where I had found him, and his hunting-knife was sticking in his belt when I brought him home.— Whether to take these away from him, was the question. Suppose I did, a billet of wood would answer the purpose pretty near as well. I thought the matter over while I watched him. Thought runs mighty quick in time of danger! Well, after turning it over on every side, I concluded 'twas better to trust him jest as if he had been a sure friend. I couldn't think, after all we had done for him, that he'd be false, so I said to him—' Lenatawá !—'twas so he called himself—' those are your people !' ' Yes !' he answered slowly, and lifting himself up as if he had been a lord—he was a stately-looking lad, and carried himself like the son of a Micco,* as he was— ' Yes, they are the people of Lenatawá—must he go to them ?' and he made a motion of going out. But I stopped him. I was not willing to lose the security which I had from his being a sort of prisoner. ' No,' said I; ' no, Lenatawá, not to-night

* A prince or chief.

To-morrow will do. To-morrow you can tell them I am a
friend, not an enemy, and they should not come to burn my
wigwam.' ' Brother—friend!' said the lad, advancing with a
sort of freedom, and taking my hand. He then went to my
wife, and did the same thing,—not regarding she was a woman,—' Brother—friend!' I watched him closely, watched
his eye and his motions, and I said to Betsy, ' The lad is true ;
don't be afeard!' But we passed a weary night. Every now
and then we could hear the whoop of the Indians. From the
loop-holes we could see the light of three fires on different
sides, by which we knew they were prepared to cut off any
help that might come to us from the rest of the settlement.—
But I didn't give in or despair. I worked at one thing or
another all night, and though Lenatawá gave me no help, yet
he sat quietly, or laid himself down before the fire, as if he
had nothing to do in the business. Next morning, by daylight, I found him already dressed in the same bloody clothes
which he had on when I found him. He had thrown aside all
that I gave him, and though the hunting-shirt and leggins
which he now wore, were very much stained with blood and
dirt, he had fixed them about him with a good deal of care
and neatness, as if preparing to see company. I must tell you
that an Indian of good family always has a nateral sort of
grace and dignity that I never saw in a white man. He was
busily engaged looking through one of the loop-holes, and
though I could distinguish nothing, yet it was cl'ar that he
saw something to interest him mightily. I soon found out
that, in spite of all my watchfulness, he had contrived to have
some sort of correspondence and communication with those
outside. This was a wonder to me then, for I did not recollect his bow and arrows. It seems to me that he had shot an
arrow through one of the loop-holes, to the end of which he
had fastened a tuft of his own hair. The effect of this was
considerable, and to this it was owing that, for a few hours
afterwards, we saw not an Indian. The arrow was shot at

the very peep of day. What they were about, in the mean
time, I can only guess, and the guess was only easy, after I
had known all that was to happen. That they were in council
what to do was cl'ar enough. I was not to know that the
council was like to end in cutting some of their own throats
instead of ours. But when we did see the enemy fairly, they
came out of the woods in two parties, not actually separated,
but not moving together. It seemed as if there was some
strife among them. Their whole number could not be less
than forty, and some eight or ten of these walked apart under
the lead of a chief, a stout, dark-looking fellow, one half of
whose face was painted black as midnight, with a red circle
round both his eyes. The other party was headed by an old
white-headed chief, who couldn't ha' been less than sixty
years—a pretty fellow, you may be sure, at his time of life, to
be looking after scalps of women and children. While I was
kneeling at my loop-hole, looking at them, Lenatewá came to
me, and touching me on the arm, pointed to the old chief, saying—'Micco Lenatewá Glucco,' by which I guessed he was
the father or grandfather of the lad.' 'Well,' I said, seeing
that the best plan was to get their confidence and friendship if
possible—'Well, lad, go to your father, and tell him what
Daniel Nelson has done for you, and let's have peace. We can
fight, boy, as you see ; we have plenty of arms and provisions ;
and with this rifle, though you may not believe it, I could pick
off your father, the king, and that other chief, who has so de-
villed himself up with paint.' 'Shoot!' said the lad, quickly,
pointing to the chief of whom I had last spoken. 'Ah! he is
your enemy, then ?" The lad nodded his head, and pointed to
the wound on his temple, and that in his side. I now began
to see the true state of the case. 'No,' said I ; 'no, Lenatewá, I will shoot none. I am for peace. I would do good
to the Indians, and be their friend. Go to your father and tell
him so. Go, and make him my friend. The youth caught my
hand, placed it on the top of his head, and exclaimed, ' Good!'

whole Cherokee people were in arms. Many persons, living still, remember that terrible war, and how the Carolinians humbled them at last; but there's no telling how much blood was shed in that war, how many sculps taken, how much misery suffered by young and old, men, women, and children. Our settlement had become so large and scattered that we had to build a sizeable blockhouse, which we stored, and to which we could retreat whenever it was necessary. We took possession of it on hearing from our scouts that Indian trails had been seen, and there we put the women and children, under a strong guard. By day we tended our farms, and only went to our families at night. We had kept them in this fix for five weeks or thereabouts, and there was no attack. The Indian signs disappeared, and we thought the storm had blown over, and began to hope and to believe that the old friendship of Lenatewá, had saved us. With this thinking, we began to be less watchful. The men would stay all night at the farms, and sometimes, in the day, would carry with them the women, and sometimes some even the children. I cautioned them agin this, but they mocked me, and said I was gitting old and scary. I told them, 'Wait and see who'll scare first.' But, I confess, not seeing any Indians in all my scouting, I began to feel and think like the rest, and to grow careless. I let Betsy go now and then with me to the farm, though she kept it from me that she had gone there more than once with Lucy, without any man protector. Still, as it was only a short mile and a half from the block, and we could hear of no Indians, it did not seem so venturesome a thing. One day we heard of some very large b'ars among the thickets—a famous range for them, about four miles from the settlement; and a party of us, Simon Lorris, Huge Darling, Jake Ransom, William Harkless, and myself, taking our dogs, set off on the hunt. We started the b'ar with a rush, and I got the first shot at a mighty big she b'ar the largest I had ever seen—lamed the critter slightly, and dashed into the thickets after her! The others pushed, in another direction, after the rest, leaving me to finish my work as I could.

"I had two dogs with me, Clap and Claw, but they were young things, and couldn't be trusted much in a close brush with a b'ar. Old Clinch was dead, or he'd ha' made other guess-work with the varmint. But, hot after the b'ar, I didn't think of the quality of the dogs till I found myself in a fair wrestle with the brute. I don't brag, my friends, but that *was* a fight. I tell you my breath was clean gone, for the b'ar had me about the thin of my body, and I thought I was doubled up enough to be laid down without more handling. But my heart was strong when I thought of Betsy and the children, and I got my knife, with hard *jugging*—though I couldn't use my arm above my elbow—through the old critter's hide, and in among her ribs. That only seemed to make her hug closer, and I reckon I was clean gone, if it hadn't been that she blowed out before me. I had worked a pretty deep window in her waist, and then life run out plentiful. Her nose dropped agin my breast, and then her paws; and when the strain was gone, I fell down like a sick child, and she fell on top of me. But she warn't in a humour to do more mischief. She roughed me once or twice more with her paws, but that was only because she was at her last kick. There I lay a matter of half an hour, with the dead b'ar alongside o' me. I was almost as little able to move as she, and I vomited as if I had taken physic. When I come to myself and got up, there was no sound of the hunters. There I was with the two dogs and the b'ar, all alone, and the sun already long past the turn. My horse, which I had fastened outside of the thicket, had slipped his bridle, and, I reckoned, had either strayed off grazing, or had pushed back directly for the block. These things didn't make me feel much better. But, though my stomach didn't feel altogether right, and my ribs were as sore as if I had been sweating under a coating of hickory, I felt that there was no

use and no time to stand there grunting. But I made out to
skin and to cut up the b'ar, and a noble mountain of fat she
made. I took the skin with me, and, covering the flesh with
bark, I whistled off the dogs, after they had eat to fill, and
pushed after my horse. I followed his track for some time,
till I grew fairly tired. He had gone off in a scare and at a
full gallop, and, instead of going home, had dashed down the
lower side of the thicket, then gone aside, to round some of
the hills, and thrown himself out of the track, it mout be seven
miles or more. When I found this, I saw there was no use to
hunt him that day and afoot, and I had no more to do but turn
about, and push as fast as I could for the block. But this was
work enough. By this time the sun was pretty low, and there
was now a good seven miles, work it how I could, before me.
But I was getting over my b'ar-sickness, and though my legs
felt weary enough, my stomach was better, and my heart
braver; and, as I was in no hurry, having the whole night
before me, and knowing the way by night as well as by light,
I began to feel cheerful enough, all things considering. I
pushed on slowly, stopping every now and then for rest, and
recovering my strength this way. I had some parched meal
and sugar in my pouch which I ate, and it helped me mightily.
It was my only dinner that day. The evening got to be very
still. I wondered I had seen and heard nothing of Jake Ransom and the rest, but I didn't feel at all oneasy about them,
thinking that, like all other hunters, they would naterally follow the game to any distance. But, jest when I was thinking
about them, I heard a gun, then another, and after that all got
to be as quiet as ever. I looked to my own rifle and felt for
my knife, and put forward a little more briskly. I suppose I
had walked an hour after this, when it came on close dark,
and I was still four good miles from the block. The night was
cloudy, there were no stars, and the feeling in the air was
damp and oncomfortable. I began to wish I was safe home,
and felt queerish, almost as bad as I did when the b'ar

was 'bracing me ; but it warn't so much the body-sickness as
the heart-sickness. I felt as if something was going wrong.
Jest as this feeling was most worrisome, I stumbled over a
human. My blood cruddled, when, feeling about, I put my
hand on his head, and found the sculp was gone. Then I knew
there was mischief. I couldn't make out who 'twas that was
under me, but I reckoned 'twas one of the hunters. There was
nothing to be done but push for'ad. I didn't feel any more
tire. I felt ready for fight, and when I thought of our wives
and children in the block, and what might become of them, I
got wolfish, though the Lord only knows what I was minded
to do. I can't say I had any raal sensible thoughts of what
was to be done in the business. I didn't trust myself to think
whether the Indians had been to the block yet or no ; though
ugly notions came across me when I remembered how we let
the women and children go about to the farms. I was in a
complete fever and agy. I scorched one time and shivered
another, but I pushed on, for there was now no more feeling
of tire in my limbs than if they were made of steel. By this
time I had reached that long range of hills where I first saw
that strange camp-fire, now eleven years gone, that turned out
to be a deception, and it was nateral enough that the thing
should come fresh into my mind, jest at that moment. While
I was thinking of the wonder, and asking myself, as I had
done over and often before, what it possibly could mean, I
reached the top of one of the hills, from which I could see, in
daylight, the whole country for a matter of ten miles or more
on every side. What was my surprise, do you reckon, when
there, jest on the very same hill opposite where I had seen that
apparition of a camp, I saw another, and this time it was a
raal one. There was a rousing blaze, and though the woods
and undergrowth were thicker on this than on the other side,
from which I had seen it before, yet I could make out that
there were several figures, and them Indians. It sort o' made
me easier to see the enemy before, and then I could better tell

what I had to do. I was to spy out the camp, see what the red-devils were thinking to do, and what they had already done. I was a little better scout and hunter this time than when I made the same sort o' search before, and I reckoned that I could get nigh enough to see all that was going on, without stirring up any dust among 'em. But I had to keep the dogs back. I couldn't tie 'em up, for they'd howl; so I stripped my hunting-shirt and put it down for one to guard, and I gave my cap and horn to another. I knew they'd never leave 'em, for I had l'arned 'em all that sort of business—to watch as well as to fetch and carry. I then said a sort of short running prayer, and took the trail. I had to work for'ad slowly. If I had gone on this time as I did in that first camp transaction, I'd ha' lost my sculp to a sartainty. Well, to shorten a long business, I tell you that I got nigh enough, without scare or surprise, to see all that I cared to see, and a great deal more than I wished to see; and now, for the first time, I saw the meaning of that sight which I had, eleven years before, of the camp that come to nothing. I saw that first sight over again, the Indians round the fire, a young woman in the middle, and that young woman my own daughter, my child, my poor, dear Lucy. !

CHAPTER VIII.

"That was a sight for a father. I can't tell you—and I won't try—how I felt. But I lay there, resting upon my hands and knees, jest as if I had been turned into stone with looking. I lay so for a good half hour, I reckon, without stirring a limb; and you could only tell that life was within me, by seeing the big drops that squeezed out of my eyes now and then, and by a sort of shivering that shook as you some-times see the canebrake shaking with the gust of the pond in-side. I tried to pray to God for help, but I couldn't pray, and as for thinking, that was jest as impossible. But I could do nothing by looking, and, for that matter, it was pretty cla'r to me, as I stood, with no help—by myself—one rifle only and knife—I couldn't do much by moving. I could have lifted the gun, and in a twinkle, tumbled the best fellow in the gang, but what good was that guine to me? I was never fond of blood-spilling, and if I could have been made sure of my daughter, I'd ha' been willing that the red devils should have had leave to live for ever. What was I to do? Go to the block? Who know'd if it warn't taken, with every soul in ¡t? And where else was I to look for help? Nowhere, nowhere, but to God! I groaned—I groaned so loud that I dreadful 'feared that they'd hear me; but they were too busy among themselves, eating supper, and poor Lucy in the midst, not eating, but so pale, and looking so miserable—jest as I had seen her, when she was only a child—in the same fix, though 'twas only an appearance—eleven years ago! Well, at last I turned off. As I couldn't say what to do, I was too miserable to look, and I went down to the bottom of the hill and rolled about on the ground, pulling the hair out of my head and groaning, as if that was to do me any good. Before I knew where I was, there was a hand on my shoulder. I jumped up to my feet, and flung my rifle over my head, meaning to bring the butt down upon the stranger—but his voice stopped me.

"'Brother,' said he, ' me Lenatewá!'

" The way he talked, his soft tones, made me know that the young prince meant to be friendly, and I gave him my hand; but the tears gushed out as I did so, and I cried out like a man struck in the heart, while I pointed to the hill — 'My child, my child!'

"' Be man!' said he, ' come!' pulling me away.

"' But, will you save her, Lenatewá?'

" He did not answer instantly, but led me to the little lake and pointed to the old tree over which I had borne his lifeless body so many years ago. By that I knew he meant to tell me, he had not forgotten what I had done for him; and would do for me all he could. But this did not satisfy me. I must know how and when it was to be done, and what was his hope! for I could see from his caution, and leading me away from the camp, that he did not command the party, and had no power over them. He then asked me, if I had not seen the paint of the warriors in the camp. But I had seen nothing but the fix of my child. He then described the paint to me, which was his way of showing me that the party on the hill were his deadly enemies. The paint about their eyes was that of the great chief, his uncle, who had tried to murder him years ago, and who had been shot, in my sight, by the party of his father. The young chief, now in command of the band on the hill was the son of his uncle, and sworn to revenge the death of his father upon him, Lenatewá. This he made me onderstand in a few minutes. And he gave me further to onderstand, that there was no way of getting my child from them onless by cunning. He had but two followers with him, and they were even then busy in making preparations. But of those preparations he either would not or could not give any account; and I had to wait on him with all the patience I could muster; and no easy trial it was, for an Indian is the most cool and slow-moving creature in the world, unless he's actually fighting, and then he's about the quickest. After awhile, Lenatewá led me round the hill. We fetched a pretty smart reach, and before I knew where I was, he led me into a hollow that I had never seen before. Here, to my surprise, there were no less than twelve or fourteen horses fastened, that these red devils had stolen from the settlement that very day, and mine was among them. I did not know it till the young prince told me.

" ' Him soon move,' said he, pointing to one on the outside, which a close examination showed me to be my own—' Him

sheet, beside their ugly painted skins. Well, I hadn't long to
wait, when there was such an uproar among the stolen horses
in the hollow on the opposite side of the hill—such a tramp-
ling, such a whinnying and whickering, you never heard the
like. Now, you must know, that a stolen horse, to an Indian, is jest as precious as a sweetheart to a white man; and
when the rumpus reached the camp, there was a rush of every
man among them, for his critter. Every redskin, but one,
went over the hill after his horses, and he jumped up with the
rest, but didn't move off. He stood over poor Lucy with his
tomahawk, shaking it above her head, as if guine to strike
every minute. She, poor child—I could see her as plain as
the fire-light, for she sat jest on one side of it—her hands were
clasped together. She was praying, for she must have looked
every minute to be knocked on the head. You may depend, I
found it very hard to keep in. I was a'most biling over, the
more when I saw the red devil making his flourishes, every
now and then, close to the child's ears, with his bloody we'pon.
But it was a needcessity to keep in till the sounds died off
pretty much, so as not to give them any scarce this side, till
they had dashed ahead pretty far 'pon the other. I don't know
that I waited quite as long as I ought to, but I waited
as long as my feelings would let me, and then I dropped the
sight of my rifle as close as I could fix it on the breast of the
Indian that had the keeping of my child. I took aim, but I
felt I was a little tremorsome, and I stopped. I know'd I had
but one shoot, and if I didn't onbutton him in that one, it
would be a bad shoot for poor Lucy. I didn't fear to hit *her*,
and I was pretty sure I'd hit him. But it must be a dead shot
to do good, for I know'd if I only hurt him, that he'd sink the
tomahawk in her head with what strength he had left him. I
brought myself to it again, and this time I felt strong. I could
jest hear a little of the hubbub of men and horses afar off. I
knew it was the time, and, resting the side of the muzzle
against a tree, I give him the whole blessing of the bullet. I

drawed off his warriors, and we saw no more of him until the
peace. That followed pretty soon after General Middleton gave
the nation that licking at Echotee,—a licking, I reckon, that
they'll remember long after my day. At that affair Lenatewá
got an ugly bullet in his throat, and if it hadn't been for one
of his men, he'd ha' got a bag'net in his breast. They made
a narrow run with him, head foremost down the hill, with a
whole swad of the mounted men from the low country at
their heels. It was some time after the peace before he got
better of his hurt though the Indians are naterally more skil-
ful in cures than white men. By this time we had all gone to
our farms, and had planted and rebuilt, and begun to forget
our troubles, when who should pop into our cabin one day, but
Lenatewá. He had got quite well of his hurts. He was a
monstrous fine-looking fellow, tall and handsome, he was
dressed in his very best. He wore pantaloons, like one of us,
and his hunting shirt was a raally fine blue, with a white
fringe. He wore no paint, and was quite nice and neat with
his person. We all received him as an old friend, and he
stayed with us three days. Then he went, and was gone for a
matter of two weeks, when he came back and stayed with us
another three days. And so, off and an, he came to visit us,
until Betsy said to me one day, 'Daniel, that Indian, Lenatewá, comes here after Lucy. Leave a woman to guess these
things.' After she told me, I recollected that the young
prince was quite watchful of Lucy, and would follow her
out into the garden, and leave us, to walk with her. But
then, again, I thought—'What if he is favourable to my
daughter? The fellow's a good fellow; and a raal, noble-
hearted Indian, that's sober, is jest as good, to my thinking,
as any white man in the land.' But Betsy wouldn't hear to
it. 'Her daughter never should marry a savage, and a heathen, and a redskin, while her head was hot:'—and while her
head was so hot, what was I to do? All I could say was
this only, 'Don't kick, Betsey, till you're spurred. 'Twill be

time enough to give the young Chief his answer when he asks
the question; and it won't do for us to treat him rudely,
when we consider how much we owe him.' But she was of the
mind that the boot was on the other leg,—that it was he and
not us that owed the debt; and all that I could do couldn't
keep her from showing the lad a sour face of it whenever he
came. But he didn't seem much to mind this, since I was
civil and kind to him. Lucy too, though her mother warned
her against him, always treated him civilly as I told her;
though she naterally would do so, for she couldn't so easily
forget that dreadful night when she was a prisoner in the
camp of the enimy, not knowing what to expect, with an Indian tomahawk over her head, and saved, in great part, by
the cunning and courage of this same Lenatewá. The girl
treated him kindly, and I was not sorry she did so. She
walked and talked with him jest as if they had been brother
and sister, and he was jest as polite to her as if he had been a
born Frenchman.

"You may be sure, it was no pleasant sight to my wife to
see them two go out to walk. 'Daniel Nelson,' she says, 'do
you see and keep an eye on those people. There's no knowing
what may happen. I do believe that Lucy has a liking for
that redskin, and should they run!'—'Psho!' said I,—but that
wouldn't do for her, and so she made me watch the young
people sure enough. 'Twarn't a business that I was overfond
of, you may reckon, but I was a rough man and didn't know
much of woman natur'. I left the judgment of such things
to my wife, and did pretty much what she told me. Whenever they went out to walk, I followed them, rifle in hand; but
it was only to please Betsy, for if I had seen the lad running
off with the girl, I'm pretty sure, I'd never ha' been the man
to draw trigger upon him. As I said before, Lenatewá was
jest as good a husband as she could have had. But, poor fellow, the affair was never to come to that. One day, after he
had been with us almost a week, he spoke softly to Lucy,

and she got up, got her bonnet and went out with him. I didn't see them when they started, for I happened to be in the upper story,—a place where we didn't so much live, but where we used to go for shelter and defence whenever any Indians came about us. 'Daniel,' said my wife, and I knew by the quickness and sharpness of her voice what 'twas she had to tell me. But jest then I was busy, and, moreover, I didn't altogether like the sort of business upon which she wanted me to go. The sneaking after an enimy, in raal warfare, is an onpleasant sort of thing enough; but this sneaking after one that you think your friend is worse than running in a fair fight, and always gave me a sheepish feeling after it. Besides, I didn't fear Lenatewá, and I didn't fear my daughter. It's true, the girl treated him kindly and sweetly, but that was owing to the nateral sweetness of her temper, and because she felt how much sarvice he had been to her and all of us. So, instead of going out after them, I thought I'd give them a look through one of the loop-holes. Well, there they went, walking among the trees, not far from the picket, and no time out of sight. As I looked at them, I thought to myself, 'Would n't they make a handsome couple !' Both of them were tall and well made. As for Lucy, there wasn't, for figure, a finer set girl in all the settlement, and her face was a match for her figure. And then she was so easy in her motion, so graceful, and walked, or sate, or danced,—jest for all the world, as if she was born only to do the particular thing she was doing. As for Lenatewá, he was a lad among a thousand. Now, a young Indian warrior, when he don't drink, is about the noblest-looking creature, as he carries himself in the woods, that God ever did make. So straight, so proud, so stately, always as if he was doing a great action —as if he knew the whole world was looking at him. Lenatewá was pretty much the handsomest and noblest Indian I had ever seen ; and then, I know'd him to be raally so noble. As they walked together, their heads a little bent downwards, and Lucy's pretty low, the thought flashed across me that, jest then, he was telling her about his feelings; and perhaps, said I to myelf, the girl thinks about it pretty much as I do. Moutbe now, she likes him better than any body she has ever, seen and what more nateral? Then I thought, if there is any picture in this life more sweet and beautiful than two young people jest beginning to feel love for one another, and walking together in the innocence of their hearts, under the shady trees, —I've never seen it! I laid the rifle on my lap, and sat down on the floor and watched 'em through the loop until I felt the water in my eyes. They walked backwards and for'ads, not a hundred yards off, and I could see all their motions, though I couldn't hear their words. An Indian don't use his hands much generally, but I could see that Lenatewá was using his, —not a great deal, but as if he felt every word he was saying. Then I began to think, what was I to do, if so be he was raally offering to marry Lucy, and she willing! How was I to do? what was I to say?—how could I refuse him when I was willing! how could I say 'yes,' when Betsy said 'no!'

Well, in the midst of this thinking, what should I hear but a loud cry from the child, then a loud yell,—a regular war-whoop,—sounded right in front, as if it came from Lenatewá himself. I looked up quickly, for, in thinking, I had lost sight of them, and was only looking at my rifle; I looked out, and there, in the twinkling of an eye, there was another sight. I saw my daughter flat upon the ground, lying like one dead, and Lenatewá staggering back as if he was mortally hurt; while, pressing fast upon him, was an Indian warrior, with his tomahawk uplifted, and striking—once, twice, three times—hard and heavy, right upon the face and forehead of the young prince. From the black paint on his face, and the red ring about his eyes, and from his figure and the eagle feathers in his head, I soon guessed it was Oloschottee, and I knew it was the old revenge for the killing of his father; for

an Indian never forgets that sort of obligation. Of course, I
didn'nt stand quiet to see an old friend, like Lenatewá, tumbled in that way, without warning, like a bullock ; and there
was my own daughter lying flat, and I wasn't to know that he
hadn't struck her too. It was only one motion for me to draw
sight upon the savage, and another to pull the trigger; and I
reckon he dropped jest as soon as the young Chief. I gave
one whoop for all the world as if I was an Indian myself, and
run out to the spot ; but Lenatewá had got his discharge from
further service. He warn't exactly dead, but his sense was
swimming. He couldn't say much, and that warn't to the
purpose. I could hear him, now and then, making a sort of
singing noise, but that was soon swallowed up in a gurgle
and a gasp, and it was all over. My bullet was quicker in its
working than Oloschottee's hatchet ; he was stone dead before
I got to him. As for poor Lucy, she was not hurt, either by
bullet or hatchet ; but she had a hurt in the heart, whether
from the scare she had, or because she had more feeling for the
young prince than we reckoned, there's no telling. She warn't
much given to smiling after that. But, whether she loved
Lenatewá, we couldn't know, and I never was the man to
ask her. It's sartan she never married, and she had about as
many chances, and good ones, too, of any girl in our settlement. You've seen her—some among you—and warn't she a
beauty—though I say it myself—the very flower of the forest!"

THE LAST WAGER.

OR THE GAMESTER OF THE MISSISSIPPI.

———"I have set my life upon a cast,
And I will stand the hazard of the die."
SHAKSPEARE.

CHAPTER I.

OUR story will be found to illustrate one of the current commonplaces of the day. Ever since my Lord Byron, in that poem of excellently expressed commonplaces, Don Juan, declared that "truth was stranger than fiction," every newspaper witling rings the changes upon the theme, until there is no relief to its dull-toned dissonance. That truth should frequently be found to be much stranger than any fiction, is neither so strange nor out of the course of things; but is just in accordance, if we bestow any thought upon the matter, with the deliberate convictions of every reasoning mind. For, what is fiction, but the nice adaptation, by an artist, of certain ordinary occurrences of life, to a natural and probable conclusion? It is not the policy of a good artist to deal much in the merely extravagant. His real success, and the true secret of it, is to be found in the *naturalness* of his story, its general seemliness, and close resemblance of its events to those which may or must take place in all instances of individuals subjected to like influences with those who figure in this narrative. The naturalness must be that of life as it is, or with life as it is shown in such picturesque situations as are probable—seemingly real—and such as harmonize equally with the laws of nature, and such as the artist has chosen for his guide. Ex-

D 5

cept in stories of broad extravagance—ghost stories for example—in which the one purpose of the romancer — that of exciting wonder—is declared at the outset—except in such stories, or in others in the broad grin—such as are common and extravagant among the frontier *raconteurs* of the West, it were the very worst policy in the world for the writer of fiction to deal much in the marvellous. He would soon wear out the patience of the reader, who would turn away, with a dissatisfaction almost amounting to disgust, from any author who should be found too frequently to employ what is merely possible in human progress. We require as close reasoning, and deductions as logically drawn, in tale or novel, as in a case at law or in equity; much more close, indeed, than is often found to be the case in a Congressional harangue, and a far more tenacious regard to the *interest* of the reader than is shown in the report of a modern secretary. Probability, unrestrained, must be made apparent at every step; and if the merely possible be used at all, it must be so used only, as, in looking like the probable, it is made to lose all its ambiguous characteristics. What we show must not only be the truth, but it must also seem like the truth; for, as the skill of the artist can sometimes enable him to make what is false appear true, so it is equally the case, that a want of skill may transmute the most unquestionable truth into something that nine persons in ten shall say, when they behold it, " it looks monstrous like a lie !"

That we are not at liberty to use too freely what is merely possible in the material brought before us, is a fact more particulary known to painters, who have often felt the danger of any attempt to paint the sky as it sometimes appears to them. They dread to offend the suspicious incredulity of the cold and unobserving citizen. They see, with equal amazement and delight—but without daring to delineate—those intenser hues and exquisite gradations of light and shadow, those elaborate and graceful shapes of cloud, born of the rainbow—carnation,

green, and purple, which the sun sometimes, in fantastic
mood, and as if in equal mockery of human faith and art,
makes upon the lovely background of the sky which he leaves
at setting. The beautiful vision gone from sight, who would
believe the poor artist, whatever his accuracy and felicity of
touch and taste, who had endeavoured to transfer, before it
faded, the vanishing glory to his canvass? Who could suppose,
and how admit, that there had ever been such a panorama, of
such super-artistical splendour, displayed before his eyes,
without commanding his admiration and fixing his attention?
The very attempt to impose such an exhibition upon him as
natural, would be something of a sarcasm, and a commentary
upon the dull eye and drowsy mind which had failed to discern
it for themselves. Nay, though the artist grappled the dull
citizen by the arm at the very instant, and compelled his gaze
upon the glorious vision ere it melted into the thin gray haze
of evening, would he not be apt to say, "How strange! how
very unnatural!" Certainly, it would be a truth infinitely
more strange than the most audacious fiction that ever grew
up at the touch of the most fantastic votary of art.

CHAPTER II.

THE sketch which I propose will scarcely justify this long di-
gression; and its character will be still less likely to corres-
pond with the somewhat poetic texture of the introduction. It
is simply a strange narrative of frontier life; one of those narratives in which a fact will appear very doubtful, unless the
artist shall exhibit such sufficient skill in his elaborations, as
to keep its rude points from offending too greatly the suspicious judgment of the reader. This is the task before me.
The circumstances were picked up, when, a lad of eighteen, I
first wandered over the then dreary and dangerous wastes of

the Mississippi border. Noble, indeed, though wild and savage, was the aspect of that green forest country, as yet only slightly smitten by the sharp edges of the ranger's axe. I travelled along the great Yazoo wilderness, in frequent proximity with the Choctaw warriors. Most frequently I rode alone. Sometimes, a wayfarer from the East, solitary with myself, turned his horse's head, for a few days' space, on the same track with mine ; but, in most cases, my only companion was some sullen Choctaw, or some still more sullen half-breed, who, emerging suddenly from some little foot-path, would leave me half in doubt whether his introduction would be made first with the tomahawk or the tongue. Very few white men were then settled in the country ; still fewer were stationary. I rode forty and fifty miles without sign of human habitation, and found my bed and supper at night most generally in the cabin of the half-breed. But there was one, and that a remarkable exception to this universal necessity ; and in this exception my story takes its rise. I had at length reached the borders of the nation, and the turbid waters of the Mississippi, at no great distance, flowed down towards the Gulf. The appearances of the white settler, some doubtful glimmerings of a more civilized region, were beginning to display themselves. Evening was at hand. The sun was fast waning along the mellow heights of heaven ; and my heart was beginning to sink with a natural sense of loneliness which such a setting is apt to inspire in the bosom of the youthful wanderer. It was also a question with me, where I should find my pillow for the night. My host of the night before, a low, dark-looking white squatter, either was, or professed to be, too ignorant to give me any information on this head, which would render the matter one of reasonable certainty. In this doubtful and somewhat desolate state of mind, I began to to prick my steed forward at a more rapid pace, to cast my eyes up more frequently to the fading light among the tree-tops, and, occasionally, to send a furtive glance on either hand, not altogether assured that my road was as safe as it was lonely. The question " where shall I find my bed to-night ?" was beginning to be one of serious uncertainty, when I suddenly caught a glimpse of an opening on my right, a sort of waggon-path, avenue like, and which reminded me of those dear, dim passages in my own Carolina, which always promised the traveller a hot supper and happy conclusion to his wanderings of the day. Warmed with the notion, and without a farther doubt or thought, I wheeled my sorrel into the passage, and pressed him forward with a keener spur. A cheery blast of the horn ahead, and the dull heavy stroke of an axe imme-diately after, were so many urgent entreaties to proceed ; and now the bellow of a cow, and next the smoke above the cot-tage roof-trees, assured me that my apprehensions were at an end. In a few seconds I stood before one of the snuggest little habitations which ever kindled hope and satisfied hunger.

This was one of those small log-cabins which are common to the country. Beyond its snug, trim and tidy appearance, there was nothing about it to distinguish it from its class. The clearing was small, just sufficient, perhaps, for a full supply of corn and provisions. But the area in front of the dwelling was cleanly swept, and the trees were trim-med, and those which had been left were evergreens, and so like favourite domestics, with such an air of grace, and good-nature, and venerableness about them, that one's heart warmed to see them, as at sight of one of " the old familiar faces." The aspect of the dwelling within consisted happily with that without. Every thing was so neat, and snug, and comfortable.

The windows were sashed and glassed, and hung with the whitest curtains of cotton, with fringes fully a foot deep. The floors were neatly sanded, the hearth was freshly brightened with the red ochrous clay of the country, and chairs and tables, though made of the plainest stuffs, and by a very rude mechanic, were yet so clean, neat and well-arranged, that the eye involuntarily surveyed them again and again with a very pleased sensation. Nor was this all in the shape of unwonted comforts. Some other matters were considered in this cottage, which are scarcely even dreamed of in the great majority. In one corner of the hall stood a hat-stand; in another there were pins for cloaks; above the fire-place hung a formidable rifle, suspended upon tenter-hooks made of three monstrous antlers, probably those of gigantic bucks which had fallen beneath the weapon which they were now made to sustain. Directly under this instrument, and the only object beside which had been honoured with a place so conspicuous, *was a pack of ordinary playing cards*—not hung or suspended against the wall, *but nailed to it ;*—driven through and through with a tenpenny nail, and so fastened to the solid log, the black head of the nail showing with a particular prominence in contrast with the red spot of the ace of hearts, through which it had been driven. Of this hereafter. On this pack of cards hangs my story. It is enough, in this place, to add, that it was only after supper was fairly over, that my eyes were drawn to this very unusual sort of chimney decoration.

At the door of the cottage sat a very venerable old man, between seventy and eighty. His hair was all white, but still thick, betraying the strength of his constitution and the excellence of his health. His skin was florid, glowing through his white beard, which might have been three days old, and his face bore the burden of very few wrinkles. He had a lively, clear blue eye, and good-humour played about his mouth in every movement of his lips. He was evidently one of those fortunate men, whose winters, if frosty, had always proved kindly. A strong man in his youth, he was now but little bent with years; and when he stood up, I was quite ashamed to find he was rather more erect than myself, and quite as tall. This was the patriarch of the family, which consisted of three members besides himself. The first of these was his only son, a man thirty-eight or forty years of age, of whom it will be quite explicit enough to say, that the old man, in his youth, must very nearly have resembled him. Then, there was the wife of the son, and her son, a lad now ten years old, a smart-looking lad enough, but in no wise resembling his male parent. Instead of the lively, twinkling blue eye of his father, he had the dark, deep, oriental sad ones of the mother; and his cheeks were rather pale than rosy, rather thin than full; and his hair was long, black and silky, in all respects the counterpart of his mother's. A brief description of his lady may assist us in our effort to awaken the interest of the reader.

Conducted into the house by the son, and warmly welcomed by the old man as well as himself, I was about to advance with the bold dashing self-possession of a young cavalier, confident in his course, and accustomed to win " golden opinions of all sorts of people." But my bold carriage and sanguine temper were suddenly checked, not chilled, by the appearance of the lady in front of whom I suddenly stood. She sat beside the fire-place, and was so very different a looking person from any I had expected to see in such a region, that the usual audacity of my temperament was all at once abashed. In place of the good, cheerful, buxom, plain country housewife whom I looked to see, mending Jacky's breeches, or knitting the good man's hose, I found myself confronted by a dame whose aristocratic, high-bred, highly composed, easy and placid demeanour, utterly confounded me. Her person was small, her complexion darkly oriental, her eye flashing with all the spiritual fires of that region; habitually bright and searching, even while the expression of her features would have made her seem utterly emotionless. Never did features, indeed, appear so thoroughly inflexible. Her beauty,—for she was all beauty, —was not, however, the result of any regularity of feature. Beauties of her order, brunette and piquant, are most usually wanting in preciseness, and mutual dependance and sympathy of outline. They are beautiful in spite of irregularity, and in consequence of the paramount exquisiteness of some particular feature. The charm of the face before me grew out of the piercing, deep-set, and singularly black eye, and the wonderful vitality about the lips. Never was mouth so small, or so admirably delineated. There was witchcraft enough in the web of it to make my own lips water. But I speak like the boy I was then, and am no longer.

Let me not be understood to mean that there was any levity, any lightness of character betrayed in the expression of those lips. Very far otherwise. While soft, sweet, beautiful, and full of life, they were the most sacred and sad-looking forms,—drooping blossoms of beauty, mourning, as it would seem, because beauty does not imply immortality; and this expression led me to observe more closely the character of the eye, the glance of which, at first, had only seemed to denote the brilliance of the diamond, shining through an atmosphere of jet. I now discerned that its intense blaze was not its only character. It was marked with the weight of tears, that, freezing as they had birth, maintained their place in defiance of the light to which they were constantly exposed. It was the brightness of the ice-palace, in the Northern Saga, which, in reflecting the bright glances of Baldar, the God of Day, still gives defiance to the fervour of his beams.

But a truce to these frigid comparisons, which suit any age but ours. Enough to say that the lady was of a rare and singular beauty, with a character of face and feature not common to our country, and with a deportment seldom found in the homely cabin of the squatter. The deep and unequivocal sadness which marked her looks, intense as it was, did not affect or impair the heightened aristocratic dignity of her subdued and perfectly assured manner. To this manner did she seem to have been born; and, being habitual, it is easy to understand that she could not be divested of it, except in a very small degree, by the pressure of any form of affliction. You could see that there had been affliction, but its effect was simply to confirm that elevated social tone, familiar to all mental superiority, which seems, however it may feel, to regard the confession of its griefs as perhaps something too merely human to be altogether becoming in a confessedly superior caste. Whether the stream was only frozen over, or most effectually crystallized, it does not suit our purpose to inquire. It is, at all events, beyond my present ability to determine the doubt.

She was introduced to me, by the husband, as Mrs. Bayner. I afterwards discovered that her Christian name was Rachel; a circumstance that tended to strengthen the impression in my mind that she might be of Jewish parents. That she was a Christian herself, I had reason to believe, from her joining freely and devoutly, and on bended knee, in the devotions of the night. She spoke seldom, yet looked intelligence throughout the conversation, which was carried on freely between the old man, the husband, and myself. When she spoke, her words and accents were marked by the most singular propriety. There was nothing in her utterance to lessen the conviction that she was familiar with the most select circles of city life; and I could see that the husband listened to her with a marked deference, and, though himself, evidently a rough honest backwoodsman, I detected him, in one or two instances, checking the rude phrase upon his lips, and substituting for it some other, more natural to the ear of civilization and society. There was a touching something in the meekness and quiet deportment of the boy who sat by his mother's knee in silence, her fingers turning in his hair, while he diligently pored over some little trophy of juvenile literature, looking up timidly at moments, and smiling sadly, when he met the deep earnest gaze of the mother's eyes, as she seemed to forget all around in the glance at the one object. I need not say that there was something in this family picture so entirely out of the common run of my woodland experience in the Southwest, at that early day, that I felt my curiosity equally excited with my pleasure. I felt assured that there was some thing of a story to be learned, which would amply and the three rival houses. The corners of the cards were curled, and the ends smoked to partial blackness. They had evidently been in that situation for several years. I turned inquiringly to my hosts—

"You have a very singular ornament for your mantle-place, Mr. Rayner;" was my natural remark, the expression of curiosity in my face being coupled with an apologetic sort of smile. But it met with no answering smiles from any of the family. On the contrary, every face was grave to sadness, and in a moment more Mrs. Rayner rose and left the room. As soon as she was gone, her husband remarked as follows:

"Why, yes, sir, it is uncommon; but there's a reason why it's there, which I'll explain to you after we've gone through prayers."

By this time the wife had returned, bringing with her the family Bible, which she now laid upon a stand beside the venerable elder. He, good old man, with an action that seemed to be perfectly habitual, drew forth the spectacles from the sacred pages, where they seemed to have been left from the previous evening, and commenced reading the third chapter of Ecclesiastes, beginning, "Hear me, your father, O children! and do thereafter, that ye may be safe." Then, this being read, we all sunk devoutly upon our knees, and the patriarch put up as sweet and fervent a prayer as I should ever wish to listen to. The conceited whipster of the school might have found his pronunciation vulgar, and his sentences sometimes deficient in grammatical nicety; but the *thought* was there, and the *heart*, and the ears of perfect wisdom might well be satisfied with the good sense and the true morality of all that was spoken. We rose refreshed, and, after a lapse of a very few moments which were passed in silence, the wife, leading the little boy by the hand, with a kind nod and courtesy took her leave, and retired to her chamber. Sweetness and dignity were most happily blended in her parting movements; but I fancied, as I caught the glance of her eye, that there had been a freshening and overflowing there of the deep and still gathering fountains. Her departure was followed by that of the old man, and the husband and myself were left alone. It was not long after this, before he, himself, without waiting for any suggestion of mine, brought up the subject of the cards, which had been so conspicuously elevated into a mantel ornament.

CHAPTER III.

"STRANGER," said he, "there is a sort of history in those cards which I am always happy to tell to any young man that's a beginner in the world like yourself. I consider them as a sort of Bible, for, when I look at them and remember all that I know concerning them, I feel as if I was listening to some prime sermon, or may be, hearing just such a chapter as the old man read to us out of the good book to-night. It's quite a long history, and I'll put on a fresh handful of lightwood before I begin."

The interruption was brief, and soon overcome, and the narrative of the husband ran as follows :

"It is now," said he, "going on to twelve years since the circumstances took place which belong to the story of those cards, and I will have to carry you back to that time before you can have a right knowledge of what I want to tell. I was then pretty much such a looking person as you now see me, for I haven't undergone much change. I was a little sprightlier, perhaps—always famous for light-headedness and laughing—fond of fun and frolic, but never doing anything out of mischief and bad humour. The old man, my father, too, was pretty much the same. We lived here where you find us now, but not quite so snugly off—not so well settled—rather poor, I may say, though still with a plentiful supply to live on and keep warm and feel lively. There was only us two, and we had but two workers, a man and woman, and they had two children, who could do nothing for us and precious little for themselves. But we were snug, and worked steadily, and were comfortable. We didn't make much money, but we always spent less than we made. We didn't have very nice food, but we had no physic to take, and no doctor's bills to pay. We had a great deal to make us happy, and still more to be thankful for; and I trust in God we were thankful for all of his blessings. I think we were, for he gave us other blessings; and for these, stranger, we are trying to be thankful also.

"Well, as I was saying, about twelve years ago, one hot day in August, I rode out a little piece towards the river bluff to see if any goods had been left for us at the landing. We had heard the steamboat gun the night before, or something like it, and that, you know, is the signal to tell us when to look after our *plunder*. When I got there I found a lot of things, some for us, and some for other people. There was a bag of coffee, a keg of sugar, three sacks of salt, and a box of odds and ends for us. But the chaps on board the steamboat—which was gone—had thrown the stuff any where, and some of the salt was half melted in a puddle of water. I turned in, and hauled it out of the water, and piled it up in a dry place. What was wet belonged chiefly to our neighbours, and the whole of it might have been lost if I had not got there in season. This kept me a good hour, and as I had no help, and some of the sacks were large and heavy, I was pretty nigh tired out when the work was done. So I took a rest of half an hour more in the shade. The heat was powerful, and I had pretty nigh been caught by sleep—I don't know but I did sleep, for in midsummer one's not always sure of himself in a drowsy moment—when I was suddenly roused up by a noise most like the halloo of a person in distress. I took the saddle on the spur, and went off in the quarter that the sound came from. It so happened that my route homeward lay the same way, and on the river road, the only public road in the settlement; and I had only gone two hundred yards or thereabout, when in turning an elbow of the path, I came plump upon a stranger, who happened to be the person whom I heard calling. He was most certainly in distress. His horse was flat upon his side, groaning powerfully, and the man was on his knees, rubbing the creature's legs with a pretty hard hand. A little way behind him lay a dead rattlesnake, one of the largest I ever did see, counting twenty-one rattles besides the button; and the sight of the snake told me the whole story. I jumped down to see what I could do in the way of help, but I soon discovered that the nag had the spasms, and was swelled up to her loins. I however cut into her leg with my knife, just where she was bitten, and when I had dug out the poisoned flesh, as much as I thought was reasonable, I got on my horse and rode back to the salt bags at full speed, and brought away a double handful of the salt. I rubbed it into the animal's wound, I really believe, a few minutes after she had groaned her last and stiffened out, but I wasn't rubbing very long. She was about the soonest killed of any creature that I ever saw snakebit before.

"It was only after I was done with the mare, that I got a fair look at her owner. He was a small and rather oldish man, with a great stoop of the shoulders, with a thin face, glossy black hair, and eyes black too, but shining as bright, I reckon, as those of the rattlesnake he had killed. They had a most strange and troublesome brightness, that made me look at them whether I would or not. His face was very pale, and the wrinkles were deep, like so many seems, and, as I have said, he was what I would call a rather oldish man; but still he was very nicely dressed, and wore a span-new velvet vest, a real English broad-cloth coat, gold watch with gold seals; and every now and then he pulled out a snuff-box made like a horn, with a curl at the end of it, which was also set with

a gold rim, and had a cap of the same precious stuff upon it.
He was taking snuff every moment while I was doctoring his
mare, and when the creature went dead, he offered it to me;
but I had always thought it work enough to feed my mouth,
and had no notion of making another mouth of my nose, so I
refused him civilly.

" He didn't seem to be much worried by the death of his
creature, and when I told him how sorry I was on his account,
he answered quickly,

" ' Oh! no matter; you have a good horse; you will let me
have him; you look like a good fellow.'

" I was a little surprised, you may reckon. I looked at the
old man, and then at my creature. He *was* a good creature;
and as prime an animal as ever stepped in traces; good at any
thing, plough, waggon, or saddle; as easy-going as a girl of
sixteen, and not half so skittish. I had no notion of giving
him up to a stranger, you may be sure, and didn't half like the
cool, easy, impudent manner with which the old man spoke to
me. I had no fears—I didn't think of his taking my nag from
me by force—but, of a sudden, I almost begun to think he
might be a wizard, as we read in Scripture, and hear of from
the old people, or mou't be, the old devil himself, and then I
didn't well know what I had to expect. But he soon made
the matter clear to me. Perhaps he saw that I was a little
beflustered.

" ' Young man,' says he, ' your horse *is* a fine one. Will
you sell him? I am willing to pay you a fair price—give you
his full value.'

" There was something to consider in that. When did you
ever find a Western man unwilling for a horse-barter? Besides, though the creature was a really first-rate nag, he was
one more than I wanted. One for the plough, and one for the
saddle—as the old man did'nt ride often—was enough for us;
and we had three. But Rainbow—that was his name—was
so sleek an animal! He could a'most do any thing that you'd

tell him. I didn't want to sell him, but I didn't want to keep
a mouth too many. You know a horse that you don't want
begins by gnawing through your pockets, and ends by eating
off his own head. That's the say, at least. But I raised
Rainbow, fed him with my own hands, curried him night and
morning myself, and looked upon him as a sort of younger
brother. · I hated powerful bad to part with him; but then
there was no reason to keep him when he was of no use.
'Twas a satisfaction, to be sure, to have such a creature; and
'twas a pleasure to cross him, and streak it away, at a brush-
ing canter, of a bright morning, for a good five miles at a
stretch; but poor people can't afford such pleasures and satis-
factions; and when I thought of the new waggon that we
wanted, and such a smart chance of other things about the
farm, I looked at the old man and thought better of his offer.
I said to him, though a little slowly,

"'It's a famous fine horse this, stranger.'

"'I know it,' said he; 'I never saw one that better pleased
my eyes. I'll pay you a famous fine price for him.'

"'What'll you give?' said I.

"'Pshaw!' said he, 'speak out like a man. I'm no baby,
and you are old enough to know better. What's your price?'

"He's low,' said I, 'at one hundred and seventy dollars.'

"'He is,' said he, 'he's worth more—will you take that?'

"'Yes.'

"'You shall have it,' he answered, 'and I'll throw the dead
horse into the bargain; she was a famous fine animal too, in
her day, and her skin's worth stuffing as a keepsake. You
can stuff it and put it up in your stables, as an example to
your other horses.

CHAPTER IV.

" ALL the time he was talking, he was counting out the money, which was almost all in gold. I was a little dub'ous that it wasn't good money; but I smelt it, and it had no smell of brass, and I was a leetle ashamed to let on that I didn't know good money from bad ; besides, there was a something about the old gentleman so much like a gentleman, so easy, and so commanding, that I couldn't find the heart to doubt or to dispute any thing he said. And then, every thing about him looked like a gentleman: his clothes, his hat, the watch he wore, the very dead horse and his coverings, saddle, bridle, and so forth, all convinced me that there was nothing of make-believe.

" ' There,' said he, ' my good fellow,' putting the money in my hand, ' I reckon you never handled so much gold in your life before.'

" ' No,' said I, ' to tell you the truth, though I've hearn a good deal of gold, and know it when I see it by what I've hearn, I never set eyes on a single piece till now.

" ' May it do your eyes good now, then,' said he ; ' you look like a good fellow. Your horse is sound ?'

" ' Yes,' said I, ' I can answer better for him than I can for your gold.'

" ' That's good.'

" ' Well,' said ' I, I'm not sure that I've dealt fairly with you, stranger. I've asked you little more than I've been asking other people. My price on Rainbow has been only one hundred and fifty dollars, before.'

" ' And your conscience troubles you. You *are* an honest fellow,' said he, ' but never mind, my lad, I'll show you a way to relieve it.'

" With these words he pulled out a buckskin roll from his
pocket, and out of this he tumbled a pack of cards ; the very
cards which you see nailed above my fireplace.

" ' We'll play for that twenty dollars,' said he, throwing
down two gold pieces on the body of the dead mare, and, beginning to shuffle the cards immediately. Somehow, I did as
he did. I put down two ten dollar pieces along with his. I
couldn't help myself. He seemed to command me. I felt
scared—I felt that I was doing wrong ; but he seemed to take
every thing so much as a matter of course, that I hadn't the
courage to say ' no ' to any thing he did or said.

" ' What do you play ?' said he, and he named some twenty
games of cards, some in French, I believe, and some in Spanish, but no one of which did I know any thing about. He
seemed beflustered.

" ' Do you play any thing at all ?' he asked.

" ' Yes—a little of *old sledge*—that's all.'

" ' Oh! that will do. A common game enough. I wonder
I should have omitted it! Here! you may shuffle them, and
we'll cut for deal.'

" I didn't shuffle, but cut at once. He cut after me, and
the deal fell to him. He took up and then put the cards down
again—put his hand into his pocket, and drew out a little
silver box, about the size of a small snuff-box,—that had in
it a good many little pills of a dark gray gummy look. One
of these he swallowed, then began to deal, his eye growing
brighter every moment, and looking into mine till I felt quite
dazzled and strange. Our table was the belly of the dead
horse. He sat on one of the thighs. I knelt down upon the
grass on the opposite side, and though it pained me, I couldn't
take my eyes from him to save my life. He asked me a great
many questions while he was throwing out the cards—how
old I was—what was my name—what family I had—how far
I lived—where I came from—every thing, indeed, about me,
and my way of life, and what I had and what I knew :—and

all this in no time—as fast as I tell it to you. Then he said, 'You are an honest fellow, take up your cards, and let us see if you are as lucky as you are honest.' It seemed as if I was, for I beat him. I played a pretty stiff game of *old sledge*, or as he called it, '*all fours*,' for I used to play, as long as I could remember, with the old man, my father, every night. Old people like these plays, and it's good for them to play. It keeps 'em lively, keeps them from sleeping too much, and from drinking. It's good for them, so long as it makes their own fireside sweet to them. Well! I was lucky. I won the game, and it worried me mightily when I did so. I didn't touch the money. *169165*

" ' I suppose,' said the stranger, ' that I must cover those pieces,' and before I could guess what he was about, he flung down four other gold pieces, making forty dollars, in the pile with mine, and began again shuffling the cards. If I was scared and unhappy before, I was twice as much so now. I could scarcely breathe, and why, I can't say exactly. It wasn't from any anxiety about the winning or the losing, for I preferred not to have the stranger's money; but it was his very indifference and unconcern that worried and distressed me. It seemed so unnatural, that I half the time thought that I was dealing with nothing human; and though I could shuffle, and cut, and play, yet it seemed to me as if I did it without altogether knowing why, or how. As luck would have it, I won the second time; and the third time he pulled out his purse and put down as many more pieces as lay there. I looked at the growing heap with a heart that seemed ready to burst. There was eighty dollars before me, and I felt my face grow red when I caught his eye looking steadily at mine. I began to feel sort 'o desperate, and flung about the cards like a person in liquor. The old man laughed, a low chuckle like, that made my blood crawl in my veins, half frozen, as it were. But, neither his skill and coolness, nor my fright, altered the luck at all. I again won, and trembled all over, to see the pile, and to see him take out his purse, and empty every thing upon it.

" ' Stranger,' said I, ' don't think of it; keep your money, and let me go home.'

" ' Pshaw! said he, ' you're a good fellow, and as lucky as you are good. Why shouldn't you be my heir? I prefer that a good fellow should win my money if any body. It'll do your sight good.'

" ' But not my heart, I'm afraid,' was my answer.

" ' That's precisely as you use it,' said he; ' money's a good creature, like every other good creature that God gives us. It's a good thing to be rich, for a rich man's always able to *do* good, when a poor man can only wish to do it. Get money, my lad, and be wise with it; wiser, I trust, than I have been.'

" With these words, he took out his silver box, swallowed another of the pills, and was busy dealing out the cards in another moment. I, somehow, was better pleased with him for what he said. The mention of God convinced me that he wasn't the devil, and what he said seemed very sensible. But I didn't feel any more right and happy than before. I only wanted the strength to refuse him. I couldn't refuse him. I took up the cards as he threw them, and it did seem to me that I scarcely saw to make out the spots when I played them. I hardly knew how the game was played; I didn't count; I couldn't tell what I made. I only heard him say at the close of the second hand,

' " The money's yours. You are a lucky fellow.'

" With these words he pushed the gold heap to me, and threw me the empty purse.

" ' There's something to put it in.'

" ' No!' said I: ' no, stranger—I can't take this money.'

" ' Why, pray ?'

" ' It's not right. It don't seem to me to be got honestly. I haven't worked for it.'

" ' Worked, indeed! If nobody used money but those who

worked for it, many a precious fellow would knaw his finger ends for a dinner. Put up your money !'

" I pushed it to him, all but the two eagles which I begun with ; but he pushed it back. I got up without touching it. ' Stay,' said he, ' you *are* a good fellow ! Sit down again ; sit down.' I sat down. ' I can't take that money,' said he, ' for it is yours. According to my way of thinking, it is yours—it is none of mine. There is only one way in which it may become mine ; only one way in which I could take it or make use of it, and that is by winning it back. That may be done, I will put the horse against the gold.'

CHAPTER V.

My heart beat quicker than ever when he pointed to Rainbow. Not that I expected or wished to win him back, for I would only have taken him back by giving up all the money, or all except the hundred and fifty dollars ; but it now seemed to me as if I looked on the old man with such feelings as would have made me consent to almost any thing he wished. I had a strange sort of pity for him. I considered him a sort of kind-hearted rich old madman. I said, ' Very well ;' and he took another pill out of his box, and begun again at the cards.

" ' You are a very fortunate fellow,' said he, ' and seem a very good one. I really see no reason why you should not be my heir. You say you are not married.'

" ' No.'

" ' But you have your sweetheart, I suppose. A lad of twenty-five, which I suppose is much about your age, is seldom without one.'

" ' It's not the case with me,' said I. ' In these parts we have mighty few folks and fewer women, and I don't know the girl among them that's ever seemed to me exactly the one that I should be willing to make my wife.'

" ' Why, you're not conceited, I hope? You don't think yourself too fine a fellow for a poor girl, do you?'

" ' No, by no means, stranger; but there's a sort of liking that one must have before he can think of a wife, and I haven't seen the woman yet to touch me in the right way.'

" ' You are hard to please, and properly. Marriage is easier found than lost. A man is too noble an animal to be kept in a mouse-trap. But there *are* women——'

" He stopped short. I waited for him to say something more, but by this time the cards had been distributed, and he was sorting his hand.

" ' There are women!' he said again, though as if he was talking to himself. There he stopt for a minute, then looking up, and fixing his bright eyes upon mine, he continued:

" ' Come, Rayner,' said he, good-humouredly. ' The cards are in your hands, and remember to play your best, for that famous fine horse may become your own again. I warn you, I have a good hand. What do you do?'

" ' Good or not,' said I, something more boldly, ' I will stand on mine.'

" I had a most excellent hand, being sure of high and low, with a strong leading hand for game.

" ' Play then!' he answered; and at the word, I clapped down the ace of hearts, the very ace you see atop of the pack over the chimney now.

" ' You *are* a lucky fellow, Rayner,' said he, as he flung down the Jack upon it, the only heart he held in his hand. The game ended: I was owner of horse and money. But I jumped to my feet instantly.

" ' Stranger,' said I, ' don't think I'm going to rob you of your horse or money. I don't exactly know why I played with you so long, unless it be because you insisted upon it, and I didn't wish to disoblige an old gentleman like yourself.

Take your money, and give me my horse ; or, if you want the
horse, leave me the hundred and fifty, which is a fair price for
him, and put the rest in your own pocket.   I won't touch a
copper more of it.'

" ' You *are* a good fellow, Rayner, but, with some persons,
younger and rasher persons than myself, your words would be
answered with a bullet.   Nay, were I the boy I have been, it
would be dangerous for you to speak, *even to me,* in such a
manner.   Among gentlemen, the obligation to pay up what is
lost by cards is sacred.   The loser *must* deliver, and the winner *must* receive.   *There* is your money, and that is your horse
again ; but I am not yet done with you.   As I said before, you
are a good fellow, and most certainly a lucky one.   I like you,
though your principles are scarcely fixed yet—not certain !
Still, I like you : and there's some chance that you will be my
heir yet.   A few more trials at the cards must determine that.
I suppose you are not unwilling to give me a chance to win
back my losses ?'

" I caught at the suggestion.

" ' Surely not,' I replied.

" ' Very good,' says he. ' Don't suppose that, because you've
emptied my purse, you've cleaned me out quite.   I have a diamond ring and a diamond breast-pin yet to stake.   They are
worth something more than your horse and your heap of money.   We will place them against your eagles and horse.'

" 'No,' said I, quickly. ' I'm willing to put down all the
eagles, but not the horse ; or I'll put down the horse and all
the money, except a hundred and fifty.'

" ' As you please,' said he; ' but, my good fellow, you must
take my word for the ring and breast-pin.   I do not carry
them with me.   I know it's rather awkward to talk of playing
a promised stake against one that we see, but I give you the
honour of a gentleman that the diamonds shall be forthcoming
if I lose.'

" I began to think that what he said **was** only a **sort** of

come-off—but I didn't want his money, and was quite willing
that he should win it back. If he had said, 'I'll stake my
tooth-pick against the money,' I'd have been just as willing,
for all that I now aimed at was to secure my horse, or the
price of him! I felt very miserable at the thoughts of winning
the man's money—such a heap of it! I had never played cards
for money in all my life before, and there's something in the
feeling of winning money, for the first time, that's almost like
thieving. As I tell you, if he had said his tooth-pick, or any
worthless thing, instead of his diamonds, I'd have been willing. I didn't say so, however, and I thought his offer to stake
diamonds that he couldn't show, was pretty much like a come-
off. But I was willing enough, for the money seemed to scald
my eyes to look upon. He took out a pencil, the case of
which I saw was gold also, and wrote on a slip of paper,
' Good for two brilliants, one a ring, the other a breast-pin, the
latter in form of a Maltese cross, both set in gold, with an
inner rim of silver, valued at seven hundred dollars.' This was
signed with two letters only, the initials of his name. I have
the paper now. He bade me read it, and when I did so, I
thought him madder than a March hare; but if I thought so
then, I was more than ever convinced of it, when, a moment
after, and when we were about to play, he spoke to this
effect:

"' There's one thing, Rayner. There's a little incumbrance
on these jewels.'

" ' Well, sir,' I said.

" I didn't care a fig for the incumbrance, for I didn't believe
a word of the jewels.

"' If you win them, you win a woman along with them.—
You win a wife.'

" I laughed outright.

"' Don't laugh,' said he; 'you don't see me laugh. I'm serious; never more so. You are unmarried. You need a wife.
Don't you want one?'

" ' Yes, if I could get a good one—one to my liking.'

" ' You *are* a good fellow. You deserve a good wife, Rayner; and such is the very one I propose to give you.'

" ' Ay, ay,' said I; ' but will she be to my liking ?'

" ' I hope so; I believe so. She has all the qualities which should command the liking of a sensible and worthy young man. She, too, is sensible; she is intelligent; she has knowledge; she has read books; she has accomplishments; she sings like an angel; plays on several instruments—piano and guitar!'

" ' Piano and guitar!' said I.

" I didn't know what they were. I felt sure that the old fellow was mad, just out of a hospital, perhaps; but then, where did he get the money and the gold things? I begun to think more suspiciously of him than ever.

" ' Yes, piano and guitar,' said he; 'she draws and paints, too, the loveliest pictures—she can make these trees live on canvass; ah! can she not? Money has not been spared, Rayner, to make Rachel what she is.'

" ' Rachel—is that her name ?' I asked.

" ' Yes, it is.'

" ' What's the other name ?'

" ' You shall know, if you win the diamonds.'

" ' Yes—but how old is she? how does she look? is she young and handsome? I wouldn't want an ugly wife, because she happened to be wise. I've heard that your wise women are generally too ugly for any thing else than wisdom.'

" ' You are a fool, Rayner, though a good fellow. But Rachel is beautiful and young—not more than seventeen—the proper age for you. You, I think you say, are twenty-eight In this climate a man's wife should always be ten or twelve years younger than himself—provided he be a sober and healthy man, and if he be not, he has no business with a wife,

E 5

nor a wife with him. You are both sober and healthy. You
are a good fellow—I see that. I like you, Rayner, and for
this reason I am willing to risk Rachel on the cards, playing
against you. My loss will probably be her gain, and this
makes me rather regardless how it ends. You shall be my
heir yet.'

"'Thank you, old gentleman,' said I, beginning to feel a
little bold and saucy, for I now couldn't help thinking that the
stranger was no better than a good-natured madman who had
got away from his friends. 'Thank you,' said I. 'If Rachel's
the girl you make her out to be, you can't bring her along a
day too soon. But, may I ask, is she your daughter?'

"'My daughter!' he answered sharply, and with something
of a frown on his face, 'do I look like a man to have children?—to be favoured with such a blessing as a daughter?—
a daughter like Rachel?'

"'Now,' said I to myself, 'his fit's coming on,' and I began
to look about me for a start.

"'No, Rayner,' he continued, 'she is no daughter of mine,
but she is the daughter of a good man, and of honourable parents. You shall have sufficient proof of that. Have you any
more questions?'

"'No, sir.'

"'And you will take Rachel as your wife? You have heard
my description of her. If she comes up to it, I ask you, will
you be willing to take her as your wife?'

"I looked at him queerly enough, I reckon. He fixed his
keen black eyes upon me, so that I couldn't look upon him
without shutting my own. I didn't know whether to laugh
or to run. But, thinking that he was flighty in the upper
story, I concluded it was best to make a short business of it,
and to agree with any thing he wished; so I freely told
him 'yes,' and he reached out his hand to mine, which he
squeezed nervously for a minute, and then took out his box
of pills, swallowed a couple of them, and began dealing out

the cards. I had the strangest luck—the same sort of luck that had kept with me from the start. I won the diamonds, and won Rachel!

" ' Well,' said he, ' I'm glad, Rayner, that you are the man. I've long been looking for an heir to my diamonds. They are yours—all is yours; and I shall have to be indebted to you for the loan of the horse, in order to go and bring you your wife.'

" ' Ay,' said I, ' stranger, the horse is at your service, and half of the money, too. I never thought to take them from you, at the first; I shouldn't have felt easy in my conscience to have used the money that I got in this way.'

" ' Help yourself to the rest,' said I, taking, as I spoke, fifteen of the eagles to myself, and leaving the rest on the dead body of the horse, where they had been growing from our first commencing to play.

" ' You are my heir,' he answered, ' and behave yourself as you should. Between persons so related there should be no paltry money scruples ;' and, while he said these words, he stooped to take the money. I turned away, that he shouldn't suppose I watched him, but I couldn't help laughing at the strange sort of cunning which he showed in his conceit. Says I to myself, ' You will take precious good care, old fellow, I see that, that I will carry off no more than my own poor hundred and fifty.' But he was too quick in mounting and riding off, to give me much time to think about it, or to change in my disposition. It was only after he was off, out of sight, and in a full gallop, that, looking round upon the dead horse, I saw the eagles still there, nearly all of them, just as I had heaped them up. He had only taken two of them, just enough, as he said, to bear his necessary expenses.

" I was a little surprised, and was now more sure than ever that the stranger had lost his wits. I gathered up the money, and walked home, mighty slowly, thinking all the way of what had taken place. It seemed more like a strange dream than

any thing else. Was there any man? Had I played *old sledge*
with a stranger? I was almost inclined to doubt; but there
was the dead horse. I went back to look at it, and when I
thrust my hand down into my breeches pocket, I brought it
up full of the precious metal; but was it precious metal? I
began to tremble at this thought. It might be nothing better
than brass or copper, and my horse was gone—gone off at a
smart canter. My heart grew chilled within me at this reflec-
tion. I felt wild—scared half out of my wits, and instead of
regarding the old man as a witless person escaped from his
keepers, I now began to consider him a cunning sharper, who
had found one more witless than I had fancied him.

CHAPTER VI.

BUT such reflections, even if well founded, came too late for
remedy. The old man was gone beyond present reach, and
when I reflected that he had taken two of the gold pieces for
his own expenses, I began to feel a little reassured on the
subject of their value. When I got home, I told my father of
the sale of the horse, and the price, though I took precious
good care to say nothing of the gambling. The old man,
though he himself had taught me to play cards, was mighty
strict against all play for money. I showed him only the fifteen
pieces that I got for Rainbow, and the rest I put away quietly,
meaning to spend them by degrees upon the farm, as chances
offered, so as to prevent him from ever getting at the real
truth. I felt myself pretty safe with regard to the strange
gentleman. I never counted on his coming back to blow me,
though, sometimes, when I wasn't thinking, an odd sort of
fear would come over me, and I would feel myself trembling
with the notion that, after all, he might return. I had heard
of rich people having strange ways of throwing away their

money, and taking a liking for poor people like myself; and then, there was a serious earnest about the strange gentleman, in spite of all his curiousnesses, that made me a little apprehensive, whenever the recollection of him came into my head.

"But regular work, day after day, is the best physic for mind and body; and, after three days had gone by, I almost ceased to bother myself with the affair. I passed the time so actively that I didn't think much about any thing. I took a trip down the river, some eighteen miles, to a wheelwright's, and bought a prime two-horse waggon, for ninety-five dollars, which made a considerable hole in the price of Rainbow; and, one thing with another, the week went by almost without giving me time to count if the right number of days was in it. Sunday followed, and then Monday. That Monday I was precious busy. I was always an industrious man—doing something or other—making this, or mending that. To be doing nothing was always the hardest work for me. But that Monday I out-worked myself, and I was really glad when I saw the sun sink suddenly down behind the woods. I threw down the broad-axe, for I had been hewing out some door-facings for a new corn-crib and fodder-house, and went towards the gallery (piazza) where the old man was sitting, and threw myself, at full length, along the entrance, just at his feet. I was mighty tired. My jacket was off. My sleeves rolled up, my neck open, and the perspiration standing thick on my breast and forehead. At that very moment, while I was lying in this condition, who should I see ride into the opening but the strange old gentleman. I knew him at a glance, and my heart jumped into my mouth, as if it was trying to get out of it. Behind him came another person riding upon a pretty little bay filly. Though it was darkening fast, I could make out that this other person was a woman, and I never felt so scared in all my life. I looked up at my father, and he at me. He saw that I was frightened, but he hadn't time to ask me a question, and I shouldn't have had the

strength to answer if he had.   Up rode the strange old gentleman, and close behind him came the lady.   Though I was
mightily frightened, I looked curiously at her.   I could make
out that she was a small and delicate-framed person, but her
face was covered with a thick veil.   I could see that she
carried herself well, sat her horse upright like a sort of queen,
and when the old man offered to take her off, yielded herself
to him with a slow but graceful stateliness, not unlike that of
a young cedar bending to the wind.

"For my part, though I could see this, I was never more
confounded in my life.   I was completely horror-struck.   To
see the old gentleman again was a shocking surprise; but that
he should really bring the lady that I had won, and that she
should catch me in that condition—my coat off, my breast
open, my face covered with dust and perspiration!   If the
work made me sweat before, this surprise increased it.   I got
up, and made out to get a few steps towards the strangers.
I said something by way of apology for being caught in that
shabby fix; but the old gentleman stopped me.

" 'Never mind, no apologies, Mr. Rayner.   The proofs of
labour are always honourable, and if the heart can show that
it works as well as the body, then the labourer is a gentleman.
How are you—and this is your father?'

"I introduced him to the old man as the person who had
bought Rainbow, and we conducted them into the house.

" ' My ward, Mr. Rayner,' said the stranger, when we had
entered, ' this is the young friend of whom I spoke to you.'

" At these words the young lady threw up her veil.   I stag-
gered back at the sight.   I won't talk of her beauty, my
friend, for two reasons; one of which is, that I haven't got
words to say what I thought and felt—what I think and feel
now.   The other—but I needn't speak of the other reason.
This one is sufficient.   The old gentleman looked at me inquiringly, and then he looked at my father.   I could see that
there was a little doubt and anxiety upon his face, but they

soon passed away as he examined the face of my father. There was something so good, so meek, so benevolent about the looks of the old man, that nobody could mistrust that all was right in the bottom of his heart. As for my heart, the strange gentleman seemed to see into it quite as quickly as into that of my father. He was not so blunt and abrupt now in his manner of speaking to me as he had been when we first met. His manner was more dignified and reserved. There was something very lofty and noble about it, and in speaking to the lady his voice sunk almost into a whisper.

" ' Mr. Rayner,' said he, looking to my father, ' I trust that you will give my ward a chamber for the night. I have heard of you, sir, and have made bold to presume on your known benevolence of character in making this application.'

" ' Our home is a poor one, stranger,' said the old man ; ' but such as it is, it is quite at the service of the young lady.'

" ' Good !' said the other ; ' you are the man after my own heart. I am known,' he continued, where men speak of me at all, as Mr. Eckhardt. My ward is the daughter of a very near and dear friend. Her name is Herder—Rachel Herder. So much is necessary for convenience in conversation ; and now, sir, if you can tell Rachel where she is to find her chamber, so that she may arrange her dress, and get rid of the dust of travel, she will be very much obliged to you.'

" All this was soon arranged and attended to, and while the lady disappeared in our best chamber, Mr. Eckhardt proceeded to disburthen the horses, on both of which were saddle-bags that were stuffed almost to bursting. These were brought into the house, and sent to the chamber after the lady. Then the stranger sat down with my father, the two old men chatting quite briskly together, while I stripped the horses of their saddles, and took them to the stable. When I returned to the house I found them as free-spoken and good-humoured as if they had been intimate from the first day of clearing in that country.

CHAPTER VII.

" You may suppose what my confusion must have been, for I can't describe it to you. I can only say that I felt pretty much like a drunken man. Every thing swum around me. I was certain of nothing; didn't know what to believe, and half the time really doubted whether I was asleep or awake. But there were the horses—there was Rainbow. I couldn't mistake him, and if I had, he didn't mistake me. When he heard my voice as I led him to the stable, he whinnied with a sort of joy, and pricked up his ears, and showed his feeling as plainly as if he had a human voice to speak it in words. And I reckon, too, it was a more true feeling than many of those that are spoken in words. I threw my arms round the good creature's neck, and if it hadn't been for thinking of Rachael Herder, I reckon I should have kissed him, too, it did me so much good to see him again. But I hadn't much time for this sort of fondness, and when I remembered the whole affair between the strange old gentleman, Mr. Eckhardt, and myself, I was too much worried to think any more of Rainbow. I couldn't bring myself to believe it true about the diamonds and the wife; and when I remembered the sight that I had caught, though a glimpse only, and for a single moment, of the great beauty of the young lady, I couldn't help thinking that the stranger was only making merry with me—running his rigs upon a poor, rough, backwoodsman. But this notion roused up my pride and feeling. ' Not so rough,' says I to myself; ' poor it may be, but not mean : not more rough than honest labour makes a man. And poor as you please, and rough as you please, when the heart's right, and the head's no fool's head, the man's man enough for any woman, though she walks in satin!' With this I considered that I ought, at least, to make myself rather decent before I sat down to supper. My cheeks burned me when I looked at myself and remembered how she had caught me. I knew that good soft spring water, and my best suit, would turn me into quite another sort of looking man: but here again was difficulty. It was my chamber which my father had given up to the young lady, and all my clothes were in it. My new coat and blue pantaloons hung upon pegs behind the door; and all my shirts were in an old chest of drawers on which the looking-glass stood; and to get these things without her seeing was impossible. But it had to be done; so I called up the old negro woman servant we had, and told her what to do, and sent her for the clothes, while I waited for them at the back of the house. When she brought them, I hurried down to the branch (brooklet) and made a rapid and plentiful use of the waters. I then got in among the bushes, and made a thorough change in my dress, taking care to hide the old clothes in the hollow of a gum. I combed my hair smoothly over the branch, which answered me at the same time for a looking-glass, and had the effect of making me much more satisfied with my personal appearance. I needn't blush, my friend, at my time of life, to say that I thought myself then, and was, a tolerable comely fellow; and I couldn't help feeling a sneaking secret notion that the young lady would think so too. Well, I got in time enough for supper. Mr. Eckhardt looked at me, as I thought, with real satisfaction. He and my father had been keeping company all the time I was gone, and I could see, among other things, that they were mightily pleased with one another. By and by, supper was brought in, and Rachel Herder came out of her chamber. If I thought her beautiful before, I thought her now ten times more so. Once I caught her eyes fixed upon me, but she turned them away without any flurry or confusion, and I don't think that I

it's not beauty altogether that makes a good wife, and I
ha'n't had time yet to judge whether she'll suit me.'

" ' How much time do you want ?' said he shortly.

" ' Well, I can't say.'

" ' Will a week or ten days answer ?'

" ' That's as it happens,' said I. ' Some men you can understand in an hour, just as if you had been with 'em all your life·
I'm pretty much such a person myself,—but with some you
can't get on so rapidly. You'll be with them a year, and
know just as little of their hearts at the end of it, as you did
at the beginning.'

" ' Humph! and whose fault will that be but your own ?
There's an eye to see, Rayner, as well as a thing to be seen.
It depends very much upon the seeker whether he shall ever
find. But enough. There's no need in this case for much
philosophy. You are easily read, and so is Rachel. A week
will answer to make you both acquainted, and I'll leave her
with you for that time.'

" ' But are you serious ?' I asked.

" ' Serious! But your question is natural. I am a man of
few words, Rayner. You see something in my proceedings
which is extraordinary. As the world goes, and acts, and
thinks, perhaps it is; but nothing was ever more deliberate or
well advised, on my part, than this proceeding. Hear me,
lad! this lady is a ward of mine ; the daughter of a very dear
friend, who gave her to my trust. I swore to do by her as a
father. I am anxious to do so; but I am an old man, not
long for this world,—an erring man, not always sure of doing
right while I am in it. I wish to find the child a protector,—
a good man,—a kind man,—a man whom I can trust. This
has been my desire for some time. I fancy I have found in
you the very person I seek. I am a man to look keenly, judge
quickly, and act in the same manner. As you yourself have
remarked, you are a person easily understood. I understood
you in a little time, and was pleased with what I saw of you.

I have chosen you out as the husband of Rachel. She knows nothing yet of my purpose. You, I see, have kept your father in partial ignorance of our adventure. Perhaps you were right in this case, though, as a general rule, such secrecy between two persons placed as you are would have been an error. Well, Rachel shall stay with you a week. I know her so well that I fancy you will in that time become intimate and remain pleased with each other—sufficiently pleased to make the rest easy.'

"There was some more talk between us, as we went toward the house, but this was the substantial part of what was said. Once I made some remark on the strangeness of such a preference shown to me, when in the great cities he might have found so many young men better suited by education for a young lady whom he represented to be so accomplished ; but he had his answer for this also ; and so quickly uttered, and with such a commanding manner, that, even if I had not been satisfied, I should still have been silenced.

"'Your remark is natural. Half the world, having such a child to dispose of, would have gone to the great city, and have preferred a fashionable husband. But I know her heart. It is her heart, and not her accomplishments, that I wish to provide for. I want a man, not a dandy,—a frank, noble-hearted citizen, however plain, not a selfish, sophisticated calculator, who looks for a wife through the stock market. Enough, my good fellow ; no more words.'

CHAPTER VIII.

" THAT very night Mr. Eckhardt contrived, after the young lady had gone to bed, to let my father know that he would be pleased if his ward could be suffered to remain in his family for a few days, until he should cross the river, in order to look after a man on the west of the Mississippi, who owed him money. He was unwilling to carry her with him into so very wild a region. He made every thing appear so natural to the old man, that he consented out of hand, just as if it had been the most reasonable arrangement in the world; and it was only after Mr. Eckhardt had set out,—which he did by daylight the next morning,—that my father said to me:

"It's very strange, now I come to think of it, that Mr. Eckhardt should leave the young lady in a family where there's none but men.'

" ' But she's just as safe here, father,' said I, ' as if she had fifty of her own sex about her.'

" ' That's true enough, William,' said the old man, ' and if the child feels herself at home, why there's nothing amiss. I'm thinking she's about the sweetest looking creature I ever laid eyes on.'

" I thought so too, but I said nothing, and followed the old man into the house, with my feelings getting more and more strange and worrisome every moment. I was in the greatest whirl of expectation—my cheeks a-burning,—my heart as cold as ice, and leaping up and down, just as scarily as a rabbit's when he's finding his way through the paling into a garden patch. I felt as if the business now upon my hands was about the most serious and trying I had ever undertaken; and it took all my thinking, I tell you, to bring my courage to the right pitch, so as to steady my eyes while I spoke to the young lady as she came out to the breakfast-table. My father had a message to her from Mr. Eckhardt, telling her of his absence; and though she looked a little anxious when she heard that he was already gone, she soon seemed to become quiet and at ease in her situation. Indeed, for that matter, she was the most resigned and easy person I ever met in my life. She seemed quite too gentle ever to complain, and I may say now with some certainty, that, whatever might be her hurts of mind or body, she was the most patient to submit, and the most easy to be pacified of all human beings.

"Now, if you know any thing of a man of my description, if you're any thing of a judge of human nature, you'll readily understand that, if I was scary and bashful at first, in meeting with a young and beautiful creature like her, and knowing what I did know of what was before me, it didn't take very long for the fright to wear off. The man whose feelings are very quick, gets mightily confused at first, but give him time, don't hurry him, and he'll come to his senses pretty soon, and they'll come to him, and they'll be the sharper and the more steady, from the scare they had at first—you can't scare them in the same manner a second time. Before that day was well out, I could sit down and talk with Rachel, and hear her talk, without growing blind, dumb, and deaf in an instant. Her mildness gave me encouragement, and when I got used to the sound of my own voice, just after hers, I then found out, not only that I had a good deal to say, but that she listened very patiently, and I think was pleased to hear it. I found her so mild, so kind, so encouraging, she seemed to take so much interest in every thing she saw, that I was for showing her every thing. Our cows, the little dairy, the new waggon, even to the fields of corn, cotton, and potatoes, were all subjects of examination one after the other. Then, I could carry her along the hill slopes, through as pretty a grove, too, as you would wish to lay eyes on; and down along just such another, even to the river banks; and we had odd things enough to show, here and there, to keep up the spirits and have something to talk about. These rambles we'd take either in the cool of the morning, or towards sunset in the afternoon; and, sometimes the old man would go along with us—but, as he couldn't go very far at one time, we had pretty much the whole chance to ourselves; and what with talking and walking with Rachel, and thinking about her when I wasn't with her, I did precious little work that week. To shorten a long story, my friend, I now began to think that there was nothing wrong in my gambling with Mr. Eckhardt, and to agree in his notion that the loser was always bound to pay, and the winner to receive. Before he got back, which he did not until ten days were fully over, I had pretty much concluded that I should find it the most trying business in nature to have to give up my winnings. I don't mean the diamonds; for them I had not seen, and hadn't cared to see ; but I mean the incumbrance that came with them, which, by this time, was more than all the gold or diamonds, in my sight, that the whole world could show.

———

CHAPTER IX.

" I was now as anxious to see Mr. Eckhardt as I had before been afraid of his coming. He overstayed his time a little, being nearer two weeks gone than one. He was a keensighted man. His first words, when we were again alone together, were, '' Well, all's right on your part, Rayner. You are a good fellow—I see that you will be my heir. You find that what I said of Rachel is true ; and nothing now remains but to see what she will say. Have you been much together ?'

" ' Pretty often. I reckon I've done little else than look after her since you've been gone.'

" ' What! you hav'n't neglected your business, Rayner ?' said he, with a smile—' the cows, the horses ?'

" ' They've had a sort of liberty,' says I.

" ' Bad signs for farming, however good for loving. You must change your habits when you are married.'

" ' Ah ! that's not yet,' said I, with a sigh. ' I'm dub'ous, Mr. Eckhardt, that Miss Rachel won't fancy me so soon as I do her !''

" He looked a little anxious, and didn't answer so quickly

as usual, and my heart felt as heavy then as if it was borne
down by a thousand pounds of lead. It wasn't much light-
ened when he answered, with a sort of doubting,—

"'Rachel,' said he, 'has always heeded my counsel. She
knows my love for her—she has every confidence in my judgment. You, Rayner, have some of those advantages which
young women are apt to admire. You are well made, youthful, manly, and with a masculine grace and beauty which you
owe to the hunter life. These are qualities to recommend the
young of one sex to the young of the other. You have something more. You are a sensible youth, with a native delicacy
of feeling which, more than any thing beside, will be apt to
strike Rachel. It struck me. I will not presume to say that
you have won either her eye or her heart—the eye of a woman is easy won at all times, the heart slowly. Perhaps it
may be safe to say that hearts are not often won till after
marriage. But, at all events, with your personal claims,
which I think considerable, and the docility of Rachel, I have
hopes that I can bring about an arrangement which, I confess
to you, I regard as greatly important to my future purposes.
We shall see.'

"At that moment I was quite too full of Rachel and my
own hopes, to consider the force of the remark which he last
made. I never troubled myself to ask what his purposes
might be, beyond the single one which we both had in view.
When Mr. Eckhardt met with Rachel, and, indeed, while he
spoke with me, I could observe that there was a gravity, like
sadness, in his voice and manner, which was not usual with
him, or at least had not shown itself in our previous meetings.
He hesitated more frequently in what he had to say. His
eye was less settled, though even brighter than before; and
I noted the fact that he took his pills three times as frequently
as ever. Even when he spoke with a show of jesting or
playfulness, I noted that there was a real sadness in what he
looked, and even something of sadness in what he said, or in

his manner of saying it. Nothing but this seriousness of look and manner kept me from thinking that he was playing upon my backwoods ignorance, when he was speaking my own good name and good qualities to my teeth. But when I doubted and began to suspicion that he was running rigs upon me, I had only to look into his face and see that he was talking in the way of downright, matter-of-fact business.

"When he came, Rachel went to him and put her hand in his, but she didn't speak. Nor did he at first. He only bent down and kissed her forehead; and so he stood awhile, holding her hand in his, and talking to my father. It was a sight to see them two. I couldn't stand it. There was something in it, I can't tell you what, that looked so sadful. I went out and wiped the water from my eyes. It seemed to me then, as if the old gentleman was meditating something very distressing, and as if poor Rachel was half dub'ous of it herself. After a little while, my father came out and joined me, and we walked off together to the stable.

"'William,' says the old man, 'these are strange people. They seem very sweet, good people; at least the girl seems very good; and is a very sweet girl; but there's something very strange and very sorrowful about them.'

"I conld't say any thing, for my heart was very full, and the old man went forward.

"'Now what's more strange than for him to leave her here with us? though, to be sure, we wouldn't see her harmed even to the falling of a hair of her head—and I can answer for you, Bill, as I can for myself; but it's not every body that will say for us what we might feel for ourselves, and precious few fathers would leave an only daughter here, in strange woods, with such perfect strangers.'

"'But she's not his daughter,' said I.

"'It don't matter. It's very clear that he loves her as if she was his daughter, and I reckon she's never known any
F

other father. Poor girl!—I'm sure I like her already so much
that I wish he would leave her here altogether.'

" These last words of my father seemed to untie my tongue,
and I up and told him every syllable of what had taken place
between me and Mr. Eckhardt, from my first meeting with
him the day when I went to the river landing, up to the very
moment when we were talking. I didn't hide any thing, but
told the whole story of the cards, the gold, and the diamonds ;
and ended by letting him know that if he should be so sorry to
lose Rachel, now that we both knew so much about her, it
would go a mighty deal harder with me. I told him all that
Mr. Eckhardt had said since his return, and what hopes I had
that all would go as he wished it. But the old man shook
his head. He did't like what he heard about Mr. Eckhardt's
gambling, and was very tight upon me for letting myself be
tempted to deal with him in the same business. He didn't
think the worse of Rachel, of course, but he looked upon it
as a sort of misfortune to be in any way connected with a
gambler.

" We hadn't much longer time for confabulating, for Mr.
Eckhardt now came from the house and joined us. He was
a man who came always jump to the business, whatever it
was, that he had in hand. But he wasn't a rough man,
though a quick one. He had a way of doing the bluntest
things without roughing the feelings. When he drew nigh,
he took my father's arm to lead him aside, speaking to me at
the same time—' Rayner, go to Rachel ;—I have prepared her
to see you. I will explain every thing to your father, if you
have not already done it; and if you have, I still have something to say.'

" You may reckon I didn't stop to count the tracks after
that. I verily think that I made the door of the house in a
hop-skip-and-jump from the stable. Yet, when I got to the
threshold, I stuck—I stuck fast. I heard a low sweet sort of
moaning from within, and oh! how my heart smote me when

I heard it. I thought to myself, it's so cruel to force this poor girl's inclination. What can she see in me? That was my question to myself, and it made me mighty humble, I tell you, when I asked it. But that very humbleness did me good, and gave me a sort of strength. 'If she don't see any thing in me to favour,' was my thought, 'at least I'll show her that I'm not the mean-spirited creature to take advantage of her necessity;' and when I thought in this manner, I went forward with a bound, and stood before her. I took her hand in mine, and said,—but Lord bless me, it's no use to try and tell you what I said, for I don't know myself. The words poured from me free enough. My heart was very full. I meant to speak kindly and humbly, and do the thing generously, and I reckon that, when the heart means what is right, and has a straight purpose before it, the tongue can't go very far out of the way. Nor did mine, if I am to judge of the effects which followed it. It's enough for me to tell you, that, though the tears wasn't altogether dried up in Rachel's eyes, her lips began to smile; she let her hand rest in mine, and she said something, but what it was, I can't tell you. It's enough to say that she let me know that she thought that all that had been proposed by Mr. Eckhardt was for her good and happiness, and she was willing to consent to whatever he had said. He came in a little while after, and seemed quite satisfied. He talked, as if he himself was particularly pleased, but there was a very great earnestness in his looks that awed and overpowered me. His eyes seemed very much sunk, even in the short time he had been gone, the wrinkles seemed to have doubled in number on his face; his form trembled very much, and I could perceive that he took his pills from the little box of silver twice as often as ever. He didn't give himself or me much time to think over what was to happen, for he hadn't been ten minutes returned to the house, after the matter was understood all round, before he said to me in a whisper:

" ' Rayner, my lad, you are a good fellow ; suppose you ride
eff at once for your parson. You have one, your father tells
me, within a few miles. A smart gallop will bring him back
with you before sunset, and I would see you married to-night.
I shall have to leave you in the morning.'

" Ah ! stranger, don't wonder if I made the dust fly after
that ! That night we were married.

CHAPTER X.

" The next morning, just as breakfast was over, Mr. Eckhardt rose and buttoned his coat.

" ' Rachel, my child,' said he, ' I shall now leave you. It
will be perhaps some time before I see you again. For that
matter, I may never see you again. But I have fulfilled my
promise to your dear father. You are the wife of a good man
—a gentle and kind-hearted man. He will make you a good
husband, I believe and hope. You, I know, will make him a
good wife. The seeds of goodness and happiness are here in
this cottage—may they grow to fruits. Kiss me, my child !
Kiss me ! It may be for the last time !'

' " No !' said she ; ' oh, no !' and she caught and she clung
to him. It was a time to bring tears, stranger, not to talk.
There was a good many words said by all of us, but not much
talking. It was a cry and an exclamation like, with poor
Rachel, and then she sunk off in the arms of Mr. Eckhardt.
I was monstrous frightened ; but he carried her into the room
and laid her on the bed. ' She will soon get over it,' said he,
' and in the mean time I'll steal away. When she recovers,
follow me. You will find me ——' He told me where to
find him—at the place where we had played together on the
dead horse—but the sentence he finished in a whisper. Then
he stooped and kissed her, gave her one long look, and his

lips moved as if he was speaking a blessing over her. After this he turned from me hurriedly, as if to conceal the tear in his eye. But I saw it. It couldn't be concealed. It was about the largest tear I ever did see in the eye of a man, but I reckon there was only that one. He was gone before Rachel come to herself. Till that happened I was about the most miserable creature on earth. When she opened her eyes and found that he was already gone, her troubles somewhat softened; and when I found that, I set off to follow Mr. Eckhardt, as he had directed me. I found him at the place appointed, but he had no horse and no cloak, and didn't appear to have made any of the usual arrangements for travelling. I expressed my surprise. 'Where's your horse?' I demanded.—'I shall need none. Besides, I *have* none. You seem to forget, Rayner, that the horse is yours.'—'Mine!'— 'Yes! you won him!'—'But you can't mean, sir——' I was beginning to expostulate, when he put his hand on my mouth. 'Say no more, Rayner. You are a good fellow. The horse *is* yours, whether you have him by your skill or my generosity. Did I not tell you that I intended to make you my heir?'

"I looked bewildered, and felt so, and said, 'Well, you don't intend to leave us then?'—'Yes, I do.'—'How do you mean to go—by water?' Remember, the river was pretty near us, and though I didn't myself expect any steamboat, yet I thought it likely he might have heard of one. 'Very possible, he answered, with something of a smile upon his countenance. He continued, after a short pause, 'It is difficult to say by what conveyance a man goes when he goes out of the world, Rayner. The journey I propose to take is no other. Life is an uncertain business, Rayner. Uncertain as it is, most people seem never to have enough of it. I am of a different thinking. I have had only too much. I am neither well in it, nor fit for it, and I shall leave it. I have made all my arrangements, settled my concerns, and, as I promised, you shall be my heir.' I began to speak and expostulate with bands have sought for her. Men of rank and substance, for whose attentions the mothers of most daughters would have worked their wits and fingers to the bone. But if I squandered Rachel's fortune—mark me—I was resolved that *she* should not be sacrificed. I resolved that I would do her justice, at least in that one respect—that she should never be yielded, if I could help it, to the shallow witling, the profligate, or the brute—let their social rank and worldly possessions be what they might. I knew her, and fancied I could tell what sort of person would suit her. I have found that person in you—so I believe—and my work is ended. The labourer knocks off when his work is done, and so will I. There is one thing, Rayner——'

" He took from his pocket the buckskin roll which contained his pack of cards.

" ' Do you see these? I will not say that they have been my bane. I were a fool to say so. My own weakness was my bane. They were only the unconscious instruments in my hands, as innocent as the dirk or pistol in the hands of the assassin. But they have their dangers, Rayner; and I would protect you against them. Take them; I promised you should be my heir. Take them, but not to play with them. Keep them in your eyes as an omen. Show them to your children as a warning. Tell them what I have told you; and while you familiarize their eyes with their forms, familiarize their hearts with their dangers. There! do not lose sight of them. Leave me now. Farewell! You see I am at the bottom of my box.'

" He thrust the cards into my hands, and as he spoke, he drew out his little silver box, and took from it the only pill which remained. This he swallowed, and then handed me the box also. I refused to take it. ' Pshaw!' said he, ' why not? your refusal to take it can have no effect on my determination! Take it and leave me!' But I still refused. He turned from me, saying: ' You're a foolish fellow, Rayner ;

and walked down the road leading to the river. I followed
him closely. He turned half round, once or twice, muttered,
and seemed discontented. I still kept close with him, and
and began to expostulate. But he interrupted me fiercely ;
and I now perceived that his eyes began to glisten and to
glare very wildly. It had not escaped my observation, that
the last pill which he he had taken was greatly larger than
any he had used before ; and I then remembered, that before
the marriage ceremony was performed, on the previous night,
he had opened the box more than once, in my presence, and I
noted that it contained a good many. By this time we
reached the banks of the river. He turned full upon me.
' Rayner,' said he, ' you're a good fellow, but you must go
home to your wife.'—' It's impossible,' said I, ' to leave you.'
—' We'll see to that,' said he, and he turned towards the
river. I took it for certain he was going to plunge in, and I
jumped forward to seize him, but, just as my arms were extended to embrace him, he wheeled about and clapped a pistol
to my head. I started back, quickly enough, as you may
suppose ; and he exclaimed—' Ah ! Rayner, you are a good
fellow, but you cannot prevent the journey. Farewell !'
With these words he flung me the pistol, which I afterwards
found was unloaded, and, before I could speak or think, he
sprang from the bluff into the stream. It appeared to me as
if I heard the splash before I saw the motion. I ran up the
bluff where he had stood, as soon as I could recover myself,
and saw where the water-rings were spreading in great
circles where he had gone down. I didn't give myself a moment after that. I could swim like a duck and dive like a
serpent, and had no fear of the water for myself ; so in I
jumped, and fished about as long as I could stand it underneath ; but I could find nothing of him. He had given himself
up to the currents so entirely, that they whirled him out of
sight in a minute. When I rose and got to the shore, I saw
his hat floating among some bushes on the other shore. But as

for poor Mr. Eckhardt, he was gone, sure enough, upon his last journey!

"You see our little family. The boy is very much like him in looks, and I reckon in understanding. He's very thoughtful and smart. We are happy, stranger, and I don't believe that Mr. Eckhardt was wrong in his notion that I would make Rachel happy. She tells me she is, and it makes me happy to believe her. It makes her sad to see the cards, and sad to hear of them, but she thinks it best for our boy to learn the tale, and learn it all by heart; and that makes her patient, and patience brings a sort of peace along with it that's pretty much like happiness. I could tell you more, my friend, but it's not needful, and your eyes look as if they had kept open long enough for one sitting. So come with me, and let me show you where you are to lie down!"

These words roused me! I half suspect that I was drowsing in my chair. I can hardly suppose that, dear reader, you could be capable of an act of like forgetfulness.

THE ARM-CHAIR OF TUSTENUGGEE.

A TRADITION OF THE CATAWBA.

CHAPTER I.

THE windy month had set in, the leaves were falling, and the light-footed hunters of Catawba, set forth upon the chase.— Little groups went off in every direction, and before two weeks had elapsed from the beginning of the campaign, the whole nation was broken up into parties, each under the guidance of an individual warrior. The course of the several hunting bands was taken according to the tastes and habits of these leaders. Some of the Indians were famous for their skill in hunting the otter, could swim as long with head under water as himself, and be not far from his haunches, when he emerged to breathe. These followed the course of shallow waters and swamps, and thick, dense bays, in which it was known he found his favourite haunts. The bear hunter pushed for the cane brakes and the bee trees, and woe to the black bear whom he encountered with his paws full of honeycomb, which he was unwilling to leave behind him. The active warrior took his way towards the hills, seeking for the brown wolf and the deer; and, if the truth were known, smiled with wholesale contempt at the more timorous, who desired less adventurous triumphs. Many set forth in couples only, avoiding with care all the clamorous of the tribe; and some few, the more surly or successful, the inveterate bachelors of the nation, were content to make their forward progress alone. The old men prepared their traps and nets, the boys their blow guns and followed with the squaws slowly, according to the division made by the hunters among themselves. They carried the blankets and bread stuffs, and camped nightly in noted places, to which, according to previous arrangement, the hunters might repair at evening, and bring their game. In this way, some of the tribes followed the course of the Catawba, even to its source. Others darted off towards the Pacolet and Broad rivers, and there were some, the most daring and swift of foot, who made nothing of a journey to the Tiger river, and the rolling mountains of Spartanburg.

There were two warriors who pursued this course. One of them was Conattee, and a braver man and more fortunate hunter never lived. But he had a wife who was a greater scold than Xantippe. She was the wonder and terror of the tribe, and quite as ugly as the one-eyed squaw of Tustenuggee, the grey demon of Enoree. Her tongue was the signal for "slinking" among the bold hunters of Turkeytown; and when they heard it, "Now," said the young women, who sympathised, as all proper young women will do, with the handsome husband of an ugly wife, "now," said they, "we know that poor Conattee has come home." The return of the husband, particularly if he brought no game, was sure to be followed by a storm of that "dry thunder," so well known, which never failed to be heard at the farthest end of the village.

The companion of Conattee on the present expedition was named Selonee—one of the handsomest lads in the whole nation. He was tall and straight like a pine tree; had proved his skill and courage in several expeditions against the Chowannee red sticks, and had found no young warriors of the Cherokee, though he had been on the war path against them, and had stricken all their posts, who could circumvent him in stratagem, or conquer him in actual blows. His renown as a hunter was not less great. He had put to shame the best wolf-takers of the tribe, and the lodge of his venerable father, Chifonti, was never without meat. There was no good reason why Conattee, the married man, should be so intimate with Selonee, the single; there was no particular sympathy between

the two ; but, thrown together in sundry expeditions, they had
formed an intimacy, which, strange to say, was neither de-
nounced nor discouraged by the virago wife of the former.—
She who approved of but few of her husband's movements,
and still fewer of his friends and fellowships, forbore all her
reproaches, when Selonee was his companion. She was the
meekest, gentlest, sweetest tempered of all wives, whenever
the young hunter came home with her husband ; and he, poor
man, was consequently never so well satisfied, as when he
brought Selonee along with him. It was on such occasions,
only, that the poor Conattee could persuade him to regard
Macourah as a tolerable personage. How he came to marry
such a creature—such a termagant, and so monstrous ugly—
was a mystery which none of the damsels of Catawba could
elucidate, though the subject was one on which, when mending the young hunter's mocassins, they expended no small
quantity of conjecture. Conattee, we may be permitted to
say, was still quite popular among them, in spite of his bad
taste, and manifest unavailableness : possibly, for the very reason that his wife was universally detested ; and it will, perhaps, speak something for their charity, if we pry no deeper
nto their motives, to say that the wish was universal among
them, that the Optichi Maneyto, or Black Devil of their belief, would take the virago to himself, and leave to the poor
Conattee some reasonable hope of being made happy by a
more indulgent spouse.

CHAPTER II.

WELL, Conattee and Selonee were out of sight of the smoke of " Turkey-town," and, conscious of his freedom as he no longer heard the accents of domestic authority, the henpecked husband gave a loose to his spirits, and made ample amends to himself, by the indulgence of joke and humour, for the sober restraints which fettered him at home. Selonee joined with him in his merriment, and the resolve was mutual that they should give the squaws the slip and not linger in their progress till they had thrown the Tiger-river behind them. To trace their course till they came to the famous hunting ground which bordered on the Pacolet, will scarcely be necessary, since, as they did not stop to hunt by the way, there were necessarily but few incidents to give interest to their movements. When they had reached the river, however, they made for a cove, well known to them on previous seasons, which lay between the parallel waters of the Pacolet, and a little stream called the Thicketty—a feeder of the Eswawpuddenah, in which they had confident hopes of finding the game which they desired. In former years the spot had been famous as a sheltering place for herds of wolves ; and, with something like the impatience of a warrior waiting for his foe, the hunters prepared their strongest shafts and sharpest flints, and set their keen eyes upon the closest places of the thickest, into which they plunged fearlessly. They had not proceeded far before a single boar-wolf, of amazing size, started up in their path ; and, being slightly wounded by the arrow of Selonee, which glanced first upon some twigs beneath which he lay, he darted off with a fearful howl in the direction of Conattee, whose unobstructed shaft, penetrating the side beneath the fore shoulders, inflicted a fearful, if not a fatal wound, upon the now thoroughly enraged beast. He rushed upon Conattee in his desperation, but the savage was too quick for him; leaping behind a tree, he avoided the rushing stroke with which the white tusks threatened him, and by this time was enabled to fit a second arrow to his bow. His aim was true, and the stone blade of the shaft went quivering into the shaggy monster's heart; who, under the pang of the last convulsion, bounded into the muddy water of the Thicketty Creek, to the edge of which the chase had now brought all the parties. Conattee beheld him plunge furiously forward—twice—thrice— then rest with his nostrils in the water, as the current bore him from sight around a little elbow of the creek. But it was not often that the Indian hunter of those days lost the game which he had stricken. Conatte stripped to it, threw his fringed hunting shirt of buckskin on the bank, with his bow and arrows, his mocasins and leggings beside it, and reserving only his knife, he called to Selonee, who was approaching him, to keep them in sight, and plunged into the water in pursuit of his victim. Selonee gave little heed to the movements of his companion, after the first two or three vigorous strokes which he beheld him make. Such a pursuit, as it promised no peril, called for little consideration from this hard and fearless race, and Selonee amused himself by striking into a thick copse which they had not yet traversed, in search of other sport. There he started the she-wolf, and found sufficient employment on his own hands to call for all his attention to himself. When Selonee first came in sight of her, she was lying on a bed of rushes and leaves, which she had prepared under the roots of a gigantic oak. Her cubs, to the number of five, lay around her, keeping a perfect silence, which she had no doubt enforced upon them after her own fashion, and which was rigidly maintained until they saw him. In was then the instincts of the fierce beasts could no longer be suppressed, and they joined at once in a short chopping bark, or cry, at the stranger, while their little eyes flashed fire, and their red jaws, thinly sprinkled with the first teeth, were cial care to place himself in the rear of some moderately sized tree, sufficiently large to shelter him from her claws, yet small enough to enable him to take free aim around it. Still he did not, at any time, withdraw more than twenty steps from his enemy. Divided in her energies by the necessity of keeping near her young, he was conscious of her inability to pursue him far. Carrying on the war in this manner he had buried no less than five arrows in her body, and it was not until his sixth had penetrated her eye, that he deemed himself safe in the nearer approach which he now meditated. She had left her cubs, on receiving his last shot, and was writhing and leaping, blinded, no less than maddened by the wound, in a vain endeavour to approach her assailant. It was now that Selonee determined on a closer conflict. It was the great boast of the Catawba warriors to grapple with the wolf, and while he yet struggled, to tear the quick quivering heart from his bosom. He placed his bow and arrows behind the tree, and taking in his left hand a chunk or fragment of a bough, while he grasped his unsheathed knife in his right, he leapt in among the cubs, and struck one of them a severe blow upon the head with the chunk. Its scream and the confusion among the rest, brought back the angry dam, and though she could see only imperfectly, yet guided by their clamour, she rushed with open jaws upon the hunter. With keen, quick eyes, and steady resolute nerves, he awaited for her approach, and when she turned her head aside, to strike him with her sharp teeth, he thrust the pine fragment which he carried in his left hand, into her extended jaws, and pressing fast upon her, bore back her haunches to the earth. All this while the young ones were impotently gnawing at the heels of the warrior, which had been fearlessly planted in the very midst of them. But these he did not heed. The larger and fiercer combatant called for all his attention, and her exertions, quickened by the spasms of her wounds, rendered necessary all his address and strength to preserve the advan-

in certain conditions of the body. Selonee reproached himself
that he had not waited beside the stream until the result of
Conattee's experiment was known. The mind of the young
hunter was troubled with many fears and doubts. He went
down the bank of the river, and called aloud with all his lungs,
until the woods and waters re-echoed, again and again, the
name of Conattee. He received no other response. With a
mind filled with increasing fears, each more unpleasant than
the last, Selonee plunged into the creek, and struck off for
the opposite shore, at the very point at which the tiger had
been about to turn, under the influence of the current, when
Conattee went in after him. He was soon across, and soon
found the tracks of the hunter in the gray sands upon its margin. He found, too, to his great delight, the traces made by the
carcass of the tiger—the tract was distinct enough from the
blood which dropped from the reeking skin of the beast, and
Selonee rejoiced in the certainty that the traces which he followed would soon lead him to his friend But not so. He
had scarcely gone fifty yards into the wood when his tracks
failed him at the foot of a crooked, fallen tree, one of the most
gnarled and complicated of all the crooked trees of the forest;
here all signs disappeared. Conattee was not only not there
but had left no sort of clue by which to follow him further.
This was the strangest thing of all. The footprints were distinct enough till he came to the spot where lay the crooked
tree, but there he lost them. He searched the forest around
him, in every direction. Not a copse escaped his search—not
a bay—not a thicket—not an island—and he came back to the
spot where the tiger had been skinned, faint and weary, and
more sorrowful than can well be spoken. At one time he
fancied his friend was drowned, at another, that he was
taken prisoner by the Cherokees. But there were his tracks
from the river, and there were no other tracks than his own.
Besides, so far as the latter supposition was concerned, it was
scarcely possible that so brave and cunning a warrior would

suffer himself to be so completely entrapped and carried off by
an enemy, without so much as being able to give the alarm;
and, even had that been the case, would it be likely that the
enemy would have suffered him to pass without notice.
"But," here the suggestion naturally arose in the mind of
Selonee, "may they not even now be on the track!" With
the suggestion the gallant youth bounded to his feet. "It is
no fat turkey that they seek!" he exclaimed, drawing out an
arrow from the leash that hung upon his shoulders, and fitting
it to his bow, while his busy, glancing eye watched every
shadow in the wood, and his keen, quick ear noted every
sound. But there were no signs of an enemy, and a singular
and mournful stillness hung over the woods. Never was
creature more miserable than Selonee. He called aloud, until
his voice grew hoarse, and his throat sore, upon the name of
Conattee. There was no answer, but the gibing echoes of his
own hoarse accents. Once more he went back to the river,
once more he plunged into its bosom, and with lusty sinews
struck out for a thick green island that lay some quarter of a
mile below, to which he thought it not improbable that the
hunter might have wandered in pursuit of other game. It
was a thickly wooded but small island, which he traversed in
an hour. Finding nothing, he made his weary way back to
the spot from which his friend had started on leaving him.
Here he found his clothes where he had hidden them. The
neighbourhood of this region he traversed in like manner with
the opposite—going over ground, and into places, which it
was scarcely in the verge of physical possibility that his friend's
person could have gone.

The day waned and night came on, and still the persever-
ing hunter gave not up his search. The midnight found him
at the foot of the tree, where they had parted, exhausted but
sleepless, and suffering bitterly in mind from those apprehensions which every moment of hopeless search had necessarily
helped to accumulate and strengthen. Day dawned, and his

towards the smoke of the camp. Nobody ventured to approach him while in this situation; but, at night, when the hunters came dropping in, one by one, Selonee drew nigh to them. He called them apart from the women, and then told them his story.

"This is a strange tale which the wolf-chief tells us," said one of the old men, with a smile of incredulity.

"It is a true tale, father," was the reply.

"Conattee was a brave chief!"

"Very brave, father," said Selonee.

"Had he not eyes to see?"

"The great bird, that rises to the sun, had not better," was the reply.

"What painted jay was it that said Conattee was a fool?"

"The painted bird lied, that said so, my father," was the response of Selonee.

"And comes Selonee, the wolf-chief, to us, with a tale that Conatte was blind, and could not see; a coward that could not strike the she-wolf; a fool that knew not where to set down his foot; and shall we not say Selonee lies upon his brother, even as the painted bird that makes a noise in my ears. Selonee has slain Conattee with his knife. See, it is the blood of Conattee upon the war-shirt of Selonee."

"It is the blood of the she-wolf," cried the young warrior, with a natural indignation.

"Let Selonee go to the woods behind the lodges, till the chiefs say what shall be done to Selonee, because of Conattee, whom he slew."

"Selonee will go, as Emathla, the wise chief, has commanded," replied the young warrior. "He will wait behind the lodges, till the chiefs have said what is good to be done to him, and if they say that he must die because of Conattee, it is well. Selonee laughs at death. But the blood of Conattee is not upon the war-shirt of Selonee. He has said it is the blood of the wolf's mother." With these words the young chief drew forth the skin of the wolf which he had slain, together with the tips of the ears taken-from the cubs, and leaving them in the place where he had sat, withdrew, without further speech, from the assembly which was about to sit in judgment upon his life.

CHAPTER V.

THE consultation that followed was close and earnest. There was scarcely any doubt in the minds of the chiefs that Conattee was slain by his companion. He had brought back with him the arms and all the clothes of the hunter. He was covered with his blood, as they thought; and the grief which filled his heart and depressed his countenance, looked, in their eyes, rather like the expression of guilt than suffering. For a long while did they consult together. Selonee had friends who were disposed to save him; but he had enemies also, as merit must have always, and these were glad of the chance afforded them to put out of their reach, a rival of whom they were jealous, and a warrior whom they feared. Unfortunately for Selonee, the laws of the nation but too well helped the malice of his foes. These laws, as peremptory as those of the Medes and Persians, held him liable in his own life for that of the missing hunter; and the only indulgence that could be accorded to Selonee, and which was obtained for him, was, that he might be allowed a single moon in which to find Conattee, and bring him home to his people.

" Will Selonee go seek Conattee—the windy moon is for Selonee—let him bring Conattee home to his people." Thus said the chiefs, when the young warrior was again brought before them.

" Selonee would die to find Conattee," was the reply.

"He will die if he finds him not!" answered the chief Emathla.

"It is well!" calmly spoke the young warrior. "Is Selonee free to go?"

"The windy moon is for Selonee. Will he return to the lodges if he finds not Conattee?" was the inquiry of Emathla.

"Is Selonee a dog, to fly!" indignantly demanded the warrior. "Let Emathla send a young warrior on the right and on the left of Selonee, if he trusts not what is spoken by Selonee."

"Selonee will go alone, and bring back Conattee."

—

CHAPTER VI.

THE confidence thus reposed in one generally esteemed a murderer, and actually under sentence as such, is customary among the Indians; nor is it often abused. The loss of caste which would follow their flight from justice, is much more terrible among them than any fear of death—which an Indian may avoid, but not through fear. Their loss of caste among themselves, apart from the outlawry which follows it, is, in fact, a loss of the soul. The heaven of the great Manneyto is denied to one under outlawry of the nation, and such a person is then the known and chosen slave of the demon, Opitchi-Manneyto. It was held an unnecessary insult on the part of Emathla, to ask Selonee if he would return to meet his fate. But Emathla was supposed to favour the enemies of Selonee.

With such a gloomy alternative before him in the event of his proving unsuccessful, the young hunter retraced his steps to the fatal waters where Conattee had disappeared. With a spirit no less warmly devoted to his friend, than anxious to avoid the disgraceful doom to which he was destined, the youth spared no pains, withheld no exertion, overlooked no

single spot, and omitted no art known to the hunter, to trace
out the mystery which covered the fate of Conattee. But days
passed of fruitless labour, and the last faint slender outlines of
the moon which had been alloted him for the search, gleamed
forth a sorrowful light upon his path, as he wearily traced it
onward to the temporary lodges of the tribe.

Once more he resumed his seat before the council and
listened to the doom which was in reserve for him. When the
sentence was pronounced, he untied his arrows, loosened the
belt at his waist, put a fillet around his head, made of the
green bark of a little sapling which he cut in the neighbouring woods, then rising to his feet, he spoke thus, in language,
and with a spirit, becoming so great a warrior.

"It is well. The chiefs have spoken, and the wolf-chief
does not tremble. He loves the chase, but he does not weep
like a woman, because it is forbidden that he go after the deer
—he loves to fright the young hares of the Cherokee, but he
laments not that ye say ye can conquer the Cherokee without
his help. Fathers, I have slain the deer and the wolf—my
lodge is full of their ears. I have slain the Cherokee, till the
scalps are about my knees when I walk in the cabin. I go
not to the dark valley without glory—I have had the victories
of grey hairs, but there is no grey hair in my own. I have no
more to say—there is a deed for every arrow that is here. Bid
the young men get their bows ready, let them put a broad
stone upon their arrows that may go soon into the life—I wil[l]
show my people how to die."

They led him forth as he commanded, to the place of execution—a little space behind the encampment, where a hole had
been already dug for his burial. While he went, he recited his
victories to the youths who attended him. To each he gave
an arrow which he was required to keep, and with this arrow,
he related some incident in which he had proved his valour,
either in conflict with some other warrior, or with the wild
beasts of the woods. These deeds, each of them was required

to remember and relate, and show the arrow which was given with the narrative on occasion to this great state solemnity. In this way, their traditions are preserved. When he reached the grave, he took his station before it, the executioners, with their arrows, being already placed in readiness. The whole tribe had assembled to witness the execution, the warriors and boys in the foreground, the squaws behind them. A solemn silence prevailed over the scene, and a few moments only remained to the victim; when the wife of Conattee darted forward from the crowd bearing in her hands a peeled wand, with which, with every appearance of anger, she struck Selonee over the shoulders, exclaiming as she did so:

"Come, thou dog, thou shalt not die—thou shalt lie in the door-way of Conattee, and bring venison for his wife. Shall there be no one to bring meat to my lodge? Thou shalt do this, Selonee—thou shalt not die."

A murmur arose from the crowd at these words.

"She hath claimed Selonee for her husband, in place of Conattee—well, she hath the right."

The enemies of Selonee could not object. The widow had, in fact, exercised a privilege which is recognized by the Indian laws almost universally; and the policy by which she was governed in the present instance, was sufficiently apparent to all the village. It was evident, now that Conattee was gone, that nobody could provide for the woman who had no sons, and no male relations, and who was too execrably ugly, and too notorious as a scold, to leave it possible that she could ever procure another husband so inexperienced or so flexible as the one she had lost. Smartly striking Selonee on his shoulders, she repeated her command that he should rise and follow her.

"Thou wilt take this dog to thy lodge, that he may hunt thee venison?" demanded the old chief, Emathla.

"Have I not said?" shouted the scold—"hear you not? The dog is mine—I bid him follow me."

G

" Is there no friendly arrow to seek my heart ?" murmured the young warrior, as, rising slowly from the grave into which he had previously descended, he prepared to obey the laws of his nation, in the commands of the woman who claimed him to replace the husband who was supposed to have died by his hands. Even the foes of Selonee looked on him with lessened hostility, and the pity of his friends was greater now than when he stood on the precipice of death. The young women of the tribe wept bitterly as they beheld so monstrous a sacrifice. Meanwhile, the exulting hag, as if conscious of her complete control over the victim, goaded him forward with repeated strokes of her wand. She knew that she was hated by all the young women, and she was delighted to show them a conquest which would have been a subject of pride to any among them. With this view she led the captive through their ranks. As they parted mournfully, on either hand, to suffer the two to pass, Selonee stopped short and motioned one of the young women who stood at the greatest distance behind the rest, looking on with eyes which, if they had no tears, yet gave forth an expression of desolateness more woful than any tears could have done. With clasped hands, and trembling as she came, the gentle maiden drew nigh.

" Was it a dream," said Selonee sorrowfully, " that told me of the love of a singing bird, and a green cabin by the rickling waters ? Did 1 hear a voice that said to me sweetly, wait but a little, till the green corn breaks the hill, and Medoree will come to thy cabin and lie by thy side ? Tell me, is this thing true, Medoree ?"

" Thou sayest, Selonee—the thing is true," was the reply of the maiden, uttered in broken accents that denoted a breaking heart.

" But they will make Selonee go to the lodge of another woman—they will put Macourah into the arms of Selonee."

" Alas ! Alas !"

"Wilt thou see this thing, Medoree? Can'st thou look upon it, then turn away, and going back to thy own lodge, can'st thou sing a gay song of forgetfulness as thou goest?"

"Forgetfulness!—Ah, Selonee."

"Thou art the beloved of Selonee, Medoree—thou shalt not lose him. It would vex thy heart that another should take him to her lodge!"—

The tears of the damsel flowed freely down her cheeks, and she sobbed bitterly, but said nothing.

"Take the knife from my belt, Medoree, and put its sharp tooth into my heart, ere thou sufferest this thing! Wilt thou not?"

The girl shrunk back with an expression of undisguised horror in her face.

"I will bless thee, Medoree," was the continued speech of the warrior. She turned from him, covering her face with her hands.

"I cannot do this thing, Selonee—I cannot strike thy heart with the knife. Go—let the woman have thee. Medoree cannot kill thee—she will herself die."

"It is well," cried the youth, in a voice of mournful self-abandonment, as he resumed his progress towards the lodge of Macourah.

CHAPTER VI.

IT is now time to return to Conattee, and trace his progress from the moment when, plunging into the waters, he left the side of Selonee in pursuit of the wolf, whose dying struggles in the stream he had beheld. We are already acquainted with his success in extricating the animal from the water, and possessing himself of its hide. He had not well done this when he heard a rushing noise in the woods above him, and fancying that there was a prospect of other game at hand, and inflated with the hope of adding to his trophies, though without any weapon but his knife, Conattee hastened to the spot. When he reached it, however, he beheld nothing. A gigantic and singularly deformed pine tree, crooked and most irregular in shape, lay prostrate along the ground, and formed such an intricate covering above it, that Conattee deemed it possible that some beast of prey might have made its den among the recesses of its roots. With this thought, he crawled under the spreading limbs, and searched all their intricacies. Emerging from the search, which had been fruitless, he took a seat upon the trunk of the tree, and spreading out the wolf's hide before him, proceeded to pare away the particles of flesh which, in the haste with which he had performed the task of flaying him, had been suffered to adhere to the skin. But he had scarcely commenced the operation, when two gigantic limbs of the fallen tree upon which he sat, curled over his thighs and bound him to the spot. Other limbs, to his great horror, while he strove to move, clasped his arms and covered his shoulders. He strove to cry aloud, but his jaws were grasped covered in his primitive integrity. But how improbable that this discovery should be made. He had no voice to declare his bondage. He had no capacity for movement by which he

before he could well open them, by other branches; and, with
his eyes, which were suffered to peer through little openings
in the bark, he could see his legs encrusted by like coverings
with his other members. Still seeing, his own person yet escaped his sight. Not a part of it now remained visible to
himself. A bed of green velvet-like moss rested on his lap.
His knees shot out a thorny excrescence: and his hands, flattened to his thighs, were enveloped in as complete a casing of
bark as covered the remainder of the tree around him. Even
his knife and wolf skin, to his great surprise, suffered in like
manner, the bark having contracted them into one of those
huge bulging knobs that so numerously deformed the tree.
With all his thoughts and consciousness remaining, Conattee
had yet lost every faculty of action. When he tried to scream
aloud, his jaws felt the contraction of a pressure upon them,
which resisted all their efforts, while an oppressive thorn
growing upon a wild vine that hung before his face, was
brought by every movement of himself or of the tree into his
very mouth. The poor hunter immediately conceived his situation—he was in the power of Tustenuggee, the Grey Demon of Enoree. The tree upon which he sat was one of these
magic trees which the tradition of his people entitled the
" Arm-chair of Tustenuggee." In these traps for the unwary
the wicked demon caught his victim, and exulted in his mi-
series. Here he sometimes remained until death released
him; for it was not often that the power into whose clutches
he had fallen, suffered his prey to escape through a sudden
feeling of lenity or good humour. The only hope of Conattee
was that Selonee might suspect his condition; in which event
his rescue was simple and easy enough. It was only to hew
off the limbs, or bare away the bark, and the victim was un-
might reveal the truth to his comrade's eyes; and unless some
divine instinct should counsel his friend to an experiment
which he would scarcely think upon, of himself, the poor prisoner felt that he must die in the miserable bondage into

his friend behind him. Life was sweet, and great was the temptation. At one moment he almost wished that Selonee would draw nigh, and seat himself after his fatigue. As if the young hunter knew his wish, he drew nigh at that instant; but the better feelings in Conattee's heart grew strong as he approached, and, striving to twist and writhe in his bondage, and labouring at the same time to call out in warning to his friend, he manifested the noble resolution not to avail himself of his friend's position to relieve his own; and, as if the warning of Conattee had really reached the understanding of Selonee, the youth retraced his steps, and once more hurried away from the place of danger. With his final departure the fond hopes of the prisoner sunk within him; and when hour after hour had gone by without the appearance of any of his people, and without any sort of change in his condition, he gave himself up utterly for lost. The mocks and jeers of the Grey Demon and his one-eyed squaw filled his ears all night, and the morning brought him nothing but flat despair. He resigned himself to his fate with the resolution of one who, however unwilling he might be to perish in such a manner, had yet faced death too frequently not to yield him a ready defiance now.

CHAPTER VII.

BUT hope had not utterly departed from the bosom of Selonee. Perhaps the destiny which had befallen himself had made him resolve the more earnestly to seek farther into the mystery of that which hung above the fate of his friend. The day which saw him enter the cabin of Macourah saw him the most miserable man alive. The hateful hag, hateful enough as the wife of his friend, whose ill treatment was notorious, was now doubly hateful to him as his own wife; and now, when, alone together, she threw aside the harsh and termagant features which had before distinguished her deportment, and, assuming others of a more amorous complexion, threw her arms about the neck of the youth and solicited his endearments, a loathing sensation of disgust was coupled with the hate which had previously possessed his mind. Flinging away from her embrace, he rushed out of the lodge with feelings of the most unspeakable bitterness and grief, and bending his way towards the forest, soon lost sight of the encampment of his people. Selonee was resolved on making another effort for the recovery of his friend. His resolve went even farther than this. He was bent never to return to the doom which had been fastened upon him, and to pursue his way into more distant and unknown forests—a self-doomed exile—unless he could restore Conattee to the nation. Steeled against all those ties of love or of country, which at one time had prevailed in his bosom over all, he now surrendered himself to friendship or despair. In Catawba, unless he restored Conattee, he could have no hope; and without Catawba he had neither hope nor love. On either hand he saw nothing but misery; but the worst form of misery lay behind him in the lodge of Macourah. But Macourah was not the person to submit to such a determination. She was too well satisfied with the exchange with

which fortune had provided her, to suffer its gift to be lost so
easily; and when Selonee darted from the cabin in such fearful haste, she readily conjectured his determination. She hurried after him with all possible speed, little doubting that
those thunders—could she overtake him—with which she had
so frequéntly overawed the pliant Conattee, would possess
an effect not less influential upon his more youthful successor.
Macourah was gaunt as a greyhound, and scarcely less fleet of
foot. Besides, she was as tough as a grey-squirrel in his
thirteenth year. She did not despair of overtaking Selonee,
provided she suffered him not to know that she was upon his
trail. Her first movements therefore were marked with caution. Having watched his first direction, she divined his aim
to return to the hunting grounds where he had lost or slain
his companion; and these hunting grounds were almost as
well known to herself as to him. With a rapidity of movement, and a tenacity of purpose, which could only be accounted
for by a reference to that wild passion which Selonee had
unconsciously inspired in her bosom for himself, she followed
his departing footsteps; and when, the next day, he heard
her shouts behind him, he was absolutely confounded. But
it was with a feeling of surprise and not of dissatisfaction
that he heard her voice. He—good youth—regarding Conattee as one of the very worthiest of the Catawba warriors,
seemed to have been impressed with an idea that such also
was the opinion of his wife. He little dreamed that she had
any real design upon himself; and believed that, to show her
the evidences which were to be seen, which led to the fate of
her husband, might serve to convince her that not only he was
not the murderer, but that Conattee might not, indeed, be
murdered at all. He coolly waited her approach, therefore,
and proceeded to renew his statements, accompanying his
narrative with the expression of the hope which he entertained
of again restoring her husband to herself and the nation. But
she answered his speech only with upbraidings and entreaties;

G 5

and when she failed, she proceeded to thump him lustily with
the wand by which she had compelled him to follow her to
the lodge the day before. But Selonee was in no humour to
obey the laws of the nation now. The feeling of degradation
which had followed in his mind, from the moment when he
left the spot where he had stood up for death, having neither
fear nor shame, was too fresh in his consciousness to suffer
him to yield a like acknowledgment to it now; and though
sorely tempted to pummel the Jezabel in return for the lusty
thwacks which she had already inflicted upon his shoulders,
he forebore, in consideration of his friend, and contented himself with simply setting forward on his progress, determined
to elude her pursuit by an exercise of all his vigour and elas-
ticity. Selonee was hardy as the grisly bear, and fleeter than
the wild turkey; and Macourah, virago as she was, soon discovered the difference in the chase when Selonee put forth his
strength and spirit. She followed with all her pertinacity,
quickened as it was by an increase of fury at that presumption
which had ventured to disobey her commands; but Selonee
fled faster than she pursued, and every additional moment
served to increase the space between them. The hunter lost
her from his heels at length, and deemed himself fortunate
that she was no longer in sight and hearing, when he again
approached the spot where his friend had so mysteriously disappeared. Here he renewed his search with a painful care
and minuteness, which the imprisoned Conattee all the while
beheld. Once more Selonee crawled beneath those sprawling
limbs and spreading arms that wrapped up in their solid and
coarse rinds the person of the warrior. Once more he emerged from the spot disappointed and hopeless. This he had
hardly done when, to the great horror of the captive, and the
annoyance of Selonee, the shrill shrieks and screams of the too
well-known voice of Macourah rang through the forests. Selonee dashed forward as he heard the sounds, and when

Macourah reached the spot, which she did unerringly in following his trail, the youth was already out of sight.

"I can go no further," cried the woman—"a curse on him and a curse on Conattee, since in losing one I have lost both. I am too faint to follow. As for Selonee, may the one-eyed witch of Tustenuggee take him for her dog."

With this delicate imprecation, the virago seated herself in a state of exhaustion upon the inviting bed of moss which formed the lap of Conattee. This she had no sooner done, than the branches relaxed their hold upon the limbs of her husband. The moment was too precious for delay, and sliding from under her with an adroitness and strength which were beyond her powers of prevention, and, indeed, quite too sudden for any effort at resistance, she had the consternation to behold her husband starting up in full life before her, and, with the instinct of his former condition, preparing to take flight. She cried to him, but he fled the faster,—she strove to follow him, but the branches which had relaxed their hold upon her husband had resumed their contracted grasp upon her limbs. The brown bark was already forming above her on every hand, and her tongue, allotted a brief term of liberty, was alone free to assail him. But she had spoken but few words when the bark encased her jaws, and the ugly thorn of the vine which had so distressed Conattee, had taken its place at their portals.

CHAPTER VIII.

THE husband looked back but once, when the voice ceased—then, with a shivering sort of joy that his own doom had undergone a termination, which he now felt to be doubly fortunate—he made a wide circuit that he might avoid the fatal neighbourhood, and pushed on in pursuit of his friend, whom his eyes, even when he was surrounded in the tree, had followed in his flight. It was no easy task, however to overtake Selonee, flying, as he did, from the supposed pursuit of the termagant. Great however was the joy of the young warriors when they did encounter, and long and fervent was their mutual embrace. Conattee described his misfortunes, and related the manner in which he was taken; showed how the bark had encased his limbs, and how the intricate magic had even engrossed his knife and the wolf skin which had been the trophy of his victory. Conattee said not a word of his wife and her entrapment, and Selonee was left in the conviction that his companion owed his escape from the toils to some hidden change in the tyrannical mood of Tustenuggee, or the one-eyed woman, his wife.

"But the skin and the knife, Conattee, let us not leave them," said Selonee, "let us go back and extricate them from the tree."

Conattee showed some reluctance. He soon said, in the words of Macbeth, which he did not use however as a quotation, "I'll go no more." But Selonee, who ascribed this reluctance to very natural apprehensions of the demon from whose clutches he had just made his escape, declared his readiness to undertake the adventure if Conattee would only point out to his eyes the particular excrescence in which the articles were enclosed. When the husband perceived that his friend was resolute, he made a merit of necessity."

"If the thing is to be done," said he, "why should you have the risk, I myself will do it. It would be a woman-fear were I to shrink from the danger. Let us go."

The process of reasoning by which Conattee came to this determination was a very sudden one, and one, too, that will not be hard to comprehend by every husband in his situation. It was his fear that if Selonee undertook the business, an unlucky or misdirected stroke of his knife might sever a limb, or remove some portions of the bark which did not merit or need removal. Conattee trembled at the very idea of the revelations which might follow such an unhappy result. Strengthening himself, therefore, with all his energies, he went forward with Selonee to the spot, and while the latter looked on and witnessed the operation, he proceeded with a nicety and care which amused and surprised Selonee, to the excision of the swollen scab upon the tree in which he had seen his wolf skin encompassed. While he performed the operation, which he did as cautiously as if it had been the extraction of a mote from the eye of a virgin; the beldam in the tree, conscious of all his movements, and at first flattered with the hope that he was working for her extrication, maintained the most ceaseless efforts of her tongue and limbs, but without avail. Her slight breathing, which Conattee knew where to look for, more like the sighs of an infant zephyr than the efforts of a human bosom, denoted to his ears an overpowering but fortunately suppressed volcano within; and his heart leaped with a new joy, which had been unknown to it for many years before, when he thought that he was now safe, and, he trusted, for ever, from any of the tortures which he had been fain to endure patiently so long. When he had finished the operation by which he had re-obtained his treasures, he ventured upon an impertinence which spoke surprisingly for his sudden acquisition of confidence; and looking up through the little aperture in the bark, from whence he had seen every thing while in the same situation, and from whence he concluded she was also suffered to see, he took a peep—a quick, quizzical and taunting peep, at those eyes which he had not so dared to offend before. He drew back suddenly from the contact—so suddenly, indeed, that Selonee, who saw the proceeding, but had no idea of the truth, thought he had been stung by some insect, and questioned him accordingly.

"Let us be off, Selonee," was the hurried answer, "we have nothing to wait for now."

"Yes," replied Selonee, "and I had forgotten to say to you that your wife, Macourah, is on her way in search of you. I left her but a little way behind, and thought to find her here. I suppose she is tired, however, and is resting by the way."

"Let her rest," said Conattee, "which is an indulgence much greater than any she ever accorded me. She will find me out soon enough, without making it needful that I should go in search of her. Come."

Selonee kindly suppressed the history of the transactions which had taken place in the village during the time when the hunter was supposed to be dead, but Conattee heard the facts from other quarters, and loved Selonee the better for the sympathy he had shown, not only in coming again to seek for him, but in not loving his wife better than he did himself. They returned to the village, and every body was rejoiced to behold the return of the hunters. As for the termagant Macourah, nobody but Conattee knew her fate; and he, like a wise man, kept his secret until there was no danger of its being made use of to rescue her from her predicament. Years had passed, and Conatte had found among the young squaws one that pleased him much better than the old. He had several children by her, and years and honours had alike fallen numerously upon his head, when, one day, one of his own sons, while hunting in the same woods, knocked off one of the limbs of the Chair of Tustenuggee, and to his great horror discovered the human arm which they enveloped. This led him to search farther, and limb after limb became detached under the unscrupulous action of his hatchet, until the entire but unconnected members of the old squaw became visible. The lad knocked about the fragments with little scruple, never dreaming how near was his relation to the form which he treated with so little veneration. When he came home to the lodge and told his story, Selonee looked at Conattee, but said nothing. The whole truth was at once apparent to his mind. Conattee, though he still kept his secret, was seized with a sudden fit of piety, and taking his sons with him, he proceeded to the spot which he well remembered, and gathering up the bleached remains, had them carefully buried in the trenches of the tribe.

It may properly end this story, to say that Selonee wedded the sweet girl who, though willing to die herself to prevent him from marrying Macourah, yet positively refused to take his life to defeat the same event. It may be well to state, in addition, that the only reason Conattee ever had for believing that Selonee had not kept his secret from every body, was that Medoree, the young wife of the latter, looked on him with a very decided coolness. "But we will see," muttered Conattee as he felt this conviction. "Selonee will repent of this confidence, since now it will never be possible for him to persuade her to take a seat in the Arm-chair of Tustenuggee. Had he been a wise man he would have kept his secret, and then there would have been no difficulty in getting rid of a wicked wife."

THE SNAKE OF THE CABIN.

CHAPTER I.

" They talk," said the stranger somewhat abruptly, " They talk of the crimes of wealthy people, and in high life. No doubt there are very great and many wrong doers among the rich. People in possession of much wealth, and seeing how greatly it is worshipped, will very naturally presume upon and abuse its powers :—but it is not among the rich only, and in the great city, that these things happen. The same snake, or one very much like it, winds his way into the wigwam and the cabin—and the poor silly country girl is as frequently the victim, as the dashing lady of the city and city fashions. For that matter she is the more easily liable to imposition, as are all persons who occupy insulated positions, and see little of the great struggles of busy life. The planter and the farmer who dwell in the remote interior find the face of the visitor too interesting, to scrutinize it very closely. A pleasant deportment, a specious outside, a gentle and attractive manner, will win their way in our forest world, without rendering necessary those formal assurances, that rigid introduction, and those guarantees of well known persons, which the citizen requires before you partake of his bread and salt. With us, on the contrary, we confide readily ; and the cunning stranger, whom other communities have expelled with loathing, rendered cautious and conciliatory by previous defeat, adopts the subtlety of the snake, and winds his way as artfully as that reptile, when he comes among us. We have too many sad stories of this sort. Yours is one of them. This poor girl, Ellen Ramsay, was abused thus, as I have shown you by this scoundrel, Stanton. But finish your nar-

rative. She had a short time of it, and a sad one, I do not
doubt, with a creature so heartless and so vile."

"But a poor eleven months; and the change was too
rapid," said young Atkins, "not to let us see that she was
any thing but happy. To-day, the gayest of all God's creatures, as much like a merry bird in spring-time, singing over
its young;—to-morrow as gloomy and miserable as if there
was neither song nor sunshine in God's whole earth."

"Poor thing!" exclaimed Walter.

"It was the shortest life," said the other, "to begin so
well, that I ever saw, and the story which you have heard is
pretty much the truth."

"But the funeral?" said Walter.

"Ah! that was not exactly as you heard it," was the reply
of Atkins. "I was at the funeral of Ellen Ramsay, as indeed
was very nearly all the village, and I could refer you to
twenty who will tell you the matter just as it occurred. In
the first place, it is not true that any body expected Robert
Anderson to be present. He sent no message of any kind to
Stanton. It was very well known that he was sick—actually
in bed, and had been so for more than a week before the death
of Ellen. People almost thought they might go off together.
There was a sort of sympathy between them, though I don't
think, from the hour of her unlucky marriage, that the eyes of
the two ever met, till they met in the world of spirits—unless
it were, indeed, in their dreams. But they seemed to pine
away, both of them, about the same time, and though he
stood it longest, he did not outlast her much. When she died
as I tell you, he was very feeble and in bed. Nobody ever
expected him to leave it alive, and least of all that he should
leave it then, to stand among the people at her grave. The
circumstances of her marriage with Stanton, were too notorious, and too much calculated to embitter his feelings and his
peace, to make it likely that he would be present at such a
scene. She had cast him off, slightingly, to give a preference

to the more showy stranger, and she had spoken to him in a manner not soon to be forgiven by a man of sensibility. But he did forgive—that I know—and his love for Ellen was unimpaired to the last. She did not doubt this, when she married Stanton, though she expressed herself so. That was only to find excuses to him, if not to her own conscience, for her conduct. I'm sure she bitterly repented of all before very long. She was just the girl to do wrong in a hurry, and be sorry for it the next minute."

"But the funeral?" said Walter.

"Ah, true—the funeral. Well, as I was telling you, when the coffin was brought round to the burial place—you know the spot, among a thick grove of stunted oaks, and the undergrowth is always kept down by old Ramsay—who should come out from behind one of the largest old trees, but Robert Anderson. He was pale as a ghost, and his limbs trembled and tottered as he walked, but he came forward as resolutely as if he felt no pain or weakness. Stanton started when he saw him. He never expected his presence, I assure you. Every eye saw his agitation as Robert came forward; and I tell you, there was not a person present who did not see, as well as myself, that the husband of the poor girl looked much paler at that moment than her sick lover. Robert did not seem to see Stanton, or to mind him as he came forward; indeed, he did not seem to see any body, His eyes were fixed on the coffin, which was carried by me, Ralph Mason, Dick Rawlins, and I think Hiram Barker. He did not shed a tear, which we all wondered at, for all of us expected to see him crying like any child, because we knew how soft-hearted he always was, and how fond he had been of Ellen. At first, we thought his not crying was because of his anger at being so ill-treated, which was natural enough; but what he said afterwards soon did away with that notion. He came close to my side, and put his hand on the lid of the coffin near the name, and though he said not a single word, to us, we seemed to understand that he meant we should stop till he read it. We did stop, and he then read the plate aloud, something in this manner—'Ellen'—and then he stopped a little as he came to the word 'Stanton'—and you could see a deep red flush grow out upon his cheek and forehead, and then he grew pale as death—and held upon the coffin as if to keep himself from falling—then he seemed to muster up strength, and he read on, in very deliberate and full accents, as if he had thrown all his resolution into the effort—"Ellen Stanton!' These words he repeated twice, and then he passed on to the rest—' WIFE OF GEORGE STANTON, BORN APRIL 7, 1817. DIED,'—Here he stopped again, poor fellow! as if to catch his breath. He only gasped when he tried to go on with the reading. He could only say—'Died. Died!' and there he stopped like a man choking. By this time, Stanton came up close to him and looked at us, as if to say 'Why don't you go forward—why do you suffer him to stop you'—but he said nothing. Robert did not seem to mind or to notice him, but, with another effort, recovering his strength and voice, he read on to the end— ' DIED MARCH 27, 1836—AGED EIGHTEEN YEARS, ELEVEN MONTHS AND NINETEEN DAYS.' Old John Ramsay by this time came up, and stood between him and Stanton. He looked up from the coffin, first at one and then at the other—and said quietly—without any appearance of anger or passion:"—

" This, Mr Ramsay, is your daughter, Ellen—she was to have been my wife—she was engaged to me by her own promise, and you gave me your consent to our marriage. Is not this true, Mr. Ramsay?"

" True," said the old man very mildly, but with a deep sigh that seemed to come from the bottom of his soul;—" but you know, Robert, ——"

Then it was that Robert seemed to lose himself for a moment. His eye brightened with indignation and his speech came quick.

"I know that she is here!" he exclaimed—"here, in her

coffin, dead to you, your daughter—dead to me, my **wife**—
your Ellen! my Ellen—My Ellen—my poor Ellen!" And then
he sobbed bitterly upon the coffin. I believe that most of the
persons present—and all had crowded round us—sobbed too.
But I could not see them, for my own heart was overflowing.
The interruption did not continue long. Robert was the first
to recover himself. He had always a right idea of what was
proper; and no doubt, just then, he felt, that, according to
the world's way of thinking, he was doing wrong in stopping
the dead in its last progress to the place of rest. He raised
up his head from the coffin plate, and said to us, speaking very
slowly, for his breath seemed only to come in sobs, and then
after great efforts—

"Do not think, my friends, when I speak of the pledges
Ellen Ramsay made to me, that I am come here to utter any
reproaches of the dead, or to breathe a single syllable of complaint against the blessed creature, who was always a sweet
angel, now looking up in heaven. God forbid that I should
speak, or that you should hear, any harm of a woman that I
have always looked upon as the purest and truest-hearted
creature under the sun. No! in telling you of this pledge, I
come here only to acquit her of any wrong, or evil thought, or
action, when she ceased to think it binding upon her. It is to
say to you at her grave, for you all knew that we were to be
married, that, as I never gave her any reason for believing me
to be false, or more unworthy of her heart than when she promised it to me, so, also, I believe that nothing but some such
persuasion could have made her deprive me of it. While I acquit her, therefore of having done me any intentional injustice,
I tell you, in the presence of her heavenly spirit, which knows
the truth of what I declare, that she has been abused by some
false slanderer, to do me wrong, and herself wrong, and
to—"

By this time Stanton put in, and stopped whatever more
Robert had to say. He had been getting more and more angry

succeeded in doing so. No doubt his mind deluded him, and
he thought so—for you could hear him whispering—" Ellen!
dear Ellen!" Then he gave way to us, and reading the plate,
he said—" But eighteen—but eighteen. But—it is all well
now! all well!" He suffered us then to go forward, and followed close, and made no objection, and said no more words.
While we let the coffin down, he stood so nigh, that the earth
shelved with him, and he would have gone in with it, for he
made no resistance, if we had not caught him in our arms and
dragged him from the brink. But we could not soon get him
from the spot. When all was done, he did not seem to mind
that the rest were going, but stood looking down as earnestly
as if he could still read the writing through six feet of earth.
Stanton, too, did not seem willing to go, but we very well
knew it was for no love he had for the poor girl that he wished
to remain ; and Maxcy whispered to me that he would bring
him off before he left the ground, for fear he might do some
harm to Robert, who was no fighter, and was too feeble to
stand one so strong. This he did, and after he was gone I
tried to get Robert away also. It was sometime before I did
so, and then it seemed he went with me only to get rid of my
presence, for he was back at the grave as soon as night set in,
and there he might be found every evening at the same hour,
just about sunset, for several months afterwards—for he lingered strangely—until they brought him to sleep beside her.
Though sick, and pining away fast, the poor fellow never let
an evening go by, whatever weather it might be, without paying the grave a visit; and one day, perhaps two weeks after
the funeral, old Mrs. Anderson called me into her cottage as I
was riding by, and said she would show me something. She
took me up into her son's room, a little chamber in the loft,
and what should it be but a head-board, that the dying lad
had sawed out with his own hands, from a thick plank, and
had smoothed, and planed, and painted, all in secret, so that
he could print on it an inscription for the poor girl's grave ;

and you would be surprised to see how neatly he had worked it all. The poor old woman cried bitterly all the time, but you could still see how proud she was of her son. She showed me his books—he had more than a hundred—and she sighed from the bottom of her heart when she told me that it was the books that has made him sickly.

"But he will read," she said, " say all I can ; though he knows it's a-doing him no good. ' Ah, mother,' he says, when I tell him about it, ' though it may shorten my life to read, it will shorten my happiness not to read, and I have too little happiness now left me to be willing to lose any of it.' And when he speaks so," said the old woman, " I can't blame him, for I know it's all true. But I blame myself, Mr. Atkins, for you see it was all my doing that he got so many books, and is so fond of them. I loved to see him learning, and made him read to me so constantly of an evening, and it did my heart so much good to think that one day my Robert might be a great lawyer, or a parson, for I could see how much smarter he was than all the other boys of the village—and so I never looked at his pale cheeks, and had no guess how poorly he was getting, till, all of a sudden, he was laid up, on my hands, and pining away every hour, as you now see him. Things looked better for a while when he got fond of Ellen Ramsay, and she of him. But that Stanton, ever since he came among us, Robert has gone backward, and I shan't wonder if it's not very long before he wants his own tombstone !"

Poor old woman ! I saw in a corner, half hidden behind an old trunk in the youth's chamber, what it was evident she had not seen, a head board, the very fellow to that which he had been making for Ellen !—but I said nothing to her at the time. When they were found after his death—for he said nothing of them while he lived—they were both neatly finished, with a simple but proper inscription. On his own was but one line above his name. It was this—

" Mine *was* wo, but mine *is* hope.
                            Robert Anderson."

" You tell me of a remarkable young man," said Walter—
" and he was but twenty when he died ?"

" No more !"

" We will go and look upon his grave."

" You will see the head board there, but that for Ellen was
never put up—Stanton would not allow it."

" Ah ! but we shall mend that. I will pluck that scoundrel's
comb. Is the head-board preserved ?"

" It is : his mother keeps it in his chamber, standing up beside his little book-case ; but see, yonder is Stanton now. He
is on his way to Ramsay's house. They do not live together.
He boards at a little farm-yard about a mile from the village.
They say that there has been a quarrel between him and his
brother-in-law, young John Ramsay, something about his sister's property. There are eleven negroes, which were owned
by young John and herself, in their own right, from the grandmother's gift, which they have suffered the old man to work
until now. Stanton wants a division, and young John tried
to persuade him not to touch them till his death, which must
happen before long, he sharing as before from the crop. But
Stanton persists, and the young fellow did not stop to tell him
that he thought him a cruelly base fellow. This is the report.
It is very certain that they are separate now, and there is a
difference between them."

" Very likely on the score of the negroes. But we will save
them to the old man, and drive him from a spot which he had
made wretched."

" Can you do this ? Are your proofs sufficient ?"

" Ample."

" You are yourself a lawyer ?"

" Yes ! But I shall have the assistance, if necessary, of Col.
Dawson, whom probably you know."

" A first-rate gentleman, and one of our best lawyers."

" I bring letters to him—have already seen him on the subject, and he concurs with me as to the conclusiveness of my proofs. Would I had been with you a year ago. Could I have traced him, this poor girl had not been his victim. I should at least have driven the snake from this one cabin."

"Yes, if you had come a year ago, poor Ellen would have been saved. But nothing could have saved the poor young man. The rot was in the heart of the tree."

" Yet!" said the other, putting his hand upon the arm of Atkins—" though the tree perished, it might have been kept green to the last. Some hurts might have been spared it. The man who died in hope, might not have found it necessary to declare, at the last moment, that he had utterly lived in we. Yes—a little year ago, we might have done much for both parties."

" You will do great good by your coming now. The poor old man loves his negroes as he does his children. They say he looks upon the giving up the eleven to be sold, like a breaking up of the establishment. His son says it will hurry him to the grave. This was what he said to Stanton, which led to the quarrel. Stanton sneered at the young man, and he, being pretty passionate, blazed out at him in a way that pretty soon silenced the fellow."

" This class of reptiles are all, more or less, cowards. We must not burn daylight, as, if they consent to a division, the scoundrel may make off with his share. Let us go forward," continued the speaker, with a show of feeling for which Atkins could not well account—" I long to tread upon the viper—to bruise his head, and above all to tear the fangs from his jaws. You will, if Stanton be there, draw the old man aside and introduce me to him, with some quiet hint of what I may be able to do."

" You say you have the papers with you ?"

" Ay, ay,—here,"—striking his bosom—" I have here that which shall confound him! Fear not! I do not deceive you.

H

At least I cannot deceive myself. I too have wrongs that need avenging—I and mine! I and mine! Remember, I am Mr. Jones from Tennessee — I must surprise and confound the fellow, and would see how the land lies before I declare myself."

CHAPTER II.

YOUNG John Ramsay was in the front piazza as they entered the little farm-yard. He was alone, and pacing the floor in evident agitation. His brow was dark and discontented, and he met the salutations of his visitors with the manner of a person who is ill pleased with any witnesses of his disquiet. But he was civil, and when Atkins asked after his father, he led the way into the house, and there they discovered the old man and George Stanton in close and earnest conversation. Several papers were before them, and Stanton held the pen in his hand. The tears stood in old Ramsay's eyes. His thin white hairs, which fell, glossy and long, upon his shoulders, gave a benign and patriarchal expression to a face that was otherwise marked with the characters of benevolence and sensibility. He rose at the appearance of the visitors. Stanton did not, but looked up with the air of one vexed at interruption in the most interesting moment. Young Ramsay, to whom the stranger had been introduced by Atkins, introduced him in turn to his father, but to his father only. He gave no look to the spot where Stanton was seated. Atkins took the old man into another room, leaving the three remaining in the apartment. Stanton appeared to busy himself over his papers. Young Ramsay requested the stranger to be seated, and drew a chair for himself beside him. There was no conversation. The youth looked down upon the floor, in abstract contemplation, while the stranger, unobserved by either, employed himself in

a most intense watch of the guilty man. The latter looked up
and met this survey seemingly with indifference. He too was
thinking of matters which led him somewhat from the present
company. He resumed his study of the papers before him,
and scarcely noticed the return of old Ramsay to the room. His
appearance was the signal to the son to go out, and resume
his solitary promenade in the piazza. The old man promptly
approached the stranger, whose hand he took with a cordial
pressure that proved how well Atkins had conveyed his suggestion. There was a bright hopefulness in his old eyes, which
had it been seen by Stanton, might have surprised him, particularly as, just before, they had been overflowing with tears
and clouded with despondency. He was, however, still too
busy in his calculations, and possibly, in his own hopes, to
note any peculiar change in the aspect or manner of his fa-
ther-in-law. But when some minutes had passed, consumed
by the old man and the stranger, in the most common-place
conversation — when he heard the former institute long inquiries into the condition of crops in Tennessee—the value of
grain, the modes of cultivation, the price of lands and negroes ;
—the impatient son-in-law began to show his restiveness. He
took up and threw down his papers, turned from them to the
company, from the company to the papers again, renewed his
calculations, again dismissed them, and still without prompt-
ing the visitor to bring to a close a visit seemingly totally deficient in object and interest, but which, to his great annoyance, all parties besides himself seemed desirous to prolong.
At length, as with a desperate determination, he turned to the
old man and said—

"Sir—Mr. Ramsay, you are aware of my desire to bring this
business to a close at once."

The words reached the ears of young Ramsay, who now appeared at the door.

"Father, pray let it be as this person desires. Give him
all which the law will allow—give him more, if need be, and

let him depart. Make any arrangement about the negroes
that you please, without considering me—only let him leave
us in our homes at peace !"

" I am sorry to disturb the peace of any home," said Stanton,
" but am yet to know that to claim my rights is doing so. I
ask nothing but what is fair and proper. My wife, if I understand it, had an equal right with Mr. John Ramsay, the
younger, to certain negroes, eleven in number, namely, Zekiel,
Abram, Ben, Bess, Maria, Susannah, Bob, Harry, Milly, Bainbridge and Nell, with their increase. This increase makes the
number seventeen. But you have never denied the facts, and
I repeat to you the proposition which I have already made to
you, to divide the property into two equal parts, thus :"—

Here he read from the strips of paper before him, enumera-
ting the negroes in two lots—this done, he proceeded :

" I am willing that your son should have the first choice of
hese lots. I will take the other. I am prepared to listen to
any other arrangement for a division, rather than be subject
to any delay by a reference to the law. I have no wish to
compel the sale of the property, as that might distress you."

" Distress !" exclaimed the young man—" spare your sympathy if you please. I consent to your first arrangement. Nay,
sir, you shall choose, first, of the lots as divided by yourself.
My simple wish now, sir, is to leave you wholly without
complaint."

" But, my son"—began the old man.

" Pray, my father, let it be as I have said. We shall never
have an end of it otherwise. The division is a tolerably equal
one, and if there be any loss it is mine."

The old man folded his hands upon his lap and looked to the
stranger. He, meanwhile, maintained a keen and eager watch
upon the features of Stanton. It could be seen that his lip
quivered and there was in his eye an expression of exultation
and scorn which, perhaps, none perceived but young Atkins.
Stanton, meanwhile, was again busy with his papers.

"It is admitted also," the latter continued, "that I have a right to one half of a tract of uncleared land, lying on the Tombeckbe, containing six hundred and thirty acres, more or less; to one half of a small dwelling house in Linden, and to certain household stuff, crockery, plate and kitchen ware. Upon these I am prepared to place a low estimate, so that the family may still retain them, and the value may be given me in negro property. I value the land, which I am told is quite as good as any in the country, at 5 dollars an acre—the house and lot at 500 dollars—and the plate, crockery, kitchen ware, etc., at 250 dollars more. I make the total of my share, at these estimates, to be 2075 dollars—we will say 2000 dollars —and I am willing to take in payment of this amount, the four fellows, Zekiel, Bob, Henry and Ben—named in one lot, or the two fellows, Abram and Bainbridge, and the two women, Milly and Maria, with their three children, named in the other parcel."

"You are extremely accommodating," said young Ramsay, bitterly, "but I prefer that we should sell the land on the Tombeckbe, the lot in Linden, and the crockery, plate, and kitchen stuff—unless you prefer that these last should be divided. This arrangement will occasion you some delay in getting your money, but it will save me much less loss than I should suffer by your estimates. Permit me to say that of the negroes in the lot which you may leave me, you shall not have a hair, and I would to God it were in my power to keep the rest, by any sacrifice, from your possession."

"No doubt you do, sir, but your wishes are not the law. I demand nothing from you but what is justice, and justice I will have. My rights are clear and ample. You do not, I trust, propose to go to law to keep me out of my wife's property."

"To law!" exclaimed the young man with indignation.— He then strode fiercely across the floor, and confronted Stanton, who had now risen. The strife in his soul was showing itself in storm upon his countenance, when the stranger from Tennessee rose and placed himself between them.

"Stay, my friend—let me speak a moment. I have a question to ask of Mr. Stanton."

"You, sir," said Stanton—"by what right do you interfere?"

"By the right which every honest man possesses to see that there is no wrong done to his neighbour, if he can prevent it. You are making a demand upon Mr. Ramsay, for certain property, which you claim in right of your wife. Now, sir, let me ask you which of your wives it is, on whose account you claim?"

"The person thus addressed recoiled as if he had been struck by an adder. A deep flush passed over his face, succeeded by an ashey paleness. He tried to speak, stammered, and sunk paralyzed back into his chair.

"What, sir, can you say nothing? Your rights by your wives ought to be numerous. You should have some in every State in the Union."

"You are a liar and a slanderer," exclaimed the criminal, rising from his seat, and, with a desperate effort, confronting his accuser.—Shaking his fist at him, he cried—"You shall prove what you say! You shall prove what you say!"

The other coldly replied, while a smile of scorn passed over his lips—"I am here for that very purpose."

"You!—and who are you?" demanded the accused, once again stammering, and showing trepidation.

"A man!—one who has his hand upon your throat, and will stifle you in the very first struggle that you propose to make. Sit down, sir—sit down all—this business is opened before us, and we will go to it as a matter of business. You sir"—to Stanton—"will please school your moods and temper, lest it be worse for you. It is only by behaving with proper modesty, under a proper sense of your position and dan-

ger, that you can hope to escape from the sharpest clutches of
the law."

"You shall not bully me—I am not the man to submit——"

"You are!" said the other, sternly interrupting him—"I
tell you, William Ragin, *alias* Richard Weston, *alias* Thomas
Stukely, *alias* Edward Stanton—you are the man to submit to
all that I shall say to you, to all that I shall exact from you,
in virtue of what I know of you, and in virtue of what you
are."

The sweat poured in thick streams from the brow of the
criminal. The other proceeded.

"I am not a bully. It is not by swagger that I hope to put
you down, or to punish you. On the contrary, I come here
prepared to prove all that I assert, satisfactorily, before a
court of justice. It is for you to determine whether, by your
insolence and madness, you will incur the danger of a trial, or
whether you will submit quietly to what we ask, and leave
the country. I take for granted that you are no fool, though
in a moral point of view, your career would show you to be
an enormous one, since vice like yours is almost conclusive
against all human policy, and might reasonably be set down
by a liberal judgment, as in some degree a wretched insanity
If I prove to you that I can prove to others what I now assert, will you be ready, without more ado, to yield your
claims here, and every where, and fly the country?"

"You can prove nothing: you know nothing. I defy you."

"Beware! I am no trifler; and, by the God of heaven, I
tell you, that were I to trust my own feelings, you should
swing upon the gallows, or be shut in from life, by a worse
death, in the penitentiary, all your days. I can bring you to
either, if I will it, but there are considerations, due to the
feelings of others, which prompt me to the gentler course I
have indicated. It is enough for me that you have been connected by the most solemn ties with Maria Lacy. Her wishes
and her memory are sacred in my sight, and these move me to

spare the villain whom my own personal wrongs would prompt
me to drag to the gallows. You see how the matter stands.
Speak!"

"You then—you are——'

"Henry Lamar, of Georgia, the cousin, aud once the be-
trothed of Maria Lacy."

There was a slight tremour in the speaker's voice, as he
made this answer, but his soul was very firm. He continued:
"I complain not of your wrong to me. It is enough that I
am prepared to avenge it, and I frankly tell you, I am half indifferent whether you accede to my proposition or not. Your
audacity here has aroused a feeling in me, which leaves it
scarcely within my power to renew the chances of escape. I
renew the offer, while I am yet firm to do it. Leave the country—leave all the bounds—all the territories of the United
States—and keep aloof from them; for, as surely as I have
power to pursue, and hear of your presence in any of them, so
surely shall I hunt you out with shot and halter, as I would
the reptile that lurks beside the pathway, or the savage beast
that harbours in the thicket."

The speaker paused, resumed his seat, and, by a strong effort of will, maintained a calm silence, looking sternly upon
the criminal. Violent passions were contending in the breast
of the latter. His fears were evidently aroused, but his cupidity was active. It was clear that he apprehended the danger—it was equally clear that he was loth to forego his grasp
upon the property of his last victim. He was bewildered,
and, more in his confusion, than because of any thought or
courage—he once more desperately denied the charges made
against him.

"You are a bold man," said he to the stranger, affecting
coolness—" considering you deal in slander. You may impose
upon these, but it is only because they would believe any
thing against me now. But you have no proofs. I defy you
to produce any thing to substantiate one of your charges."

"Fool!" said the other coolly, I have but to call in the slaves—to have you stripped to the buff, and to discover and display to the world the marks upon your body, to which your wife swore in open court in New York State, on the trial of Reuben Moore, confounded in identity with yourself as William Ragin. Moore was only saved, so close was the general resemblance between you, as the scar of the scythe was not apparent upon his leg—to which all parties swore as certainly on yours. Are you willing that we should examine your left leg and foot?"

"My foot is as free from scar as yours; but I will not suffer myself to be examined."

"Did it need, we should not ask you. But it does not need. We have the affidavit of Samuel Fisher, to show that he detected the scar of the scythe upon your leg, while bathing with you at Crookstone's mill-pond; that he asked you how you got such a dreadful cut, and that you were confused, but said that it was a scythe cut. This he alleged of you under your present name of Stanton. Here, sir, is a copy of the affidavit. Here also is the testimony of James Green, of Liberty county, Georgia, who knew you there as the husband of Maria Lacy. He slept with you one night at Berry's house, on the way to the county court house. You played *poker* with a party of five, consisting of the said Green, of Jennings, Folker, and Stillman—their signatures are all here. You got drunk, quarrelled with Folker and Stillman, whom you accused of cheating you, were beaten by them severely, and so bruised, that it was necessary you should be put to bed, and bathed with spirits. When stripped for this purpose, while you lay unconscious, the scythe cut on your leg, and a large scar from a burn upon your right arm, to both of which, your wife, Elizabeth Ragin, swore in New York, with great particularity— as appears in that reported case—were discovered—and attracted the attention of all present."

H 5

"Man or devil!" exclaimed the criminal in desperation,—
"by what means have you contrived to gather these damnable
proofs?"

"You admit them, then?"

"I admit nothing. I defy them, and you, and the devil.—
Let me go. I will hear nothing more—see nothing farther.—
As for you, John Ramsay, let me ask, am I to have any of my
wife's property? Let me have it, and I leave the cursed country for ever."

John Ramsay, the younger, was about to reply, when the
stranger silenced him.

"Stay! You leave not this spot, unless with my consent,
or in the hands of the sheriff. He is here in readiness. Are
you willing that I should call him in? I am serious! There
must be no trifling. Here are proofs of your identity with
William Ragin, who married Elizabeth Simpson, of Minden,
Connecticut;— with Richard Weston, who married Sarah
Gooch, of Raleigh, N. C.;—with Thomas Stukeley, who married with Maria Lacy, of Liberty county, Geo.;—with Edward Stanton, now before us, who married with Ellen Ramsay,
of Montgomery county, Alabama. Of these wretched wives
whom you have wronged and dishonoured, two of them are
still living. I do not stipulate for your return to either.
They are sufficiently fortunate to be rid of you for ever. But
this I insist upon, that you leave the country. As for taking
the property of this wife or that, you must consider yourself
particularly fortunate that you escape the halter. You can
take nothing. Your fate lies in these papers."

In an instant the desperate hands of the criminal had
clutched the documents where the other laid them down. He
clutched them, and sprang towards the door, but a single
blow from the powerful fist of young John Ramsay brought
him to the floor. The stranger quietly repossessed himself of
the papers."

"You are insane, William Ragin," he remarked coolly—

" these are all copies of the originals, and even were they originals, their loss would be of little value while all the witnesses are living. They are brought for your information—to show you on what a perilous point you stand—and have been used only to base the warrant upon which has been already issued for your arrest. That warrant is even now in this village in the hands of the sheriff of the county. I have but to say that you are the man whom he must arrest under it, and he does his duty. You are at my mercy. I see that you feel that. Rise and sign this paper, and take your departure. If, after forty-eight hours, you are found east of the Tombeckbe, you forfeit all the chances which it affords you of escape. Rise, sir, and sign. I have no more words for you."

The criminal did as he was commanded—passively, as one in a stupor. The stranger then waved him to the door, and he took his departure without any more being spoken on either side. When he was gone—

" These papers," said Lamar to old John Ramsay, " are yours. I leave them for your protection from this scoundrel. The proofs are all conclusive, and, with his re-appearance, you have but to seek the sheriff and renew the warrant."

The old man clasped the hands of the stranger and bedewed them with tears.

" You will stay with us while you are here. We owe you too much to suffer it otherwise. We have no other way of thanking you."

" I have another day's business here," said Lamar, " and will cheerfully partake your hospitality for that time. For the present I must leave you. I have an engagement with Mr. Atkins.

The engagement with Atkins led the stranger to the grave of poor Ellen Ramsay and to that of Robert Anderson. They next visited the cottage of the widow Anderson, and obtained her consent to the use of the head board which the devoted youth had framed and inscribed, while himself dying, for the grave of his beloved. The next day was employed, with the consent of old Ramsay, in putting it up—an occasion which brought the villagers together as numerously as the burial of the poor girl had done. The events of the day had taken wind—the complete exposure of the wretch who had brought ruin and misery into the little settlement, was known to all, and deep were the imprecations of all upon his crime, and warm the congratulations at a development which saved the venerable father from being spoiled and left in poverty in his declining years. But there is yet finish to the story—another event, perhaps necessary to its finish, which, as it was the offspring of another day, we must reserve for another chapter.

CHAPTER III.

THAT night, while the little family at Ramsay's were sitting over their evening meal, Abram, one of the plantation negroes, appeared at the door of the apartment, and abruptly addressed young Ramsay after the following fashion :—

" Look ya, Mass Jack, I want for see you out ya a minute."

Abram was the *driver* of the plantation—a sort of superintendent of details. He was a faithful negro, such as is to be found on every long established plantation at the South—shrewd, cool, sensible—perhaps forty years of age—honest, attentive to his business, and, from habit, assuming the interest which he managed to be entirely his own. His position gave him consequence, which he felt and asserted, but never abused. A trick of speaking very much what was uppermost in his mind, was the fruit of a just consciousness of duties well performed, leaving him in no fear of any proper authority. Young Ramsay rose instantly and obeyed the summons. With some little mystery in his manner, Abram conducted the youth from the piazza into the yard, and thence into the shadow of one of the gigantic shade trees by which the house was literally embowered. Here, looking around him with the air of one anxious neither to be seen nor overheard, he thrust a paper into the hands of John Ramsay, with this inquiry—

"Dis ya money, Mass Jack,—good money?"

"I will tell you when I look at it by the candle. Why?— where did you get it?"

"You look at 'em first—I tell you all 'bout 'em arter-ward."

John did as was required, returned and reported the bank note—for it was such, and for twenty dollars—to be utterly worthless—that, in short, of a broken bank.

"I bin tink so," said the negro.

"Where did you get it, Abram?"

"Who you speck gib me, Mass Jack?"

"I don't know!"

"Who but Mass Ned Stanton."

"Ha!—why—when did he give you this money?"

"To-day—when you bin all busy wid de tomb stone of young Missis. He come by de old creek field, call me out, say I must come to 'em in de wood, and den he say to me dat he sorry for see me ya working for Massa. Him will help me git off work—I shall be free man, if I will only go wid him, and bring off many of de brack people as I kin. He promise me heap of tings, git me 'nuff tobacco for las' a mont', gib me knife—see dis ya—and dis money which you say no good money. I bin speck 'em for bad when he tell me its twenty dollars. Twenty dollars is heap money, I say to myself. Wha' for he gib me twenty dollars now. Wha' for he con-siders my freedom, jes' now, and he nebber bin tink 'pon 'em before. Someting's wrong, I say to myself, and Massa for know—but I nebber let on to 'em I 'spec 'em. I say 'da's all right. I will come, Mass Ned. I will see you in de bush to-night.' Den he shake my hand—say he always bin lub me—

will take me to country whay brack man is gentleman and hab white wife, and is lawyer, and schoolmosser, and preacher, and hab white man for dribe he carriage. I yerry em berry well, but I never le' him see I laugh. But I hab my tongue ya (thrust to one side of his jaws) and the white ob my eye grow large as I look 'pon 'em. I know 'em of ole. I bin speck on 'em when he first came ya courting poor Miss Nelly. I no like 'em den—I no like 'em now. But I mak' blieb I lub 'em too much. Das for you now to fix 'em. He's for see me to-night by ole Robin tree in de swamp. Wha' mus do—wha' mus say—how you gwine fix 'em ?"

" You have done right, 'Bram. Before I say any thing, I will consult my father, and a stranger who is with us."

" I yerry bout 'em. He's a man, I ya. Flora bin tell me how he fixed Ned Stanton."

" Well, I'll consult him and my father. Do you remain here in the meantime. Do not let yourself be seen. Stanton *is* a villain, but we have found him out. Stanton is not his real name, but Ragin."

" Ragin, eh? Well, we must Ragin 'em. I'll wait 'pon you ya. But mak' haste—de time is pretty close, and he'll 'spec' somet'ing ef I aint by de tree when he come."

John Ramsay re-entered the house, and, in few words, repeated the substance of the negro's story.

" The scoundrel's bent on being hung," was the exclamation of Lamar, with something like a look of exultation. " Let 'Bram encourage him, and give him a meeting for to-morrow night, promising to bring all the negroes that he can. We shall be at the meeting. 'Bram shall carry us, though we go as his comrades, not as his superiors."

The scheme of Lamar was soon laid. Young Ramsay and himself were to smut their faces, and, in negro habiliments, were to impose upon the villain. Lamar promised that the sheriff should take his hand at the game.

"Our mercy is thrown away upon such a thrice-dyed scoun-

drel. His destiny forces the task of vengeance upon us. Go
to Abram, and give him his cue."

CHAPTER IV.

THERE is a fatality about the wicked that, sooner or later,
whatever may be their precautions and their adroitness, inva-
riably brings about their confusion and defeat. The criminal
in the present instance, was one who had enjoyed a long
swing of good fortune—using these words only to mean that
he had been able to gratify his wishes, of whatever sort, without yet having been made to pay the usual penalties. This
very success is most commonly the source of final disaster.
The fortunate man is apt to presume upon his good fortune—
to hold himself, like Sylla, a sort of favourite with the capri-
cious goddess, until he loses himself irrevocably in the blind
presumption which his confidence provokes. Edward Stanton,
for so we shall continue to call him, had been too often in
straits like the present, and had too often emerged from them
with profit, to fancy that he had much at hazard in the new
game that he had determined to pursue. He had been tempo-
rally daunted by the complete exposure of his career, which
had been made by Lamar, and felt, from all he saw and all he
heard, that the chances were entirely up with him where he
then stood. But he had not long gone from sight of his enemy,
before his mind began once more to recover, and to unravel
new schemes and contrivances for the satisfaction of his selfish
passions. He was a person soon to cast aside his apprehensions, and to rise with new energies after defeat. It is a very
great misfortune that this admirable quality of character
should be equally shared, upon occasion, by the rogue and the
ruffian, with the honest man and the noble citizen. Stanton
was resolved to make the most of the forty-eight hours which

were allowed him. He took for granted that, having attained his object, Lamar would be satisfied ;—he may have discovered, indeed, that the latter would return in another day to Georgia. We have seen, from the revelations of Abram, what direction his scheming mind was disposed to pursue. His plans were laid in a few minutes, and, while the family of Ramsay, its guest, and the people of the village generally, were raising the simple head board over the grave of his injured wife, the mise-rable wretch, totally insensible to all honourable or human feeling, was urging the ignorant negro to a desertion of the ancient homestead, in the vain hope of attaining that freedom with which, when acquired, he knew not well what to do. Of course, this was all a pretext of the swindler, by which to get the property within his grasp. He had but to cross the Tombecbe with his unsuspecting companions, and they would have been sold, by public outcry, at the first popular gathering. His plans laid, his artifices all complete, he waited with anxi-ety the meeting with the negro. He had already taken his leave of the family with which he lodged, had mounted his horse, and turned his head towards the west, using particular care that his departure should be seen by several. He little fancied that his return to the neighbourhood by another route, and after night had set in, had also been perceived. But the vigilance of Lamar had arranged for this. Young Atkins had volunteered to observe the movements of Stanton, and, born a hunter, and familiar with all the woods for twenty miles round, he was able to report on the return of the fugitive, within half an hour of the moment when it took place. Con-cealing his horse in a neighbouring *bay*, ready for use in the first emergency, Stanton proceeded, at the appointed time, to the place of rendezvous.

Meanwhile, the preparations of Lamar were also in progress. The sheriff had been brought, after night-fall, to the house of old Ramsay. The coarse garments of the negro had been provided for himself and his deputy—for Lamar and the younger Ramsay. Young Atkins also insisted on going as a volunteer, and old Ramsay could with difficulty be persuaded to forbear accompanying the party. The blood of the veteran blazed up as fiercely as it had done twenty years before, when he heard the call for volunteers, from the lips of Andrew Jackson, to avenge the butcheries of Indian warfare. The good sense of Lamar succeeded in persuading him to leave the affair to younger men. Abram was of the party, and, with his assistance, a greasy preparation was procured, in which soot and oil were the chief ingredients, by which our free citizens were made to assume, in a very few moments, the dark and glossy outside of the African. Prime stout fellows were they—able field hands—such as would delight the unsuspecting eye of the kidnapper as soon as he beheld them. They were all armed with pistols—all but Abram, who carried however the knife— a formidable *couteau de chasse*, which had been one of the bribes of Stanton, presented to him with the bank note and tobacco, at their first interview. Abram undertook the conduct of the party. They were led forth secretly, in profoundest silence, by a circuitous path, to the swamp thicket, in the neighbourhood of which the meeting was to take place. It is needless to describe the route. Suffice it that they were there in season, snugly quartered, and waiting with due impatience for the signal. It was heard at last; a shrill whistle, thrice repeated, followed by the barking of a hound. To this Abram answered, going forth as he did so, and leaving the party in the close covert to which he had conducted them. The night was a bright star-light. The gleams, however, came but imperfectly through the thick foliage, and our conspirators could distinguish each other only by the sound of their voices. Their faces shone as glossy as the leaves, when suddenly touched by the far light of the stars. Gradually, they heard approaching footsteps. It was then that Lamar said, seizing the hand of young Ramsay,—

"No haste, now,—no rashness,—we must let the fellow hobble himself fairly."

Deep silence followed, broken only by the voice of the negro, and his companion.

"You have brought them?" said Stanton.

"Da's ya!" replied the black.

"How many?"

"Some tree or four, 'side myself."

"Could you bring no more?" asked the eager kidnapper.

"Hab no chance—you no gib me time 'nuff. Ef you left tell Saturday night now, and Sunday, I get 'em all."

"No!—no! that's impossible. I dare not. These must do. Where are they?"

"In de bush! jes' ya! But look ya, Mass Ned, you are gwine do wha' you promise?"

"On my honour, 'Bram."

"You will take your Bible oat', Mass Ned?"

"I swear it."

"Dis ya nigger I bring you is no common nigger, I tell you. Mossa hab heaby lose for loss 'em. Wha' you 'spose he gwine say,—wha', he tink, when he get up to-morrow mornin', and can't find 'Bram and the rest ob 'em. Wha' he gwine do?"

"What can he do? We will have the start of him by twenty-five miles, and in one day more you will be free, 'Bram, your own master, and able to put him at defiance. I will see to that."

"He will push arter us, Mass Ned,—and dese ya nigger in de bush—look ya, Massa Ned, dese all prime nigger. Da's one on 'em, a gal ya, most purty nuff for white man wife. You 'member little Suzy, Mass Ned?"

"Don't I, 'Bram? Little Luzy is a pretty girl—pretty enough to be the wife of any man. Bring her out, bring them all out, and let us be off. We understand each other."

"Suzy is good gal, Mass Ned. I want to see 'em doing

prime when he git he freedom. You will marry 'em yourself, wid parson?"

"If she wishes it."

"He will wish 'em for true! But wha' dis I yer 'em say 'bout you habing tree wife a'ready?"

"No more of that, 'Bram."

"Wha'! he aint true, den?"

"A lie, 'Bram! a black, a bloody lie!"

"What for den you let dat Georgy man run you out ob de country?"

"Ha! who told you this?"

"I yer dem house sarbant talk ob 'em."

"They do not understand it. I am not driven. I choose to go."

"Well! you know bes', but dat's whá' I yer dem say."

"No more, 'Bram! Where are the people?"

"Let me dog bark tree time, and dey come. You kin bark like dog, Mass Ned. Try for 'em."

The imitation was a good one. Sounds were heard in the bushes, and one by one the supposed negroes appeared in the starlight. They looked natural enough, and the kidnapper approached them with some interest.

"These are all men, are they not? Are there no women? Where's Little Suzy?"

"Ha! Mass Ned,—I speck its true wha' dem people say. You lub gal too much. I call little Suzy now, him take you 'bout de neck. Come ya, my people. Mass Ned hab make 'greement wid me to carry us all to fine country. He swear Bible 'oat to make we all free, and gib we plenty whiskey and tobacco. I tell 'em you's ready to go. You ready, eh?"

There was a general grunt of assent.

'Bram was disposed to be satirical. His dry chuckle accompanied every syllable.

"Gib um you hand den on de bargain. Shake hand like

brudderin. Ha! ha! I nebber bin speck to be bruder ob my my young mossa. Shake hands, niggers, on de bargain."

"You have heard what 'Bram has said, my boys. I promise the same things to you. You shall go with me to a country where you shall be free. I will give you plenty of whiskey and tobacco. Here is my hand. Who is this— Zeke?"

The hand was clutched by Lamar, with a grasp that somewhat startled the criminal. The voice of the supposed negro in the next moment, terribly informed him of his danger.

"Villain" exclaimed the Georgian, "I have you! You are sworn for the gallows! You shall not escape us now."

A short struggle followed—the doubtful light, and their rapid movements, not suffering the other persons around so to distinguish between them as to know where to take hold. The criminal put forth all his strength, which was far from inconsiderable. The combatants were nearly equally matched, but in the struggle they traversed a fallen tree, over which Lamar stumbled and fell, partly dragging his enemy with him to the ground. To save himself only did he relax his hold. Of this Stanton nimbly availed himself. He recovered his feet, and, before the rest of the party could interfere, had gained a dozen paces on his way to the thicket. Once within its shadows, he might with good heart and good fortune, have baffled their pursuit. But this was not destined. He was intercepted by no less a person than Abram, who rolled himself suddenly like a huge ball in the path of the fugitive, and thus broke the fall which yet precipitated him to the ground. In the next moment, the negro had caught him by the leg, yelling at the same time to the rest of the party to come to his succour.

"Ah! dog it is you then to whom I owe all this."

Such was the speech, muttered through his closed teeth, with which Stanton declared his recognition of the assailant. His words were followed by a pistol shot. Abram gave a cry, released his hold, and leapt to his feet. Stanton had only half risen when the whole weight of the negro was again upon him.

"Where is he, 'Bram?" demanded Lamar.

"I hab em ya, Mossa,—he safe," responded the other with a groan.

"You are hurt?" said young Ramsay, inquiringly.

"One arm smash wid he pistol, Mass Jack."

His young master helped the poor fellow up, while Lamar and the sheriff, with young Atkins, prepared to secure the criminal.

"What is this! He is lifeless!" said the former, as he touched the body. "What have you done, 'Bram?"

"I don't know, Mossa. I hab my knife in my han', and when he shoot me, I be so bex and so scare, I don't know wha' I do wid em. I gib um he knife, I speck. It's he own knife."

Sure enough! the weapon was still sticking in the side of the criminal. The one blow was fatal, and his dying groan, if any was uttered, was drowned in the furious exclamation with which the negro accompanied the blow.

"It is a loss to the gallows," said Lamar, with an expression of chagrin.

"Better so!" replied young Ramsay.

"It saves me a very dirty job!" muttered the sheriff. We may add that he took care to pay the usual fees to Abram, who was otherwise well provided for by the Ramsay family, and still lives to relate the events of that night of conflict with the Snake of the Cabin.

OAKATIBBE,

OR THE CHOCTAW SAMPSON.

CHAPTER I.

It was in the year 182—, that I first travelled in the valleys of the great south-west. Circumstances, influenced in no slight degree by an "errant disposition," beguiled me to the Choctaw nation, which, at that time, occupied the greater part of the space below the Tennessee line, lying between the rivers Tombeckbe and Mississippi, as low, nearly, as the town of Jackson, then, as now, the capital of the State of Mississippi. I loitered for several weeks in and about this region, without feeling the loss or the weight of time   Yet, the reader is not to suppose that travelling at that day was so simple a matter, or possessed many, if any of the pleasant facilities of the present. *Au contraire ·* It was then a serious business.   It meant *travail* rather than *travel.*   The roads were few and very hard to find.   Indian foot-paths—with the single exception of the great military traces laid out by General Jackson, and extending from Tennessee to Lake Ponchartrain—formed almost the only arteries known to the "Nation;" and the portions of settled country in the neighbourhood, nominally civilized only, were nearly in the same condition.   Some of the Indian paths, as I experienced, seemed only to be made for the perplexity of the stranger.   Like Gray's passages which "led to nothing," they constantly brought me to a stand.   Sometimes they were swallowed up in swamps, and, in such cases, your future route upon the earth was to be discovered only by a deliberate and careful survey of the skies above.   The openings in the trees over head alone instructed

you in the course you were to pursue. You may readily imagine that this sort of progress was as little pleasant as edify-
ing, yet, in some respects, it was not wanting in its attractions, also. To the young and ardent mind, obstacles of this
nature tend rather to excite than to depress. They contain
the picturesque in themselves, at times, and always bring out
the moral in the man. "To learn to rough it," is an educational phrase, in the dialect of the new countries, which
would be of great service, adopted as a rule of government
for the young in all. To " coon a log"—a mysterious process
to the uninitiated—swim a river—experiment, at a guess, upon
the properties of one, and the proprieties of another route—
parley with an Indian after his own fashion—not to speak of
a hundred other incidents which the civilized world does not
often present—will reconcile a lad of sanguine temperament
to a number of annoyances much more serious than will attend him on an expedition through our frontier countries.

It was at the close of a cloudy day in November, that I
came within hail of the new but rude plantation settlements
of Colonel Harris. He had but lately transferred his interests
to Mississippi, from one of the "maternal thirteen"—had
bought largely in the immediate neighbourhood of the Choctaw
nation, and had also acquired, by purchase from the natives,
certain reserves within it, to which he chiefly owes that large
wealth, which, at this day, he has the reputation of possessing.
In place of the stately residence which now adorns his homestead, there was then but a miserable log-house, one of the
most ordinary of the country, in which, unaccompanied by his
family, he held his temporary abiding place. His plantation
was barely rescued from the dominions of nature. The trees
were girdled only the previous winter, for his first crop, which
was then upon the ground, and an excellent crop it was for
that immature condition of his fields. There is no describing
the melancholy aspect of such a settlement, seen in winter, on
a cloudy day, and in the heart of an immense forest, through

which you have travelled for miles, without glimpse of human
form or habitation. The worm-fence is itself a gloomy spectacle, and the girdled trees, erect but dead, the perishing
skeletons of recent life, impress you with sensations not entirely unlike those which you would experience in going over
some battle-field, from which the decaying forms of man and
horse have not yet been removed. The fences of Colonel Harris
were low in height, though of great extent. They were simply
sufficient to protect the fields from the random assaults of cattle. Of his out-houses, the most respectable in size, solidity
and security, was the corn crib. His negro-houses, like the
log-house in which he himself dwelt, were only so many temporary shanties, covered with poles and thatched with bark
and pine-straw. In short, every thing that met my eye only
tended the more to frown upon my anticipations of a cheerful
fireside and a pleasant arrangement of the creature-comforts.
But my doubts and apprehensions all vanished at the moment
of my reception. I was met by the proprietor with that ease
and warmth of manner which does not seem to be conscious
of any deficiencies of preparation, and is resolved that there
shall be none which sincere hospitality can remedy. I was
soon prepared to forget that there were deficiencies. I felt myself very soon at home. I had letters to Colonel Harris, which
made me particularly welcome, and in ten minutes we were
both in full sail amongst all the shallows and deeps of ordinary
conversation.

Not that we confined ourselves to these. Our discourse,
after a little while, turned upon a circumstance which I had
witnessed on riding through his fields and while approaching
his dwelling, which struck me with considerable surprise, and
disturbed, in some degree, certain pre-conceived opinions in
my mind. I had seen, interspersed with his negro labourers,
a goodly number of Indians of both sexes, but chiefly young
persons, all equally and busily employed in cotton picking.
The season had been a protracted one, and favourable, accord-

ingly, to the maturing of great numbers of the bolls which an early and severe winter must have otherwise destroyed. The crop, in consequence, had been so great as to be beyond the ability, to gather in and harvest, of the "force" by which it was made. This, in the new and fertile vallies of the southwest, is an usual event. In ordinary cases, when this happens, it is the custom to buy other negroes from less productive regions, to consumate and secure the avails of labour of the original "force." The whole of these, united, are then addressed to the task of opening additional lands, which, should they yield as before, necessarily demand a second purchase of an extra number to secure and harvest, in season, the surplus fruits of their industry. The planter is very readily persuaded to make this purchase so long as the seeming necessity shall re-occur; and in this manner has he continued expanding his interests, increasing the volume of his lands, and incurring debt for these and for his slaves, at exorbitant prices, in order to the production of a commodity, every additional bag of which, disparages its own value, and depreciates the productive power, in an estimate of profit, of the industry by which it is produced. It will not be difficult, keeping this fact in mind as a sample of the profligacy of western adventure —to account, in part, for the insolvency and desperate condition of a people in possession of a country naturally the most fertile of any in the world.

The crop of Colonel Harris was one of this description. It far exceeded the ability of his "force" to pick it in; but instead of buying additional slaves for the purpose, he conceived the idea of turning to account the lazy Choctaws by whom he was surrounded. He proposed to hire them at a moderate compensation, which was to be paid them weekly. The temptation of gain was greedily caught at by these hungering outcasts, and, for a few dollars, or an equivalent in goods, groceries, and so forth, some forty-five of them were soon to be seen, as

I

busy as might be, in the prosecution of their unusual labour. The work was light and easy—none could be more so—and though not such adepts as the negro, the Indian women soon contrived to fill their bags and baskets, in the course of the day. At dark, you might behold them trudging forward under their burdens to the log-house, where the proprietor stood ready to receive them. Here he weighed their burdens, and gave them credit, nightly, for the number of pounds which they each brought in. The night of my arrival was Saturday, and the value of the whole week's labour was then to be summed up and accounted for. This necessarily made them all punctual in attendance, and nothing could be more amusing than the interest which they severally displayed as Colonel Harris took out his memorandum book, and proceeded to make his entries. Every eye was fixed upon him, and an old Indian, who, though he did not work himself, represented the interests of a wife and two able-bodied daughters, planted himself directly behind this gentleman, and watched, with looks of growing sagacity, every stroke that was made in this—to him—volume of more than Egyptian mystery and hieroglyphics. Meanwhile, the squaws stood about their baskets with looks expressive of similar interest, but at the same time of laudable patience. The negroes in the rear, were scarcely less moved by curiosity, though a contemptuous grin might be seen on nearly all their countenances, as they felt their superiority in nearly every physical and intellectual respect, over the untutored savages. Many Indians were present who neither had nor sought employment. Of those employed, few or none were of middle age. But these were not wanting to the assemblage. They might be seen prowling about the rest— watchful of the concerns of their wives, sons and daughters, with just that sort and degree of interest, which the eagle may be supposed to feel, who, from his perch on the tree-top or the rock, beholds the fish-hawk dart into the water in pursuit of that prey which he meditates to rend from his jaws as soon

as he shall re-ascend into the air. Their interest was decidely
greater than that of the poor labourer. It was in this manner
that these vultures appropriated the fruits of his industry, and
there was no remedy. They commonly interfered, the moment
it was declared what was due to the *employée*, to resolve the
pay into a certain number of gallons of whiskey; so many
pounds of tobacco; so much gunpowder and lead. If the em-
ployer, as was the case with Colonel Harris, refused to furnish
them whiskey, they required him to pay in money. With this,
they soon made their way to one of those moral sinks, called
a grog-shop, which English civilization is always ready to
plant, as its first, most familiar, and most imposing standard
among the hills and forests of the savage.

It may be supposed that this experiment upon the inflexibility of Indian character and habit—for it was an experiment
which had been in trial only a single week—was a subject of
no little curiosity to me, as it would most probably be to almost every person at all impressed with the humiliating moral
and social deterioration which has marked this fast decaying
people. Could it possibly be successful? Could a race, proud,
sullen, incommunicative, wandering, be persuaded, even by
gradual steps, and with the hope of certain compensation, to
renounce the wild satisfaction afforded by their desultory and
unconstrained modes of life? Could they be beguiled for a
season into employments which, though they did not demand
any severe labours, at least required pains-taking, regular industry, and that habitual attention to daily recurring tasks,
which, to their roving nature, would make life a most mono-
tonous and unattractive possession? How far the lightness
of the labour and the simplicity of the employment, with the
corresponding recompense, would reconcile them to its tasks,
was the natural subject of my inquiry. On this head, my
friend, Colonel Harris, could only conjecture and speculate like
myself. His experiment had been in progress but a few days.
But our speculations led us to very different conclusions. He

was a person of very ardent character, and sanguine, to the last degree, of the success of his project. He had no question but that the Indian, even at his present stage, might be brought under the influence of a judicious civilization. We both agreed that the first process was in procuring their labour —that this was the preliminary step, without taking which, no other could be made; but how to bring them to this was the question.

"They can be persuaded to this," was his conclusion. "Money, the popular god, is as potent with them as with our own people. They will do any thing for money. You see these now in the field. They have been there, and just as busy and in the same number, from Monday last."

"How long will they continue?"

"As long as I can employ and pay them."

"Impossible! They will soon be dissatisfied. The men will consume and squander all the earnings of the females and the feeble. The very motive of their industry, money, to which you refer, will be lost to them after the first payment. I am convinced that a savage people, not as yet familiar with the elements of moral prudence, can only be brought to habitual labour, by the one process of coercion."

"We shall see. There is no coercion upon them now, yet they work with wonderful regularity."

"This week will end it. Savages are children in all but physical respects. To do any thing with them, you must place them in that position of respectability, and teach them that law, without the due employment of which, any attempt to educate a child, must be an absurdity—you must teach them obedience. They must be made to know, at the outset, that they know nothing—that they must implicitly defer to the superior. This lesson they will never learn, so long as they possess the power, at any moment, to withdraw from his control."

"Yet, even were this to be allowed, there must be a limit.

Suppose, in order that the experiment may be fairly tried, that they withhold from him all knowledge of his origin. He is brought up precisely as the other lads around him. But what is the first discovery which he makes? That he is a copper-coloured boy—that he is, alone, the only copper-coloured boy—that wherever he turns he sees no likeness to himself. This begets his wonder, then his curiosity, and finally his suspicion. He soon understands—for his suspicion sharpens every faculty of observation—that he is an object of experiment. Nay, the most cautious policy in the world could never entirely keep this from a keen-thoughted urchin. His fellow-pupils teach him this. He sees that, to them, he is an object of curiosity and study. They regard him, and he soon regards himself, as a creature set apart, and separated, for some peculiar purposes, from all the rest. A stern and singular sense of individuality and isolation is thus forced upon him. He asks —Am I, indeed, alone?—Who am I?—What am I?—These inquiries naturally occasion others. Does he read? Books give him the history of his race. Nay, his own story probably meets his eye in the newspapers. He learns that he is descended from a nation dwelling among the secret sources of the Susquehannah. He pries in all corners for information. The more secret his search, the more keenly does he pursue it. It becomes the great passion of his mind. He learns that his people are fierce warriors and famous hunters. He hears of their strifes with the white man—their successful strifes, when the nation could send forth its thousand bow-men, and the whites were few and feeble. Perhaps, the young pale faces around him, speak of his people, even now, as enemies; at least, as objects of suspicion, and perhaps antipathy. All these things tend to elevate and idealize, in his mind, the history of his people. He cherishes a sympathy, even beyond the natural desires of the heart, for the perishing race from which he feels himself, "like a limb, cast bleeding and torn." The curiosity to see his ancestry—the people of his tribe and to a white maiden! What a revulsion of the moral and social sense would have followed his proposition in the mind of the Saxon damsel;—and, were she to consent, what a commotion in the community in which she lived. And this revulsion and commotion would have been perfectly natural, and, accordingly, perfectly proper. God has has made an obvious distinction between certain races of men, setting them apart, and requiring them to be kept so, by subjecting them to the resistance and rebuke of one of the most jealous sentinels of sense which we possess—the eye. The prejudices of this sense, require that the natural barriers should be maintained, and hence it becomes necessary that the race in subjection, should be sufficiently numerous to carry out the great object of every distinct community, though, perchance, it may happen to be an inferior one. In process of time, the beneficial and blessed effects of labour would be felt and understood by the most ignorant and savage of the race. Perhaps, not in one generation, or in two, but after the fifth and seventh, as it is written, " of those who keep my commandments." They would soon discover that, though compelled to toil, their toils neither enfeebled their strength nor impaired their happiness—that, on the contrary, they still resulted in their increasing strength, health, and comfort;—that their food, which before was precarious, depending on the caprices of the seasons, or the uncertainties of the chase, was now equally plentiful, wholesome and certain. They would also perceive that, instead of the sterility which is usually the destiny of all wandering tribes, and one of the procseses by which they perish—the fecundity of their people was wonderfully increased. These discoveries— if time be allowed to make them—would tacitly reconcile them to that inferior position of their race, which is proper and inevitable, so long as their intellectual inferiority shall continue. And what would have been the effect upon our Indians —decidedly the noblest race of aborigines that the world has ever known—if, instead of buying their scalps at prices varying from five to fifty pounds each, we had conquered and subjected them? Will any one pretend to say that they would not have increased with the restraints and enforced toils of our superior genius?—that they would not, by this time, have formed a highly valuable and noble integral in the formation of our national strength and character? Perhaps their civilization would have been comparatively easy—the Hebrews required four hundred years—the Britons and Saxons, possibly, half that time after the Norman Conquest. Differing in colour from their conquerors, though I suspect, with a natural genius superior to that of the ancient Britons, at the time of the Roman invasion under Julius Cæsar, the struggle between the two races must have continued for some longer time, but the union would have been finally effected, and then, as in the case of the Englishmen, we should have possessed a race, in their progeny, which, in moral and physical structure, might have challenged competition with the world."

" Ay, but the difficulty would have been in the conquest."

" True, that would have been the difficulty. The American colonists were few in number and feeble in resource. The nations from which they emerged put forth none of their strength in sending them forth. Never were colonies so inadequately provided—so completely left to themselves; and hence the peculiar injustice and insolence of the subsequent exactions of the British, by which they required their colonies to support their schemes of aggrandizement and expenditure by submitting to extreme taxation. Do you suppose, if the early colonists had been powerful, that they would have ever deigned to treat for lands with the roving hordes of savages whom they found on the continent? Never! Their purchases and treaties were not for lands, but tolerance. They bought permission to remain without molestation. The amount professedly given for land, was simply a tribute paid to the superior strength of the Indian, precisely as we paid it to Algiers and the Mussel-

I 5

tried upon a scale sufficiently extensive to make it a fair one. But your Indian student, drawn from

" Susquehannah's farthest springs,"

and sent to Cambridge, would present you with some such moral picture as that of the prisoner described by Sterne. His chief employment, day by day, would consist in notching upon his stick, the undeviating record of his daily suffering. It would be to him an experiment almost as full of torture, as that of the Scottish Boot, the Spanish Thumb-screw—or any of those happy devices of ancient days, for impressing pleasant principles upon the mind, by impressing unpleasant feelings upon the thews, joints and sinews. I wish that some of our writers, familiar with mental analysis, would make this poem of Freneau, the subject of a story. I think it would yield admirable material. To develope the thoughts and feelings of on Indian boy, taken from his people, ere yet he has formed such a knowledge of them, or of others, as to have begun to discuss or to compare their difference—follow him to a college such as that of Princeton or Cambridge—watch him within its walls—amid the crowd, but not of it—watch him within himself while all others are looking into him, or trying to do so—surrounded by active, sharp-witted lad of the Anglo-Norman race ; undergoing an hourly repeated series of moral spasms, as he hears them wantonly or thoughtlessly dwell upon the wild and ignorant people from whom he is chosen ;—listening, though without seeming to listen, to their crude pseculations upon the great problem which is to be solved only by seeing how well he can endure his spasms, and what use he can make of his philosophy if he survives it— then, when the toils of study and the tedious restraints and troubles of prayer and recitation are got over, to behold and describe the joy with which the happy wretch flings by his fetters, when he is dismissed from those walls which have witnessed his tortures—even supposing him to remain (which is very unlikely,) until his course of study is pronounced to be complete! With what curious pleasure will he stop in the shadow of the first deep forest, to tear from his limbs those garments which make him seem unlike his people! How quick will be the beating at his heart as he endeavours to dispose about his shoulders the blanket robe in the manner in which it is worn by the chief warrior of his tribe! With what keen effort—should he have had any previous knowledge of his kindred—will he seek to compel his memory to restore every, the slighest, custom or peculiarity which distinguished them when his eyes were first withdrawn from the parental tribe; and how closely will he imitate their indomitable pride and lofty, cold, superiority of look and gesture, as at evening he enters the native hamlet, and takes his seat in silence at the door of the Council House, waiting, without a word, for the summon of the Elders!"

" Quite a picture, I think with you, that in good hands, such a subject would prove a very noble one."

" But the story would not finish here. Supposing all this to have taken place, just as we are told it did—supposing the boy to have graduated at the college, and to have flung away the distinction—to have returned, as has been described, to his savage costume—to the homes and habits of his people. —it is not so clear that he will fling away all the lessons of wisdom, all the knowledge of facts, which he will have acquired for the tuition of the superior race. A natural instinct, which is above all lessons, must be complied with; but this done—and when the first tumults of his blood have subsided, which led him to defeat the more immediate object of his social training—there will be a gradual resumption of the educational influence in his mind, and his intellectual habits will begin to exercise themselves anew. They will he provoked necessarily to this exercise by what he beholds around him. He will begin to perceive, in its true aspects, the wretchedness of that hunter-state, which, surveyed at a distance, appeared only the embodiment of stoical heroism and the most elevated pride. He will see and lament the squalid poverty of his people; which, his first lessons in civilization must have shown him, is due only to the mode of life and pursuits in which they are engaged. Their beastly intoxication will offend his tastes—their superstition and ignorance—the circumscribed limits of their capacity for judging of things and relations beyond the life of the bird or beast of prey—will awaken in him a sense of shame when he feels that they are his kindred. The insecurity of their liberties will awaken his fears, for he will instantly see that the great body of the people in every aboriginal nation are the veriest slaves in the world ; and the degrading exhibitions which they make in their filth and drunkenness, which reduce the man to a loathsomeness of aspect which is never reached by the vilest beast which he hunts or scourges, will be beheld by the Indian student in very lively contrast with all that has met his eyes during that novitiate among the white sages, the processes of which have been to him so humiliating and painful. His memory reverts to that period with feelings of reconciliation. The torture is over, and the remembrance of former pain, endured with manly fortitude, is comparatively a pleasure. A necessary reaction in his mind takes place ; and agreeably to the laws of nature, what will, and what should follow, but that he will seek to become the tutor and the reformer of his people? They themselves will tacitly raise him from this position, for the man of the forest will defer even to the negro who has been educated by the white man. He will try to teach them habits of greater method and industry—he will overthrow the altars of their false gods—he will seek to bind the wandering tribes together under one head and in one nation—he will prescribe uniform laws of government. He will succeed in somethings—he will fail in others ; he will offend the pride of the self-conceited and the mulish—the priesthood will be the first to declare against him—and he will be murdered still tardy, adoption of the laws and guidance of the superior race."

CHAPTER II.

I AM afraid that my reader will suffer quite as much under this long discussion, as did my excellent companion, Colonel Harris. But he is not to suppose that all the views here expressed, were uttered consecutively, as they are above set down. I have simply condensed, for more easy comprehension, the amount of a conversation which lasted some two hours. I may add, that, at the close, we discovered, as is very often the case among disputants, there was very little substantial difference between us. Our dispute, if any, was rather verbal than philosophical. On the subject of his experiment, however, Colonel Harris fancied, that, in employing some forty or fifty of the Indians, of both sexes, he had brought together a community sufficiently large for the purposes of a fair experiment. Still, I thought that the argument remained untouched. They were not subordinate; they were not subdued; they could still exercise a free and absolute will, in despite of authority and reason. He could resort to no method for compelling their obedience; and we know pretty well what will result—even among white men—from the option of vagrancy.

"But," I urged, "even if the objections which I have stated, fail of defeating your scheme, there is yet another agent of defeat working against it, in the presence of these elderly Indians, who do not join in the labour, and yet, according to your own showing, still prowl in waiting to snatch from the hands of the industrious all the fruits of their toil. The natural effect of this will be to discourage the industry of those who work; for, unless the labourer is permitted to enjoy a fair proportion of the fruits of his labour, it is morally impossible that he should long continue it."

Our conference was interrupted by the appearance of the labourers, Indians and Negroes, who now began to come in, bringing with them the cotton which they had severally gathered during the day. This was accumulated in the courtyard, before the dwelling; each Indian, man or woman, standing beside the bag or basket which contained the proofs of his industry. You may readily suppose, that, after the dialogue and discussion which is partially reported above, I felt no little interest in observing the proceedings. The parties present were quite numerous. I put the negroes out of the question, though they were still to be seen, lingering in the background, grinning spectators of the scene. The number of Indians, men and women, who had *that day* been engaged in picking, was thirty-nine. Of these, twenty-six were females; three, only, might be accounted men, and ten were boys—none over sixteen. Of the females the number of elderly and young women was nearly equal. Of the men, one was very old and infirm; a second of middle age, who appeared to be something of an idiot; while the third, whom I regarded for this reason with more consideration and interest than all the party beside, was one of the most noble specimens of physical manhood that my eyes had ever beheld. He was fully six feet three inches in height, slender but muscular in the extreme. He possessed a clear, upright, open, generous cast of countenance, as utterly unlike that sullen, suspicious expression of the ordinary Indian face, as you can possibly imagine. Good nature and good sense were the predominant characteristics of his features, and—which is quite as unusual with Indians when in the presence of strangers—he laughed and jested with all the merry, unrestrainable vivacity of a youth of Anglo-Saxon breed. How was it that so noble a specimen of manhood consented to herd with the women and the weak of his tribe, in descending to the mean labours which the warriors were accustomed to despise?

"He must either be a fellow of great sense, or he must be a coward. He is degraded."

Such was my conclusion. The answer of Colonel Harris was immediate.

"He is a fellow of good sense, and very far from being a coward. He is one of the best Choctaws that I know."

"A man, then, to be a leader of his people. It is a singular proof of good sense and great mental flexibility, to find an Indian, who is courageous, voluntarily assuming tasks which are held to be degrading among the hunters. What is his name?"

"His proper name is Oakatibbé; but that by which he is generally known among us—his English name—is Slim Sampson, a name which he gets on the score of his superior strength and great slenderness. The latter name, in ordinary use, has completely superseded the former, even among his own people. It may be remarked, by the way, as another proof of the tacit deference of the inferior to the superior people, that most Indians prefer to use the names given by the whites to those of their own language. There are very few among them who will not contrive, after a short intimacy with white men, to get some epithet—which is not always a complimentary one— but which they cling to as tenaciously as they would to some far more valuable possession."

This little dialogue was whispered during the stir which followed the first arrival of the labourers. We had no opportunity for more.

The rest of the Indians were in no respect remarkable. There were some eight or ten women, and perhaps as many men, who did not engage in the toils of their companions, though they did not seem the less interested in the result. These, I noted, were all, in greater or less degree, elderly persons. One was full eighty years old, and a strange fact for one so venerable, was the most confirmed drunkard of the tribe. When the cotton pickers advanced with their baskets, the hangers-on drew nigh also, deeply engrossed with the prospect of reaping the gains from that industry which they had no mood to emulate. These, however, were very moderate, in most cases. Where a negro woman picked from one to two hundred weight of cotton, *per diem*, the Indian woman, at the utmost, gathered sixty-five; and the general average among them, did not much exceed forty-five. Slim Sampson's basket weighed eighty-six pounds—an amount considerably greater than any of the rest—and Colonel Harris assured me, that his average during the week had been, at no time, much below this quantity.

The proceedings had gone on without interruption or annoyance for the space of half an hour. Colonel Harris had himself weighed every basket with scrupulous nicety, and recorded the several weights opposite to the name of the picker, in a little memorandum book which he kept exclusively for this purpose; and it was amusing too see with what pleasurable curiosity, the Indians, men and women, watched the record which stated their several accounts. The whole labour of the week was to be settled for that night (Saturday), and hence the unusual gathering of those whose only purpose in being present, was to grasp at the spoils.

Among these hawks was one middle-aged Indian—a stern, sulky fellow, of considerable size and strength—whose skin was even then full of liquor, which contributing to the usual insolence of his character, made him at times very troublesome. He had more than once, during the proceedings, interfered between Colonel Harris and his *employees*, in such a manner as to provoke, in the mind of that gentleman, no small degree of irritation. The English name of this Indian, was Loblolly Jack· Loblolly Jack had a treble motive for being present and conspicuous. He had among the labourers, a wife and two daughters. When the baskets of these were brought to be weighed, he could no longer be kept in the background, but, resolutely thrusting himself before the rest, he handled basket, book and steelyards in turn, uttered his suspicions of foul play, and insisted upon a close examination of every movement which was made by the proprietor. In this manner, he made it very difficult for him to proceed in his duties; and his conduct, to do the Indians justice, seemed quite as annoying to them as to Colonel Harris. The wife frequently expostulated with him, in rather bolder language than an Indian squaw is apt to use to her liege lord; while Slim Sampson, after a few words of reproach, expressed in Choctaw, concluded by telling him in plain English, that he was "a rascal dog." He seemed the only one among them who had no fear of the intruder. Loblolly Jack answered in similar terms, and Slim Sampson, clearing the baskets at a single bound, confronted him with a show of fight, and a direct challenge to it, on the spot where they stood. The other seemed no ways loth. He recoiled a pace, drew his knife—a sufficient signal for Slim Sampson to get his own in readiness—and, thus opposed, they stood, glaring upon each other with eyes of the most determined expression of malignity. A moment more—an additional word of provocation from either—and blows must have taken place. But Colonel Harris, a man of great firmness, put himself between them, and calling to one of his negroes, bade him bring out from the house his double-barreled gun.

"Now," said he, "my good fellows, the first man of you that lifts his hand to strike, I'll shoot him down; so look to it. Slim Sampson, go back to your basket, and don't meddle in this business. Don't you suppose that I'm man enough to keep Loblolly Jack in order? You shall see."

It is not difficult for a determined white man to keep an Indian in subordination, so long as both of them are sober. A few words more convinced Loblolly Jack who had not yet reached the reckless stage in drunkenness, that his wiser course was to give back and keep quiet, which he did. The storm subsided almost as suddenly as it had been raised, and Colonel Harris resumed his occupation. Still, the Indian who had proved so troublesome before, continued his annoyances, though in a manner somewhat less audacious. His last pro-ceeding was to get as nigh as he could to the basket which was about to be weighed—his wife's basket—and, with the end of a stick, adroitly introduced into some little hole, he contrived to press the basket downwards, and thus to add so much to the weight of the cotton, that his squaw promised to bear off the palm of victory in that day's picking. Nobody saw the use to which the stick was put, and for a few mo-ments no one suspected it. Had the cunning fellow been more moderate, he might have succeeded in his attempt upon the steelyards; but his pressure increased with every ap-proach which was made to a determination of the weight, and while all was wondering that so small a basket should be so heavy, Slim Sampson discovered and pointed out the trick to Colonel Harris, who suddenly snatching the stick from the grasp of the Indian, was about to lay it over his head. But this my expostulation prevented; and, after some delay, the proceed-ings were finally ended; but in such a manner as to make my friend somewhat more doubtful than he had been before, on the subject of his experiment. He paid off their accounts, some in cloths and calicoes, of which he had provided a small supply for this purpose; but the greater number, under the evil influence of the idle and the elder, demanded and received their pay in money.

CHAPTER III.

It was probably about ten o'clock that evening. We had finished supper, and Col. H. and myself had resumed the sub-ject upon which we had been previously engaged. But the discussion was languid, and both of us were unquestionably lapsing into that state, when each readily receives an apology for retiring for the night, when we were startled from our drowsy tendencies by a wild and terrible cry, such as made me thrill instinctively with the conviction that something terrible had taken place. We started instantly to our feet, and threw open the door. The cry was more distinct and piercing, and its painful character could not be mistaken. It was a cry of death—of sudden terror, and great and angry excitement. Many voices were mingled together—some expressive of fury, some of fear, and many of lamentation. The tones which finally prevailed over, and continued long after all others had subsided, were those of women.

"These sounds come from the shop of that trader. These rascally Choctaws are drunk and fighting, and ten to one but somebody is killed among them!" was the exclamation of Col. H. "These sounds are familiar to me. I have heard them once before. They signify murder. It is a peculiar whoop which the Indians have, to denote the shedding of blood—to show that a crime has been committed."

The words had scarcely been uttered, before Slim Sampson came suddenly out into the road, and joined us at the door. Col. H. instantly asked him to enter, which he did. When he came fully into the light, we discovered that he had been drinking. His eyes bore sufficient testimony to the fact, though his drunkenness seemed to have subsided into something like stupor. His looks were heavy, rather than calm. He said nothing, but drew nigh to the fireplace, and seated himself upon one corner of the hearth. I now discovered that his hands and hunting shirt were stained with blood. His eyes beheld the bloody tokens at the same time, and he turned his hand curiously over, and examined it by the fire-light.

"Kurnel," said he, in broken English, "me is one dog fool!"

"How, Sampson?"

"Me drunk—me fight—me kill Loblolly Jack! Look ya!

Dis blood 'pon my hands. 'Tis Loblolly Jack blood! He
dead! I stick him wid de knife!"

"Impossible! What made you do it?"

"Me drunk! Me dog fool!—Drink whiskey at liquor shop
—hab money—buy whiskey—drunk come, and Loblolly Jack
dead!"

This was the substance of the story, which was confirmed a
few moments after, by the appearance of several other Indians, the friends of the two parties. From these it appeared
that all of them had been drinking, at the shop of Ligon, the
white man; that, when heated with liquor, both Loblolly
Jack and Slim Sampson had, as with one accord, resumed the
strife which had been arrested by the prompt interference of
Col. H.; that, from words they had got to blows, and the former had fallen, fatally hurt, by a single stroke from the other's
hand and knife.

The Indian law, like that of the Hebrews, is eye for eye,
tooth for tooth, life for life. The fate of Slim Sampson was
ordained. He was to die on the morrow. This was well
understood by himself as by all the rest. The wound of Loblolly Jack had proved mortal. He was already dead; and it
was arranged among the parties that Slim Sampson was to
remain that night, if permitted, at the house of Col. H., and
to come forth at early sunrise to execution. Col. H. declared
his willingness that the criminal should remain in his house;
but, at the same time, disclaimed all responsibility in the
business; and assured the old chief, whose name was "Rising
Smoke," that he would not be answerable for his appearance.

"He won't run," said the other, indifferently.

"But you will not put a watch over him—I will not suffer
more than the one to sleep in my house.

The old chief repeated his assurance that Slim Sampson
would not seek to fly. No guard was to be placed over him.
He was expected to remain quiet, and come forth to execution
at the hour appointed.

"He got for dead," continued Rising Smoke—"he know the law. He will come and dead like a man. Oakatibbé got big heart." Every word which the old fellow uttered went to mine.

What an eulogy was this upon Indian inflexibility! What confidence in the passive obedience of the warrior! After a little farther dialogue, they departed,—friends and enemies— and the unfortunate criminal was left with us alone. He still maintained his seat upon the hearth. His muscles were composed and calm—not rigid. His thoughts, however, were evidently busy; and, once or twice, I could see that his head was moved slowly from side to side, with an expression of mournful self-abandonment. I watched every movement and look with the deepest interest, while Col. H. with a concern necessarily deeper than my own, spoke with him freely, on the subject of his crime. It was, in fact, because of the affair of Col. H. that the unlucky deed was committed. It was true, that, for this, the latter gentleman was in no wise responsible; but that did not lessen, materially, the pain which he felt at having, however unwittingly, occasioned it. He spoke with the Indian in such terms of condolence as conventional usage among us has determined to be the most proper. He proffered to buy off the friends and relatives of the deceased, if the offence could be commuted for money. The poor fellow was very grateful, but at the same time, told him that the attempt was useless.—The tribe had never been known to permit such a thing, and the friends of Loblolly Jack were too much his enemies, to consent to any commutation of the penalty.

Col. H., however, was unsatisfied, and determined to try the experiment. The notion had only suggested itself to him after the departure of the Indians. He readily conjectured where he should find them, and we immediately set off for the grogshop of Ligon. This was little more than a quarter of a mile from the plantation. When we reached it, we found

the Indians, generally, in the worst possible condition to be
treated with. They were, most of them, in the last stages of
intoxication.   The dead body of the murdered man was
stretched out in the piazza, or gallery, half covered with a
bear-skin. The breast was bare—a broad, bold, manly bosom
—and the wound, a deep narrow gash, around which the
blood stood, clotted, in thick, frothy masses. The nearer relations of the deceased, were perhaps the most drunk of the
assembly. Their grief necessarily entitled them to the greatest
share of consolation, and this took the form of whiskey. Their
love of excess, and the means of indulgence, encouraged us
with the hope that their vengeance might be bought off without much difficulty, but we soon found ourselves very much
deceived. Every effort, every offer, proved fruitless : and
after vainly exhausting every art and argument, old Rising
Smoke drew us aside to tell us that the thing was impossible.

"Oakatibbé hab for die, and no use for talk. De law is
make for Oakatibbé, and Loblolly Jack, and me, Rising Smoke,
and all, just the same. Oakatibbé will dead to-morrow "

With sad hearts we left the maudlin and miserable assembly. When we returned, we found Slim Sampson employed
in carving with his knife upon the handle of his tomahawk.
In the space thus made, he introduced a small bit of flattened
silver, which seemed to have been used for a like purpose on
some previous occasion. It was rudely shaped like a bird,
and was probably one of those trifling ornaments which
usually decorate the stocks of rifle and shot-gun. I looked
with increasing concern upon his countenance. What could
a spectator—one unacquainted with the circumstances—have
met with there ? Nothing, surely, of that awful event which
had just taken place, and of that doom which now seemed so
certainly to await him. He betrayed no sort of interest in
our mission. His look and manner denoted his own perfect
conviction of its inutility ; and when we told him what had
taken place, he neither answered nor looked up.

It would be difficult to describe my feelings and those of my companion. The more we reflected upon the affair, the more painful and oppressive did our thoughts become. A pain, little short of horror, coupled itself with every emotion. We left the Indian still beside the fire. He had begun a low chanting song just before we retired, in his own language, which was meant as a narrative of the chief events of his life. The death song—for such it was—is neither more nor less than a recital of those deeds which it will be creditable to a son or a relative to remember. In this way the valour of their great men, and the leading events in their history, are transmitted through successive ages. He was evidently refreshing his own memory in preparation for the morrow. He was arranging the narrative of the past, in proper form for the acceptance of the future.

We did not choose to disturb him in this vocation, and retired. When we had got to our chamber, H., who already had one boot off, exclaimed suddenly—" Look you, S., this fellow ought not to perish in this manner. We should make an effort to save him. We must save him!"

" What will you do?"

" Come—let us go back and try and urge him to flight. He can escape easily while all these fellows are drunk. He shall have my best horse for the purpose."

We returned to the apartment.

" Slim Sampson."

" Kurnel!" was the calm reply.

" There's no sense in your staying here to be shot."

" Ugh!" was the only answer, but in an assenting tone.

" You're not a bad fellow—you didn't mean to kill Loblolly Jack—it's very hard that you should die for what you didn't wish to do. You're too young to die. You've got a great many years to live. You ought to live to be an old man and have sons like yourself; and there's a great deal of happiness

K

in this world, if a man only knows where to look for it. But
a man that's dead is of no use to himself, or to his friends, or
his enemies. Why should you die—why should you be shot?"

"Eh ?"

"Hear me ; your people are all drunk at Ligon's—blind
drunk—deaf drunk—they can neither see nor hear. They
won't get sober till morning—perhaps not then. You've been
across the Mississippi, hav'nt you ? You know the way ?"

The reply was affirmative.

"Many Choctaws live over the Mississippi now—on the
Red River, and far beyond, to the Red Hills. Go to them—
they will take you by the hand—they will give you one of
their daughters to wife—they will love you—they will make
you a chief. Fly, Sampson, fly to them—you shall have one
of my horses, and before daylight you will be down the country, among the white people, and far from your enemies—Go,
my good fellow, it would be a great pity that so brave a man
should die."

This was the substance of my friend's exhortation. It was
put into every shape, and addressed to every fear, hope, or
passion which might possibly have influence over the human
bosom. A strong conflict took place in the mind of the Indian,
the outward signs of which were not wholly suppressible. He
started to his feet, trod the floor hurriedly, and there was a
tremulous quickness in the movement of his eyes, and a dilation of their orbs, which amply denoted the extent of his emotion. He turned suddenly upon us, when H. had finished
speaking, and replied in language very nearly like the following :—

"I love the whites—I was always a friend to the whites. I
believe I love their laws better than my own. Loblolly Jack
laughed at me because I loved the whites, and wanted our
people to live like them. But I am of no use now. I can
love them no more. My people say that I must die. How
can I live ?"

Such was the purport of his answer. The meaning of it
was simple. He was not unwilling to avail himself of the
suggestions of my friend—to fly—to live—but he could not
divest himself of that habitual deference to those laws to
which he had given implicit reverence from the beginning.
Custom is the superior tyrant of all savage nations.

To embolden him on this subject was now the joint object
of Col. H. and myself. We spared no argument to convince
him that he ought to fly. It was something in favour of
our object that the Indian regards the white man as so infinitely his superior; and, in the case of Slim Sampson, we
were assisted by his own inclinations in favour of those cus-
toms of the whites, which he had already in part begun to
adopt. We discussed for his benefit that which may be considered one of the leading elements in civilization—the duty
of saving and keeping life as long as we can—insisted upon
the morality of flying from any punishment which would deprive us of it; and at length had the satisfaction of seeing
him convinced. He yielded to our arguments and solicitations,
accepted the horse, which he promised voluntarily to find
some early means to return, and, with a sigh—perhaps one of
the first proofs of that change of feeling and of principle
which he had just shown, he declared his intention to take
the road instantly.

" Go to bed, Kurnel. Your horse will come back." We
retired, and a few moments after heard him leave the house.
I am sure that both of us felt a degree of light-heartedness
which scarcely any other event could have produced. We
could not sleep, however. For myself I answer—it was almost dawn before I fell into an uncertain slumber, filled with
visions of scuffling Indians—the stark corse of Loblolly Jack
being the conspicuous object, and Slim Sampson standing up
for execution.

CHAPTER IV.

NEITHER Col. H. nor myself arose at a very early hour. Our first thoughts and feelings at waking were those of exultation. We rejoiced that we had been instrumental in saving from an ignominious death, a fellow creature, and one who seemed so worthy, in so many respects. Our exultation was not a little increased, as we reflected on the disappointment of his enemies; and we enjoyed a hearty laugh together, as we talked over the matter while putting on our clothes. When we looked from the window the area in front of the house was covered with Indians. They sat, or stood, or walked, all around the dwelling. The hour appointed for the delivery of Slim Sampson had passed, yet they betrayed no emotion. We fancied, however, that we could discern in the countenances of most among them, the sentiment of friendship or hostility for the criminal, by which they were severally governed. A dark, fiery look of exultation— grim anticipation of delight— was evident in the faces of his enemies; while, among his friends, men and women, a subdued concern and humbling sadness, were the prevailing traits of expression.

But when we went below to meet them—when it became known that the murderer had fled, taking with him the best horse of the proprietor, the outbreak was tremendous. A terrible yell went up from the party devoted to Loblolly Jack; while the friends and relatives of Slim Sampson at once sprang to their weapons, and put themselves in an attitude of defence. We had not foreseen the effects of our interposition and advice. We did not know, or recollect, that the nearest connection of the criminal, among the Indian tribes, in the event of his escape, would be required to suffer in his place; and this, by the way, is the grand source of that security which they felt the night before, that flight would not be attempted by the destined victim. The aspect of affairs looked squally. Already was the bow bent and the tomahawk lifted. Already had the parties separated, each going to his own side, and ranging himself in front of some one opponent. The women sunk rapidly into the rear, and provided themselves with billets or fence rails, as they occurred to their hands; while little brats of boys, ten and twelve years old, kept up a continual shrill clamour, brandishing aloft their tiny bows and *blow-guns*, which were only powerful against the lapwing and the sparrow. In political phrase, " a great crisis was at hand." The stealthier chiefs and leaders of both sides, had sunk from sight, behind the trees or houses, in order to avail themselves of all the arts of Indian strategy. Every thing promised a sudden and stern conflict. At the first show of commotion, Col H. had armed himself. I had been well provided with pistols and bowie knife, before leaving home; and, apprehending the worst, we yet took our places as peacemakers, between the contending parties.

It is highly probable that all our interposition would have been fruitless to prevent their collision; and, though our position certainly delayed the progress of the quarrel, yet all we could have hoped to effect by our interference would have been the removal of the combatants to a more remote battle ground. But a circumstance that surprised and disappointed us all, took place, to settle the strife for ever, and to reconcile the parties without any resort to blows. While the turmoil was at the highest, and we had despaired of doing any thing to prevent bloodshed, the tramp of a fast galloping horse was heard in the woods, and the next moment the steed of Col. H· made his appearance, covered with foam, Slim Sampson on his back, and still driven by the lash of his rider at the top of his speed. He leaped the enclosure, and was drawn up still quivering in every limb, in the area between the opposing Indians. The countenance of the noble fellow told his story. His heart had smitten him by continual reproaches, at the

adoption of a conduct unknown in his nation; and which all
its hereditary opinions had made cowardly and infamous.
Besides, he remembered the penalties which, in consequence
of his flight, must fall heavily upon his people. Life was sweet
to him—very sweet! He had the promise of many bright
years before him. His mind was full of honourable and—
speaking in comparative phrase—lofty purposes, for the im-
provement of himself and nation. We have already sought to
show that, by his conduct, he had taken one large step in resistance to the tyrannous usages of custom, in order to introduce the elements of civilization among his people. But he
could not withstand the reproaches of a conscience formed
upon principles which his own genius was not equal to overthrow. His thoughts, during his flight, must have been of a
very humbling character; but his feature now denoted only
pride, exultation and a spirit strengthened by resignation
against the worst. By his flight and subsequent return, he
had, in fact, exhibited a more lively spectacle of moral firmness, than would have been displayed by his simple submis-
sion in remaining. He seemed to feel this. It looked out
from his soul in every movement of his body. He leaped from
his horse, exclaiming, while he slapped his breast with his
open palm :

"Oakatibbé heard the voice of a chief, that said he must
die. Let the chief look here—Oakatibbé is come.

A shout went up from both parties. The signs of strife disappeared. The language of the crowd was no longer that of
threatening and violence. It was understood that there would
be no resistance in behalf of the condemned. Col. H. and myself, were both mortified and disappointed. Though the return of Slim Sampson, had obviously prevented a combat *á
outrance*, in which a dozen or more might have been slain,
still we could not but regret the event. The life of such a
fellow seemed to both of us, to be worth the lives of any hundred of his people.

Never did man carry himself with more simple nobleness He was at once surrounded by his friends and relatives. The hostile party, from whom the executioners were to be drawn, stood looking on at some little distance, the very pictures of patience. There was no sort of disposition manifested among them, to hurry the proceedings. Though exulting in the prospect of soon shedding the blood of one whom they esteemed an enemy, yet all was dignified composure and forbearance. The signs of exultation where no where to be seen. Meanwhile, a conversation was carried on in low, soft accents, unmarked by physical action of any kind, between the condemned and two other Indians. One of these was the unhappy mother of the criminal—the other was his uncle. They rather listened to his remarks, than made any of their own. The dialogue was conducted in their own language. After a while this ceased, and he made a signal which seemed to be felt, rather than understood, by all the Indians, friends and enemies. All of them started into instant intelligence. It was a sign that he was ready for the final proceedings. He rose to his feet and they surrounded him. The groans of the old woman, his mother, were now distinctly audible, and she was led away by the uncle, who, placing her among the other women, returned to the condemned, beside whom he now took his place. Col. H. and myself, also, drew nigh. Seeing us, Oakatibbé simply said, with a smile:

"Ah, kurnel, you see Injun man ain't strong like white man!"

Col. H. answered with emotion.

"I would have saved you, Sampson."

"Oakatibbé hab for dead!" said the worthy fellow, with another, but a very wretched smile.

His firmness was unabated. A procession was formed, which was headed by three sturdy fellows, carrying their rifles conspicuously upon their shoulders. These were the appointed executioners, and were all near relatives of the man

who had been slain. There was no mercy in their looks·
Oakatibbé followed immediately after these. He seemed
pleased that we should accompany him to the place of execution. Our way lay through a long avenue of stunted pines,
which conducted us to a spot where an elevated ridge on
either hand produced a broad and very prettily defined valley.
My eyes, in all this progress, were scarcely ever drawn off
from the person of him who was to be the principal actor in
the approaching scene. Never, on any occasion, did I behold
a man with a step more firm—a head so unbent—a countenance
so sweetly calm, though grave—and of such quiet unconcern,
at the obvious fate in view. Yet there was nothing in his deportment of that effort which would be the case with most
white men on a similar occasion, who seek to wear the aspect
of heroism. He walked as to a victory, but he walked with a
staid, even dignity, calmly, and without the flush of any excitement on his cheek. In his eye there was none of that
feverish curiosity, which seeks for the presence of his execu-
tioner, and cannot be averted from the contemplation of the
mournful paraphernalia of death. His look was like that of
the strong man, conscious of his inevitable doom, and prepared, as it is inevitable, to meet it with corresponding indifference.

The grave was now before us. It must have been prepared
at the first dawn of the morning. The executioners paused,
when they had reached a spot within thirty steps of it. But
the condemned passed on, and stopped only on the edge of its
open jaws. The last trial was at hand with all its terrors.
The curtain was about to drop, and the scene of life, with all
its hopes and promises and golden joys—even to an Indian
golden—was to be shut forever. I felt a painful and numbing
chill pass through my frame, but I could behold no sign of
change in him. He now beckoned his friends around him.
His enemies drew nigh also, but in a remoter circle. He was
about to commence his song of death—the narrative of his

performances, his purposes, all his living experience. He began a low chant, slow, measured and composed, the words
seeming to consist of monosyllables only. As he proceeded,
his eyes kindled, and his arms were extended. His action became impassioned, his utterance more rapid, and the tones
were distinguished by increasing warmth. I could not understand a single word which he uttered, but the cadences were
true and full of significance. The rise and fall of his voice,
truly proportioned to the links of sound by which they were
connected, would have yielded a fine lesson to the European
teacher of school eloquence. His action was as graceful as
that of a mighty tree yielding to, and gradually rising from,
the pressure of a sudden gust. I felt the eloquence which I
could not understand. I fancied, from his tones and gestures,
the play of the muscles of his mouth, and the dilation of his
eyes, that I could detect the instances of daring valour, or good
conduct, which his narrative comprised. One portion of it, as
he approached the close, I certainly could not fail to comprehend. He evidently spoke of his last unhappy affray with the
man whom he had slain. His head was bowed—the light
passed from his eyes, his hands were folded upon his heart, and
his voice grew thick and husky. Then came the narrative of
his flight. His glance was turned upon Col. H. and myself,
and, at the close, he extended his hand to us both. We grasped
it earnestly, and with a degree of emotion which I would not
now seek to describe. He paused. The catastrophe was at
hand. I saw him step back, so as to place himself at the very
verge of the grave—he then threw open his breast—a broad,
manly, muscular bosom, that would have sufficed for a Her-
cules—one hand he struck upon the spot above the heart,
where it remained—the other was raised above his head. This
was the signal. I turned away with a strange sickness. I
could look no longer. In the next instant I heard the simul-
taneous report, as one, of the three rifles ; and when I again

looked, they were shoveling in the fresh mould, upon the noble
form of one, who, under other more favourable circumstances,
might have been a father to his nation.

JOCASSEE.

A CHEROKEE LEGEND.

CHAPTER I.

" KEOWEE Old Fort," as the people in that quarter style it, is
a fine antique ruin and relic of the revolution, in the district
of Pendleton, South Carolina. The region of country in which
we find it is, of itself, highly picturesque and interesting. The
broad river of Keowee, which runs through it, though comparatively small as a stream in America, would put to shame, by
its size not less than its beauty, one half of the far-famed
and boasted rivers of Europe;—and then the mountains,
through and among which it winds its way, embody more of
beautiful situation and romantic prospect, than art can well
figure to the eye, or language convey to the imagination. To
understand, you must see it. Words are of little avail when
the ideas overcrowd utterance; and even vanity itself is content to be dumb in the awe inspired by a thousand prospects,
like Niagara, the ideals of a god, and altogether beyond the
standards common to humanity.

It is not long since I wandered through this interesting region, under the guidance of my friend, Col. G——, who does
the honours of society, in that quarter, with a degree of ease
and unostentatious simplicity, which readily makes the visiter
at home. My friend was one of those citizens to whom one's
own country is always of paramount interest, and whose mind
and memory, accordingly, have been always most happily em-

ployed when storing away and digesting into pleasing narrative those thousand little traditions of the local genius, which give life to rocks and valleys, and people earth with the beautiful colours and creatures of the imagination. These, for the gratification of the spiritual seeker, he had forever in readiness; and, with him to illustrate them, it is not surprising if the grove had a moral existence in my thoughts, and all the waters around breathed and were instinct with poetry. To all his narratives I listened with a satisfaction which book-stories do not often afford me. The more he told, the more he had to tell; for nothing staled

" His infinite variety."

There may have been something in the style of telling his stories; there was much, certainly, that was highly attractive in his manner of doing every thing, and this may have contributed not a little to the success of his narratives. Perhaps, too, my presence, upon the very scene of each legend, may have given them a life and a *vraisemblance* they had wanted otherwise.

In this manner, rambling about from spot to spot, I passed five weeks, without being, at any moment, conscious of time's progress. Day after day, we wandered forth in some new direction, contriving always to secure, and without effort, that pleasurable excitement of novelty, for which the great city labours in vain, spite of her varying fashions, and crowding, and not always innocent indulgences. From forest to river, from hill to valley, still on horseback,—for the mountainous character of the country forbade any more luxurious form of travel,—we kept on our way, always changing our ground with the night, and our prospect with the morning. In this manner we travelled over or round the Six Mile, and the Glassy, and a dozen other mountains; and sometimes, with a yet greater scope of adventure, pushed off on a much longer ramble,—such as took us to the falls of the White Water, and

gave us a glimpse of the beautiful river of Jocassée, named
sweetly after the Cherokee maiden, who threw herself into its
bosom on beholding the scalp of her lover dangling from the
neck of his conqueror.   The story is almost a parallel to that
of the sister of Horatius, with this difference, that the Cherokee girl did not wait for the vengeance of her brother, and altogether spared her reproaches.   I tell the story, which is
pleasant and curious, in the language of my friend, from whom
I first heard it.

   " The Occonies and the Little Estatoees, or, rather, the
Brown Vipers and the Green Birds, were both minor tribes of
the Cherokee nation, between whom, as was not unfrequently
the case, there sprung up a deadly enmity.   The Estatoees
had their town on each side of the two creeks, which, to this
day, keep their name, and on the eastern side of the Keowee
river.   The Occonies occupied a much larger extent of territory, but it lay on the opposite, or west side of the same
stream.   Their differences were supposed to have arisen from
the defeat of Chatuga, a favourite leader of the Occonies, who
aimed to be made a chief of the nation at large.   The Estatoee
warrior, Toxaway, was successful; and as the influence of
Chatuga was considerable with his tribe, he laboured success-
fully to engender in their bosoms a bitter dislike of the Estatoees.   This feeling was made to exhibit itself on every possible occasion.   The Occonies had no word too foul by which
to describe the Estatoees.   They likened them, in familiar
speech, to every thing which, in the Indian imagination, is accounted low and contemptible.   In reference to war, they were
reputed women—in all other respects, they were compared to
dogs and vermin ; and, with something of a Christian taste
and temper, they did not scruple, now and then, to invoke the
devil of their more barbarous creed, for the eternal disquiet of
their successful neighbours, the Little Estatoees, and their
great chief, Toxaway.

   " In this condition of things there could not be much

in and form this beautiful valley. With the first glimpse of
his prey flew the keen shaft of Nagoochie; but, strange to say,
though renowned as a hunter, not less than a warrior, the
arrow failed entirely and flew wide of the victim. Off he
bounded headlong after the fortunate buck; but though, every
now and then getting him within range,—for the buck took
the pursuit coolly,—the hunter still most unaccountably failed
to strike him. Shaft after shaft had fallen seemingly hurtless
from his sides; and though, at frequent intervals, suffered to
approach so nigh to the animal that he could not but hope
still for better fortune, to his great surprise, the wary buck
would dash off when he least expected it, bounding away in
some new direction, with as much life and vigour as ever.
What to think of this, the hunter knew not; but such repeated
disappointments at length impressed it strongly upon his
mind, that the object he pursued was neither more nor less
than an Occony wizard, seeking to entrap him; so, with a
due feeling of superstition, and a small touch of sectional
venom aroused into action within his heart, Nagoochie, after
the manner of his people, promised a green bird—the emblem
of his tribe—in sacrifice to the tuelar divinity of Estato, if he
could only be permitted to overcome the potent enchanter,
who had thus dazzled his aim and blunted his arrows. He
had hardly uttered this vow, when he beheld the insolent deer
mincingly grazing upon a beautiful tuft of long grass in the
valley, just below the ledge of rock upon which he stood.
Without more ado, he pressed onward to bring him within
fair range of his arrows, little doubting at the moment that
the Good Spirit had heard his prayer and had granted his
desire. But, in his hurry, leaping too hastily forward, and
with eyes fixed only upon his proposed victim, his foot was
caught by the smallest stump in the world, and the very next
moment found him precipitated directly over the rock and into
the valley, within a few paces of the deer, who made off with
the utmost composure, gazing back, as he did so, in the eyes

of the wounded hunter, for all the world, as if he enjoyed the
sport mightily. Nagoochie, as he saw this, gravely concluded
that he had fallen a victim to the wiles of the Occony
wizard, and looked confidently to see half a score of Occonies
upon him, taking him at a vantage, Like a brave warrior,
however, he did not despond, but determining to gather up
his loins for battle and the torture, he sought to rise and put
himself in a state of preparation. What, however, was his
horror, to find himself utterly unable to move;—his leg had
been broken in the fall, and he was covered with bruises from
head to foot.

"Nagoochie gave himself up for lost; but he had scarcely
done so, when he heard a voice,—the sweetest, he thought, he
had ever heard in his life,—singing a wild, pleasant song, such
as the Occonies love, which, ingeniously enough, summed up
the sundry reasons why the mouth, and not the eyes, had been
endowed with the faculty of eating. These reasons were
many, but the last is quite enough for us. According to the
song, had the eyes, and not the mouth, been employed for this
purpose, there would soon be a famine in the land, for of all
gluttons, the eyes are the greatest. Nagoochie groaned aloud
as he heard the song, the latter portion of which completely
indicated the cause of his present misfortune. It was, indeed,
the gluttony of the eyes which had broken his leg. This sort
of allegory the Indians are fond of, and Jocassée knew all
their legends. Certainly, thought Nagoochie, though his leg
pained him wofully at the time, 'certainly I never heard such
sweet music, and such a voice.' The singer advanced as she
sung, and almost stumbled over him.

"'Who are you?' she asked timidly, neither retreating nor
advancing; and as the wounded man looked into her face, he
blessed the Occony wizard, by whose management he deemed
his leg to have been broken.

"'Look!' was the reply of the young warrior, throwing
aside the bearskin which covered his bosom,—'look, girl of

Occony! 'tis the *totem* of a chief;' and the green bird stamped
upon his left breast, as the badge of his tribe, showed him a
warrior of Estato, and something of any enemy.   But his eyes
had no enmity, and then the broken leg! Jocassée was a
gentle maiden, and her heart melted with the condition of the
warrior.   She made him a sweet promise, in very pretty language, and with the very same voice the music of which was
so delicious; and then, with the fleetness of a young doe, she
went off to bring him succour.

CHAPTER II.

" NIGHT, in the meanwhile, came on; and the long howl of
of the wolf, as he looked down from the crag, and waited for
the thick darkness in which to descend the valley, came freez-
ingly to the ear of Nagoochie. ' Surely,' he said to himself,
' the girl of Occony will come back. She has too sweet a
voice not to keep her word. She will certainly come back.'
While he doubted, he believed. Indeed, though still a very
young maiden, the eyes of Jocassée had in them a great deal
that was good for little beside, than to persuade and force
conviction ; and the belief in them was pretty extensive in the
circle of her rustic acquaintance.   All people love to believe
in fine eyes, and nothing is more natural than for lovers to
swear by them.   Nagoochie did not swear by those of Jocassée, but he did most religiously believe in them ; and though
the night gathered fast, and the long howl of the wolf came
close from his crag, down into the valley, the young hunter of
the green bird did not despair of the return of the maiden.

" She did return, and the warrior was insensible. But the
motion stirred him; the lights gleamed upon him from many
torches ; he opened his eyes, and when they rested upon Jocassée, they forgot to close again. She had brought aid

enough, for her voice was powerful as well as musical; and, taking due care that the totem of the green bird should be carefully concealed by the bearskin, with which her own hands covered his bosom, she had him lifted upon a litter, constructed of several young saplings, which, interlaced with withes, binding it closely together, and strewn thickly with leaves, made a couch as soft as the wounded man could desire. In a few hours, and the form of Nagoochie rested beneath the roof of Attakulla, the sire of Jocassée. She sat beside the young hunter, and it was her hand that placed the fever balm upon his lips, and poured into his wounds and bruises the strong and efficacious balsams of Indian pharmacy.

"Never was nurse more careful of her charge. Day and night she watched by him, and few were the hours which she then required for her own pleasure or repose. Yet why was Jocassée so devoted to the stranger? She never asked herself so unnecessary a question; but as she was never so well satisfied, seemingly; as when near him, the probability is she found pleasure in her tendance. It was fortunate for him and for her, that her father was not rancorous towards the people of the Green Bird, like the rest of the Occonies. It might have fared hard with Nagoochie otherwise. But Attakulla was a wise old man, and a good; and when they brought the wounded stranger to his lodge, he freely yielded him shelter, and went forth himself to Chinabee, the wise medicine of the Occonies. The eyes of Nagoochie were turned upon the old chief, and when he heard his name, and began to consider where he was, he was unwilling to task the hospitality of one who might be disposed to regard him, when known, in an unfavourable or hostile light. Throwing aside, therefore, the habit of circumspection, which usually distinguishes the Indian warrior, he uncovered his bosom, and bade the old man look upon the totem of his people, precisely as he had done when his eye first met that of Jocassée.

" ' Thy name ? What do the people of the Green Bird call the young hunter ?' asked Attakulla.

" ' They name Nagoochie among the braves of the Estato : they will call him a chief of the Cherokee, like Toxaway,' was the proud reply.

" This reference was to a sore subject with the Occonies, and perhaps it was quite as imprudent as it certainly was in improper taste for him to make it. But, knowing where he was, excited by fever, and having—to say much in little—but an unfavourable opinion of Occony magnanimity, he was more rash than reasonable. At that moment, too, Jocassée had made her appearance, and the spirit of the young warrior, desiring to look big in her eyes, had prompted him to a fierce speech not altogether necessary. He knew not the generous nature of Attakulla ; and when the old man took him by the hand, spoke well of the Green Bird, and called him his ' son,' the pride of Nagoochie was something humbled, while his heart grew gentler than ever. His ' son !'—that was the pleasant part ; and as the thoughts grew more and more active in his fevered brain, he looked to Jocassée with such a passionate admiration that she sunk back with a happy smile from the flame-glance which he set upon her. And, day after day she tended him until the fever passed off, and the broken limb was set and had re-knitted, and the bruises were all healed upon him. Yet he lingered. He did not think himself quite well, and she always agreed with him in opinion. Once and again did he set off, determined not to return, but his limb pained him, and he felt the fever come back whenever he thought of Jocassée ; and so the evening found him again at the lodge, while the fever-balm, carefully bruised in milk, was in as great demand as ever for the invalid. But the spirit of the warrior at length grew ashamed of these weaknesses ; and, with a desperate effort, for which he gave himself no little credit, he completed his determination to depart with the coming of the new moon. But even this decision was only

effected by compromise. Love settled the affair with conscience, after his own fashion ; and, under his direction, following the dusky maiden into the little grove that stood beside the cottage, Nagoochie claimed her to fill the lodge of a
young warrior of the Green Bird. She broke the wand which
he presented her, and seizing upon the torch which she carried,
he buried it in the bosom of a neighbouring brook; and thus,
after their simple forest ceremonial, Jocassée became the be-
trothed of Nagoochie.

CHAPTER III.

" BUT we must keep this secret to ourselves, for as yet it remained unknown to Attakulla, and the time could not come
for its revealment until the young warrior had gone home to
his people. Jocassée was not so sure that all parties would
be so ready as herself to sanction her proceeding. Of her father's willingness, she had no question, for she knew his good
nature and good sense; but she had a brother of whom she
had many fears and misgivings. He was away, on a great
hunt of the young men, up at Charashilactay, or the falls of
the White Water, as we call it to this day—a beautiful cas-
cade of nearly forty feet, the water of which is of a milky
complexion. How she longed, yet how she dreaded, to see
that brother ! He was a fierce, impetuous, sanguinary youth,
who, to these characteristics, added another still more dis-
tasteful to Jocassée ;—there was not a man among all the
Occonies who so hated the people of the Green Bird as
Cheochee. What hopes, or rather what fears, were in the
bosom of that maiden !

" But he came not. Day after day they looked for his return, and yet he came not; but in his place a runner, with a
bearded stick, a stick covered with slips of skin, torn from

the body of a wolf. The runner passed by the lodge of Attakulla, and all its inmates were aroused by the intelligence he brought. A wolf-hunt was commanded by Moitoy, the great war-chief or generalissimo of the Cherokee nation, to take place, instantly, at Charashilactay, where an immense body of wolves had herded together, and had become troublesome neighbours. Old and young, who had either taste for the adventure, or curiosity to behold it, at once set off upon the summons; and Attakulla, old as he was, and Nagoochie, whose own great prowess in hunting had made it a passion, determined readily upon the journey. Jocassee, too, joined the company,—for the maidens of Cherokee were bold spirits, as well as beautiful, and loved to ramble, particularly when, as in the present instance, they went forth in company with their lovers. Lodge after lodge, as they pursued their way, poured forth its inmates, who joined them in their progress, until the company had swollen into a goodly caravan, full of life, anxious for sport, and carrying, as is the fashion among the Indians, provisions of smoked venison and parched grain, in plenty, for many days.

" They came at length to the swelling hills, the long narrow valleys of the Keochee and its tribute river of Toxaway, named after that chief of the Little Estatoees, of whom we have already heard something. At one and the same moment they beheld the white waters of Charashilactay, plunging over the precipice, and the hundred lodges of the Cherokee hunters. There they had gathered—the warriors and their women— twenty different tribes of the same great nation being represented on the ground ; each tribe having its own cluster of cabins, and rising up, in the midst of each, the long pole on which hung the peculiar emblem of the clan. It was not long before Nagoochie marshalled himself along with his brother Estatoees—who had counted him lost—under the beautiful green bird of his tribe, which waved about in the wind, over the heads of their small community.

" The number of warriors representing the Estato in that great hunt was inconsiderable—but fourteen—and the accession, therefore, of so promising a brave as Nagoochie, was no small matter. They shouted with joy at his coming, and danced gladly in the ring between the lodges—the young women in proper taste, and with due spirit, hailing, with a sweet song, the return of so handsome a youth, and one who was yet unmarried.

" Over against the lodges of the Estatoees, lay the more imposing encampment of the rival Occonies, who turned out strongly, as it happened, on this occasion. They were more numerous than any other of the assembled tribes, as the hunt was to take place on a portion of their own territory. Conscious of their superiority, they had not, you may be sure forborne any of the thousand sneers and sarcasms which they were never at a loss to find when they spoke of the Green Bird warriors ; and of all their clan, none was so bitter, so uncompromising, generally, in look, speech, and action, as Cheochee, the fierce brother of the beautiful Jocassée. Scorn was in his eye, and sarcasm on his lips, when he heard the rejoicings made by the Estatoees on the return of the long-lost hunter.

" ' Now wherefore screams the painted bird to-day ? why makes he a loud cry in the ears of the brown viper than can strike ?' he exclaimed contemptuously yet fiercely.

" It was Jocassée that spoke in reply to her brother, with the quickness of woman's feeling, which they wrong greatly who hold it subservient to the strength of woman's cunning. In her reply, Cheochee saw the weakness of her heart.

" ' They scream for Nagoochie,' said the girl ; ' it is joy that the young hunter comes back that makes the great bird to sing to-day.'

" ' Has Jocassée taken a tongue from the green bird, that she screams in the ears of the brown viper ? What has the

girl to do with the thoughts of the warrior ?   Let her go—go,
bring drink to Cheochee.'

"Abashed and silent, she did as he commanded, and brought
meekly to the fierce brother, a gourd filled with the bitter
beverage which the Cherokees love. She had nothing further
to say on the subject of the Green Bird warrior, for whom she
had already so unwarily spoken. But her words had not
fallen unregarded upon the ears of Cheochee, nor had the look
of the fond heart which spoke out in her glance, passed unseen by the keen eye of that jealous brother. He had long before this heard of the great fame of Nagoochie as a hunter,
and in his ire he was bent to surpass him. Envy had grown
into hate, when he heard that this great reputation was that
of one of the accursed Estatoees; and, not satisfied with the
desire to emulate, he also aimed to destroy. This feeling
worked like so much gall in his bosom; and when his eyes
looked upon the fine form of Nagoochie, and beheld its sym-
metry, grace and manhood, his desire grew into a furious passion which made him sleepless. The old chief, Attakulla, his
father, told him all the story of Nagoochie's accident—how
Jocassée had found him; and how, in his own lodge, he had
been nursed and tended. The old man spoke approvingly of
Nagoochie ; and, the better to bring about a good feeling for
her lover, Jocassée humbled herself greatly to her brother,—
anticipated his desires, and studiously sought to serve him.
But all this failed to effect a favourable emotion in the breast
of the malignant young savage towards the young hunter of
the Green Bird. He said nothing, however, of his feelings ;
but they looked out and were alive to the sight, in every aspect, whenever any reference, however small, was made to
the subject of his ire. The Indian passion is subtlety, and
Cheochee was a warrior already famous among the old chiefs
of Cherokee.

CHAPTER IV.

" THE next day came the commencement of the great hunt, and the warriors were up betimes and active. Stations were chosen, the keepers of which, converging to a centre, were to hem in the wild animal on whose tracks they were going. The wolves were known to be in a hollow of the hills, near Charashilactay, which had but one outlet; and points of close approximation across this outlet were the stations of honour; for, goaded by the hunters to this passage, and failing of egress in any other, the wolf, it was well known, would then be dangerous in the extreme. Well calculated to provoke into greater activity the jealousies between the Occonies and the Green Birds, was the assignment made by Moitoy, the chief, of the more dangerous of these stations to these two clans. They now stood alongside of one another, and the action of the two promised to be joint and corresponsive. Such an appointment, in the close encounter with the wolf, necessarily promised to bring the two parties into immediate contact; and such was the event. As the day advanced, and the hunters, contracting their circles, brought the different bands of wolves into one, and pressed upon them to the more obvious and indeed the only outlet, the badges of the Green Bird and the Brown Viper—the one consisting of the stuffed skin and plumage of the Carolina parrot, and the other the attenuated viper, filled out with moss, and winding, with erect head, around the pole, to the top of which it was stuck—were, at one moment, in the indiscriminate hunt, almost mingled over the heads of the two parties. Such a sight was pleasant to neither, and would, at another time, of a certainty, have brought about a squabble. As it was, the Occonies drove their badge-carrier from one to the other end of their ranks, thus studiously avoiding the chance of another collision between the viper so adored, and the green bird so detested. The pride of the Estatoees was exceedingly aroused at this exhibition of impertinence, and though a quiet people enough, they began to think that forbearance had been misplaced in their relations with their presumptuous and hostile neighbours. Had it not been for Nagoochie, who had his own reasons for suffering yet more, the Green Birds would certainly have plucked out the eyes of the Brown Vipers, or tried very hard to do it; but the exhortations to peace of the young warrior, and the near neighbourhood of the wolf, quelled any open show of the violence they meditated; but, Indian-like, they determined to wait for the moment of greatest quiet, as that most fitted for taking away a few scalps from the Occony. With a muttered curse, and a contemptuous slap of the hand upon their thighs, the more furious among the Estatooees satisfied their present anger, and then addressed themselves more directly to the business before them.

" The wolves, goaded to desperation by the sight and sound of hunters strewn all over the hills around them, were now, snapping and snarling, and with eyes that flashed with a terrible anger, descending the narrow gully towards the outlet held by the two rival tribes. United action was therefore demanded of those who, for a long time past, had been conscious of no feeling or movement in common. But here they had no choice—no time, indeed, to think. The fierce wolves were upon them, doubly furious at finding the only passage stuck full of enemies. Well and manfully did the hunters stand and seek the encounter with the infuriated beasts. The knife and the hatchet, that day, in the hand of Occony and Estato, did fearful execution. The Brown Vipers fought nobly, and with their ancient reputation. But the Green Birds were the hunters, after all; and they were now stimulated into double adventure and effort, by an honourable ambition to make up for all deficiencies of number by extra valour, and the careful exercise of all that skill in the arts of hunting for which they

have always been the most renowned of the tribes of Cherokee.
As, one by one, a fearful train, the wolves wound into sight
along this or that crag of the gully, arrow after arrow told
fearfully upon them, for there were no marksmen like the Estatoees. Nor did they stop at this weapon. The young Nagoochie, more than ever prompted to such audacity, led the
way ; and dashing into the very path of the teeth-gnashing
and claw-rending enemy, he grasped in desperate fight the
first that offered himself, and as the wide jaws of his hairy foe
opened upon him, with a fearful plunge at his side, adroitly
leaping to the right, he thrust a pointed stick down, deep, as
far as he could send it, into the monster's throat, then pressing back upon him, with the rapidity of an arrow, in spite of
all his fearful writhings he pinned him to the ground, while
his knife, in a moment after, played fatally in his heart.
Another came, and, in a second, his hatchet cleft and crunched
deep into the skull of the angry brute, leaving him senseless,
without need of a second stroke. There was no rivalling
deeds of valour so desperate as this ; and with increased bitterness of soul did Cheochee and his followers hate in proportion as they admired. They saw the day close, and heard the
signal calling them to the presence of the great chief Moitoy,
conscious, though superior in numbers, they could not at all
compare in skill and success with the long-despised, but now
thoroughly-hated Estatoees.

" And still more great the vexation, still more deadly the
hate, when the prize was bestowed by the hand of Moitoy,
the great military chief of Cherokee—when, calling around
him the tribes, and carefully counting the number of their
several spoils, consisting of the skins of the wolves that had
been slain, it was found that of these the greater number, in
proportion to their force, had fallen victims to the superior
skill or superior daring of the people of the Green Bird. And
who had been their leader ? The rambling Nagoochie—the
L

young hunter who had broken his leg among the crags of Occony, and, in the same adventure, no longer considered luck-
less, had won the young heart of the beautiful Jocassée.

" They bore the young and successful warrior into the centre of the ring, and before the great Moitoy. He stood up in
the presence of the assembled multitude, a brave and fearless,
and fine looking Cherokee. At the signal of the chief, the
young maidens gathered into a group, and sung round him a
song of compliment and approval, which was just as much as
to say,—' Ask, and you shall have.' He did ask; and before
the people of the Brown Viper could so far recover from their
surprise as to interfere, or well comprehend the transaction,
the bold Nagoochie had led the then happy Jocassée into the
presence of Moitoy and the multitude, and had claimed the
girl of Occony to fill the green lodge of the Estato hunter.

" That was the signal for uproar and commotion. The Occonies were desperately angered, and the fierce Cheochee,
whom nothing, not even the presence of the great war-chief,
could restrain, rushed forward, and dragging the maiden vio-
lently from the hold of Nagoochie, hurled her backward into
the ranks of his people; then, breathing nothing but blood
and vengeance, he confronted him with ready knife and uplifted hatchet, defying the young hunter in that moment to
the fight.

" ' E-cha-e-cha, e-herro—echa-herro-echa-herro,' was the
war-whoop of the Occonies; and it gathered them to a man
around the sanguinary young chief who uttered it. ' Echa-
herro, echa-herro,' he continued, leaping wildly in air with
the paroxysm of rage which had seized him,—' the brown viper has a tooth for the green bird. The Occony is athirst—
he would drink blood from the dog-heart of the Estato.
Echa-e-cha-herro, Occony.' And again he concluded his
fierce speech with that thrilling roll of sound, which, as the so
much dreaded warwhoop, brought a death feeling to the
heart of the early pioneer, and made the mother clasp closely,

in the deep hours of the night, the young and unconscious infant to her bosom. But it had no such influence upon the fearless spirit of Nagoochie. The Estato heard him with cool composure, but, though evidently unafraid, it was yet equally evident that he was unwilling to meet the challenger in strife. Nor was his decision called for on the subject. The great chief interposed, and all chance of conflict was prevented by his intervention. In that presence they were compelled to keep the peace, though both the Occonies and Little Estatoees retired to their several lodges with fever in their veins, and a restless desire for that collision which Moitoy had denied them. All but Nagoochie were vexed at this denial; and all of them wondered much that a warrior, so brave and daring as he had always shown himself, should be so backward on such an occasion. It was true, they knew of his love for the girl of Occony; but they never dreamed of such a feeling acquiring an influence over the hunter, of so paralyzing and unmanly a character. Even Nagoochie himself, as he listened to some of the speeches uttered around him, when he reflected upon the insolence of Cheochee—even he began to wish that the affair might happen again, that he might take the hissing viper by the neck. And poor Jocassee—what of her when they took her back to the lodges? She did nothing but dream all night of Brown Vipers and Green Birds in the thick of battle.

CHAPTER V.

" THE next day came the movement of the hunters, still under the conduct of Moitoy, from the one to the other side of the upper branch of the Keowee river, now called the Jocassée, but which, at that time, went by the name of the Sarratay.— The various bands prepared to move with the daylight; and,

still near, and still in sight of one another, the Occonies and
Estatoees took up their line of march with the rest. The long
poles of the two, bearing the green bird of the one, and the
brown viper of the other, in the hands of their respective
bearers—stout warriors chosen for this purpose, with reference to strength and valour—waved in parallel courses, though
the space between them was made as great as possible by the
common policy of both parties. Following the route of the
caravan, which had been formed of the ancient men, the women, and children, to whom had been entrusted the skins taken
in the hunt, the provisions, utensils for cooking, &c., the great
body of hunters were soon in motion for other and better
hunting-grounds, several miles distant, beyond the river.

"The Indian warriors have their own mode of doing business, and do not often travel with the stiff precision which
marks European civilization. Though having all one point of
destination, each hunter took his own route to gain it, and in
this manner asserted his independence. This had been the
education of the Indian boy, and this self-reliance is one
source of that spirit and character which will not suffer him
to feel surprise in any situation. Their way, generally, wound
along a pleasant valley, unbroken for several miles, until you
came to Big-knob, a huge crag which completely divides it,
rising formidably up in the midst, and narrowing the valley on
either hand to a fissure, necessarily compelling a closer march
for all parties than had heretofore been pursued. Straggling
about as they had been, of course but little order was perceptible when they came together in little groups, where the
mountain forced their junction. One of the Bear tribe found
himself alongside a handful of the Foxes, and a chief of the
Alligators plunged promiscuously into the centre of a cluster
of the Turkey tribe, whose own chief was probably doing
the proper courtesies among the Alligators. These little cross-
ings, however, were amusing rather than annoying, and were,
generally, productive of little inconvenience, and no strife.—

But it so happened there was one exception to the accustomed harmony. The Occonies and Estatoees, like the rest, had broken up into small parties, and, as might have been foreseen, when they came individually to where the crag divided the valley into two, some took the one, and some the other hand, and it was not until one of the paths they had taken opened into a plain in which the woods were bald—a sort of prairie—that a party of seven Occonies discovered that they had among them two of their detested rivals, the Little Estatoees. What made the matter worse, one of these stragglers was the ill-fated warrior who had been chosen to carry the badge of his tribe; and there, high above their heads—the heads of the Brown Vipers—floated that detestable symbol—the green bird itself.

"There was no standing that. The Brown Vipers, as if with a common instinct, were immediately up in arms. They grappled the unoffending stragglers without gloves. They tore the green bird from the pole, stamped it under foot, smothered it in the mud, and pulling out the cone-tuft of its head, utterly degraded it in their own, as well as in the estimation of the Estatoees. Not content with this, they hung the desecrated emblem about the neck of the bearer of it, and, spite of all their struggles, binding the arms of the stragglers behind their backs, the relentless Vipers thrust the long pole which had borne the bird, in such a manner between their alternate arms, as effectually to fasten them together. In this manner, amidst taunts, blows, and revilings, they were left in the valley to go on as they might, while their enemies, insolent enough with exultation, proceeded to join the rest of the party.

CHAPTER VI.

" A HUNDRED canoes were ready on the banks of the river
Sarratay, for the conveyance to the opposite shore of the assembled Cherokees. And down they came, warrior after warrior, tribe after tribe, emblem after emblem, descending from
the crags around, in various order, and hurrying all with
shouts, and whoops, and songs, grotesquely leaping to the
river's bank, like so many boys just let loose out of school.—
Hilarity is, indeed, the life of nature. Civilization refines the
one at the expense of the other, and then it is that no human
luxury or sport, as known in society, stimulates appetite for
any length of time. We can only laugh in the woods—society
suffers but a smile, and desperate sanctity, with the countenance of a crow, frowns even at that.

" But, down, around, and gathering from every side, they
came—the tens and the twenties of the several tribes of Cherokee. Grouped along the banks of the river, were the boats
assigned to each. Some, already filled, were sporting in every
direction over the bosom of that beautiful water. Moitoy
himself, at the head of the tribe of Nequassée, from which he
came, had already embarked ; while the venerable Attakulla,
with Jocassée, the gentle, sat upon a little bank in the neigh-
hourhood of the Occony boats, awaiting the arrival of Cheochee and his party. And why came they not ? One after
another of the several tribes had filled their boats, and were
either on the river, or across it. But two clusters of canoes
yet remained, and they were those of the rival tribes—a green
bird flaunted over the one, and a brown viper, in many folds'
was twined around the pole of the other.

" There was sufficient reason why they came not. The strife
had begun ;—for, when gathering his thirteen warriors in a
little hollow at the termination of the valley through which

they came, Nagoochie beheld the slow and painful approach
of the two stragglers upon whom the Occonies had so practised—when he saw the green bird, the beautiful emblem of
his tribe—disfigured and defiled—there was no longer any measure or method in his madness. There was no longer a thought
of Jocassée to keep him back; and the feeling of ferocious indignation which filled his bosom, was the common feeling with
his brother warriors. They lay in wait for the coming of the
Occonies, down at the foot of the Yellow Hill, where the
woods gathered green and thick. They were few—but half
in number of their enemies—but they were strong in ardour,
strong in justice, and even death was preferable to a longer
endurance of that dishonour to which they had already been
too long subjected. They beheld the approach of the Brown
Vipers, as, one by one, they wound out from the gap of the
mountain, with a fierce satisfaction. The two parties were
now in sight of each other, and could not mistake the terms
of their encounter. No word was spoken between them, but
each began the scalp-song of his tribe, preparing at the same
time his weapon, and advancing to the struggle.

" ' The green bird has a bill,' sang the Estatoees, ' and he
flies like an arrow to his prey,'

" ' The brown viper has poison and a fang,' responded the
Occonies;' and he lies under the bush for his enemy.'

" Give me to clutch the war-tuft,' cried the leaders of each
party, almost in the same breath.

" ' To taste the blood,' cried another.

" ' And make my knife laugh in the heart that shrinks,' sung
another and another.

" ' I will put my foot on the heart,' cried an Occony.

" I tear away the scalp,' shouted an Estato, in reply; while
a joint chorus from the two parties promised—

" ' A dog that runs, to the black spirit that keeps in the
dark.'

" ' *Echa-herro, echa-herro, echa-herro,*' was the grand cry or fearful war-whoop, which announced the moment of onset, and the beginning of the strife.

" The Occonies were not backward, though the affair was commenced by the Estaotees. Cheochee, their leader, was quite as brave as malignant, and now exulted in the near prospect of that sweet revenge, for all the supposed wrongs, and more certain rivalries, which his tribe had suffered from the Green Birds. Nor was this more the feeling with him than with his tribe. Disposing themselves, therefore, in readiness to receive the assault, they rejoiced in the coming of a strife, in which, having many injuries to redress, they had the advantages, at the same time, of position and numbers.

" But their fighting at disadvantage was not now a thought with the Little Estatoees. Their blood was up, and like all usually patient people, once aroused, they were not so readily quieted. Nagoochie, the warrior now, and no longer the lover, led on the attack. You should have seen how that brave young chief went into battle—how he leapt up in air, slapped his hands upon his thighs in token of contempt for his foe, and throwing himself open before his enemies, dashed down his bow and arrows, and waving his hatchet, signified to them his desires for the conflict, *à l'outrance*, and, which would certainly make it so, hand to hand. The Occonies took him at his word, and throwing aside the long bow, they bounded out from their cover to meet their adversaries. Then should you have seen that meeting—that first rush—how they threw the tomahawk—how they flourished the knife—how the brave man rushed to the fierce embrace of his strong enemy— and how the two rolled along the hill in the teeth-binding struggle of death.

" The tomahawk of Nagoochie had wings and a tooth. It flew and bit in every direction. One after another, the Occonies went down before it, and still his fierce war cry of ' *Echa-mal-Occony*,' preceding every stroke, announced another and another victim. They sank away from him like sheep before

the wolf that is hungry, and the disparity of force was not so
great in favour of the Occonies, when we recollect that
Nagoochie was against them. The parties, under his fierce
valour, were soon almost equal in number, and something
more was necessary to be done by the Occonies before they
could hope for that favourable result from the struggle which
they had before looked upon as certain. It was for Cheochee
now to seek out and to encounter the gallant young chief of
Estato. Nagoochie, hitherto, for reasons best known to himself, had studiously avoided the leader of the Vipers ; but he
could no longer do so. He was contending, in close strife
with Okonettee, or the One-Eyed—a stout warrior of the
Vipers—as Cheochee approached him. In the next moment,
the hatchet of Nagoochie entered the skull of Okonettee. The
One-Eyed sunk to the ground, as if in supplication, and,
seizing the legs of his conqueror, in spite of the repeated
blows which descended from the deadly instrument, each of
which was a death, while his head swam, and the blood filled
his eyes, and his senses were fast fleeting, he held on with a
death-grasp which nothing could compel him to forego. In
this predicament, Cheochee confronted the young brave of
Ettato. The strife was short, for though Nagoochie fought as
bravely, as ever yet he struck in vain, while the dying wretch,
grappling his legs, disordered, by his convulsions, not less
than by his efforts, every blow which the strong hand of
Nagoochie sought to give. One arm was already disabled, and
still the dying wretch held on to his legs. In another moment,
the One-Eyed was seized by the last spasms of death, and in
his struggles, he dragged the Estato chief to his knees. This
was the fata disadvantage. Before any of the Green Bird
warriors could come to his succour, the blows was given, and
Nagoochie lay under the knee of the Brown Viper. The knife
was in his heart, and the life not yet gone, when the same
instrument encircled his head, and his swimming vision could

L 5

M R.   G R E E N.

CHAPTER I.

" And to him Euronome, Ocean's girl, gave three fair-cheeked wenches, very comely-looking creature, to wit : Aglaia, and Euphrosyne, and Thalia the lovely."—HESIOD

IN relating some anecdotes of the life of Mr. Green, recent as the occurrences are, and true as recent, we have no fear of giving offence to himself. But as he has respectable relations and connections, who might not relish our taking such liberties with him, we have been careful as to the designation of localities, and as to the use of names.

As it is inartificial, even in telling a true story, to begin at the beginning, the reader will please to allow himself to be introduced to the family of Mr. Brown, a respectable merchant, flourishing in business, and residing in the town of Short-hills, He had an excellent wife, and three captivating daughters, Miss Barbara, Miss Betsey, and Miss Bella Brown. Miss Brown was the tallest, fairest in complexion, and stateliest in carriage. The black-eyed, black-haired brunette Betsey had a more immediate and probably more enduring witchcraft about her than her elder sister. But the fairy, blue-eyed, yellow-haired Bella bade fair to eclipse the pretensions of both. This brief description must suffice, for the present, for the " cat'log of their perfections." In the words of the heathen poet, quoted at the head of our chapter ; " Love leaked from their eyelids when they *looked*, melting the frame ;—yea, beautifully did they *look* from under their brows."

No wonder that there was no lack of young gentlemen for them to look *at* jointly and severally. Not only from the immediate neighbourhood, but from remote towns and cities, did swains repair to pay their homage ; or, at least, if they came on other special business, they strove to avail themselves of the opportunity of so doing.

The family circle had assembled around Mr. Brown's hearth, one evening, after tea. Two young gentlemen, Mr. White and Mr. Black, were present—very unexceptionable young men, and promising to do well in the world—the one a country merchant, and the other a country lawyer. It would seem that there could have been no objection to their paying proper and civil attention to the young ladies ; and certainly they did seem to do so with unaffected heartiness and sincerity.

But this *con-amore* mode of proceeding brought a thoughtful cloud over the honest brow of Mr. Brown, after he had been for some time quietly observing the delighted, and apparently delightful manner, in which Mr. Black balanced himself over and roundabout the fair Barbara, as she played, or tried to play, one of her favourite pieces of music, which of course was also his ; and also observing how Mr. White, under pretext of playing chess with Betsey, was enacting the part of Ferdinand in the Tempest, when engaged in enjoying a similar amusement with Miranda.

" Pray, my dear," said he, " when do you suppose we shall see Mr. Green ?"

The abrupt mode in which the question was put startled the young ladies ; or it might have been some association with the person referred to. But Miss Barbara made a very vile (musical) shake; Miss Betsey put her king in check; and pretty Miss Bella, who was sitting on a little Ottoman (which in Short-hills was called a stool,) and was knitting a purse, glancing occasionally with her kind and laughter-loving eyes at the erotic net-work in which her sisters were employed, lost a row of her stitches, and wounded her rosy fingers.

" Why, my love," replied Mrs. Brown, " you know brother wrote that he was to come back by spring ; and we are now in April. I expect you will hear from him, or we shall see him in a few days."

"Green?" asked Mr. White—"is it Sap Green you speak of?"

"No sir," said Brown, dryly; "it is Mr. George Green; a near relation of my family; and likely," he added, with a look intended for one of significant revelation, "to be still nearer."

"I beg your pardon, sir; but I knew him at school, and the boys gave him that nickname."

"And I was acquainted with him at college," said Black. "He came there in a green coat, and never had one, according to my recollection, of any other colour. When one got rusty, they twitted him with '*ver non semper viret*,' and then he got another. He said he was indifferent about colours; and about most matters of indifference he would follow anybody's advice. But in many things he was sensible enough."

"There certainly always was something peculiar about George Green," said Mrs. Brown. "But as the Baronet says, in the Man of Feeling, 'I suppose he has worn it off by travel.'"

The rather sparkling serenity of the little party became manifestly dulled after this interlogue. The young ladies looked restrained. Good Mr. Brown, who was generally fond both of talking and of hearing a little gossip, retained the thoughtfulness of his expression, which operated as a spell upon his daughters; and his dame even resisted a strong propensity she had for making quotations. The young men withdrew early, and in making their congees, felt, for the first time at Brown's house, that it was a formal affair. No doubt they found parting much sweeter sorrow, when leaving the piazzaed entrance of the mansion, to which two of the young ladies accompanied them, as they do in the country towns very often, particularly when the nights are fine. A gentle pressure of the soft hand, not altogether unphilosophically unreactive,— a motion for leave to sit again, which could not be denied,

according to "the rules of the house,"—mitigated therefore
the dolour of these disciples of the "porch." But they did not
feel as happy as they had done before the visit, because both
were, or thought they were, in love—a speculation in which
it is vexatious to be crossed, as it is indeed in any speculation
whatever.

"Those young men," said Mr. Brown, after the re-union of
his family (that is, after the two young ladies had returned
into the sitting-room,) "seem, by all I learn, to be unexceptionable and clever in every respect. But you know, girls,
that if they have any serious intentions, as I believe you call
it, they must not for the present receive the slightest encouragement."

"Certainly not," said Mrs. Brown. "Miss Hannah More
truly observes, that 'it is important not only to possess the
mind with the affair which is under consideration, but to bestow on it an *undivided* attention.'"

"We can't divide this affair among us, mamma," said Bella
—"can we?"

"You will be a good girl, I know," said her father, patting
her forehead, with an affectionate regard for her curls, which
were only a little differently arranged from what they would
have been, had there been no importation of foreign fashions,
in living or graven caricatured images of head-dresses, into
the town of Short-hills, because the fashion happened to be
after that of nature. "You will be a good girl, always, I
know, Bella. If *you* should be *the rich lady*, you must not
crack your jokes on your old father and mother, my little gip-
sey. I am going to bed directly, so kiss me for good night.
I know that *you* will do nothing without your father's and
mother's advice.

So much he knew about the state of *his* "foreign and domestic relations!"

CHAPTER II.

Early to bed and early to rise.

Falsely luxurious, will not man awake,
And, springing from the bed of sloth, enjoy
The cool, the fragrant, and the silent hour
To meditation due, and sacred song?

THOMSON.

MR. LEWIS LAKE had been informed by a gentleman who had just returned from Europe, and whom he casually met, that his cousin, Mr. Green, was certainly in town, and had gone that evening to take up his quarters in a certain hotel, coffee-house, or drinking-shop. The gentleman added that he believed he had " come on shore on a raft," as the other passengers, who came together, knew nothing about the manner of his deportation from the packet. When these tidings were communicated, Lake was under the necessity of escorting a party home, long after the " noon of night."

But when the light crept through his shutters in the morning, and moving shadows came on the wall opposite to them, he arose with a resolute effort, and indued himself drowsily in his morning vestimental gear. The domestics had not yet begun to kick up a dust, and he was the morning-star of the family. The chimney-sweeps were singing their matins as he issued forth into the street; and the first steamboat bells had just begun to agonise the ears of those who had no immediate occasion or desire to be reminded of the flues of either chimneys or boilers. A solitary milkman was watering his commodity at a pump, without any fear of public criticism.

" Is it possible," mentally soliloquised Lewis, as, with a sleepy and reflective look, he trod the flags of a broad street, "is it possible that Green is the same ' two-and-sixpence, after all his travels? If so, I should not be surprised to find him in the watch-house." Presently he met with a couple of dyspeptic lovers, who were walking for health and sentiment to a promenade by the water's side. They looked more sleepy than himself, and while he was making his manners to the lady, the whole trio yawned as if they would have become monumental specimens of oscitation. A dingy wench, whose early rising was certified to by the Society for the supply of good and useful servants, dissolved the dream, and adjourned the interesting meeting, by discharging into a cross-gutter, from behind an iron-railed area, a quantity of liquid miscellanies, which lubricated their soles, and gave them an immediate idea of separation.

The next animated object of which Lake became aware was a Mercury of the Press, whose wings stuck out of his coat pockets in the shape of goose-quill feathers. He was going towards a building in which mistakes of the night were corrected in the morning; and by perusing his table of errata, many honest people were enabled to find out in the evening, how they had woke up in the morning with their throats cut, after their most valuable property had been abstracted, without any consciousness on their part of either accident. This spectral appearance naturally led Mr. Lake to cast, what our great novelist would call a furtive glance at the portal of the building in question. He saw there a group of wild-looking vagabonds, and was strongly tempted to make one of them himself, with a view of ascertaining whether his cousin, who had just crossed the Atlantic Styx, might not be trembling before the Rhadamanthus of the morning, without any credentials. But he resisted this suggestion of fancy, and kept on his way until he arrived in front of the hostelrie of which he was in quest. All its windows and its solitary door were closed. But as the adjacent houses gave faint signs of the expergiscence of some of their inhabitants, he made bold to knock emphatically. The unwashed face of a sandy-haired little girl, protruding through a broken window, in a hovel called a grocery, which adjoined the hotel, regarded him

during this operation, and during his subsequent state of ex-
pectance, which lasted beyond the decent time during which
patience is a comfortable virtue. She then screamed out,
"It's too late to go there now, Mister. They always locks
up at four."

However, Mr. Lake thought he heard a heteroclitical noise
and motion in the room into which the door opened, and took
the liberty of trying his open-sesame upon it again. An odd
confusion of noises, mingled with crashings, and with what
sounded too much like hard swearing, followed; and one of
the valves was slowly turned inward by a lout three-fourths
asleep and one-fourth dressed, who was worse off than the
pilgrims who had not boiled their peas; as his bare feet had
been imperfectly thrust into slippers to which their proportions
bore no resemblance, and he was undergoing a new species of
ordeal—of treading among bits of broken glass, to show himself to be awake, when he was not. The appearance of the
bar-room, for such it was, was rueful, and disgusting was the
odour thereof.

"I sot up for you," said the sweet porter of this establishment, suffering the valve to relapse briskly, and locking it,
while his one eye that did not squint winked dimly, like a
star of the least magnitude through a floating fog—"I sot up
for you, Mr. Tardy, till a half-past four, I'm darned if I
didn't."

"If I was Mr. Tardy," said Lake, "I ought to be very
much obliged to you, and as I am his substitute, here is something for your trouble. But I want to see Mr. Green, who
lodges here, as I learn. I am his near relation, and you may
show me his bedroom, without any ceremony."

It was strange to see the blanket-curtains of the fellow's
odd eyes struggling sluggishly to uplift themselves a little, as
his features were exhibited in the swarthy and smoky light of
a foul lamp, hanging from the centre of the ceiling, and looking, as the glorious sunshine contrived to peep in through im-

perceptible crannies, like some irregular ghost which had forgotten cock-crow. The expression of those features was indescribably mystified—being at once inquisitive, communicative, minatory, timorous, sharp, puzzled, and ridiculous.

But oh, Sleep and Death!—as your flashy novelists would exclaim, in handling this matter—as the blankets fell over the poor lad's windows again, what a yawn he did give! It could not have been performed by the Sleeping Beauty in the Wood, on the first centennial anniversary of her enchantment; nor by the Rev. Mr. Tennant, when he first objected to enjoying the rites of sepulture. And as to poor Lake, no old hero could have been as much scared by the looks of the grisly mouth of Avernus, when projecting a jaunt to the pleasing banks of Acheron—no naked Egyptian, bathing for pleasure, was ever as much discommoded by the uplifted upper-jaw of a crocodile. It was a yawn which nature and art both contributed to make superlative in its way. And Lake shrewdly interpreted it. He told him that he was no sheriff's officer nor constable ; but simply what he represented himself to be, a relation of Mr. Green, who wished to see him as soon as possible, and would be responsible for the liberty he took in disturbing him at so unseasonable an hour. The valet, therefore, stretched himself and yawned, yawned and stretched, stretched and yawned, and yawned again. Then, hitching up his lower garments, he shuffled himself out of the room, and up three pair of uncarpeted and uncleaned stairs, followed by the young gentleman.

He opened the door of an apartment, into which the broad light of day was shining through the uncurtained windows. The floor, and a few melancholy chairs, that had been entire strangers to each other when introduced, were strewn with various garments, lying in all the graceful negligence of attitude in which they had been left when cast off from the persons of their proprietors. There were three beds in the apartment, each of which was occupied by an extempore tenant; and two pictures, or coloured engravings, exactly alike and the same, ornamented the chimney-piece.

"Mr. Green is in that there bed in the corner, Mister," said the Virgil of our Dante.

One of the snoring triad here made a movement; rubbed his eyes, and contrived to speak as follows: "I say, Peter, fetch me some cider." Peter departed to execute this commission, and went down stairs much faster than he had come up; for his slippers playing him a trick, he went down one whole flight at once.

Lake advanced to the couch in which his cousin was recumbent, whose slumbers his intrusion had not disturbed, and succeeded, with some difficulty, in waking him. Speculation came gradually to his optics; and when it did, he showed no signs of surprise, or of any other emotion, at the apparition before him. "Ah!" said he, is that you Lake? What o'clock is it?"

"It is rather early. But how do you do? And what in the devil's name brought you *here*?"

"It was a coach. Bistre said this was a good place; and I was perfectly indifferent about it."

"Who is Mr. Bistre? I don't admire his taste?"

"He's a singer. He came out with me in the packet. But oh! how sleepy I am!"

"I can easily account for your not having rested well!"

"Oh! I am indifferent about sleeping; but we must do it sometimes. They were singing and halloo-hallooing in the room underneath all night; and the people were coming into and going out of this one. One man blundered half of himself into my bed. When the other noises ceased, they began to kill rats with a dog. I am indifferent as to noises: but I confess I don't much like that kind. But oh! how sleepy I am!"

"I thought that you would perhaps accompany me to breakfast. They all want to see you very much.

"If any man would bring me any thing to dress with, I would as leave go as not. I might sleep it out afterwards."

St. Peter reappeared with a bottle of cider and a pint tumbler, for the gentleman who thirsted. Lake asked him to look after Mr. Green's servant.

"Why," said he "he's gone. He went to the play, and when he came in here, he said he'd go to a better house, and the boss told him he might go to * *, and they had like to have fit about it."

"Ah, well," said Green, "he'll come back by-and by. Suppose you come and breakfast with me."

"Where?"

"Here. I suppose they have some breakfast. Come about ten o'clock. Oh! how I could sleep!—though I don't care any thing about it."

"I will leave you then to your *snooze*," said Lake as he turned on his heel, with rather a vexed and mortified air. He was young and enthusiastic, and had a natural regard for Green; besides private reasons of his own for wishing to intercommune with him before anybody else should do so. But he ought to have reflected that it is highly improper to disturb any gentleman's slumbers at such an hour; particularly when he has just returned from a voyage.

Still the utter nonchalance of Green, and his not inquiring *at all* about any of *the all* who were so anxious to see him, vexed Lake particularly. And at the breakfast-table of the family poor Green was decided to be worse than a dolt and a mooncalf, by a unamious vote.

CHAPTER III.

CELIA. Bonjour, Monsieur Le Beau, what's the news.
LE BEAU. Why, this that I speak of.—As You Like It.

AT ten o'clock, not without covertly and shamefacedly peering about, to watch whether he was observed by any of the decent people of his acquaintance, Master Lake popped into the indifferent establishment, patronised by Messrs. Bistre and Green. Things had assumed a little more regular and respectable aspect in this anti-temperance chapel; and Lake immediately recognised an old acquaintance, in the person of the body servant of his cousin, whose Christian name was Abel; but who was generally called " Slow-and Easy,"—and sometimes more classically " Festina Lente." He looked mightily spruce, showing, that foreign travel had at least made him more ambitious, as regarded his apparel. He was not only finer (as was proper), but was more genteel in his appearance than his master, which was decidedly incorrect. The latter was sitting in a box, in an adjoining apartment, reading a newspaper. He wore a green frockcoat and a black velvet waistcoat, and had strings of gilt or gold chains, hanging down over his breast and below it. Though the barbers' apprentices had not adopted the same practice at that time, Lake could not help thinking that his cousin looked more like a beau-nasty than like a gentleman.

Lake insinuated the nether part of his person into the interspace of three inches in breadth, and less, between the edge o a table and the partition, opposite to his cousin, and sat himself down on the bench. On the table there was a cloth, which, by no conscientious stretch of courtesy, could have been called either white, or only half-dirty. It was garnished with a broken mustard-pot, a bottle with a quill thrust into a cork, professing to hold pepper-vinegar, and other appliances

which it is unnecessary to particularise, as it has been done so
much more minutely than we have room for, in several recent
works of imagination.

Mr. Green looked askance from his newspaper at Lake, and
looked at his newspaper again. He then said—" Pray, is this
General Jackson the president now ? How did he get to be
elected ?"

" Come, now," said Lake, with some tincture of morosity,
" this is affectation; you must know he was elected by the
people somehow or other."

" Indeed, I did not know it," said Green, in a tone rather
more decisive than he usually employed. " I think I did hear
something about it in Paris. But politics is a subject about
which I am totally indifferent."

" Yes—our politics. I don't wonder at all. But tell me
where have you been ? Where have you travelled ? What
have you seen ?"

" Oh ! I have been to several places. Chiefly to London and
Paris."

" And you were in Paris during the three days ?"

" Which three ? Oh, yes—you mean when they made such
a disturbance in the streets ! I was there then."

" And where was you ? And how much of it did you
see ?"

" Oh! I was in a snug room in the back of a house, with
Nicholas Umber. You know him. He said that we had nothing to do with the scrape. He got five cold hams, and plenty
of loaves of bread and claret; and we shut up the windows.
I was perfectly indifferent, of course, about French politics ;
so I staid with him until they had done firing guns, and making it inconvenient either to walk or ride."

" And is it possible that you know nothing of it ?"

" Oh, yes. I saw the pavements all torn up, and had to
take a roundabout way to get clear of them. It was none of
my business ; but I found it very inconvenient."

" Well, cousin Green, I doubt not that they thought you shut yourself up from pure fright, You are a strange individual, Did you see General La Fayette and Mr. Cooper ?"

" Yes. I went to the general's hotel one night. I saw a parcel of people in soldier's clothes there, marching in with great fur caps on their heads. I did not stay more than five minutes. As to what they thought about me, I am entirely indifferent. It was none of *their* business."

" Perhaps you are a Carlist. Do you not believe that the elder branch of the Bourbons is effectually and for ever disinherited ? Will the new king be able to sustain himself on the throne ? Is he honest in his professions to the people ?"

" I tell you I took no interest in their local politics. I really forget, if I ever knew, which *is* the elder branch. Why, you know, they cut off the oldest one's head. They said that Charles the Tenth had run away somewhere, with several carriage loads of his family. I don't know whether he will think it an object to go back. He seemed to me to be a gentlemanly man, and they said he was something of a sportsman. How they will fix it I can't tell; and the Lord knows, I don't care."

" I don't suppose you do. Now, I believe, you are honest. But I cannot believe that you do not know the difference between good coffee and the stuff you are drinking."

It is to be noted, that the unhappy Peter, while this discourse was in progress, had put on the table a waiter, with a strange assortment of crockery, and poured into two cups, from a tea-pot, a brown liquid, which Mr. Green, after having put into it materials representative of sugar and milk, was swallowing.

" I am indifferent about the quality of coffee. But now you mention it, I doubt whether this *is* the article at all. Slow-and-Easy, is this coffee ?"

" I should say, sir," said Abel, after a deliberate inspection of Lake's rejected cup, " that there might be some coffee-

grounds in it.   But the landlord has really been so insolent to
me, that, unless you are about letting me lick him; it is of no
use to talk about it."

   " I don't care whether you lick him or not.   It will make
the coffee no better, either way."

   " Are you going to eat that egg ?" asked Lake.

   " Certainly not.   I am indifferent about eggs and chickens
too ; but I confess I do not like this one at all."

   It is unnecessary, and would be dull to record, in this place,
further specimens of the manner of the honest poco-curante
whose small gray eyes could not be made to assume expression,
by the introduction of any topic whatever ; and who showed
himself so totally destitute of curiosity as to the situation of
his own family and friends, that he did not in any way advert
to their existences.   In one point alone, Lake knew that he
was sensitive ; and that was, in his pocket.   And, with this
sensitiveness, an affair in which _he_ took a deep interest was
so intimately connected, that he determined to push his inquiries farther, before Green had fallen in with other company,
whose advice, unless it cost him something, he would be sure
to take, as he had done that of Mr. Bistre.   Green agreed to
change his lodgings forthwith, and to put up at the hotel where
Abel had seen fit to deposit the principal part of his luggage
without consulting him ; and to accompany Lake home.   Had
it not been for the reason mentioned, the latter would, with
pleasure and contempt, if the two sensations be compatible,
have left him to the enjoyment of his _nil-admirari_ philosophy.

CHAPTER IV.

" One woman is fair, yet I am well ; another is wise, yet I am well ; another
is virtuous, yet I am well."—BENEDICT.

THE father of Green, a man of substance, had directed by his
will that his son should travel for a certain time after becoming of age, and had made his right to succeed to the possession
of half of his property, contingent upon marrying one of the
daughters of Mr. Brown within a limited period after his return from abroad. In case he declined doing so, the moiety
was to be divided among the testator's other relatives. The
young gentleman had but rarely visited his country cousins
before his departure. He observed, very sensibly, that some
of them might die before it would be necessary for him to fulfil
the condition attached to the bequest ; and that it would be
time enough to see about it when he could make his selection
from the live ones. He had never written home during his
absence ; nor had the impressions made by the brief exhibitions of himself, with which he had condescended to favour
them, been such as to create any rivalship or jealous feeling in
the breasts of the fair Misses Brown. This little explanation
is necessary here.

Green's reception at the house of his uncle Lake was formal
and frigid in the extreme. That amiable family were, indeed,
almost too angry to indulge their natural curiosity to know
where their singular relative had been, and what he had been
about for two years. He was, however, perfectly at his ease,
and seemed very well pleased with himself; and when the
conversation, or rather the questioning on their part, and unsatisfactory responses on his, ceased for some minutes, and
an " awful pause " ensued, he began to read the genealogy of

M

the patriarchs, in a bible that lay on the table beside which he sat.

But Miss Lucy Lake was determined to renew the attack on a topic in which she took more interest than in the recent events of the French revolution, in which Green had borne the conspicuous part before-mentioned by himself. " George" said she, " do you mean to pay a visit soon to Shorthills ? or would it suit you better to have the Shorthills come to you ?"

" I am indifferent about it," said Green, with an off-hand air of good nature, and with perfect gravity.

Mrs. Lake regarded him with a scrutinizing glance; and seeing him unexpressive and unconcerned as before, observed—" You do not mean, then, to take your legacy, ' with the burthen annexed,' as the lawyers call it."

"Surely I do," said Green, with some little animation. " Ah !" he added, after pondering for a moment, " when Lucy spoke of Shorthills coming here, I thought she meant the people. I know the hills cannot travel."

" I must say then," said Miss Lucy, " you made as conceited and ungallant a reply as I ever heard of."

" And as abominably foolish," said her mother.

" Why," said Green, " I know nothing about their arrangements; but if it is equally convenient for them to visit the town, I cannot conceive what difference it can make, as it is a settled affair."

" A settled affair !" iterated Mr. Lewis, in surprise.

" Why, they cannot upset the will—can they ? I believe it is settled as much as the law can make it."

" But is not the consent of the lady of some little consequence in the case?" asked Miss Lucy.

" That is their business. If I am ready—as I am—to complete the arrangement on my part, some one of them must consent, or I take all the property without any condition. I have had advice on the subject."

"Do you feel no curiosity to know which one of them, if either, may be disposed to smile upon you! For I believe, you must be refused by all, or united to one, if you wish to enjoy the legacy."

"I have thought of the inconvenience of that. And since it is a matter of perfect indifference to me, who only remember that they are three wholesome-looking girls (they did think Barbara scrofulous, but it was a mistake), I am sure they had better fix it among themselves. If the affections of either are engaged, this will be decidedly more convenient. And if they are all free, it will save much trouble if they will toss it up."

"It certainly would have been far better for Troy, if the three goddesses_had settled their dispute in that manner," said Lewis.

"Cousin George is no Paris, however," said Lucy, who was considerably provoked by what she considered affectation and imperturbable impatience. "I am writing to Shorthills to-day. Perhaps you would like me to communicate your views and intentions on this subject: or will you write an 'epistle general' to the ladies yourself. I think it would be a very great curiosity."

"It *would* look odd on the back of the letter," said the single-minded Green. "If I wrote, it should be, of course, to uncle Brown, or to Aunt. But, as it will be perfectly convenient for you, while you are writing, I wish you would say that I await the commands of the family; and that any arrangement which will be most convenient to them, will be altogether indifferent to me."

"I shall do so, most assuredly."

"I am obliged to you. We have time enough to spare; but as casualties may occur, the sooner they arrange it, the better for them. As to myself, if I do not hear from them soon, I believe I will take three straws of different lengths, and draw them. And I will write three letters, to be sent in order accordingly. I will get a lawyer to make a draught for me, and request an answer, by return of mail, to each, in case I have occasion to send them all. As it is a matter of business, which must be attended to, it strikes me that this is the least inconvenient plan. I must go to see about various matters. So I wish you a good morning."

"I am sorry," said the good Mrs. Lake, "for whichever of the poor girls may be so unlucky as to become the wife of such a piece of asbestos. It will be hopeless to try either to mend his head, or to break his heart. Perhaps, however, he might be made to go tame about the house."

"Of all things," said Lucy, "to use George's favourite phrase, '*that* would be the least convenient.' But how do you like his ' arrangements,' as he calls them, Lewis?"

"Admirably well. I hope you will do him justice in reporting what they are."

"I cannot conceive," said Mrs. Lake, "why you should be particularly pleased with any way in which the bear may choose to suck his paws; and I think it may look indelicate in Lucy to say any thing about it. You have been wasting the morning to no purpose whatever, and your father will be displeased. It is of no consequence to you which of the girls is to be sacrificed; for one of them must be; or else I do not understand Mr. Brown's character."

So much the good lady knew about *her* domestic relations. Lewis withdrew to write a letter. Glowing, affectionate, and full of amaranthine hope, were its contents. Lucy's could not have been unamusing. We are authorized to publish a portion of that written by Mr. Lake, senior.

"Dear Brother Brown;—

"Yours of the 16th ult. was duly received. I note what you say about George Green. He has just returned from France. I have not seen him, but by what I learn from my family, he is as great a fool as ever; and can give no account

of himself since his departure. You will recollect that I
always told you this would be the case. I never was mistaken
in my life in any opinion I formed from an observation of character. It must be ascribed to Providence alone, and to no common sense of his own, that he has come back in a whole skin.
I cannot help using plain language, though it is in reference to
one who is to be your son-in-law; for he says he will take
either of the girls you may choose to send him, when it suits
his own convenience. The puppy! I think the property be-
queathed to him on this condition is estimated at twice its
value; and that the title to the real estate is very doubtful.
He is, at any rate, an incorrigible blockead, who will soon
run through it, together with his own, if he has not squandered that already. Lewis ferreted him out of a place, which
is a low gaming house and grog-shop, this morning. It is my
duty to suggest these things, and I know you will duly appre-
preciate the disinterestedness of my motives. Cotton is
ris'g, &c."

It was true that the only pecuniary interest which Mr.
Lake had in the matter was, that in case of Green's not marrying according to the will, two-fifths of the moiety would go
to his own children. But it cannot for a moment be supposed
that such mercenary considerations were thought of, when the
happiness of one of his nieces was, as he believed, seriously at
stake.

CHAPTER V.

And so I won my Genevieve,
My bright and beauteous bride.—Coleridge.

THE sweet influence of spring, now well advanced towards her young maturity,—the fragrance of her prolific breast,—her soft delightful whispers, after she had left off the irrational crying hysterics to which she was too much addicted in March and April,—a picturesque grove where every thing was budding, and the violets yet gave forth their gentle perfume,—a pretty brook with its most insinuating susurration—the young moon and the conscious stars, with their mildest, kindliest sweetest aspects—the impalpable dew, and the gentle air which make all vegetating things quiver with joy—a clean trunk of a prostrate tree to sit down upon—no mosquitoes— and the intolerable insolence of Mr. Green—all these, together with a more than half-ripe partiality for him, conspired to favour the suit of Willis White, as he told Betsey Brown, what she had had a shrewd suspicion of before, that he loved her better than any thing else he could think of in the way of comparison.

It did not hurt her feelings to be told so; for it eased her of all doubts she might have had upon the subject. And though White sold calicoes, tape, shad, onions, &c., and would have been glad to sell any thing, except human flesh, that he could come honestly by, and could make an honest profit upon, he was perhaps as worthy of the handsome Betsey's love as any paladin could have been who ever ran in debt to a blacksmith for tinkering up his mail harness. He " told his love" with the honest simplicity of a freeman and an equal, so far as birth was concerned, to the object of his adoration, with unaffected ardour, and with a sufficiently interesting degree of embarrassment. He was not blind nor deaf to the spectacles and voices of nature; nor would he have been so had he never read any poems or romances, to which, indeed, he was very little addicted. He knew that shad, and onions, and tape, and calicoes, and every other article that is supposed to be useful or ornamental, must be sold by somebody or another in a world, of which we should have more reason to be proud, if conscience, honour, and faith were not also vendible commodities.

In the beginning of their ramble, Betsey had told her lover, with her usual frankness, the substance of the communication which had been received, relative to the arrival of Mr. Green, and the manner in which he had expressed his views and intentions. Miss Lake certainly had not given too *little* colour to her account, not to make it faithful.

" That cousin Green of yours," said White, " must be very unhappy, or must be a very foolish hypocrite, to say that he is indifferent as to all things. Is there any thing in nature that is always the same—always insensible ? Those monastic-looking evergreens—are they not greener now, when you and the spring are visiting them, Betsey ? Is not the moss on those old rocks newer and brighter ? The power that governs all the economy of creation is not indifferent even to the falling of a sparrow. How can *man* be so, who is but a little lower than the angels, and for whose companion WOMAN was made ? Nature teaches us to love, and to love in the proper season after her own examples. Does not that beautiful star seem to oscillate with a more tremulous and liquid lustre now, than it does in winter, when it coldly exhibits its diamond radiance ? Does it not now seem to smile, and to be glad ? Why do the birds sing more sweetly ? Why do the shad come up the rivers in such quantities ?" And thus he went on, innocently committing a plagiarism upon the Pastor Fido, which Betsey thought at least as pretty as she would have thought Linco's remonstrance to Sylvio, had she read it in the sweet music of Guarini.

" Good evening, Miss Brown. How do you do, Mr. White

It is a charming night, isn't it? I heard you talking about shad. Will they be plenty this season?" Thus spoke Mr. Ochre, who dealt in paints and oils, and who was one of Mr. White's best customers. He had fetched a walk to the same romantic spot which had witnessed the confession of Mr. White, and his gracious absolution by his mistress. So it is always in human life. Feeling, fancy, fun, flourish, and fact are jumbled together. But Betsey loved Willis none the less for the interruption, and assured him as they walked home together, arm in arm, that she would never marry George Green under any circumstances whatever. If her papa and mamma assented she would marry him (White); and if she did not marry him, she would not marry anybody else. Those, she said, were her sentiments. And she was as honest and whole-souled a girl, independently of her personal attractions, as any virtuous democrat could wish to boast of as his bride. And now that she is a matron, it would be improper, were not her name and her other "circumstances" so adumbrated, that the great world cannot identify her with these allusions to facts, to put up in print that prayer for her happiness which all good people who know her do in their hearts. May she be always happy in her husband's still fond regard! May she still have cause to respect him! May she attend no six-day meetings, nor any other profanities! May her children grow up wise, and strong, and beautiful! And may she live, during the natural time of life, blessing, and being blessed—and then expire with resignation and hope as her attendant angels!

CHAPTER VI.

There are maidens in Scotland, more lovely by far,
Who would gladly be bride to the young Lochinvar.
                              WALTER SCOTT.

With every pleasing, every prudent part,
Say, what can Chloe want!   She wants a heart.
                              POPE.

THE same stars and groves, and pensively murmuring rivulet, quivering ever and anon with silver light, through the overhanging branches and bushes, witnessed the suit of Lawyer Black, as the cockneys of the village called him, to the stately Barbara. He had proved himself an ingenious advocate in the causes of other people, but felt considerably more embarrassed in pressing his own. He managed, however, to make his application sufficiently intelligible. Miss Barbara cast down her eyes, and perhaps blushed. She withdrew her arm from the support of her suitor, gently however, and for the ostensible purpose of taking out her handkerchief from her reticule. Black might have thought that it was for the purpose of allowing him to make a genuflexion. He did make one, at any rate, and sought to seize the hand with the handkerchief in it; forgetting that the lady might want to wipe her bright eyes, or otherwise to employ her cambric.

"Rise, Mr. Black," she said, with no extraordinary show of agitation. "I am honoured by your preference; but I must refer you to my father, by whose decision I shall wholly be governed. You know in what peculiar circumstances we are placed."

"I know that you have heard of the arrival of Mr. Green," said Black, with anxiety, and a feeling of mortification at the coolness of her manner, and set terms of her reply; "and therefore I ventured to risk, perhaps too soon, asking you to decide on my happiness. Has he solicited *your* hand?"

M 5

Miss Barbara *did* blush in reply to this question, but Black mistook the cause of the crimson suffusion, until she answered hesitatingly—" No !" It was uttered in a tone unsatisfactory to the suitor.

" Then," said he, " indeed I know of no other peculiar reasons why I should not now urge the dearest wish of my heart. He may soon present himself—and your father may compel you either to accept him, or to be disobedient. But tell me now, Barbara, tell me—what have I to hope from yourself? I have no presumptuous hope—but I have fondly imagined that I was not utterly indifferent to you. Was it a delusion ?"

" Why, certainly, Mr. Black, I highly esteem your good qualities, and your society has afforded me pleasure. Nor— nor did I mean to intimate to the contrary. But my father's will must be law to me. Want of filial piety is a bad omen for matrimonial felicity."

" She got that bit of morality, with the other formal scrap she uttered first, by heart at school; or has heard her mother quote it," thought Black.

" I will make my application then forthwith—but, do you, Barbara, do you care about its fate ? I fear that confounded Mr. Green will be in its way." His vexation made him speak in his usual manner, and rather technically. But, as he watched the expression of the truly handsome (rather than lovely) lineaments of her to whom he spoke, admiration and warmth of another description returned. " I feel that I may be, *am* unworthy of you, Barbara, except in the sincerity of my love. Your image has lived in my heart, and floated before my eyes, waking, musing, or dreaming, since first I saw you. I have worshipped it as I have never worshipped, never can worship any other. I would fain believe that some little re-sponsive interest in the heart of the original may be awakened as to the result of the conference with your father. Pardon me if I ask too much—but do you wish me success ?"

"Indeed, I do hope that the result may be fortunate for all parties. But let us return homeward."

Even this equivocal response, delivered in rather a kindlier tone than the young lady had previously spoken in, gave some consolatiou to the lover, and he chose to construe it favourably, as she again took his proffered arm. But presently, notwithstanding the delight with which such a construction, and still more the pleasure of such contact made his veins thrill, he could not help considering the *case* as it was *made up* (to use the language of his profession), and, in making out his *points*, he did not like the looks of them. He wished, therefore, to have it *amended*.

"Should Mr. Brown make no other objection than that this invisible Green *may* claim *your* hand—and he *will* do it, that is, Green will, if he has eyes—are my hopes to be a contingent remainder? I beg pardon, are they to depend upon the caprice of Green, Barbara?" He began in uttered meditation, and ended in an interrogatory.

Barbara was perplexed—for more reasons than Black was aware of, who knew nothing about the "three straws;" on the longitude of which his contingent remainder was to depend. She had persuaded herself that this was a jest, but still the pride of her spirit felt all the humiliation of her position. She certainly did prefer an indifferent husband, who was very rich, to an impassioned and really agreeable suitor, who had his own fortune to make by a profession. She could only resort to her own formulary.

"My *actions* must depend altogether on the pleasure of my father, to which my feelings must be subdued."

Here, on turning into a path that led immediately to the village, they were met by Bella, and a young gentleman on whose arm she was leaning, who was no other than Master Lake.

"We were sent to look after you," said the latter, as Miss

Barbara welcomed his appearance, with the most unembarrassed frankness. "Where is cousin Betsey?"

As she asked the question, the images of Betsey and her swain emerged from an alley in the hanging groves, and answered it by a visible exhibition of themselves. They looked remarkably cheerful, though Miss Betsey's cheek was rather flushed, as she received her cousin's wonted salute.

"Mamma," said Bella, "sent us to find you. She thought you might be lost in the woods, and did not know you had found errant cavaliers to take care of you. She is alarmed to death about that old influenza of yours, sister Betsey; and your pulmonary symptoms, sister Barbara; and father is all but swearing about it."

"And so," said Betsey, laughing, "they sent you to get rid of your toothache, did they, to look for us?"

"I think we had better proceed homeward," said Mr. Black. "The night *is* chilly and damp."

So he took the lead with his fair and graceful partner, while White and Betsey followed at a reasonable and fluctuating distance.

"We need not 'progress backwards,' Bella," said Lake. "I have a thousand other things to tell you."

"You must tell them to me at home, Lewis, to-night or to-morrow, you know. You are in no hurry."

They did not seem to be in any special hurry; at any rate they did not tread upon the heels of Mr. White and Betsey. Mr. Black, marching at a more regulated pace, in the van, said to Barbara, after a *dumb* silence of some minutes' duration,—"Miss Brown, with your permission, I shall leave the understanding between us subject to the exception of either party. I cannot consent to the arrangement *de bene esse*—I beg pardon—Barbara, I shall not speak to your father very soon,—nor—nor—until we have a better understanding."

"As you please, Mr. Black. You have a right to consult

your own feelings—and I must comply with my duty. And I think you need not be too precipitate. You have my best wishes whenever propriety permits. *Bon soir*," and she gracefully waved her gloved hand to him, as she discharged him, and entered her father's door.

"She may remain a *femme sole*, for all I care," grumbled Mr. Black, in his thoughts, as he stalked homeward. "I want no lapsed legacies. She is a handsome girl; but she has no more *heart* than Bacon on Uses; and no more utility either. What use would she be of to me, except putting me to useless expense?" And, so moralizing, he went whistling to his quarters, striving to feel merry, or at least indifferent; and being, in sooth, quite sad.

––––––

CHAPTER VIII.

Rome in her Capitol saw Querno sit,
Throned on seven hills, the Antichrist of wit.—Pope.

Rhyme the rudder is of verses.

On the day after Mr. Green's interview with his relations, he was sitting in a large and public room, smoking a cigar, in company with Mr. Sam Sienna, clerk to a firm of wholesale druggists, and Mr. Isaac Indigo, also a clerk in another establishment. He had just received a note, delicately folded and sealed, inviting him to a soirée that evening, at the house of a most respectable family, related to, and on terms of intimacy with his own. It was lying on the table—that is, such a portion of it as had not been used to ignite the twisted nicotian.

"Do you mean to go to this scrape, Green?" said Sienna.

"I don't know. I am indifferent about parties,—perfectly."

"I wouldn't go. I know several who have been to these

soirées, as they call them, and they say it is the greatest bore in the world. They give no feed. There is nothing but coffee, and lemonade, and slops. They talk about books, and have foreigners who *parlez-vous* it in their own lingo. You understand French, however, of course."

"No, thank God, I was indifferent about it. I got along well enough without it. Slow-and-Easy picked up enough to get what we wanted."

"I can give you both an invitation to a very nice party to-night," said Indigo. "You *must* go along with me. Mrs. Vermilion is going to blaze it out. She is going the whole figure. I dare say there will be a tremendous squeeze, and there will be plenty of fun, and no ceremony. You must go, Green."

"Well, I don't care, if you say so. But I think that squeezing is inconvenient: and I am indifferent about fun."

"Oh! you won't be when you get into it. If you knew Polly Pink and Kate Cochiloe, they'd tickle the indifference out of you."

"I must say that tickling is decidedly inconvenient. I am indifferent about being introduced to them ; but I will go along with you, if you wish it."

"You will be pleased, I am sure. But, as I am alive, here is a kind of namesake of yours ;"—in an audible whisper, meant to be heard, he continued—"Mr. Green-Bice, one of the most distinguished poets and literary characters alive."

"I am indifferent about poets and literature," said Mr. Green, "though I must confess I had rather not see such verses as these"—pointing to some of the then popular lines of Coculus Indicus, in a newspaper of the day, which the judicious editor characterized as *strains* from his lyre, far sweeter than the obscurities of Wordsworth, or the foreign affectations of Scott.

"It is a great pity not to be able to relish poetry," said Sienna. "I cannot express myself exactly ; but there is something or other charming about *them* verses—that I don't understand."

"What *is* poetry?" said Mr. Green, yawning.

"Oh!" said Indigo, "if I was sufficiently familiar with you, Mr. Green, I would venture to suggest that people may treat such a question from a man who has been educated, and who has travelled, like you, as gross affectation.

"I am indifferent as to how people treat it, or as to knowing what poetry *is*. But I don't know."

"God bless me, my dear sir, don't you know that it is the language of the passions, expressed in regular numbers?"

"I did not know it, indeed. I think that cursing and swearing is inconvenient. I am indifferent as to whether it is donein regular or irregular numbers."

"You will never get along with Miss Pink, unless you can talk to her about poetry. Certainly you can see that this article about General Jackson's conduct in vetoing the grand Erie Canal is prose?"

"I suppose it is. I am indifferent about prose; but I must say that I don't like such prose as that."

"Well now—this is poetry. Hear a little of it—

> "How dimly does the phantom wing,
>   Between the moonbeam and the wave,
> Of many an embryo notion fling
>   Its radience o'er the spirit's grave!
> Like twilight, when the images
>   Extern are seen, obscure and clear,
> So weeping memory fondly says,
>   Though life be dark, there's lustre here!"

Isn't that sweet? Ain't there a kind of twang about it? *That's* poetry, Mr. Green."

"I dare say. I don't know what it means; but I don't care about knowing. Don't trouble yourself to tell me—though if you want to, I am indifferent as to hearing it. If that is poetry, I am satisfied that there is too much of it;—but what an everlasting quantity there must be that is not burnt up!" Here, whiffing off a beautiful column of blue smoke, he threw

away the unconsumed end of his cigar, and took another
from a box of real Cabanas. Though he might have professed
himself indifferent as to cigars he certainly did not like any
other than the best.

"Mr. Green," said Mr. Sienna, who had [shovelled himself
around in many eccentric circles, after and with the poet to
make his own and their mutual consequence better understood
by the democrats who were lounging or walking about the
contiguous premises—"allow me to introduce to you,—and
you to him—Mr. Green-Bice; poetry is the subject of our
conversation ; and if he cannot tell you about it, there's
nobody can."

"I was trying," said Indigo, "by the music of this charming ode, as well as I could make it out, to give Mr. Green an
idea of the mysterious harmony which makes poetry most
poetical."

"What! that stuff!" said Green-Bice (who would have
been none the worse for having been indued in less sordid in-
teguments in the linen line), "why the poor fellow that made
it doesn't understand how to count his fingers. *He* belongs to
the Lake school of poetry ?"

" I am indifferent about it," said Green, " but I did not
know that my uncle had set up a charity school. I certainly
won't subscribe to it."

" Oh, Mr. Green's uncle's name is Lake, Mr. Bice," said
Indigo. " You do not mean *him*. I have heard before of the
Lake school of poetry. What is it ?"

" Why, sir, if I was called upon to tell you what it is, I
should have to go through so much explanation, that I should
be wearied, and you would be so likewise. There are many
articles in the Edinburgh Review which show what it is. But I
can tell you one thing which you may apprehend without much
trouble. It is a school, sir, in which the *prosody* of language is
sacrificed. Now, sir, you can clearly understand what
prosody is, if you will listen to me and mark me. Hear a

passage from the first of our poets, as last revised by him in his twentieth edition. Now mark the regularity of the rymth —the *tum-ti, tum-ti,* the flowing and majestic and classical *tum-ti* which pevades it:

> " How sweet, oh, friendship ? is thy magic charm !
> Our souls to elevate,—our hearts to warm !
> Within thy realm no discord's jarring sound
> Is heard, nor Cain and Abel there are found !
> Congenial friendship brings the potent spell.
> To bid the young affections softly swell,
> The sweets of fond society impart,
> Whose cordial balm exhilarates the heart,
> The friendly bosom that can share our grief
> Is the best sanctuary to yield relief ;
> To quench the fiery aspect of despair,
> And ease the labouring mind of half its care."

Mr. Bice illustrated his recitation by making iambics on the fingers of his left hand (one of which had a crooked joint,) with the forefinger of the right.

" I am indifferent about hearing any more of that, sir," said Green. " If I cared about poetry, I believe I could make such myself. But what is that line with a ' sanctuary' in it ?"

" Is the—best sanct—twer-ry—to yield relief," recited Mr. Bice.

" Oh! very well. That is in the new dictionary, I suppose. They made me call it sanctuary when I went to school ; but I am indifferent as to pronunciation. If you call it sanktery, your *tum-ti* will answer well enough. But I thought you had to double up your *pinkie* twice when you said it first. Won't you smoke a cigar ? or are you indifferent about it ? I never swear ; but for heaven's sake, if it is not inconvenient to you to stop reading that, it will be very convenient to me."

Green actually seemed interested in this matter, and inspired too on the occasion ; for he called for a bottle of wine, of which Bice availed himself freely, while he delivered the following lecture, during which Green fell asleep—for he could smoke as well asleep as awake.

" Poetry, Mr. Green, is a natural art. It is both inspired

and mechanical. If I say that the grass is green (begging
your pardon for playing on your name, which I do not mean
to do), do I talk poetry? No. Why not? Because there is
no curious jingle, or metrical arrangement. If I say,

> " The grass is green,
>   As may be seen,"

that *is* poetry. Why? Because it rhymes. There are no
epithets in it without meaning ; and there is no sentiment in it
without pathos. It is easy, and not careless; polished, and
not laborious. Its decorations are not tawdry, and it cannot
be made more elegant without losing its simplicity. The
versification is neither sluggish nor rugged. All who have
any relish for delightful melody will be charmed with it; because it is congenial to the soul of every true bard. But,
believe me, Mr. Green, that the injudicious praise which some
poets have received from pretended friends and sciolous
editors of newspapers has been their great misfortune."

" *Sci*— what ?" said Green. "I used to have a pointer that
we called Si, because his name was Syphax; and I knew a
nigger called Si-Van Brunt. However, I am indifferent about
knowing the meaning of it; don't inconvenience yourself to
explain."

Mr. Bice regarded him with an air of commiseration, and
having got a small knot around him of tavern loungers, proceeded,—while Green incensed the oracle by puffing volumes
of aromatic smoke into his eyes, nostrils, and mouth,—as follows :

" Several of our New England poets, Mr. Green, are not
without talents. A species of cleverness marks many of their
productions ; and would, were it not deformed by the bad
style of the disagreeable school, which so unhappy infects it—"

"Infects what ?" said Mr. Green. " Oh! the species of
cleverness. But what infects that ? Oh! the disagreeable
school. Go on, sir, though I am indifferent about it."

"I say, sir," said Bice, rather testily, "that the bad style of the disagreeable school so unhappily infects the species of cleverness natural to the race, that we do not know what it means."

"Nor I either," said Mr. Green. "If the school is offensive, chloride of lime is cheap enough."

"Oh, my God!" exclaimed Bice. "Do you really *not* know, Mr. Green, that the friends of Wordsworth, Southey, Coleridge, Shelley, and the whole tribe of intellectual poets have never succeeded in making any of their works popular?"

"Really I do not. And I am really indifferent about it."

"So I presume you are," said Bice, with a satisfied air of superlative conceit. "But you have some idea of music, Mr. Green—of the melody of numbers."

"I know the difference between Yankee Doodle and Old Hundred; but I am *very* indifferent about music."

"But surely the *rhythmus* of the following charming and original metre must strike your ear:—

> "And though the wintry tempest rage the while,
> Domestic legends shall the night beguile;
> Or lite-ra-ry taste its charms impart
> To please the fancy and improve the heart."

"I am indifferent about literature," said Mr. Green, "but the last line is 'fished,' as the boys used to say when I went to school, from a poet named Searson, who was crazy. I remember it very well, because it had in it a picture of General Washington."

"*Fished* from Searson! Oh, Mr. Green!"

"Why certainly it is. I used to know a good deal of his poetry by heart. I am indifferent about remembering such things, but it ran somewhat in this fasion:—

> 'To please the fancy and divert the mind,
> Most pleasing scenes will still the thoughts refine.'"

"That is very pretty, indeed," said Mr. Verdigris, one of

the volunteers at this conclave; and the rest laughed promiscuously.

" You perceive, Mr. Green," said Bice, " that the company
are laughing, involuntarily, at your expense."

" I am indifferent as to laughter. It is but like the crackling of thorns under a pot." Here he projected " involuntarily," right up into what the fancy call the " smellers " of
Mr. Bice, which made him sneeze, according to no rhythmus,
tum-ti, or Lake school that ever was heard of, or attempted to
be defined; and the crackling of the thorns waxed louder, and
grew to be more general and obstreperous. Bice seemed to
understand it; for, after saying, " Depend upon it, Mr. Green,
that since Wordsworth published his dull and drawling poem
called the Excursion, there has been nothing published like
this poetry in twenty editions, of which I have spoken to
you,"—he wen out in what the waiter called a miscellaneous
way.

But he is a great writer in one of the leading Reviews, and
the propriety of publishing this scrap of history during his life
might be questionable, were it not that of the few passages in
Mr Green's biography which delicacy allows us to insert, this
this is one about which there can be no question.

Let all laud and exclusive glory and renown be allotted to
him and to the great Mæcenas who understands his genius.

> Fortunati ambo'! si quid mea carmina possint,
> Nulla dies uuquam memori vos eximet ævo!

CHAPTER VIII.

Nunc est bibendum, nunc pede libero
Pulsanda tellus—Hob.

Now let us tipple, and dance the double shuffle.—Trans.

Why don't you dance up to that entire stranger?
KENTUCKY SONG.

To describe social manners as they appear in the old cities of
our country, among what would be called in another the mid-
dling classes, or the *parvenus*, or by some other name here
totally inapplicable, may be an easy task to an English tourist
before he has got his land legs. It is a very hard one for a
native. At any rate, if the attempt has ever been made it has
been sufficiently successful to save the product from oblivion.
Broad burlesque, or faithful, gross, prosaic delineation might
convey a picture of particular portions of such society to the
reader; but it would not be recognised as characterizing
a species. The phases of such circles change as to their minor
characteristics with the changes of fashion; but there are no
broad outlines which mark them always distinctly. Let us not
therefore attempt to describe the re-union of people of all de-
scriptions to which Mr. Green was taken under the auspices of
Sienna and Indigo. Mr. Vermilion was to fail in two or
three weeks, at the farthest; and his excellent lady was determined that the show of wealth and pomp, if it must
temporarily expire, should do so with eclat, " and in music
and perfume die away."

Green was put into the hands of the accomplished Miss
Pink, who had him seated by her at a piano, in a corner of
one of the rooms, which was sufficiently crowded to make it
" inconvenient" for him to change his position. The lady was
small, plump, frank, and lively, and had good laughing and
languishing eyes.

" Don't you doat on music, Mr. Green ?" said she, as she

concluded the *execution* of something which she unjustly alleged to be the composition of Rossini.

"No. I don't care any thing about it. But as it is just as convenient for you to play now as not, you might as well go on."

"What shall I sing? said Miss Pink. "Every thing here is so old."

"Oh! sing any thing. It is quite immaterial to me."

"Every thing that Miss Polly sings has equal fascinations for you, Green, I suppose," said Sienna.

"Oh! yes. Sing any thing. Only I think a very great shrill noise is rather inconvenient. I believe some of the works of this instrument are out of order. Sing something simple.

Polly accordingly chanted the following lines, to some sort of an air or another, rolling her eyes occasionally at Green, in a very touching manner.

> " They talk of love that grows with years,
> And is by time matured,
> Budding in joy, bedewed by tears,
> By accidents manured.
> Mine, like Minerva, large as life,
> Was born, and cannot grow.

"I declare I forget the next line, Mr. Green. Don't you remember it?"

"No! I never care about remembering such verses. *Wife* and *wo* will rhyme to them."

"Come, Green, you must get a place for Miss Polly for this cotillion," said Sienna.

"I am totally indifferent about dancing. I don't see any room."

"Oh! there's room enough here," continued the extempore master of the ceremonies; 'ample room and verge enough,' as Milton says, just where you are. Put your chair in the corner."

So Mr. Green became the passive partner of Miss Polly,

who was determined that he should at least seem to be something more, so far as pulling, and hauling, and squeezing could
make him so. She had no idea of "treading a measure," but
was for hop, skip, and jump, flings, and rapid gyrations. The
gallopade and mazurka had not been yet quite introduced into
Mrs. Vermilion's coterie. Waltzing, however, was in fashion,
and she announced to Green her intention of performing that
exercise with him, as soon as it should be practicable. Resigned to his fate, and perhaps not altogether displeased with
having some one to take care of him, who was willing to be
at all the expense of conversation, compliment and invitation,
he acquiesced, with a protestando as to its inconvenience on
account of the want of room. "We shall certainly," said he,
"get into the fire, or tread on somebody's toes."

Simon Scarlet, the scion of a prosperous and pugnacious
butcher, had witnessed with no pleasure the flirtation in which
Green played a secondary and involuntary part. He had set
the eyes of affection on Polly, and the pretty personality
which she was supposed to possess. He had had many a
frolic of the same kind with her, and had indeed stated that
he meant to heighten the colour of her name. He was a bully
of some notoriety, and determined to give the new Adonis of
his romping Venus a taste of his manners and quality.

Accordingly, after the cotillion was no longer "being
danced," as eminent writers of the present age would say,
(for the sake of brevity, perspicuity, and grammar,) Simon
forced his way up to the spot where Green was sitting, in the
corner of a sofa, in close juxtaposition to Miss Pink—there
being, as a Hibernian lady observed, "one more in the sofa
than it would hold." Here he planted his six feet of perpen-
dicular longitude right before Polly, while his clumsy pedestals
interfered with the adjustment of her own plump but brief
extremities. He brushed up his fiery red hair with his fingers,
with an awkward attempt at ease, and at assuming an expression of contempt as he looked at Green. Miss Pink drew

in her feet as far as the circumstances would permit, and looked at him with an air of perfect innocence, expecting the opening of such polite conversation as he might be pleased to indulge in.

This was exactly what he did not know how to do ; for he remained standing with folded arms, in the same position, for several seconds, casting his eyes down upon Green, who was fastening one of Polly's bracelets, as she had desired him to do.

" Well, Mr, Scarlet," she said at length, " *comment se porte votre tante?* as the French say.

" I don't know what that means, Miss Pink," he observed, with a droll mockery of stateliness in his tone and carriage, adjusting at the same time the swathes of some coloured fabric which encircled his neck. " I wish you to dance with me— that is, if you please."

" I can't, indeed. I am going to waltz with this gentleman presently."

" Waltz with *who ?*"

" You are hurting my feet, sir," said Green, looking up to the firelocks of the querist. " It is very inconvenient."

" Maybe so, sir. I would keep them out of the way then, if I was you."

Here, in crossing his legs, Green slightly kicked the shin of Mr. Scarlet, who became immediately more " deeply red" than ever. " What do you mean, sir ?" he asked abruptly.

" Mean ? I said nothing. But I wish you would stand a little further off. It is inconvenient enough sitting here as it is."

" You are a puppy, sir," said Scarlet, in a loud enough voice to be generally heard. " I don't believe that you have any business to be here."

" Mr. Scarlet," said Sienna, coming up at this juncture, " Mr. Green came here on my introduction. You must apolo- gize—you are under a mistake.

" I apologize to no puppies, mistake or no mistake." So

saying he strutted about in the elegant attitude of Lord Castlereagh's crocodile.

Miss Pink had the crying-and-laughing hysterics. The goodly company was frightened from its propriety, or impropriety, as the refined Mrs. Trollope would probably have called it. Sienna and Indigo withdrew with Mr. Green.

" You must fight that bully," observed the first of these worthies to the last.

" I must have satisfaction certainly : but it is decidedly inconvenient for me to shoot him, or to be shot by him at present. I am indifferent about duelling, but I have got to see about getting married. I think *you* ought to challenge him first, if it is convenient; and, if necessary, I can attend to it afterward."

" I ?—no, I don't see why."

" You led me into the scrape."

" I invited you to go into ' good society,' and ' endorsed your appearance,' as the attorneys say ; but he did not know it when he affronted you."

" He called *you* a puppy when he did—however."

" I did not understand him, or" (blaspheming) " I would have knocked him down on the spot. You are altogether mistaken. You will be cut, if you do not call him to an account instantly."

" If he should kill me, I am indifferent as to what becomes of the estate after my death. But I know I can hit him, and it will be dreadfully inconvenient for me to run away just now from the country."

" Pshaw ! he will apologize on the ground. He is a coward as well as a ruffian. I know that he will have Grey for his second, and I can arrange every thing with him, for the perfect vindication of your honour, without burning any powder."

" I am indifferent, as I said before, about duelling ; but I must say, that if I have to get up before sunrise, and be put

N

to so much inconvenience, I *should* like to have a fair crack at the butcher-boy. But you may fix it as you like."

And Mr. Sienna, who desired nothing better than to have the notoriety of being confidentially employed in an affair in which a young gentleman of good family and of wealth was a principal,—and of causing Mr. Scarlet, who uniformly treated him with thorough and rude superciliousness, to be either humbled or made a *caput mortuum*, without any risk to himself,—wrote a missive forthwith for Green, of which Indigo, who was somewhat of a fire-eater, was the bearer ; as he (Sienna) alleged that he was in some sort a second principal, and must send another invitation on his own account, should it become necessary.

———

CHAPTER IX.

Dabellare Superbos.—Virg.
Arms and the man !—*Ib.*

In a plain tale, which might make two volumes duodecimo, but which must be here restricted to a *nouvelette* of some fifty pages or less, we must adopt, as Mr. Black would say, the legal maxim, and not care about minutest trifles ; otherwise we might describe the progress of a row-boat over a glorious piece of water at early dawn, and spin it out into perhaps half a dozen chapters, descriptive and narrative, of adventures leading to nothing before the catastrophe, excepting what the said Black would have called *imparlances*. The fact too is, that the morning was foggy and mizzly ; and that nothing was to be seen at more than five yards' distance from the boat, than the wave and the watery drapery of mist. It is a pity that the *crepusculum* did not happen to be more promising ; and if it had been, we should have had no room to discuss it here. Nor can we dilate upon the risk the party ran of being run down by a steamboat: or upon how a porpoise actually liked to have turned in among them, in his peculiarly clumsy manner.

Their boatmen backed water, and an exceedingly spruce, and indeed rather priggish-looking young gentleman, who was playing cockswain, looked knowingly at a pocket-compass

" I must say that this is very inconvenient," said one of the party, " though, since it can't be helped, I am indifferent about it." And, wrapping his cloak about himself more strictly, he reclined against the gunwale.

" No—nor-west, Doctor," said one of the rowers to the steersman.

" We shall be too late to get any breakfast," said the third passenger.

" I am indifferent about breakfast," responded Mr. Green ;" " but after we have settled the matter, I must say that I should decidedly like to have some refreshment; hot tea, or soda-water with hock in it."

" Take a taste of this," said Indigo, handing him a small, flat, elliptical, metal flask.

" Faugh ! It is spirits. I am indifferent about smelling spirits at any time. But I will take a suck of it, if you say so."

The rowers pulled and pulled energetically. It is marvellous in the eyes of some *dilettanti* moralists, how when men act as machines they play their part so well. If hired to do a job in the way of rowing, whether it be to carry the idle apprentice to the transport-ship which was to take him to Botany Bay, or a couple of gentlemen to shoot *selon les regles*, what do *they* care about the freight they have on board, or its ultimate destination, direct or contingent ? Hogarth does, to be sure, make one of his Charons cast a pregnant squint at the illustrious exile who was " being" ferried by him on his way to foreign parts ; which squint, coupled in the way of association with the gallows on the shore, make a very pretty unwritten morality. But your regularly-bred boatmen are generally unobservant altogether.

So they rowed and rowed, through and over the water, and in an atmosphere which was as good as water, though thinner, for the purpose of wetting people, until, through the moist fogginess, a bold shore covered with evergreens, became dimly visible. Previously, however, to this appearance, and while they were floating in and under the influence of haze and hydrogen, Mr. Green seemed to have an idea.

" This mist," said he, " puts me in mind of eternity. Did you ever think about eternity, Mr. Indigo ?"

" No—not a great deal. In Cato's play, that they used to speak at school, I remember that he says it is a pleasingly dreadful thought. What put that into your head ? O yes— but you are indifferent about most matters. Do you care any thing about religion."

" I don't know—"

Here a pause ensued, and after some time the boat shot under a fir-clad precipice, its keel grating on the pebbles. The oarsmen bestowed their implements in the usual fashion ; and looked as if they were glad that so much of their business was transacted. Messrs. Green and Indigo ascended the bank, and presently came upon a level space, where they saw bully Scarlet, with his friend Grey, sitting upon a rock. When the former saw them he looked rather uneasy, and " made his manners" very awkwardly.

" We have been expecting you, gentlemen," said Mr. Grey.

" Not long, I hope ; or if so it was unnecessary," said Indigo (looking at his watch). " It yet wants ten minutes of six. We will, however, proceed to business as soon as you please."

While these two worthies were pacing the ground and arranging the preliminaries, it would have been amusing to a spectator to see Mr. Scarlet covertly glancing upwards to the

top of the wooded eminence, at the foot of which he was
to be " set-up;" anticipating the interference of the old landlord, at whose house he had slept and breakfasted, and whom
he had taken care privately to inform of the purpose with
which he came, or rather did not come, to that locality.
Bluebeard's sister-in-law did not look more earnestly from the
top of the tower, when the truculent old curmudgeon was
trifling with her natural sister's terrors, than this poor body
gazed up the wall of earth and vegetation, expecting a revelation of his hearty old host's person, in a shape either of a
mediator, or of a preserver of the peace.   Grey told him
where to stand, put a pistol in his hand, and cautioned him to
remember his previous instructions, which there is no necessity
for our remembering, as Scarlet had forgotten them himself.
Like Guy Denzil, when he was about to be "being hanged,"
he was scarcely conscious of what he saw or heard ; and
the beautiful violet lingering in the recesses near his feet, and
the scarlet lichen which had begun to flaunt as a spring belle
among the crevices in the grey stones above him, with a small
sisterhood of early blue, and white, and pink wild-flowers;
and the trees, and the earth, and the waters swam dimly on
his sight.   Lady Morgan has a crazy notion in one of her
novels, which is out of print, about the Avatar of one of the
ugly Hindoo gods being pre-announced by the strange mysterious movement of the leaves of an old and solemn forest.
The heathen devotee who watched and interpreted for himsel
the expression of those vegetables, could not have been more
earnest in his gaze, than was our Bombastes Furioso for the
apparition of the red face of the aged and respectable Mr.
Orange Tawney, with a couple or more of constables, to ter-
minate honourably the difficulties of his position : and indeed,
presently, the jolly visage of mine host was protruded from
the bank above, between the slim trunks of two junipers, spe-
culating with great complacency and good-nature, through
vines and bushes, upon the arrangement.

" To say the truth," said Grey, " I do not know where to go. I would as lief take a run down there as not. I used to know several persons in the West Indies; and Green can get money enough any where, I have no doubt, to save us all from running aground'"

" Gentlemen," said Green, " I thank you infinitely for your excessive kindness and politeness. Good luck to both of you. I am indifferent about leading others into embarrassments, and I do not see how you would get along in foreign parts, with no more clothes, and linen, and funds, and things than you have about you. They are weighing anchor, and the longer you stay, the more inconvenient it will be for you to make your arrangements. Good-by to you both." The gentlemen shook hands very coldly with him, and looked excessively blank, as, finding there was no other alternative, they left the vessel.

" A pretty kettle of fish we have made of it," said Indigo for the sake of such a cold-blooded fellow."

" He is not so great a fool as I took him for," said Grey.

It was many months after the transactions recorded in the foregoing sketches, that an olive-coloured gentleman arrived at the village of Short-hills, and introduced himself to Mr· Brown, with a power of attorney from Mr. Green, and missives from that gentleman. In the latter he stated that he was ready to marry either of his cousins whom it would be most convenient for the family to consign to him, as it was altogether inconvenient for him to return to the country at that time and an immediate answer was required.

Whatever might have been the soundness of the legal opinion taken by Mr. Green, the time specified in the will had elapsed. Owing to the casualties of navigation which it were needless to specify, he had been detained longer in sailing from a northern Atlantic port for St. Croix, than Christopher Columbus was in finding the islands; and his plenipotentiary had not made a quick passage. The moiety of old Green's estate had been divided, with their entire consent, among the residuary legatees. Miss Betsey

> " Sat a smiling bride,
> By Mr. White's protecting side."

Miss Bella was on the eve of her nuptials with Mr. Lewis Lake, and Miss Barbara was, as she remains, " the last rose of the family, left blooming alone." She is considered, however, an advantageous speculation; but, notwithstanding she came in for her share of the contingent spoils, no inconsiderable trifle for a country practitioner of law, Black was surly and unpropitiative. It is even said that he was much closeted with Green's attorney-in-fact; who rejoiced in the name of Rufus-Flavus-y-Azur, Esq.; and talked of filing a bill in Chancery on behalf of that gentleman's principal. But the sinews of war were a-wanting, and Rufus Flavus, it is believed, had to go back to the Hesperides upon tick.

A current statement, that shortly after these adventures' Mr. Green was recognised smoking a cigar on a bald rock, on an exceedingly high mountain of Massachusetts, at a place called Peru, is of course entitled to no credit whatever. That is a place, indeed, which may be called with propriety, " the bare convex of the world's orb ;" like the one spoken of in the argument to the third book of the Paradise Lost, as the spot where Satan alighted, when on his malicious mission. And it may be a fact, as has been stated by some English travellers, who say they have ridden over it, that, in a high gale, coaches full of passengers may be blown off from it into infinite space, and never more seen or heard tell of, unless they are made fast to the rocky rim of our planet in that quarter, by strong hooks and grapples of iron. It *is* an undoubted fact that Mrs. Trollope lost the hair off from her head, and Lieutenant Lacka-day his mustachios, in *tramontanising* this sublime district, and that they might as well have rummaged all the hay-stacks in creation for a needle and tooth-pick, as to have gone in the pursuit of their property. But it is *not* a fact that Mr. Green was ever there in the whole course of his life.

He was, however, at the last accounts, much nearer the *old* Peru, travelling under the auspices of "old India's awful genius," as Warton calls it, on his way to the interesting capital of Guatimala. He was reposing for a time near the summit of a very huge eminence, called Mico, in company with a distinguished traveller, on the mud floor of a genteel unfurnished hovel. An imperfectly clad native damsel was helping him to some *pesso;* a beverage which Mr. Dunn describes as "being made of the rinds of limes, rubbed with corn, and allowed to ferment, and then mixed with honey." He adds that it is very insipid.

"What a magnificent prospect!" exclaimed the traveller looking down on the long, crooked profile of the circuitous route by which they had thus far ascended; and upward at the grand and frowning elevation which they had yet to surmount.

"I am indifferent about prospects," said Mr. Green; "but I must say that it is inconvenient to get up such hills, on such mules; and I wonder why people take the trouble to do it."

If it be indispensable that every moral tale should have a pointed moral, the reader may punctuate this with a note of exclamation or of interrogation, according to his taste. But old Mrs. Brown often took occasion to remark, in relation to her nephew—"The Countess of C—— has truly said, in her reply to Mrs. Greville's prayer,

'No grain of cold indifference
Was ever yet allied to sense.'"

N 5

"HOW WOULD *YOU* LIKE IT?"

MR. JONES had occasion, one day, to make a few trifling purchases at a dry goods store. While standing by the counter,
a young woman came in, the daughter of a neighbour, and
asked the price of a good many articles, none of which seemed
to please her. At last, she turned away and left the store,
not, however, until she had dexterously slipped a valuable
piece of lace under her cloak, unseen by any one but Mr.
Jones, who was so confounded at the act, that he could not
clearly determine in his own mind what he ought to do. He
concluded, finally, to keep silence until he had conferred with
his wife on the subject, as the young woman was a particular
friend of Mrs. Jones.

"Something happened to-day, Mary," he said, on returning
home, "that I never would have believed, if I hadn't seen it
with my own eyes."

"Indeed! What was it?" and Mrs. Jones was all interest.

"While I was at Mr. Smith's store to-day, Emily Jenkins
came in, and asked for something, that, when shown to her,
didn't seem to suit her fancy. She then asked to see something else, which pleased her about as well as the first article.
And so she kept on for ten or fifteen minutes, without buying
anything. At last, I saw her slip a whole piece of fine French
lace under her cloak, while the clerk's back was turned. She
then declined purchasing any of the articles shown to her, and
went out."

"You must surely be mistaken, Mr. Jones!" his wife replied to this, incredulously.

"O no, Mary, I am not mistaken at all. I saw it done just
as clearly as ever I saw any thing in my life."

"Emily Jenkins, did you say?"

" Yes. Emily Jenkins."

" It seems impossible, Mr. Jones !"

" So it does, Mary; but seeing, you know, is believing."

" Isn't it dreadful? What could have possessed the girl to do so wicked a thing? But have you said any thing about it to Mr. Smith?"

" No—not yet. I thought I would see and talk with you first."

" I'm glad of that," Mrs. Jones said, breathing more freely. " I wouldn't have had you exposed her for the world. It is bad enough as it is."

" But I am not sure, Mary," replied the husband, " that it will be right for me to keep this matter from Mr. Smith. He has had a piece of goods stolen, and I know the thief.'

" Don't! Don't! Mr. Jones, talk in that way. I cannot bear to hear you use such expressions in regard to Emily Jenkins."

" Still, they are true expressions, Mary, and I must use them. Mr. Smith has had his goods stolen, and I know the thief. Now, the question for me to decide is, how far I shall be justified in withholding from him the information that will lead to the recovery of his property."

" Depend upon it, Mr. Jones, to do so will occasion more harm than good. It will, of course, result in the exposure of Emily, and the ruin of her character—and what is a paltry piece of lace compared with such a consequence? No—no— you must not say a word on the subject."

" I am not so clear about that," Mr. Jones said,—" She is a thief in heart, or she never would have stolen that lace. If she is a deliberate thief, she is as bad as any other deliberate thief, and she ought to be classed with them and be treated like them."

" Why will you talk so, Mr. Jones? You distress me to death! Suppose she were your daughter, and any one should talk in that way about her, even if she had been guilty of a like indiscretion, how would *you* like it? How would you like to have *her* exposed?

This at once settled the question in Mr. Jones' mind. It was coming right down to his home and his heart, and it scattered all his abstract principles of justice to the four winds.

" Well, perhaps it would be best to remain quiet," he said, after musing for some time. " There is no telling what Mr. Smith might do, for he is a hasty man. Still Emily ought not to be suffered to go on unchecked. She will certainly be found out, sooner or later, and meet with an exposure and its dreadful consequences. Suppose you talk to her on the subject."

" Me? Goodness! No! I wouldn't name it to her for the world!"

" But she ought to be spoken to about it, Mary, and shown the evil of it, as well as the great risk she runs."

" I can readily agree to that, Mr. Jones. But *I* can't do it. Suppose you break the matter to her father?"

" I shouldn't like to do that, somehow or other," Mr. Jones replied—its rather a delicate affair. It would hurt him dreadfully."

" Not half so much as to have her exposed!"

" True—But I can't make up my mind to do it. How would *I* feel were any one to mention such a thing to me about my own child?"

" You wouldn't believe it, of course."

" No, of course not. For our daughter couldn't be guilty of stealing. And now it occurs to me, that Mr. Jenkins wouldn't believe such a story about Emily if I were to tell him. It would be natural enough for him to conclude that I was mistaken. So you see that no good could possibly grow out of my speaking to him on the subject. So upon the whole, perhaps it would be just as well not to meddle at all in the matter. Let Mr. Smith and his clerk keep a better look out, and let Mr. Jenkins teach his children how to keep the Commandments."

"I agree with you, that our best plan is not to meddle at all in the matter. We'll get no credit for our pains, depend upon it!"

And here the thing was allowed to rest by Mr. Jones and his wife—though, to tell the truth, the former did not feel by any means satisfied with himself.

"How should *I* like it?" he would often ask himself, "if Mr. Smith were to see any one stealing goods from my store, and not say any thing about it to me? Would he be acting towards me justly? I'm afraid not!"

This argument of "how would *I* like it?" had a strong influence over the mind of Mr. Jones. He could see clearly enough what would be his neighbour's duty, were he the sufferer of wrong. But when the case was reversed, his mind relapsed into its former obscurity—and he again became undecided how he should act.

About a week after the occurrence of the incident that had disturbed his mind, Mr. Jones came home one day, and found Miss Jenkins in the parlour with his wife. It was the first time he had seen her since her light-fingered operations in Mr. Smith's store. He felt confused, while the blood instantly mounted to his face; but Emily's smiling countenance, that had in it so much of conscious innocence, brought back his self-possession in a moment. Joining in the conversation, he chatted for half an hour with her, in quite a familiar way, and when she arose to go, joined with his wife in urging her to come and see them oftener than she had been in the habit of doing.

"You certainly must have been wrong about Emily," Mrs. Jones said as soon as her visitor had departed.

"I only wish I could think so. But when any one sees a thing with his own eyes, he is bound to believe it. And I saw her take a piece of Mr. Smith's lace as plainly as ever I saw any thing in my life."

"Well, it passss belief, really—how can she put on such an innocent face, and she conscious all the while of being a ——"

But Mrs. Jones could not utter the word that rose to her lips. After a pause she added—

"I'm really afraid that she'll be caught one of these days and then just to imagine the consequences. Isn't it dreadful?"

"Really, Mary, I think you ought to go to her, and tell frankly what you know. It may save her from the terrible consequences of an open exposure."

"Perhaps I ought. But then I can't do it. That's settled. How could I look her in the face, and accuse her of stealing?"

"*You* could look *her* in the face well enough, I should think. The difficulty would be for *her* to look *you* in the face."

"It's no use to talk, Mr. Jones—I can't do it!" Mrs. Jones said, at once silencing her husband on the subject. But I do think you ought to speak to her father!"

But Mr. Jones shook his head, and looked grave. He was a man of too much feeling to wound Mr. Jenkins, by making to him so painful a disclosure. Still his mind was much troubled, for he was conscious of acting unjustly towards Mr. Smith, in not taking some steps to have his property restored to him, or to apprise him of the wrong he had suffered. Thus matters went on for some months, during which time Emily Jenkins visited as usual at the house of Mr. Jones, and was treated with the same kindness and attention that she had always received, notwithstanding Mr. and Mrs. Jones had such good reasons for believing her guilty of the crime of taking what did not belong to her.

"What do you think, Mrs. Jones," said a neighbour, about this time. "I saw Emily Jenkins take a beautiful ring to-day, while we were in Armand's jewelry store. We were out shopping together, and she proposed going into Armand's to look at some rings. She asked to see a good many, and at last slipped one under her glove—I saw it distinctly—then she declined buying any, and we went away. Mr. Armand's clerk looked very hard at us—and I am much inclined to think suspected the theft."

"Did you say any thing to her about it?" eagerly asked Mrs. Jones.

"Oh no, indeed! I didn't let on that I saw her take the ring. But you'll never catch me in any store again with Emily Jenkins, I know. Suppose Armand misses the ring. He'll be just as likely to suspect me as he will her."

"Well, it is too much!" Mrs. Jones said. "That girl will get herself into trouble yet. I wonder what she can be thinking about! My husband saw her take a piece of lace from Mr. Smith's store with his own eyes."

"He did?"

"Yes, indeed! And if it hadn't been such a pity for the family, he would have exposed her. As it was, we thought it best to say nothing about it."

The lady acquaintance who had seen the purloining of the ring, came to a like conclusion. How would she like to have a member of her family—a sister, for instance—exposed, under like circumstances?—settled the question in regard to how she ought to act. It was deemed far best to say nothing further on the subject, at least not in a way that would be likely to lead to an exposure.

When Mr. Jones came home on that evening, his wife mentioned this subject, when there ensued a long discussion as to what was their duty. Mr. Jones contended, that true charity required him at least to inform Mr. Smith of the wrong he had suffered some months before. His wife did not think so. She could not bear the thought of the terrible exposure, and perhaps punishment, of Miss Jenkins that might ensue.

"But see here, Mary," argued her husband,—"Just think

for a moment how the innocent might be made to suffer for the guilty? Emily Jenkins and another lady, as the case happened to-day, might be out shopping together, and a ring or some other article be stolen. Suppose, after they had gone out, this article were missed, and suspicion falling upon one of the two ladies, the innocent were arrested for the guilty, and subjected to the mortifying exposure and suspicion consequent upon this arrest? How, for instance, would *you* like such an exposure, if you should happen to be in company with her?"

Mrs. Jones shuddered involuntarily at this suggestion; and for a moment, felt like yielding to her husband's evident desire to rid his conscience of the secret burden that rested upon it. The question of—How would *you* like it?—brightened her ideas a good deal. But a mist soon obscured her perceptions.

" How would it look, Mr. Jones," she said, " for you to inform on Emily Jenkins? What would people think? Oh, no, I wouldn't have you do it for the world."

This brought a new idea to the mind of Mr. Jones. " Sure enough! How would it look? What would be said about it? How could he ever look Mr. Jenkins in the face after having destroyed his peace, and that of his family?"

And again the subject was laid aside, and an effort made to forget it. But this was not so easily done.

One day, about six months after the period of the last mentioned incident of the ring, Mrs. Jones, per request, received from her husband a twenty dollar bill, and, with this in her pocket-book, went out upon a shopping expedition. She had completed about half her purchases, when she fell in with Miss Jenkins, who was, of course, very glad to see her, and who, as she was going the same way, and on the same errand very naturally went along with her. Mrs. Jones watched her companion very closely at every store where they called; but saw no act positively confirmatory of previous charges against her honesty,—although she could not help acknowledging to herself that Emily sometimes acted very strangely. She asked to see a great many articles, which she examined with apparent interest, and desire to be suited, and yet purchased nothing. At length Mrs. Jones completed her list of indispensables and superfluities. During the first half hour succeeding her arrival at home, with her purchases, she was engaged in the pleasing employment of examining the various articles she had bought, as to quality and style, and congratulating herself upon her fine bargains and the beautiful goods she had selected. While thus engaged a servant came in and told Mrs. Jones that a gentleman was below, who wished to speak to her, but wouldn't give his name.

"A strange way for a *gentleman* to act" muttered Mrs. Jones, as she descended to the parlour. There she found a stout, rough-looking man, who seemed slightly embarrassed, as he said to her on her entrance—

"I am sorry to disturb you, madam. But I have to do my duty."

"What do you mean, sir?" Mrs. Jones said, instantly turning pale, for the strange speech, tone, appearance, and manner of her visiter, inspired her with a sudden fear.

"I have a writ, commanding me to bring you before a magistrate, on the charge of taking unlawfully from the store of Jacob Jackson, six linen cambric handkerchiefs."

Mrs. Jones sank upon a chair, pale as death, and ready to faint.

"Surely, sir, you must be mistaken in the person! You cannot mean me?" she half gasped, after the first few moments of painful surprise had elapsed.

"Yes, ma'am. I mean Mrs. Mary Jones, at 100——street,' replied the constable—for a constable he was, sure enough. "I am very sorry, but you will have to go with me to the magistrate's."

"But I know nothing about the linen cambric. I never took

it. I am not a thief!" Mrs. Jones said, with indignant emphasis, though her face continued very pale.

"That, you will no doubt be able to make clear enough at the office," returned the officer, respectfully, but firmly.

"At the office! Surely you will not drag me to a magistrate's office?" Mrs. Jones said imploringly. "I am as innocent as a child unborn!"

"No doubt of it, madam. But I am a sworn officer, and must do my duty."

The distinct consciousness at length came to the mind of Mrs. Jones, that there was no escape for her. That she had been charged with stealing, and that she was really in the hands of the law, and must abide its behests. This brought forth a flood of tears, for the subsidence of which the constable waited with becoming patience. At length he said—

"You see, madam, that there is only one course for me to pursue, and that is to bring you before a magistrate. I am sorry that the unpleasant task has fallen to my lot, but as it has become my duty, I must discharge it. You will, therefore, please to make yourself ready as quickly as possible, and go with me."

"You will wait until I send for my husband, will you not?" the distressed woman asked, looking with tearful appealing eyes into the face of the rough minister of the law.

"O certainly madam. Send for him and I will wait until he comes."

A servant was instantly despatched with a note to Mr. Jones, who soon made his apperance. His wife flung herself into his arms, tearful and trembling, on his entrance, and with a choking voice, explained to him, incoherently, the dreadful accusation against her. Mr. Jones was painfully shocked at this. But he endeavoured to soothe the terrors of his wife, by assuring her, that no such charge could be substantiated. This was well enough, so far as it went. To be obliged to appear before a magistrate, and be tried on such a foul and disgraceul charge, was the terrible ordeal from which she shrunk. But even from this, there was no escape ; and to this, she was compelled, reluctantly, to make up her mind. While her husband went for a carriage, Mrs. Jones retired to her chamber to prepare herself to obey the imperious summons. On his return, she came down deeply veiled. Some delay occurred in the arrival of the carriage, during which time Mrs. Jones remained seated upon the sofa in a dejected attitude. The muff which she had brought down with her was placed by her side. A movement threw it down, when a small roll of something fell upon the floor. As she stooped to pick it up, the officer, whose quick eye observed it, stepped forward and lifted it before she could reach it,

" What is that ?" eagerly asked Mr. Jones.

" Six linen cambric handkerchiefs, I believe," said the officer, coolly, as he counted over the number he had named of beautiful handkerchiefs, yet uncut.

" Mary !" exclaimed the husband, turning to his wife, and regarding her for a few moments, with a fixed, sorrowful, yet rebuking look.

For a moment poor Mrs. Jones was unable to speak. Then rising quickly, she said, in a firm voice,—

" I never saw that piece of goods before ! How it came into my muff, I cannot tell. Certainly, I never put it there. And, certainly, no one could possibly believe for a moment, that if I had, I would have left it there under these circumstances.

This was conclusive to Mr. Jones, and caused the instant suspicion that had crossed his mind, as instantly to give place to a clear consciousness of his wife's innocence. She had been made the victim of a conspiracy, or the scape-goat to bear the half-discovered iniquity of some petty shop-purloiner. The carriage now drove up, and the whole party entered, and proceeded to the office of a city magistrate, where the storekeeper and his clerk stood ready to bring their accusations against poor Mrs. Jones, who, closely veiled, and in tears, presented herself before the grave looking Justice of the Peace. The production of the goods alleged to have been stolen, and which were sworn to by the clerk as the property of Mr. Jackson, at once settled, in the mind of the Justice, the question of the culprit's guilt or innocence, and he was, in quite a summary way, about to pronounce a decision, when Mr. Jones asked the right of having counsel, even in these preliminary proceedings against his wife, and also of having the testimony of her accusers adduced, so soon as his counsel should arrive, as to the causes which led them to prefer against her the charge of stealing. A moment's deliberation led the magistrate to acquiesce in this request. A messenger was then sent for a lawyer of distinction—a personal friend of Mr. Jones—who came immediately. A few brief statements gave to his intuitive mind a full knowledge of the case and its merits. And a few questions to the clerk, who was the witness for the prosecution, soon placed the whole matter in a different light.

"Did you see Mrs. Jones take that piece of goods?" was his first question to the witness.

"No, sir."

"What led you, then, to suppose that she had it in her possession?"

"I saw the lady who came into the store with her, slip it into her muff, which she had laid upon the counter a moment before, and then, so soon as this had been done, Mrs. Jones took it up again, and in a little while after they left the store together."

"Indeed! Then there was another lady with her, and this other lady took the goods?"

"Yes, sir.

"Do you know that lady?"

"Not by name. But I often see her in our store."

"What reason had you for supposing that Mrs. Jones knew the handkerchiefs had been put into her muff?"

" None other than that the two ladies came in together;—appeared acquainted with each other, and evidently, to my mind at least, were acting in concert."

" Who was that lady?" asked the counsel, turning to the accused.

" Emily Jenkins," was the reply.

" That explains the whole matter!" exclaimed Mr. Jones, striking his hand hard upon the magistrate's desk, beside which he stood.

" Let Emily Jenkins be summoned," said the lawyer.

An officer, who was handed a summons, immediately departed. In half an hour Miss Jenkins appeared, with her father; both looking pale and alarmed. As soon as the former had presented herself, the magistrate asked the clerk if she was the woman who had taken the handkerchiefs and thrust them into Mrs. Jones' muff? He replied, promptly, in the affirmative.

Poor Emily burst into tears and sank half fainting into a chair, while a thrill of joy ran through the breast of Mrs. Jones at this declaration, which she saw was leading to the establishment of her own innocence.

" Have you any reason to believe, that she was induced so to conceal the article taken, from any fear lest you had discovered the theft?" asked the lawyer of the witness.

" I am not certain of this. But I saw the goods in her hand, and from a look which I gave her, am inclined to believe that she was conscious that I had detected her slipping the article she had taken, under her cloak. She asked me, just as I had made the discovery, to let her see a piece of goods on the shelf. I reached up for it, and turned as quickly as I could to watch her. It was then that I saw her put the handkerchiefs in Mrs. Jones' muff. The muff was taken from the counter immediately after by its owner, and very soon after both ladies left the store without making any purchases."

" Is that true?" asked the father of Miss Jenkins, in an

excited tone, catching hold of the arm of his daughter with a tight grasp.

"It is," murmured the unhappy creature.

"You took the goods?"

"Yes, sir."

"And Mrs. Jones is innocent?"

"Yes, sir."

"Wretched girl!" exclaimed the father, letting go of her arm, and clasping his hands tightly upon his forehead,—"And unhappy father of so wicked a child!"

The scene was painful in the extreme to all present—though mingled with joy to Mr. and Mrs. Jones, who had so narrowly escaped wretchedness and disgrace.

"Let the innocent go"—at length Mr. Jenkins said, recovering himself. "She has suffered enough for the guilty!"

The magistrates at once dismissed the case first brought before him; but required bail for the appearance of the true culprit at the next session of the criminal court, to answer the charge of petty larceny.

"We have both been deservedly punished," was the first remark made by Mr. Jones on their arrival at home.

"How so?" asked Mrs. Jones, in surprise.

"For not having acted with true charity toward our neighbour. We knew that Emily Jenkins was addicted to stealing from the stores. We knew whom she had wronged, and when she had done it. But for fear of what others might think of us, or lest the feelings of some might be injured, we suffered this wrong to continue either unrebuked or unexposed. We knew that every lady who might happen to be seen with Emily in a store was liable to the very accusation that has been brought against you, and yet we lifted no warning voice; but left the innocent exposed, from false feelings of regard toward the guilty. Therefore, I say we have been justly punished. It is but right that we should bear the consequences of our own act."

Mrs. Jones wss silent. She felt the truth of what her husband had said; and yet she found it hard to say, or even acknowledge to herself, that her punishment had been just.

As for Emily Jenkins, when the trial came on, she could not be found in the city. Her father, who of course knew where she was, paid the bail which had become forfeited, and there the matter rested. His daughter has not, however, returned to her family, as it would not be prudent for her to do so.

FINIS.

James Clark, Printer, Aberdeen.